M000198640

KNIGHT AVENGED

Also by Coreene Callahan

Dragonfury Series
Fury of Fire
Fury of Ice
Fury of Seduction
Fury of Desire

Circle of Seven Series
Knight Awakened

Warriors of the Realm Series
Warrior's Revenge

KNIGHT AVENGED

A CIRCLE OF SEVEN NOVEL

COREENE CALLAHAN

Montlake
Romance

This is a work of fiction. Names, characters, organizations, places, events, and incidents are either products of the author's imagination or are used fictitiously.

Text copyright © 2014 Coreene Callahan
All rights reserved.

No part of this book may be reproduced, or stored in a retrieval system, or transmitted in any form or by any means, electronic, mechanical, photocopying, recording, or otherwise, without express written permission of the publisher.

Published by Montlake Romance, Seattle

www.apub.com

Amazon, the Amazon logo, and Montlake Romance are trademarks of Amazon.com, Inc., or its affiliates.

ISBN-13: 9781612187105
ISBN-10: 1612187102

Cover design by Anne Cain

Library of Congress Control Number: 2014903957

Printed in the United States of America

And then, there was you—I'm so glad I got to take this journey with you and that you finally found your happily ever after.

The Prophecy
And out of the ashes seven warriors shall rise.
Bringers of death, they shall wreak vengeance
upon the earth, until shadow is driven into darkness
and only the light remains.

—The Chronicles of Al Pacii:
written in the hand of Seer

CHAPTER ONE

GREY KEEP: AL PACII STRONGHOLD—AD 1331

Halál bolted upright in bed, a shout locked in the back of his throat. Gasping, he clawed at his bare chest, then looked down to see the damage. No blood. No gaping wound. No mark at all. Disbelief slithered in, coiling with ominous intent. Lucifer be merciful. It had felt so real. So bloody *real*—the slash, the pain, the warm trickle of his own blood. Pressing one hand over his heart, he fisted the other in the blanket. Rough wool scraped his palm as he sucked in another lungful of air. It didn't help. He couldn't catch his breath. Or think straight. Not while vivid imagery swirled inside his head and . . .

A tremor rumbled through him.

Damnation. A dream . . .

The dream.

It had shifted into something dangerous. Something darker. Drifting toward something he could no longer identify.

Another shiver rattled down his spine. Gaze riveted to the timber beam ceiling, Halál fell back onto one elbow. His bones creaked. Muscles stiff with age groaned in protest as his forearm sank into the feather mattress. Sweat beading on his chest, he shifted focus and scanned the room. Rough stone walls. Heavy wood door with the iron lock engaged. A dying fire hissed in the widemouthed hearth. The familiar arrangement grounded him. Still in the heart of night. Still safe inside his own room. Still surrounded by strength and the walls of Grey Keep.

No need to be alarmed.

Halál frowned, knowing that wasn't true. There was much to fear. Even more reason to be cautious. The return of his dream said it all. More than he wanted to acknowledge. And yet, he couldn't let it go, never mind exorcise the demons. Ignoring the latest version of the nightmare wouldn't be wise considering what it signaled . . .

Change on an infinite scale.

Not a good sign. His sleep visions were never wrong.

Unease swirled through him, ratcheting his tension up another notch. Halál snarled softly in disdain. Be damned, he didn't want change. He liked the status quo along with his current mission as leader of the Al Pacii nation: Abduct more strong boys. Fill the Al Pacii ranks. Train the most promising until Grey Keep teemed with warrior assassins and Halál's stranglehold on Transylvania tightened. Power. Glory. His coffers full of the European kings' coin and entire nations kneeling at his feet. The ultimate test of his prowess as a warlord—invincibility in the minds of his prey. He would be untouchable.

A harbinger of death. Revered and feared by one and all.

Halál huffed, enjoying the symmetry. 'Twas a worthy goal. Something to be proud of, but only if he succeeded—an outcome he began to question more with each passing day. And especially after tonight. Devil take him, the dream . . .

The dream.

It taunted him without end, showing him snippets but not the details. Every time he went to sleep, he received another piece of the puzzle. Morsels of information. Tonight, the visual riddle had ended with his chest being torn wide open. The who, when, and why, however, evaded him. How would it come to pass? With a blade held by one of his assassins? A sneak attack? An uprising among the Al Pacii ranks to overthrow him?

All good questions. None of which he could answer.

A pity in more ways than one.

Distraction from his primary goal wasn't an option. Not with The Seven—a group of former Al Pacii assassins—breathing down his neck. The crafty bastards stalked him like a pack of wolves: killing his men, interrupting supply lines, stealing potential Al Pacii inductees before the boys could reach Grey Keep. Releasing his grip on the blanket, Halál shook his head. So cunning. So skilled. Far too reckless and brutal. Henrik and his cohorts would never relent. Or bow to his command . . . ever again. Halál knew that now. The reality of it made regret rise. 'Twas a double-damned travesty.

Particularly since The Seven's prowess would be missed.

With a sigh, he flipped the covers back and swung his legs over the side of the bed. As his bare feet touched down on cold stone, he gripped the mattress edge and stared across the chamber into the fireplace beyond. Flames burning low, orange embers glowed like cats' eyes in the gloom. From the size of the coals, he knew it was well past midnight. The wee hours—where the darkness was blackest and night's menace thickest.

His favorite time of all.

Taking a deep breath, he allowed his eyes to drift closed and listened. The wind moaned, the rush low and pitiful as it pushed past mountain peaks to reach the great walls surrounding

Grey Keep. A perilous hiss played a soft accompaniment. Halál glanced to the right. His gaze narrowed on the cage sitting on a table across the room. Hinges squeaked as the steel door swung wider. His heart picked up a beat. And then another, slamming against the inside of his breastbone, making his temples throb. Each movement slow and measured, he turned toward the table and . . .

The door to the viper's enclosure stood wide open.

His mouth curved. Exhilaration followed, drowning caution beneath a wave of satisfaction. Such a superb turn of events. An interesting twist wrapped up in a lethal game of hide-and-seek. Scanning the shadows, Halál pushed to his feet. He needed to be moving—able to shift quickly when the snake slithered into view. Cunning for her kind, Beauty enjoyed the hunt too much to ever back down. Or show an ounce of mercy. She would strike fast and sink her fangs deep instead. Leave him with little defense as she filled him with poison and left him for dead.

No doubt his adversary's intention.

Beauty's escape was no accident. Someone had unlocked and opened the cage door. Which meant one thing. One of his assassins sought to kill him. Slowly. With his own snake.

Halál hummed in appreciation. Pride surfaced along with the pleasure. Finally. At last. A worthy opponent. An assassin willing to use creative means to relieve him of command. 'Twas a good sign, one that gave him hope for Al Pacii's future. He wouldn't be around forever and the Order of Assassins needed a strong leader. A man willing to do what was necessary—like mastermind a power play to eliminate him, clearing the way for a change in the ranks. All without raising a blade against him . . .

Or getting his hands dirty.

With a grace that belied his age, Halál shifted away from the bed. Bare feet brushing over the flagstone floor, he searched the shadows again: under tables and chairs, in each corner of the chamber. He caught sight of Beauty in his periphery. Black scales gliding across stone, she slithered under the bed behind him.

"My Beauty," he whispered, preparing for the attack.

The viper's tongue flicked out. She curled the forked tip, searching for his scent in the air, then drew it back in, and retreated on a smooth glide. Slithering into a coil, her horned head shifted to one side, as though preparing to strike, but . . .

Beauty stayed still and silent instead, the orange glow of fire-light reflecting in her eyes.

Halál frowned. Strange. Not like her at all. She should have struck by now.

"Come, lovely," he said, coaxing her. "Be bold. Show me your secrets."

"She has none left to give you." The deep voice rolled into the room on a malevolent wave. The air thickened and warped, tumbling into smoky froth as a sinister presence filled the chamber. "I, on the other hand, have plenty to share."

The inky intonation drove spikes into Halál's skin. As the prickle deepened, his attention split. One eye on the viper, he pivoted toward the hearth. Fire roared, exploding from the opening. The flamed tongue licked into the room. Ravenous heat rolled into the chamber like venomous swill, filling his lungs so full he couldn't breathe. Eyes watering, choking on the acrid smell, awareness struck. He recognized the scent. Had encountered it once before . . . years ago when he'd met the High Priestess of Orm and borne witness to her powerful spells.

Black magic. The calling card of evil incarnate.

"The dark one." Halál coughed, fighting for each breath in the smoky air. "Prince of Shadows."

"Very good, assassin."

Stance set, physical discomfort fading, Halál raised his fists. "Show yourself."

"Unafraid, human?" A menacing hiss spilled out of the fire. "Then I have chosen well."

Inferno-like heat crept over the hearthstone and across the floor, billowing over the tops of his bare feet. Cinders stirred in the fireplace. Two footprints became visible in the coals. Halál took an involuntary step backward as the blaze twisted into a tornado and . . .

The silhouette of a man appeared in the flames.

Boots planted in the fiery pit, the beast opened his eyes. Twin irises the hue of orange flames, the dark one met his gaze. Shock hit Halál like a mailed fist, causing his muscles to clench as surprise settled into something more. Awe. Fascination. Glory and fear. The powerful emotions mingled, sharpening his senses. Intuition stirred, and the truth struck home. Strange as it seemed, the Prince of Shadows—god of the demon realm— wanted a word. Anticipation streaked through him, making his skin tingle. Halál drew a deep breath. Incredible. His night had just gone from mundane to extraordinary.

Lucky him.

He had so many questions. Had been studying the occult for years. The bookshelves in his library, crammed full of texts on the subject, proved his obsession. Bowing his head, Halál forced his stiff muscles to bend. Pain tore at his knee joints. Ignoring the creak of his old bones, he knelt on the hard floor. "My lord . . . welcome."

The Prince of Shadows said nothing.

Without mercy, the silence expanded, beating against Halál's temples. He frowned, wondering if he'd said the wrong thing. By all accounts, the dark one lacked patience along with any semblance of peace. Mayhap he shouldn't be kneeling. Mayhap the malevolent force standing inside Grey Keep wanted him to fight instead. Mayhap he'd just ruined all chance of gaining the Prince of Shadows' favor by—

"Come," the dark one said, speaking to the snake as he stepped over the grate and out of the fireplace. His fiery feet touched down on the hearthstone. Power rolled into the chamber on a violent gust of wind. Halál flinched, heart thumping hard. The fire went out and smoke billowed, rising in a wave over the Prince of Shadows' shoulders. Flame-orange gaze riveted to him, the dark one held out his hand, and with a flick of his fingertips, gestured to the viper coiled beneath Halál's bed. "Come to me, Beauty."

The viper obeyed.

Muscles rippling along her sleek sides, she slithered around Halál to reach the devil. Laying her head in his open palm, she accepted the dark one's touch without coaxing, curling around his forearm, caressing his skin with her scales. The sign of affection rubbed Halál the wrong way. He clenched his teeth. Lucifer save him, the viper was his pet. His love. His to care for, not the devil's. And yet, she'd betrayed him without a moment's hesitation. Fisting his hands, he smothered his ire and smoothed his expression. Rebuking the Prince of Shadows was not the smart play to make. Not if he wanted to survive long enough to discover the reason behind his midnight visit.

The dark one stroked the underside of Beauty's chin. "Jealous, assassin?"

"You come into my house and steal what is mine." Refusing to show weakness, Halál squared his shoulders and looked the beast in the eye. "'Tis not jealousy I feel."

"Rage, then." Approval sparked in the deity's eyes. "An excellent emotion."

"If wielded properly."

The dark one laughed. "True enough, Halál."

"You know my name?"

"Of course. I know all about you."

"Then you will understand Beauty's importance to me." Family. Comfort. The viper represented both. So nay, her theft—no matter the power of the perpetrator—couldn't go unchallenged. Bones aching, Halál shifted his weight from one knee to the other, trying to alleviate the pressure. "I would like her returned."

"Careful, human." The Prince of Shadow bared his teeth on a snarl. Fire flared in response, roaring out of the hearth toward the ceiling. The large candles sitting on the mantelpiece melted. Wax spilled in rivulets over limestone, splattering the floor as the mantel grew black with soot. Petting the viper, the Prince of Shadows approached Halál, crossing the chamber on silent feet. The flames in his eyes grew wilder, cannibalizing his dark pupils. "Your temper does not impress me."

"Be that as it may, my lord, I—"

"Call me Armand," he said, stroking Beauty yet again. "And if you agree to my proposition . . . master."

A frisson of excitement shot through Halál.

"On your feet, assassin."

Swallowing past the knot in his throat, he obeyed and, ignoring the pain, pushed to his feet. Armand stepped in close. Halál tensed, but remained unmoving, trying to guess his game. It didn't help. His opponent gave nothing away. No sign of what he wanted. Even less of what he intended. Halál's eyes narrowed. The dark one growled, and with a quickness that defied reason, grabbed him by the throat. Armand squeezed. Halál's windpipe contracted under the pressure. Beauty hissed. Wrapping both hands around the deity's wrist, he struggled to retreat. But as the call to self-preservation sparked in his mind, his body failed to obey. Immobilized by black magic, he stood helpless in the face of power.

With a hum, Armand tightened his grip. "Agree to serve me, assassin."

Halál shook his head. "I am my own master."

"Have it your way."

Satisfaction in his fiery eyes, Armand murmured a command. Beauty rose, horned head angled with deadly intent. Halál moaned as her fangs sank into the side of his neck. The air left his lungs. Pleasure rose on an ecstasy-filled wave. He'd waited so long . . . too damned long to feel her fangs pierce his flesh. All the months spent in yearning, desperate to savor the bliss of her bite. And as she delivered her venom, delight took him to a place he'd never visited before . . .

Paradise.

"Heaven, is it not?" Armand asked, amusement in each syllable.

Halál shuddered, the murmur adding to the thick rush of euphoria.

"To bed, Beauty." His fingertips circling the puncture holes on Halál's throat, Armand lowered his arm and released the viper. She slid to the floor and slithered toward her cage. Once inside, she coiled her long length, pale eyes ever watchful, and laid her horned head on her thick body. The dark one flicked his fingers. The cage door swung closed and locked with a click. "Now, assassin, time to choose. Death by viper venom . . . or life with me."

Desperate to prolong the pleasure as long as possible, Halál shook his head.

Armand tightened his grip. "Your answer, assassin."

"Aye . . . with conditions."

"A worthy opponent. I have indeed chosen well." Mouth curved, Armand leaned closer. The tip of his nose an inch from Halál's, he gave life to temptation with a whisper. "Agree, assassin, and I will give you gifts beyond measure. All the things you crave. Strength. The power to command black magic, along with the promise of eternal youth. Imagine all you could accomplish with immortality, Halál. To cheat death . . . how divine."

Ah, and there it was: the promise of all promises. The one he craved above all others. "What price for the privilege?"

"Your heart and soul," the dark one said, fingers turning to flame. Halál cursed as fire burned the column of his throat. Pain spiraled out in a wave, making his body twitch and his senses scream. Showing no mercy, Armand brought his other hand up. He held it aloft a moment, allowing Halál to see the inferno gathering in the center of his palm. "Service to me for all eternity."

Forever under the yoke of the Prince of Shadows.

A heavy price to pay. A terrible burden to bear. Halál frowned. Or was it? Pledging himself to the dark one would be no great hardship. Aye, there were risks—the loss of independence chief among them. But as he hung from Armand's hand—suspended in glory—the path became clear. He wanted it all. Every bit of the magic. All of the acclaim. The magnificence of youth and a strong body. To be part of Armand's stable, yet free to wreak havoc upon the earth and his enemies.

"Your decision, assassin." Flames growing wilder, Armand met his gaze. "Life with me. Or death here and now."

"I choose life," he whispered, welcoming immortal chains.

"With me."

"Aye, master."

Approval flared in Armand's eyes. The inferno in his palm lengthened into a fiery blade. The dark one drew his arm back. Halál arched, twisting as the magical dagger plunged toward him. An awful crack sounded as the tip punctured his breastbone. Fire spilled into the wound. He screamed in agony as Armand tore his chest open and—

The dream.

He knew what it meant now—the who and why—as Armand spread his ribs. Blood splattered in an ugly arc, running down his belly, soaking his linen trews, dripping from his toes onto the floor. Armand fisted a hand around his heart. Ash and blood bubbled up his throat and cinders burst from his chest, flying like sparks. The smell of burning flesh putrefied the air. One moment tipped into the next, and yet numbness didn't come. Anguish ate at him, burning through his veins as Armand consumed him. A black wave rose inside his head. Consciousness expanded into certain knowledge. He was being eaten alive. It had all been a trick. A terrible lie. Armand had no intention of—

Halál roared as the fire stopped and the black mist began.

Like an insidious disease, the brume settled in his chest cavity—in the place his heart had once occupied. Armand murmured. The fog solidified, turning to sludge. Moving like a voracious wave, the slime splashed into his veins, then reached out to coat the raw edges of the hole in his chest. Suspended in horror, Halál watched the evil nectar sew the gaping wound closed one demonic thread at a time.

Armand released him.

Halál landed with a thud on the hard floor. Clawing at the flagstones, he rolled onto his back. His bones cracked, shifting under his skin. A silent scream locked in his throat, he writhed on the flagstones at Armand's feet.

His spine twisted, bending beneath the pressure. "Jesus help me."

"Leave God out of it," Armand said from above him. "That bastard hasn't been here in centuries."

Halál cracked his eyes open. Blurred by tears, he couldn't see much, but . . . something was different, as though . . .

He blinked to clear away the moisture. His vision leapt into focus, allowing him to see in the low light. Halál frowned. Odd, but 'twas as though he sat in the light of day, not in the near dark of a windowless room. Struggling to acclimate to the change, he glanced around, then shook his head, noticing the spiders for the first time. Tiny and black, at least twenty of them hung between the ceiling beams, weaving silvery webs.

Night vision. Incredible. Which begged the question . . . what else had Armand changed?

Halál looked down at his chest. No wound. Naught but youthful skin poured over hard muscle. Next, he examined his hands. No longer lined with age, both were strong, capable—the hands of a much younger man. His breath caught as he made twin fists. No stiffness. No sound of cracking joints. No pain of any kind. Testing the theory, he popped to his feet. His thigh muscles flexed, and with a growl of satisfaction, he turned to Armand.

"Signed, sealed, and delivered, assassin," Armand said, an unholy light in his eyes. "You now belong to me."

Eagerness engulfed him. "My first task?"

"White Temple," Armand said, a growl in his voice. "The pilgrimage has begun. You will stop it from taking root."

Halál raised a brow, asking for details without words.

"The Blessed return to the holy city. Servants of the Order of Orm and the Goddess of All Things, the women observe the ancient rites," Armand said. "Each time one of the sacred rituals is performed, the goddess' grip on the earthly realm strengthens. If the Blessed amass in great numbers, the rituals will be performed daily and her power will increase a thousandfold. This must be prevented if I am to triumph."

"You wish me to eliminate the Blessed?"

"I wish you to make war on the Goddess of All Things. Bring pain to all who follow her. She loves the humans, refusing me my due and her heart," he said, jealousy seeping into his tone. Rage in his eyes, Armand cracked his knuckles. "You will wipe those who serve the Order of Orm from the face of the earth. Track them down. Leave none alive."

"It will be so," he said, squaring his shoulders. "Thy will be done, master."

Armand's eyes narrowed on him. "Do not disappoint me, assassin."

He wouldn't. Ever.

'Twas the truth, plain and simple. He'd been given a second chance. The gift of immortality shaped by his favorite thing—black magic. The fact Armand's agenda complemented his own meant chance favored him. Luck stood on his side and turned against his enemy. Why? Simple. The new High Priestess of Orm called Drachaven home. The mountain fortress might be far away, but news traveled fast. And if rumor held true? Xavian—leader of The Seven and Lord of Drachaven—was now her husband. Halál growled. Two birds with one stone. His master's word obeyed and his enemies dead.

Perfect in every way that mattered.

CHAPTER TWO

WHITE TEMPLE, VALLEY OF THE BLESSED

ONE MONTH LATER

The chill of midnight descended like a wraith, leaving Henrik Lazar alone amid deep shadows and silence. Stripped of foliage, tree limbs creaked above his head as fog curled between the oak's gnarled feet to reach his own. Just as well. The phantom called night suited him. He belonged in the darkness. The blacker the abyss, the better he liked it.

Especially tonight. And for the mission to come.

Reconnaissance at its finest. The wait and see of time spent lurking in shadows, hoping the enemy showed his face. The toil and trouble of tracking those who served the Order of Assassins across the Carpathian Mountain Range. His objective? To put every one of the bastards down and rid his homeland of Al Pacii scum.

So far, his efforts had all had been for naught. Smart. Combat trained. Well aware he followed in their wake, the warriors he'd once called brethren had been careful, leaving a trail of boot prints in the snow, but little else. Not a good sign. The enemy's desire to stay ahead of him meant one of two things. Either the group wished to avoid him in order to complete a raid . . .

Or he was being lead into a trap.

Fighting his disquiet, Henrik rolled his shoulders. It didn't help. No matter how hard he tried, he couldn't shake the sharp coil of unease. The restlessness wouldn't let him go, slithering through him like a venomous snake, tightening muscle over bone until his instincts hissed, warning him to turn and walk away. The reaction was an unfamiliar one. All the more unwelcome for the fact he was a seasoned assassin at the height of his game. But a mission was a mission. No turning away. No going back. No room for failure either. Naught about seeing his duty done, however, had ever shaken him . . .

Until now.

The fortress he stood inside wasn't his friend. It hadn't been during his childhood, and it sure as hell wasn't now. Abandoned but still intact, the walled city was a beast full of bitter memories.

Henrik shook his head. So many years. So much hurt, and yet the stronghold he'd once called home hadn't changed. Thick walls still soared toward pinpoint stars, standing strong to protect the sanctuary at its center: White Temple. He could see the curved dome from his position overlooking the village square.

Leaping onto the half wall beside the old oak, he crouched low, hitting his haunches to avoid detection. Balanced on the balls of his feet, he stared at the birthplace of his boyhood misery. Less than a league away, surrounded by a cluster of white cottages, the temple shone beneath fickle moonglow, waiting patiently for order to return and chaos to fade.

Godforsaken place. The pit of hell would've been easier to bear.

At least for him.

Some might ask—feeling as he did about the temple—why he'd agreed to the mission. Hell, *he* was still wondering himself. But despising the Goddess of All Things, and her place of worship, didn't change his purpose. In the end, it came down to one thing: brotherhood. Loyalty and the common bond he shared with his comrades were more important than holding a grudge against a deity who didn't give a damn about him. Aye, that and the fact he loved to fight. So, aligning himself with the goddess? Henrik bit back a huff. He might not like it, but his capitulation offered the best of both worlds . . . the opportunity to stay with his brothers and the chance to make war on Al Pacii, the Order that had both shaped and poisoned his life.

Searching the top of the stone parapet opposite him, Henrik rechecked his weapons. Leather creaked as he adjusted the harness holding twin swords in place against his back. All good. The curved blades were ready to be used, just like him. With quick hands, he palmed his daggers, ensuring all five slid from their scabbards with ease. Steel hummed against his jerkin. His mouth curved. The hiss of knives never got old. Neither did the feel of well-worn hilts against his palms. Or the satisfaction as he threw one and felled his target.

Strength upon strength. An assassin's game. One at which he excelled.

With a hum, Henrik sheathed the last of his daggers. After adjusting his bow and quiver of poison-tipped arrows, he turned and jumped from his perch. Grass frozen by winter's chill crackled beneath his boots as he scanned the garden beyond the great oak. Nothing yet. But his comrades would arrive soon. They'd taken different directions to cover more ground after breaching the postern gate. Like him, his brothers were efficient hunter-killers, and after an hour spent searching the city from different vantage points, Henrik knew each one would be—

A whisper of sound ghosted from his left.

Sensation prickled along his spine.

Unsheathing a dagger, Henrik shifted right and gathered the gloom, disappearing behind a veil of darkness. The cloak of invisibility was new to him—a skill he hadn't possessed until a month ago. His grip on the knife hilt tightened. Goddamned goddess. Trust her to meddle—to visit him while he slept and . . . well, hell. He didn't know what she'd done. Not exactly. The result, however, was undeniable. Quantifiable. Unwelcome too. Particularly since magic now hummed in his veins: enlivening his body, sharpening his mind, making him more lethal than ever.

Terrific on one level. The added edge of aggression suited him. The downside, however, was one he struggled to accept. Henrik suppressed a shiver. Christ help him, but . . .

The wizardry fueling the new skill made his skin crawl.

The goddess didn't understand his aversion. Didn't agree with it either. All she saw was his heritage, the long line of sorcerers in his bloodline. But Henrik didn't give a damn about ancient history. He needed the magic to stay where it belonged, in the maternal line of his family, in his younger sister's veins, and out of his. Too bad the Goddess of All Things didn't care what he wanted. She no doubt relished his revulsion as she made him into something he couldn't abide.

Curse her . . . and him too for remembering. For reliving the pain of betrayal, and the goddess' refusal to protect him from his own mother. For wanting something different for the boy he'd been, and the man he'd become. But making peace with his past wasn't part of the deal. Not for him. Too much had happened. He couldn't forgive, and if given half a chance, he'd burn White

Temple to the ground. Raze the goddess' abbey until the Blessed's holy place was reduced to naught but rubble and ash.

"H?" The soft call drifted, swirling in on the frigid wind.

Henrik sighed. Goddamned Shay. His apprentice might be whipcord smart, but he had a lot to learn. First lesson among many: never compromise a comrade's position by calling his name. Unless, of course, you wanted to get your arse kicked by said assassin.

That lecture, however, would have to wait.

Separating himself from the gloom, Henrik materialized behind his apprentice.

"Jesu!" Shay swung around, settling into a fighting stance. His eyes flared with surprise, then narrowed as he debated whether to let his fists fly. Henrik hoped he chose to fight. Being inside the walled city made him ache to hit something, and Shay made an excellent target.

"Hellfire, H." Indulging in a huff, Shay lowered his hands. "I hate it when you do that."

No doubt. Henrik didn't like it much either. "And I hate it when you act like an idiot."

His apprentice tossed him a perturbed look.

"You call me out like that again . . ." he murmured, his tone without an ounce of heat. His pissy mood, after all, wasn't Shay's fault. Still he refused to let the infraction go. "I'll cut off your balls and feed them to you."

"Stop disappearing into thin air," Shay said, mouthy as ever. "And I won't have to break cover to find you."

Henrik wanted to roll his eyes. He smacked Shay instead, delivering a gentle cuff to the back of his head. "What did you find?"

"More wagon tracks."

"Fresh?"

"Less than a day old." Loosing the tension of a long hunt, Shay rolled his shoulders. "Anything to the south?"

"Naught." Leaping back onto his favorite perch, Henrik balanced on the lip of the wall, his eyes on the abandoned blacksmith's shop below him. Two years after the mass exodus and yet, the town hadn't aged a day. All the buildings stood as they always had: well trimmed and tidy, without a single stone out of place. No looting had occurred in the High Priestess of Orm's absence. Not a single squatter had moved in. And no wonder. Magic breathed inside these walls. Henrik felt it in the air—smelled the stench of it drifting upon the winter breeze—and no one, neither criminal nor regular folk, dared steal from the holy city for fear of incurring the goddess' wrath. "The bastards are covering their tracks."

"Good." A wicked glint in his eyes, Shay joined him atop the wall. "No challenge in easy prey."

Unable to help himself, Henrik grinned. "There's hope for you yet, *bratling*."

"You bet your arse, *sensei*," Shay said, returning his smile.

Henrik gritted his teeth to keep from cringing. *Sensei*. He hated the title and what it meant. But he'd agreed to teach Shay and complete the younger assassin's training. So like it or nay, the moniker now fit him like a well-shod shoe. Even so, he couldn't stop his mind from sliding into the past . . . to a time and place where another sensei ruled. Where all hope fell away, leaving naught but Halál, leader of Al Pacii, and the memory of a boy struggling to survive the brutality of Grey Keep.

"You two make for a pair of lovely targets up there." Rich and deep, the quiet voice rolled on a French accent, drifting up from below.

Henrik shoved the painful memories aside and refocused. His eyes narrowed on the man-size shadow leaning against the smithy's back wall. "You're late, Andrei."

"Not by much," the Frenchman said, amusement in his tone. "Anything?"

"Evidence of an encampment near the old stable east of here." Andrei separated himself from the shadows. Moonlight glinted in his hair, illuminating red streaks within the brown. "A large group . . . at least twenty strong. The coals in the fire pit are still warm."

"About goddamn time." Henrik growled. He couldn't help it. Finally. At last. After a month of searching and coming up empty, a group of Al Pacii assassins lay within reach. Just beyond the tips of his razor-sharp swords. But not for long if he got his way. "Find a trail?"

Andrei nodded. "Boot prints in fresh snow. Child's play to track."

"And Kazim?"

"With Tareek. Awaiting our signal from outside the city walls."

Henrik's mouth curved at the mention of his self-proclaimed protector . . . and new shadow. Well, at least, most of the time. Tonight, Tareek had opted out, refusing to enter White Temple. For a member of Dragonkind—a man able to shift from human to dragon at will—the action smacked of cowardice. Henrik knew better. He understood the rage Tareek battled day in and day out. Imprisoned for twenty years in dragon form by the former High Priestess of Orm, the dragon-shifter's history with the Order was as brutal as his own.

So nay, he didn't blame Tareek for his decision. Nor the aversion that drove it, as long as his friend kept to the code and provided backup when called.

With a quick shift, Henrik spun off his perch, falling into thin air. His hands caught on the lip of the stone wall. Dangling two hundred feet about the ground, bitter cold crept into his fingertips. He hung motionless for a moment, letting his muscles stretch, easing the tension before finding fingerholds and toeholds. Using the cracks between the chiseled blocks, he free-climbed toward the smithy's hut. As he descended the vertical drop, Henrik visualized meeting the group of Al Pacii, readying himself for the battle to come. The images centered him, and he sank into aggression, allowing the predator deep inside him out of its cage.

Too bad Halál wouldn't be among the enemy. He never was. The canny old goat didn't venture beyond the walls of Grey Keep. Not anymore. A brilliant strategist, Halál ruled his assassins with an iron fist—and a sadistic nature—coordinating Al Pacii efforts from afar. Annoying, but effective. Just like the bastard's assassins. Tonight, though, promised to be interesting. Thank God. Henrik needed a fight. Craved the flex of muscle and the chaos that always followed. Yearned to see his enemies' blood flow while he completed his primary mission and procured the information he needed . . .

Answers.

He wanted some. Before the enemy slithered back under cover. Back into darkness . . . and the silence Halál used to hide his movements.

The change in tactic was a surprising one. Halál wasn't one for subtlety. A master manipulator, the bastard always took the most direct route to reach a goal. Brazen. Straightforward. Front and center was more the Al Pacii leader's style. So aye, the covert activity piqued his interest. Narrowed his focus too. Adjusting his grip on the slick stone, Henrik descended a few more feet, his mind circling the problem. What the hell was the bastard doing? Why stay hidden for over a month? What plan would necessitate such a strategy? The questions cranked him tight. Whatever the reason, it must be notable. Dangerous to the next power. Epic in a way that put Henrik on edge.

Particularly since he suspected the goddess might be right.

At least, this time around. If what she feared proved true, Halál was now in league with her archenemy, the Prince of Shadows.

Mood set to vicious, Henrik jumped the last few feet to the ground. Ice and snow crackled beneath his boots. Unmoving, he waited until Shay landed beside him. Expression set in lethal lines, his apprentice nodded a greeting to Andrei and unsheathed one of his swords. Henrik's mouth curved. He couldn't help it. Aye, the bratling might have a lot to learn, but swordplay wasn't a lesson he needed. Shay's skill with a blade was second to none, making difficult look downright easy.

Drawing an arrow from his quiver, Henrik notched it in his bow. Weapon at the ready, he tipped his chin at Andrei. "You lead. We'll follow."

"*Merde*, H." Blue eyes glinting in the weak light, Andrei palmed his throwing stars. "Are you feeling all right? You never allow anyone else to lead, so . . . what? Got a fever? Feeling weak in the—"

"Shut it, Andrei, and get moving," Henrik said, in no mood to be teased. Most of the time, he didn't mind his friend's sense of humor . . . or the affection that accompanied it. Right now, though, he could do without that kind of razzing. "I don't want them slipping away."

"*Bien sûr.*" Andrei flashed a set of pearly whites. "Slippery bastards always run when you show up."

Shay snorted.

Henrik bared his teeth on a curse.

Andrei backed off and, footfalls silent, led the way into the mouth of a narrow alleyway. Wind gusts played in the open areas between buildings. Thin skiffs of snow blew around his legs, stripping the cobblestones, leaving icy patches on the ground. Henrik hardly noticed the cold. Eyes scanning the terrain, he slid in behind his comrades and tracked east toward the center of town. White Temple loomed, rising like a ghoul in the darkness. Unease swirled like frosty air, tightening its grip on his heart.

Pulling his bowstring taut, Henrik killed his disquiet. He could abide being this close. Could handle anything as long as he got to fight . . . to deliver a punishing blow to Halál by executing the bastards who served him. The battle couldn't come fast enough. Henrik craved the kill almost as much as he needed to breathe. Mayhap then he'd be able to forget. To let history be just that . . . *history.* Even as he stood in the shadow of a place that still gave him nightmares.

CHAPTER THREE

The headache came on without warning. They always did. The rush throbbed against Cosmina Cordei's temples, pulling at her scalp, making her jaw ache and her teeth hurt. Absorbing the pain, she forced one foot in front of the other. She must keep moving. Alone in the descending chill of midnight wasn't a good time to be idle.

Or discovered, never mind cornered.

Given a choice, she would never have ventured out after dark. Night didn't agree with her. Neither did White Temple, the one place she thought she'd never see again. And yet, after three days of traveling—and two nights spent braving the open road—here she stood, heart racing, fingertips numb, already deep inside the belly of the beast with only one thing on her mind . . .

The sacred ritual.

She must remember the words. Delve deep into the past—into unwanted history and brutal experience—and perform the rite without error before the full moon crested. If she didn't . . . if she—

Worry tightened her throat. Tension sank deep, twisting her stomach into knots. She tried to smooth out the rough edges . . . to tell herself it would be all right. That she was being silly. That no danger lay inside the holy city. That the Goddess of All Things would protect and keep her. The deity she served had always done so, but as Cosmina held the mantra inside her mind—repeating it over and over, again and again—doubt seeped in, invading her certainty. Now she couldn't quite bring herself to believe it. She swallowed past the lump in her throat. It had been so long, five full years since she'd left the temple and the Order of Orm. But despite everything—her unease, the awful stillness, the quiet desolation of White Temple—she refused to turn back.

Or allow fear to rule her.

The late-night visit couldn't be helped. She must keep going.

Footfalls quiet, she crept into the thickening shadows. Turning down another wide corridor, she tiptoed past limestone walls with raised carvings honoring the Goddess of All Things. She knew each one by heart. All the impressions. Every curved symbol. Numerous prayers etched in stone. The silence, though, was different. Once a joyous place, the hallways inside the holy city had always been filled with laughter. Now silence reigned, making her heart pound and cold air rasp against the back of her throat. Each hard-won exhale puffed between her lips, frosting the space in front of her face. Ignoring the chill, Cosmina upped her pace. Almost there. One more length of corridor. A three-stair ascent and—

A soaring archway materialized in the gloom.

Thank the gods. Finally. The entryway into High Temple.

Taking the steps two at a time, she crossed beneath the massive stone lintel high above her head. Senses keen, she veered right, away from the center of the enormous rotunda. She didn't want to traverse the middle of it. With moonlight ghosting through the many windows near the roof edge, 'twas too risky. Anyone might see her. Take aim, let fly, and make her pay for daring to enter the goddess' realm.

Cosmina swallowed a huff. The worry was ridiculous. No one was here, after all, but . . .

She glanced over her shoulder anyway. Nothing. No one. Naught to indicate she was being followed. And yet, she couldn't shake her disquiet. Or the belief she wasn't alone. A premonition? Complete paranoia? Mayhap . . . mayhap not. All she knew was that something felt wrong. 'Twas the small things. Infinitesimal, really. Signs most would've missed—a slight stirring of the air, the quiet whisper of magic within the walls, the rise of the fine hairs on the nape of her neck. All murmured, making blood rush in her ears as her senses prickled in warning.

Using night shadows for cover, she made a beeline for one of the massive pillars that circled the chamber, separating the rotunda from the wide aisle ringing it. The soft tap-tap-tap of her boots echoed, keeping time with her heart as she slid to a stop at the base of the first column. She shuffled sideways and scanned the expanse of High Temple, looking for danger inside the sacred chamber—the jewel in the Goddess of All Things' crown, a physical manifestation of her power here on earth.

Not that anyone would recognize it as such now.

Long deserted by the Blessed—those who served the goddess—High Temple reeked of abandonment. It looked the part too. Was the epitome of neglect, cobwebs hanging in corners, brittle leaves littering the mosaic floor beneath the arc of the golden dome. A pang of regret curled around Cosmina's heart. Such a mess. So unnecessary. Sad beyond words that the chamber—and a once vibrant community—lay in ruin. Almost beyond repair in a city that had always been renowned for hope, revival, and . . .

Healing magic.

But then, 'twas the very reason she'd made the journey, wasn't it? Perform the ancient ceremony. Revive the old ways. Do as the goddess demanded and recall the Blessed to White Temple.

The thought made her temples throb with renewed vigor. Swallowing a curse, Cosmina sank into a crouch. Balanced on the balls of her feet, she turned into the raised collar of her winter cloak. Rabbit fur brushed her cheek, bringing soft comfort as compulsion reared its ugly head. Unable to resist its allure, she checked her throwing knives. Tucked into her boots, the familiar hilts settled in her palms. Good. No need to panic. The twin blades were right where she needed them, close at hand, easily drawn, more quickly thrown. Her fingers flexed around the well-worn hilt as she pulled one blade free. Steel glinted in the weak light. Taking comfort in the sight, she held her breath and listened.

Naught. Barely any sound at all. Just the low moan of the wind pushing against the temple walls. All right, then. All clear. 'Twas now or never.

Time to move.

Spinning into the aisle, she hurried toward the base of the next column. The agonizing thump expanded inside her head. Her stomach pitched, then rolled. With a quiet curse, she slid to a stop and, using the square base of the round pillar for cover, leaned against the cool stone. Steel rasped against leather as she sheathed her dagger and pressed the heel of her hand to her eye socket. It didn't help. She squeezed her eyes closed. The pain persisted, becoming worse with each passing minute.

Blast it to heaven and back. Of all the rotten luck. Such bad timing too. Distraction wasn't an option. Neither was staying in one spot for too long.

Too bad the coming vision didn't care.

Ever obstinate, her gift ignored her wishes, refusing to go away. Pinching the bridge of her nose, Cosmina shook her head. *Gift*. Right. What a farce. Her talent as a Seer was more curse than boon. A plague upon her mind. A constant drain upon her body. A sickness that traveled so deep it infected her heart and soul. Normally, she was better at controlling it. Could block out the images, forestall the inevitable, and keep her visions at bay for as long as needed. Tonight was proving to be an exception. Bright light kept flaring in her mind's eye. The constant barrage sapped her strength, weakened her guard, and—

Gods. The pressure. It was so intense now, making her skin crawl and her eyes tear.

Raising her hands, Cosmina cupped both sides of her head. The cap she wore to conceal her hair shifted, pulling at her scalp. Pain drove a spike through the top of her skull. With a silent curse, Cosmina pitched forward. Her knees cracked against the marble floor. Battling the onslaught of the premonition, she barely noticed the collision. The gods keep her. She must hold the line. Needed to keep her mental barricade up and the vision from—

An image pushed its way inside her head.

Her hands curled into the leather sides of her hat. Oh nay . . . not here. Not now. But her gift for the second sight didn't care what she wanted. Without mercy, it clawed through her mind, shredding any chance of denial. The image of a man solidified in her Seer's eye. Stark details tumbled over each other.

Short hair as black as a raven's wing. Hazel-gold eyes. Armed to the teeth. Warrior strong. Twin swords raised and at the ready.

"Blast," she whispered through clenched teeth, trying to shut out the mental apparition. The beginning of a name morphed in her mind: *H* . . . his name started with an *H*. Henry or Heath, or mayhap . . . Cosmina frowned. Goddess preserve her, she couldn't tell. Couldn't steady the vision long enough to procure the information she needed. "Damn you to hell and back. Get out of my head."

Surprise, surprise, the warrior didn't listen any better than her gift. Despite the fact he'd yet to speak inside the vision, H-whatever-his-name didn't seem the obedient type. Riding roughshod over people seemed more his style. Was it unfair to make the assumption based on appearance alone? Cosmina huffed. Probably, but she didn't care. All she wanted was for him to go away and leave her in peace. But even as she prayed for him to fade, she wondered what envisioning him meant.

Was he friend or foe? Would he hurt or help her?

Damn good questions. Ones that highlighted an ever-persistent problem. As much as she wished otherwise, her visions never came with a road map. Or any kind of explanation. Instead of a complete picture, she ended up with bits and pieces. Visual snippets and broken whispers. Quick flashes that left her scrambling to fit the puzzle pieces together. Never the whole story. Always a jumbled mess inside her head.

Incredibly frustrating. Dangerous too, considering the warrior was still planted on the forefront of her brain. He was too strong. Far too capable. She could tell by the way he held himself inside the vision and knew—without a shadow of doubt—H represented a threat of disastrous proportions if he proved to be an enemy of the Order of Orm.

Too bad her mission couldn't be forestalled, never mind ignored. Turning tail and returning home would be easier. Safer too, but she'd never been a quitter. Duty called. The goddess had been clear. So instead of backtracking to the nearest exit, Cosmina lifted her head and squared her shoulders. Her boot heels pressed against her bottom, she drew a deep breath, filling her lungs to capacity, and started to count. One . . . the horror of her stupid gift. Two . . . ridiculous quest. Three . . . just kill her now and call it a night. Four . . .

She released the air on a shaky exhale, then nodded. Better. Much, much better. The handsome hazel-eyed warrior was fading along with the excruciating pain. As he disappeared, draining from her mind like grains of sand through open fingertips, her focus returned. Her gaze narrowed on her target: the towering wall beyond the golden altar at the front of the rotunda.

Almost there. A hop, skip, and a jump away. A mere stone's throw from the secret entrance into the Chamber of Whispers.

Adjusting her heavy satchel, Cosmina secured the strap against her shoulder and pushed to her feet. As her weight settled back on her frame, she shifted onto the balls of her feet. Strength infused her muscles. With a burst of speed, she charted a course and sprinted past the next column. Her gaze skipped around the space, landing on the dome rising above the rotunda. Moonlight shone through the stained-glass windows ringing the base of the cupola. Color exploded across the floor, painting the pale marble with strange patterns, revealing the hour. Almost midnight. It wouldn't be long now. Within minutes, the winter solstice would commence and her duties would begin.

Which meant she must hurry. Before she lost all possibility of redemption.

A second chance. The opportunity to belong once more. Cosmina's heart throbbed a little harder. 'Twas a gift, one presented to her by the Goddess of All Things mere days ago. Even while on the run, the dreamscape visit still haunted her, hanging on edge of conscious thought, urging her toward what the goddess wanted. The deity worked that way, invading dreams to convey a message. Or present one of her subjects with a new path.

Sprinting past another column, the exchange expanded between her temples, making her recall the unexpected conversation.

"Cosmina . . ."

The warm whisper drifted on a stream of power a moment before an image formed in her mind's eye. Glorious to behold, the goddess reached across time and space, enfolding her in majesty. And as the soft web of welcome embraced her, Cosmina knew she'd come home. That all the years of struggle had been worth it. That the powerful being who held her close needed her help and could not be denied.

Aware but still lost to sleep, Cosmina bowed her head and sank to her knees inside the dream. *"Majesty . . . you honor me with your presence. Thank you for your protection and grace through dark days and lost years."*

"Naught has been lost, child," the goddess murmured, a smile in her voice. *"You have thrived outside the Order of Orm, and I am proud to call you mine own."*

The praise tightened Cosmina's throat. *"How may I serve you, Majesty?"*

The goddess laughed, the tinkling sound one of delight. *"You always were keen of mind, Cosmina. Quick to comprehend."*

"I had a good teacher in my mother."

"Indeed." Sorrow in her eyes, the goddess' expression turned solemn. *"I am sorry for her loss and your hurt."*

"All things happen for a reason," Cosmina whispered with lingering sadness. The goddess' concern—and obvious grief—did naught to soothe her. Five years had come and gone since her mother's murder, and yet the pain persisted. Now Cosmina missed her more than ever. Wished for so many things, but most of all, to have her back. A foolish longing. Naught could bring her mother back. She knew that. Accepting the facts, however, didn't help. Her heart still ached, and the loss still hurt. *"Is that not what you teach?"*

"It is, child . . . although some things are more difficult to understand than others."

Didn't she know it. Years spent in exile had taught her well. Evil abounded in hearts and minds, tempting fate. A harsh reality, one in which destiny wove a crooked trail, refusing to spare the innocent.

Leveling her chin, Cosmina met the deity's gaze. *"What would you have me do, Majesty?"*

Brilliant green eyes returned her regard. *"Return, Cosmina. Journey to White Temple. Perform the ancient rite and recall the Blessed to the holy city. Evil rises to the west. The Order of Orm must be strong and the sacred rituals observed if we are to withstand it."*

As Cosmina pushed to her feet in the dreamscape, the image of the goddess faded. Woven in magic, her final command arrived on a smoky whisper . . .

"Rise and return, child. The future rests with you."

End of conversation. And the last she'd heard from the Goddess of All Things.

Yet, Cosmina knew the deity watched from afar. She felt her gaze, the heft and weave of a cosmic wind as the goddess tracked her progress, cheering her on, moving obstacles until her path opened and the way became clear.

Staying low, Cosmina raced past another pillar. Using each base for cover, she rounded the outskirts of the room. Gaze on the wall beyond the High Altar, the irony of her actions struck home, dragging an unwanted memory to the forefront of her mind. Her throat went tight. How many times had she been in this chamber? Hundreds? Thousands? Too many times to count? As she headed around the last corner, her eyes on the staircase in front of the altar, an image flashed in her mind's eye . . .

Four, mayhap five, years old, she was playing hopscotch on the marble tiles, beneath the golden dome, while other members of the Blessed looked on.

Such a pretty portrait. One filled with good memories despite how wrong it had gone in the end. Her banishment at the hands of Ylenia, the former High Priestess, might have separated her from the Order, but the holy city remained her home. And the goddess her one true purpose.

Some had called her exile a death sentence.

Cosmina knew better. Regardless of the fear and uncertainty, her expulsion had been her salvation. Instead of death that dark day, she'd gained her freedom. From servitude inside the temple and a High Priestess that craved her gift, but cared naught for her. From the realization that no matter how much she believed—or how hard she tried—she would never measure up to Ylenia's twisted standards.

Just as well.

She hadn't been made for music and poetry. For prayer and ceremony either. She preferred her knives to quill and parchment.

Had been made for a battlefield, not a ballroom. The years away had only strengthened her resolve and honed her ability. And yet, even in the face of confidence—of sure skill and certain knowledge—her dread refused to fade. She must do the goddess proud. She mustn't spoil the ancient rite.

She must remember the words . . .

Or die trying.

Arms and legs pumping, Cosmina vaulted onto the first step. Wasting no time, she took the treads two at a time. Her satchel banged against the outside of her thigh. An ache bloomed at the base of her skull, clanging like a warning bell. Cosmina ignored its seductive pull. She didn't have time for nonsense, never mind another vision. She was close. So close now. Twenty feet at most, and she would skirt the altar and slide to a stop in front of the wall carvings. The pictographs told the history of White Temple, but also served as a ruse. The intricate design rose in an impressive sweep, colorful images camouflaging the keyhole that unlocked the door into the Chamber of Whispers.

The ball of her foot connected on the top tread. A difficult jump. A quick shift in midair, and she leapt over the iron railing. With the quiet grace of a cat, she landed on the other side. Boot soles slapping against tarnished marble, she flipped her cloak over her shoulders. Raising her chin, she reached beneath her leather hauberk and pulled out the silver disc she wore on the end of a delicate chain. Engravings on one side, raised metal on the other, the ancient key settled in her palm as she sighted the identical indentation hidden in the wall design. She came even with the gilded corner of the huge altar.

A whisper of sound slithered through the quiet.

Cosmina's attention snapped left, but—

A man appeared in her path, materializing out of thin air.

"Gods!" Her shout rippled, slamming through the rotunda.

Arms and legs churning, she reversed course, trying to stay out of range. But it was too late. Locked on, the warrior moved in for the kill. With a quick stride and even faster hands, he fisted the front of her mantle. He growled. She squawked as he lifted her off the floor. Fear spun her around the lip of insanity. By the gods, where had he come from? A good question. One that left her head the instant her attacker spun around and let go, launching her through the air.

Breath locked in her throat, Cosmina braced for impact. Oh goddess. She was in for a terrible tumble, a hard landing, one that wasn't going to be—

She collided with the top of the altar.

Whiplashed into a death skid, she spun across the golden surface. Dust flew. Panic shrieked, banding around her rib cage. Chest tight, heart throbbing against her breastbone, Cosmina grasped for purchase. Too little, too late. She was already falling. With a gasp, she hurtled over the edge and slammed into the floor on the other side.

CHAPTER FOUR

Henrik cursed as he lost his grip on the intruder. He heard the gasp of alarm. Saw the pint-size body whirl through the air and the dark cloak billow around the hat on the boy's head. All without him moving a muscle to help. Mayhap 'twas the shock of losing control. Mayhap 'twas the idea he no longer knew his own strength. Mayhap 'twas the god-awful magic coursing through his veins. Or the combination of the three, but . . . ah hell. The reasons didn't matter. Only one thing held true . . .

He shouldn't be standing around watching it happen.

Some sort of action seemed necessary. Chief among the options included intervening to stop the scamp's violent tumble. A good plan, but for one considerable problem. The second the realization took root, the boy rotated into a death skid and plummeted off the other side of the altar. A vicious thud echoed, ricocheting through the rotunda.

A soft groan followed.

Henrik winced, feeling the boy's pain, hating that he'd caused it. Lovely. Just terrific. Completely idiotic too. Empathy wasn't his usual fare. Neither was regretting something he couldn't change.

Not that his newfound conscience cared.

The thing kept poking at him, squawking when he least expected. A problem. A serious one, considering he'd never felt guilty about anything until a few months ago. The fact he'd somehow grown a conscience in so little time annoyed the hell out of him. Assassins didn't care. His kind killed. Obliterated. Maimed and eviscerated. Concern didn't come into it. Neither did second-guessing himself. Somehow, though, the killer he kept caged—and unleashed on a regular basis—*cared* far too much now.

With a sigh, Henrik shoved the hood of his heavy cloak off his hair. As the wool folded around the base of his neck, he shook his head. There was something wrong with him. No way should he feel bad about the rough treatment. Particularly since the boy was inside the holy city, a place he shouldn't be anywhere near. White Temple wasn't for the masses. Or wayward boys who wanted a taste of adventure, but . . . goddamn it. Even as he told himself the interloper deserved his skull thumped, contrition struck, knocking the wind out of an excellent argument.

Sweet Christ. Talk about bad timing. And untapped strength. He hadn't meant to toss the boy, but well . . . hell. He'd expected a boy of that size to weigh a lot more.

Another low moan rose from behind the altar.

"Brilliant, H." Tone hushed, the French accent crept up the wide-faced staircase. Andrei followed, stepping from the shadows flanking the base of a massive column. "Taken to brutalizing infants now, have you?"

"Stow it, Andrei." Glancing over his shoulder, Henrik tossed his friend an annoyed look, then switched focus. The boy still hadn't gotten up. His brows collided as a list of potential injuries streamed into his head. Had the scamp hit his head on the edge of the altar? Had he broken a bone upon impact? Was he even now bleeding all over the marble floor? Angst tightened Henrik's chest. "Keep your eyes open."

"The bastards are here somewhere," Shay said, his quiet voice drifting down from somewhere high. Henrik scanned the narrow architectural frieze situated at the top of the pillars. He found his apprentice on the first go-around. Henrik huffed. He should've guessed. The young assassin preferred heights—enjoyed scaling monster cliffs most skilled climbers would never attempt. "The city stinks of them."

Leather rasped against steel as Andrei palmed his throwing stars.

"I sense them. 'Tis like an uncomfortable prickle, a buzz between my temples," Henrik murmured, feeling the strange slither of sensation. The zing made his skin tighten, awakening senses he hadn't known he possessed. 'Twas as though his magic reacted to another kind . . . a darker presence within the holy city. "Do you feel that?"

Andrei shook his head. "*Non*, but footprints in snow never lie."

"Neither does Henrik's gut," Shay said, speculation in his gaze. "I don't feel it either, H. Can you track it?"

"Unclear." Henrik frowned. "I feel it, but the connection is weak. I don't know if I can follow the trail."

"Allow me." Blue eyes narrowed, Andrei stepped back into the shadows. "I will go—"

"Nay. We stay together." The hum inside Henrik's veins intensified. He tuned in, tracking the slither and slide, trying to understand. He'd never felt anything like it. Another new skill? A symptom of all the goddess' meddling? Excellent questions. Ones best left for another time. The sensation kept shifting, becoming a pulse of warning, telling him Al Pacii assassins closed the gap, heading their way. "Strength in numbers."

As his comrades murmured in assent, Henrik strode around the end of the altar. He needed to get the boy moving toward the nearest exit. The sooner he left, the better. No way he wanted the scamp anywhere near the coming battle. The enemy wouldn't care that he was an innocent caught in the cross fire. Regardless of his tender age, the Al Pacii bastards would gut and leave him to bleed out on the temple floor.

No mercy. No second chances. Just a slow, hard death.

Henrik gritted his teeth. Christ help him if that happened. He had enough to feel guilty about without tossing that mess onto the ever-growing pile. Gold glimmered in the low light as he cleared the corner of the altar and stepped around—

Steel glinted in the gloom.

A six-inch blade sliced toward him.

Reflexes kicked in. His muscles coiled. Henrik leapt sideways, away from the threat. The razor-sharp tip grazed his thigh, cutting through his trews. Surprise made him stare at the gash in the leather even as he shifted into a fighting stance. He frowned. What in God's name did the boy think he was doing? Well, besides ruining his favorite pair of goddamned trews.

Fists raised and brows drawn, Henrik scowled at the little bastard. Huge green eyes met his over the points of twin daggers and . . .

Henrik sucked in a quick breath. He took a step back. "Jesus Christ."

Not the most elegant response. Then again, neither was his reaction. But both were warranted, not to mention appropriate, 'cause . . . shit. He didn't know to react—had never . . . ah hell. Another mistake on his part. He'd missed the obvious. The scamp staring him down was not a boy, but a woman dressed as one.

Unable to believe his eyes, his gaze skimmed over her again. A pretty good disguise, all things considered. Without her hat, though, the smoke screen dissipated. No one would ever mistake her for a boy with all that thick red hair. Tumbling in loose curls, the cascade reached well past her shoulders, framing her pretty face, giving her a disheveled look that only increased her appeal. Instant attraction sparked, blazing into an inferno, making his heart thump and his body tighten. Christ take him. Even dressed as a boy—trews, leather tunic, short boots, and a heavy woolen cloak—she presented an enticing picture.

One he appreciated, even though she held him at knifepoint.

The observation should've alarmed him. Her bravery charmed him instead. Not many had the balls to threaten him. Most turned tail and ran when faced with the possibility of taking him on. But not her. Courage out in full force, she stood firm, weapons raised with the wherewithal to use them. He could tell by the way she leveled the twin blades at him. Hands steady. Grip sure. Dagger tips pointed at just the right angle. His mouth curved. Incredible. A sight to behold. A warrior wrapped up in a small package.

He shifted toward her.

She adjusted her fighting stance. "Stay back."

Her hushed tone reached out to stroke him. Pleasure ghosted down his spine. Henrik quelled the reaction. No matter how appealing he found her, he must stay even. Desire was all fine and good, but not here. She felt threatened—with very good reason. So nay, 'twas no time to give the traitor behind the lacing of his trews free reign. He needed his head screwed on straight and a solid plan to disarm her. If he didn't do it right—or fast enough—he'd cause her pain. And the last thing he wanted to do was hurt her. Again.

Gaze steady on his, her back to the altar, she stepped to her right. He mirrored each of her movements, pressing the advantage of his position while weakening hers.

Not liking his proximity, she bared her teeth. "Move away."

"No need for alarm." Holding his arms out to the sides, Henrik flipped both hands palm up. The move was designed to reassure her. She didn't take the bait, keeping her guard high and him at bay. Boots sliding over marble tile, he kept pace with her and, dancing the dance, searched for an opening between her blades. He didn't have much time. The buzz between his temples told the tale, sending up a serious warning. The enemy was approaching, which meant . . . time to disarm the little hellion and send her to safety. "I mean you no harm."

"Liar."

"Leave. I will not stop you."

"I belong here. You do not . . ." She twisted a blade in her hand, leveling one at him. "Get out."

Her territorial tone rubbed him the wrong way. The words whispered through his mind. *I belong here.* Hell in a handbasket. She couldn't mean . . . wasn't admitting to . . .

Suspicion took an ugly turn, raising internal alarms bells. As the clang got going inside his head, Henrik raked her with his gaze. He clenched his teeth. Please let him be wrong. He'd hoped never to see her kind again. Didn't want anything to do with blind faith, never mind those who held it in high regard. And yet even as he hoped for the best, instinct told him to expect the worst. Swallowing the bad taste in his mouth, he tabled his hunch. Intuition was all fine and good, but facts were better. Mayhap he was just being paranoid. Mayhap she'd simply made White Temple her home when everyone else deserted the holy city. Henrik stifled a snort. And mayhap he would grow two heads on the morrow.

Her assertion—and the steely tone that carried it—left little doubt.

His eyes narrowed on her. "You are one of the Blessed."

"What I am is none of your affair." Eyes glittering with mistrust, her fingers flexed around the knife hilts as she sidestepped again. Her mistake. The slight shift unbalanced her for a split second, giving him an opening. "Get the hell—"

Lightning quick, he struck. She cursed as he slipped through her guard. She spun, trying to counter. But it was too late. He'd already invaded her space, moving in so tight she couldn't maneuver. A precise strike. A quick twist, and he blocked each of her thrusts. She lost her grip on her weapons. Steel whirled through the air. The twin blades clattered against the floor and slid, colliding with the wall behind him as he surrounded her with his body.

She lashed out. Her small fist came toward his head. Henrik dodged the blow and tightened his hold. Using gentle pressure, he spun her around, lifted her off the ground, and took a step forward. She gasped in outrage. He pressed his advantage, trapping her between him and the lip of the altar. Her hip bones pressed to the edge, he bent her forward and pinned her down: bottom up, breasts pressed to the golden surface, his thigh lodged between her own as her feet dangled inches from the floor.

"Let go!" Fighting like a wildcat, she bucked beneath him. "Get off me!"

"Little hellion, calm down." Shackling both her wrists with one hand, he immobilized her. Her breath hitched as she vibrated beneath him. Fear. A cartload of it. He smelled it on her and . . . remorse hit him chest level. Goddamn it. He was scaring the hell out of her. Which made him feel an inch tall. Particularly since he respected women too much to ever hurt one. But desperate times called for rougher methods. He needed to know. Couldn't let her go until she answered his question. So like it or nay, he would play the ruffian until she did. "I meant what I said. I am no threat to you. But tell me true, or I'll see for myself."

"Nay," she said, gritting the denial between clenched teeth. "You have no right—"

"Have it your way."

"Don't!"

He ignored her and, backing off a bit, wrenched her cloak from beneath her hips. As he held her down and tossed the thick wool to one side, she threatened to kill him . . . with a battle-axe . . . to the head. Henrik almost grinned. Almost, but not quite. He was too busy staring at the curves he'd uncovered. Christ, she was well put together, sweetly rounded in all the right places. Which—damn it to hell and back—was the wrong thought to be thinking.

Especially right now. With her pinned beneath him.

But that didn't stop him. His grip firm, he unsheathed one of his daggers and sliced the lacing running up the back of her leather tunic. The binding gave way, parting to reveal a linen undershirt. She reared, kicking out with her legs. Re-sheathing his blade, he pushed her back down and, with a sharp tug, pulled the fabric from the waistband of her trews.

She snarled at him. Henrik swallowed hard. Oh God. Christ be merciful. So soft. So sweet. A beautiful expanse of smooth, pale skin.

Desire licked through him.

He put a leash on the errant urges and clung to self-discipline. To hell with his reaction to her. He was stronger—more experienced—than that. No way would he allow baser needs to get in the way. Answers. He wanted some. Right now. Needed to see the mark and confirm her status without a shadow of a doubt. But as he shoved at the linen, pushing it up her torso—uncovering the incredible curve of her waist, the fine indent of her rib cage, seeing goose bumps spread on her skin—Henrik struggled to control his lust. All of a sudden he wanted to touch, to taste, to slip between her thighs and find the heart of her, instead of discovering the truth.

Dumb. Reprehensible. So wrong in every way.

And yet, he refused to stop. Or let her go.

Another shove. The linen rose another six inches, catching beneath her arms. She twisted, quivering with fear, raging beneath him, revealing the side of her breast. Henrik blew out a long, slow breath. Call him a wretch, then call it a night, 'cause . . . God. She was beautiful. All smooth skin, tempting curves, the taut curve of her breast so enticing, his imagination took flight and filled in the blanks, supplying an image of her in his bed. Bowed in supplication beneath him. Legs spread and lips parted as she begged for his possession.

Henrik cursed. Wrong thought. Again.

"You bastard."

Without a doubt. He qualified as the worst sort. But as he uncovered the expanse between her shoulder blades, Henrik knew he'd taken the correct tack. Been right to check because—aye, there it was—the moon-star, the symbol of the Goddess of All Things burned into her back. Literally. Unlike him, she hadn't been born with the mark. Hers had been seared into her skin the moment she'd been born inside White Temple.

Just another in a long line of the goddess' mindless servants.

"Goddamn it," he growled, brushing his thumb over the raised patch of scarred skin. He shook his head. Of all the horrible luck. "A Blessed."

The growl in his tone made her shiver. "Please let me go."

Her quiet tone pierced through his disappointment, then sank deep to touch his heart. His grip on her gentled, but he couldn't do what she asked. Not yet. Not with the past circling like a rabid dog, reminding him of his mother. Of her cruelty and all the abuse he'd suffered inside these walls. God, how he despised this place. Hated everything about it. The exquisite expanse of mosaic floors. The intricate pictographs carved into its stone walls. The golden dome rising over the rotunda's center. Some might have called the chamber beautiful. Mayhap it was, but only on the surface. Ugliness seethed beneath, infecting White Temple's underbelly, heralding a brutal history that couldn't be ignored, forgotten . . .

Or forgiven.

"H, wrap it up," Andrei said from his position behind a pillar. "Company's coming."

The reminder brought Henrik's head up.

The rasp of multiple footfalls drifted into the chamber.

His focus snapped to the rear of the rotunda. Gathering the gloom, Henrik wrapped himself and the woman in magical swirl. She shivered, reacting to the chill that always accompanied the veil of invisibility. As the air thickened and his exhale frosted into white puffs, a man-size silhouette crept into view. Others followed, one by one. More than twenty strong, the enemy assassins crossed the threshold, slipping beneath the archway that served as High Temple's only entrance. Its only exit point too.

Henrik growled in appreciation. Absolutely fantastic. Perfect in every way. Except for one thing . . .

The woman still pinned beneath him.

Some men would've said the hell with it and let her go. Turned away and left her to fend for herself in the face of the coming onslaught. Henrik couldn't do it. Aye, she might be a member of an Order he despised, but he refused to abandon her to Al Pacii. Instead, he would do his duty. Get her to safety. See that she got outside the city walls in one piece before sending her on her way.

"Please." Harried breaths coming in icy bursts, another tremor rattled through her. "Let go."

Smoothing her shirt back into place, Henrik covered her up. Groin pressed to her bottom, he leaned in close. The wall of his chest met the curve of her spine. She tensed. He set his mouth against her ear. "Listen very carefully, Blessed. I will let you go on one condition."

"W-what?"

"You must do what I say, when I say it," he said, so low only she heard the instructions. "Otherwise you will not make it out of the temple alive. Understood?"

She hesitated a moment. "Who's here?"

"Al Pacii assassins."

"I need my knives."

"Pick up your blades, then stand at my back."

Her chin dipped as she nodded.

Releasing her wrists, he tightened the veil of invisibility around her. The temperature dropped another few degrees. She shivered in the growing chill, but even as he regretted her discomfort, he held the line. The cold was a necessary thing, the only way to keep her hidden without him touching her. If she obeyed and stayed close, the enemy wouldn't see her until he lifted the veil in order to attack. As he straightened and stepped away from her, she spun to face him. Wary green eyes met his. She shuffled backward, putting more distance between them. Henrik didn't blame her. She'd been manhandled and stripped in the space of a few minutes.

Her mistrust was only natural.

Holding her gaze, he drew the yew bow from inside his quiver of arrows. "Move when I say move. Got it, Blessed?"

"Cosmina." Throwing him a nasty look, she sidestepped and, slipping between him and the altar, went in search of her blades. She found both near the base of the rear wall. After palming the pair, she stood and glared at him over her shoulder. "I am more than my calling, warrior."

He arched a brow. Well, well, well. More than just a Blessed, it seemed. One with a temper to match the fire in her eyes and the color of her hair.

"Henrik," he murmured, giving in to convention.

First names were a good idea. Comfort came with knowing. Knowing engendered trust. Both excellent things at the moment. Particularly while headed into battle with a strange woman at his back.

"Remember my instructions." Sense crackling in warning, Henrik treated her to another no-nonsense look. "Stay close, Cosmina."

Bow at the ready, he turned his back on her and drew a poison-tipped arrow from his quiver. He notched it and, pivoting toward the open expanse of the rotunda, pulled the bowstring taut. Wood whispered against wood. Inhaling through his nose, he caught the scent on the air. Oiled leather and wood smoke, Al Pacii calling cards. Excellent. The enemy was downwind and headed straight for him. About time too. After playing hide-and-seek inside White Temple for the last hour, he needed a fight. A brutal one in which he snapped necks and watched Al Pacii blood flow.

*　*　*

Heart hammering, stance set, Cosmina fought to steady her nerves along with her hands. She glanced at the tips of her twin blades. Both shook, following the tremor running beneath her skin. She swallowed a curse. Goddess help her, she needed to pull it together. Right now. Before she made a complete fool of herself.

An excellent notion.

Too bad it was chock-full of problems. First among them: the usual calm she carried like a badge of honor had vacated the premises. Henrik was to blame. He'd ambushed her, rattling her with his presence, throwing her off-balance with his quick moves and gentle touch. Cosmina frowned at his back. Odd, but . . . she recognized him now. Had put a face to his name. He was the man from her vision. The warrior with the hazel eyes, hard expression, and little mercy.

Blowing out a shaky breath, Cosmina shook her head. Gods, 'twas inconceivable. Confusing in the extreme. Henrik had not only taken liberties with her, but turned his back on her as well. Just like that. Without any hesitation, acting as if he hadn't a care in the world . . . as if she presented no threat to him at all. Her fingers flexed around the dagger hilts as she debated the best course of action.

Attack him from behind. Retreat into the gloom. Or do as instructed, stay close, and . . .

Obey a strange man who'd stripped her to the skin.

All right. So he hadn't *stripped* her. Not exactly, but . . . gods. It had been close. So very close. The memory slapped at her. Cosmina flinched, remembering the strength of Henrik's body, how easily he'd subdued her . . . the warmth of his hands on her skin. He could've hurt her without difficulty. Taken all he wanted. Kept her pinned facedown—and bottom up—against the altar. Cut away the rest of her clothing and—

The open edges of her leather tunic flapped against her back.

Cold air washed in, mocking her with what might have been.

A shiver raced up her spine, colliding with the base of her skull, causing an awful ache to bloom behind her eyes. Cosmina swallowed the lump in her throat and shook her head. Nay. No chance in heaven or hell. She refused to think about it. He'd done the right thing. Let her go. Seen what he wanted to see—the moon-star burned into her skin—and retreated. Which meant all the terrible what-ifs needed to stay the hell out of her head. Dwelling on the past served no purpose. Well, other than to distract her, which was nowhere near advisable. Not with Henrik armed and acting dangerous. The thought prompted another, forcing to her to circle back to her alternatives.

Attacking Henrik again wasn't a good idea. No real option at all. Particularly since she wanted to keep her weapons where they were . . . in her own hands.

And the second possibility?

Cosmina's focus split. Half her attention on Henrik, her gaze strayed to the stained glass circling the base of the dome. Dread coiled in the pit of her stomach, making her insides hurt. Fighting the internal burn, she chewed on the inside of her lip and faced the facts. Forget option number two. It wasn't viable either. She refused to turn tail and run.

Not while duty called and her conscience squawked.

The moon hastened its ascent into the night sky, throwing illumination through the high windows. Stained glass glowed, sending color spilling onto the mosaic tiles below. The sight jabbed at her, reminding her of her promise to the Goddess of All Things.

Rise and return, child. The future rests with you.

Cosmina's chest went tight. She couldn't fail. Must at least try to fulfill her duty and keep her word. Otherwise she was nothing but a liar and a cheat. Naught but a shell of the girl she'd once been—the one who'd braved the wildness after being turned out of White Temple to face the world alone. So forget fear. Let it all go. She must cling to faith, stay the course, and . . . get moving. The Chamber of Whispers lay just behind her, hidden behind a thick wall covered in ancient carvings. One keyhole away from disabling the lock and watching the heavy door slide open.

With a nod, she dragged her attention from the windows. Her gaze landed on Henrik. Tall and strong, he was a wide-shouldered, hard-bodied dream. So blasted handsome with his dark hair and hazel eyes. Lethal allure wrapped in aristocratic features. Not that she was noticing his appeal. Nay. She pursed her lips. Certainly not. 'Twas more of an examination, a way of weighing his character while deciding how best to proceed without angering him.

Or making him turn and come after her again.

Not the least bit desirable. She didn't want his hands on her again.

The thought made her shiver, tightening muscles over her bones. Shoving aside her rising panic, Cosmina rolled her shoulders to ease the tension and glanced down. The round key bumped against the front of her tunic. She exhaled long and slow. Still there. Her scuffle with Henrik hadn't broken the chain. Thank the gods. Her foresight too. Putting the key on a necklace—keeping it with her always—had just paid off.

Footfalls quiet, mind racing to come up with a solid plan, Cosmina shifted behind her would-be protector. She stifled a snort. *Protector*. Right. Henrik didn't want the role. 'Twas evident in the way he tensed as she moved, aware of her but unwilling to take his gaze from the wide expanse of the rotunda. Another round of unease rolled through her. Not good. For a man like him to turn his back on an armed stranger signaled serious trouble—the kind no sane person wanted. He'd said something about Al Pacii by way of explanation. Possible. Even so, she wasn't sure she believed him.

The Order of Assassins never came out into the open. They were a legendary league. Trained killers without conscience or mercy. A group that operated in the dark places most refused to tread. Ordinary folk never saw them—not coming or going. Rumor held only those marked for death ever looked an Al Pacii assassin in the eye. And then, never for very long before he became a bloody corpse.

Which posed a problem of another sort, didn't it?

If Henrik spoke true, the assassins had entered White Temple for a reason. On the eve of the winter solstice, a time of great importance to the Order of Orm. A coincidence? Cosmina's hands flexed around her dagger hilts. She didn't think so. The timing didn't bode well. Not for her.

Nor for the man who'd become her impromptu shield.

Instincts screaming a warning, Cosmina sidestepped again. The shift improved her view. She caught movement near the mouth of High Temple. Men dressed in black and armed to the teeth crept under the massive archway. Disquiet ramped into full-blown fear. Her breath caught while her mind yelled . . . *run!*

Cosmina stood her ground instead, all her focus leveled on the fighting force slithering into the rotunda. How many, she didn't know. She couldn't get an accurate count in the gloom as the enemy spread out to cover more ground.

A smart move.

Splitting into smaller groups increased their advantage, allowing the assassins multiple points of attack . . . while cutting off access to the only exit.

Alarm picked up her heart, slamming it against her breastbone. "Henrik, mayhap—"

"Quiet." His hushed tone rang with authority, pricking her skin until the hair on her nape stood on end. A fine tremor rippled through her. Knife tips quivering, Cosmina widened her stance. Henrik turned his head, giving her his profile. Bow drawn tight, chin even with his shoulder, he glanced at her from the corner of his eye. "Stay true, *iubita*. Be strong for me. I'll get you out."

Cosmina blinked. *Iubita?* Really? The gall of the man, trying to soothe her with an endearment . . . and a misplaced one at that. Her eyes narrowed on him. "Don't call me 'sweetheart.'"

"It suits you."

"Does not."

"Would you prefer hellion?" Hazel-gold eyes flashed in amusement, making her tingle, before his gaze left her. His muscles flexed, rippling in warning. Hands steady on his weapon, he swiveled and faced forward once more. "Then again, mayhap *vrăjitoare* fits you better."

His deep voice stroked her, leaving a heated trail along her spine. Cosmina sucked in a quick breath. The big dolt. Idiotic clod. Call her a witch, would he? Raising her knives, she leveled the razor-sharp blades at his back.

"All right, then," he said, without looking at her, a teasing lilt in his tone. "*Mica vrăjitoare* it is."

The insult lit a fuse on her temper. "You—"

"Hush now, Cosmina." Drawing his bowstring a notch tighter, he leveled his arrow, all his focus on the other side of the rotunda. "Put your blades to better use. Aim them at the enemy, not at my back."

"Not my enemy."

"Very soon," he whispered, "they will be."

She opened her mouth to argue the point. He cut her off.

"Do not distract me again, *iubita*," he said, using the endearment, ignoring her objections, acting like a jackass. "'Twill only leave you vulnerable. Accept the protection I am willing to provide."

The hard edge in his voice made her quiver. "At what cost?"

"Stay close," he said, refusing to answer her question. "When I unleash the arrow, they will be able to see and hear us. Move with me. Stay behind me. You'll live longer."

They will be able to see us.

The statement cranked her tight. What in God's name did that mean? Could the assassins not see them? She scanned the rotunda again. Swords drawn, a group of three approached, coming across the center of the chamber. Almost beneath the golden dome now, the trio searched the shadows, looking for a target, sweeping the open expanse with keen eyes and brutal intent. And yet, even though he stood in plain view, none saw Henrik. Or her. Each enemy gaze skipped right over them.

Impossible, and yet, absolutely true.

Magic. She knew it existed. Had lived with the consequences of it all her life. Naught else explained her *gift*—the ability to see bits and pieces of the future. Or the fact she'd seen Henrik with her Seer's eye moments before he appeared in front of her. But a *man* who wielded magic? One capable of masking his movements by gathering the gloom? 'Twas unheard of in her circle. A dangerous skill, one Cosmina didn't want any part of.

She glanced at the stained-glass windows again. Higher now, the moon pushed light across the tiled floor.

Her throat tightened. So little time left. So much danger to avoid. Not the least of which was Henrik. Despite his assurances, she knew not to trust him. Men changed their minds like the wind, one moment gentle, the next naught but brutal. So nay, his willingness to release her earlier—and protect her now—didn't mean his thoughts wouldn't turn carnal in the aftermath of the coming violence.

Which meant she needed to withdraw. Get as far away from him as possible. This instant.

Gaze glued to him, Cosmina retreated toward the wall behind her.

Henrik shifted, widening his stance. Winter cloak thrown over wide-set shoulders covered in a black leather hauberk, the muscles roping his bare arms flexed. Wood creaked as his bow stretched another inch. The chill surrounding her deepened, along with the shadows. Harried breaths coming on white puffs, she backed up another step. And then another. Stay close, her foot! She needed to go. Must unlock the chamber door and slip inside before Henrik unleashed the arrow . . .

And his enemy attacked.

Halfway between Henrik and the keyhole, she slid into a crouch. Balanced on the balls of her feet, she sheathed one of her blades inside her boot and grasped the key. A solid tug released the clasp at the nape of her neck. The delicate links rattled, tinkling against her palm and—

"Goddamn it, Cosmina." Henrik's low growl curled around her, scraping her senses raw. Her already frayed nerve endings twitched as panic vied for prominence. "Whatever you think you are doing . . . stop. Right now."

"Sorry," she whispered without knowing why. She owed him nothing, least of all an apology. Too bad her conscience didn't agree. Her plan put him at risk. The second she broke cover, all hell would break loose, leaving him in the cross fire. And her safely on the other side of a thick stone wall. "But I have to go."

"Don't you—"

Dare, she thought, finishing his sentence as she took flight. Boots scraping over stone, she scrambled toward her target. The round edges of the key bit into her palm. She sighted the keyhole within the stone pattern. With a snarl, Henrik loosed his arrow. Wood rasping against wood, the bowstring twanged. Frosty air rushed outward, burning her cheeks, pulling at her mantle, whipping its woolen tail. Time stalled. The chill around her flexed, then snapped. A sharp pop echoed. Pain flared at her temples as the cloak of invisibility burst, tearing wide open.

The arrow found its target. Cosmina cringed as an enemy assassin roared in agony.

A horrific battle cry throbbed through High Temple.

Oh gods. The enemy now had Henrik in their sights. She could tell by the way he shifted. Could see him in her periphery as he put himself between Al Pacii assassins and her. Aggressive, each movement sure, Henrik loosed another arrow. And then another. More screams of pain. More snarls of fury. Multiple scrapes of swords leaving scabbards, and the rapid fall of footsteps pounded through the rotunda. Remorse twitched its tail. Guilt joined in, making her skin crawl and her conscience scream. Feet crackling through old leaves, Cosmina shoved the shame aside.

She refused to feel bad about doing what she must . . . keeping her word and seeing her duty done.

Delicate chain links rattled in her palm. Skidding to a halt at the base of the wall, she raised the key and—

Thunk!

A silver-tipped arrow struck the wall an inch above her head. Cosmina flinched. She heard Henrik curse.

"The woman." The feral growl rolled in on inhuman intonation. "Kill the woman!"

Fear caught at the back of Cosmina's throat. Recognition sparked. The voice. Oh gods . . . that *voice*. Without warning, her Seer's eye expanded. A channel opened inside her mind. One word streamed into her head: *Druinguari*. Minions to the Prince of Shadows, not Al Pacii assassins at all.

"Cosmina—get behind me."

Ignoring Henrik's command, she slid the rest of the way on her knees. Leather trews slipping over marble tiles, eyes on the pictographs, she searched for the keyhole, but—drat and damn. She couldn't find it. Up close, the lock disappeared into the pattern. Lines looped and crisscrossed. Colorful figures blurred together. Intersections whirled into more. With a curse, hands sliding over stone, Cosmina shuffled sideways—

"Goddamn it. Andrei, Shay," Henrik yelled, swords flashing as the first wave of Druinguari struck. Steel met steel. The terrible clang rose, washing over the altar as demonic snarls burned away the chill. "Fighting triangle—now!"

Weapons drawn, two warriors slid to a stop beside Henrik.

Cosmina's fingertips dipped into a round depression in the stone. Her heart throbbed, threatening to pound its way out of her chest. Thank the gods. About blasted time.

Secret keyhole . . . dead ahead.

Flipping the disc over in her hand, she fit the key into the lock. Something whistled by her head, tearing at her hair. Pain lanced her temple. Blood welled. A thin droplet trickled down the side of her face. She cringed, but refused to acknowledge the nick. Or think too hard about the weapon that had just grazed her. Cosmina turned the key instead. Click by slow click, she counted off each tick. Five to the right. Now, seven to the left. One more number in the combination to go.

Each breath clawing at the back of her throat, Cosmina swiped at the sweat on her brow, then wiped her damp palms on her dirty trews. One more right turn. Just four clicks. *Do not hurry. Do it right.* She must go slow. Respect the sequence and the timed pauses between each rotation. Otherwise the door wouldn't open and she wouldn't make it out of High Temple alive.

CHAPTER FIVE

An arrow whizzed toward his head.

Senses keen, Henrik dodged right. The bolt blew by his ear, ruffling his hair. The razor-sharp tip hammered the wall behind him. A violent crack exploded through the rotunda. Stone dust flew. Cosmina cursed. With a snarl, he launched another arrow. And then three more in quick succession. The enemy scattered, diving behind High Temple's massive pillars to avoid the lethal volley. Adjusting his stance, he shifted to the left, putting himself between Cosmina and the enemy.

"H—duck," Andrei growled behind him.

Henrik hit one knee. His comrade launched another assault. The bladed boomerang flew, whirling across the huge chamber. Caught out in the open, an assassin cursed as Andrei's weapon clipped him. A thin line appeared at the bastard's throat. A second later his head left his shoulders and fell, thumping into a lopsided roll across the mosaic floor.

Henrik nodded in approval. "Nice."

"*Merci.*" Intense eyes met his. Andrei raised his hand, catching the boomerang as it came back around. "I aim to please."

"And kill," Shay said as he palmed his throwing stars.

Henrik snorted and, reaching up and over, stowed his bow in the quiver on his back. His hands found the twin hilts rising above his shoulders. Pushing to his feet, he drew hard, unsheathing his swords. The curved blades flashed in the low light. Aggressive. Efficient. Deadly. Henrik became all three as his comrades spread out, giving him room to work. Staying low, he spun on the balls of his feet. His black cloak whipped in his wake, blurring into a streak that stained the air around him. A dark warning in a holy place, one he barely noticed as the enemy swarmed up the steps . . .

Toward him. Sights set on Cosmina. Intent on killing a member of the Order he'd sworn to protect.

More's the pity.

Somewhere along the line, he'd lost his godforsaken mind. Or at least, taken a temporary leave of his senses. The theory made a lot of sense. 'Twas the simplest explanation—the likeliest excuse for allowing himself to become shackled to the Goddess of All Things. But an oath was just that: an *oath*. Binding. Unbreakable. The very definition of honor. He'd pledge himself alongside his brothers-in-arms. Promised the goddess his skill along with his sword. The conditions weren't negotiable, and the parameters put Cosmina firmly in his camp.

His to shield. His to keep safe.

One hundred percent his responsibility.

Which meant no matter the obstacles, he must keep his word. It was, after all, the only thing of true value he had left. So forget walking away. Leaving her behind wasn't in his immediate future. He refused to allow Cosmina to be taken. Or hurt. Aye, she might be a pain in the arse—a mouthy one with a lush body and a mind of her own—but he would do his duty. Defend in order to protect. Provide what she needed . . .

And get her out alive.

Shifting both sword hilts into one hand, Henrik palmed the dagger he kept sheathed against his lower back. Steel rasped against leather as he pulled the weapon free. Timing it to perfection, he waited for the lead assassin to crest the top step. Muscles coiled, he held his position a split second, then unleashed. The knife hurtled through the air and . . .

Thud! The blade found its home. In the center of the bastard's throat.

Knife buried to the hilt, blood spilled down the enemy's chest. The bastard teetered a moment, then buckled, falling backward into thin air. Cursing, the assassins behind the leader leapt, getting out of the way as their comrade tumbled down the steps. A few Al Pacii down, many more to go. Henrik didn't care. Outnumbered didn't mean defeated. It simply elevated the challenge. Anticipation streaked though him. He launched another dagger, then growled in satisfaction.

Bull's-eye. Right on the mark. Another idiot down for the count.

Pulling another blade free, Henrik sighted the enemy while tracking Cosmina's movements. Strange, but even over the din—the hammer of footfalls, the shouts of fury, the chorus of steel striking steel—he could hear her behind him. Senses pinpoint sharp, Henrik reached out with his mind. Magic coursed through his veins. Awareness explained, upping the intensity as he listened to her move. Sweet Christ, his fixation was odd. Locked onto her, he perceived everything—the slightest twitch of her muscles, the frantic thump of her heart, the rustle and slide as she shifted, small boots scraping over the marble floor.

Without looking, he knew Cosmina was on her knees in front of the wall carvings. Reaching up, she pressed something against a line etched in stone. Hand steady, she turned it, each movement slow and measured. A faint click echoed inside his head. Henrik frowned. Bizarre. Beyond anything he'd ever experienced before. His awareness of her was downright eerie. And yet, the whisper of sensation couldn't be denied. He felt it like a heartbeat, the throb and tear as his mind connected with hers and . . .

He read her thoughts.

Ah hell. So much for controlling the situation. Cosmina was on a mission. Had a goal and was scrambling to make sure she completed it. Words like duty, honor, and redemption whirled inside her head. *Stay the course. Be strong. Get it finished.* The mental flash inside her mind exploded between his temples and—

Terrific. Just what he didn't want. Another magic-driven skill to set at the goddess' feet—mind reading, the gift of Thrall. Tareek had warned Henrik, explaining he possessed the ability to tap into another's thoughts, but . . . goddamned son of a bitch. He despised the sorcery. Needed to shut it down. Faster than fast. Before Cosmina's fear infected him and he lost his edge. And yet, even as he told himself to do just that, Henrik checked on her anyway, reading her like an open book. Heartbeat strong. Mind set. Focus fixed. Afraid, but not seriously injured. At least, so far. But not for long if he didn't do something . . .

Like eliminate the threat.

Another assassin came within range. Weapons whirling, Henrik pinwheeled, ducking beneath razor-sharp swords. He lashed out with his own. His blades bit, cleaving through flesh to reach bone. The bastard roared. He rammed the steel tip deeper, punching through the enemy's breastbone. Impaled on his blade, the warrior's eyes widened in shock. Henrik raised his booted foot. A split second. A mere moment in time and . . .

Slam-bang. He kicked out, hammering the man in the chest.

Arms flailing, the assassin flew backward. With a yank, Henrik pulled his sword free of muscle and bone. Black blood arced through the air. Viscous liquid splattered across the top of the golden altar. Each movement sure, weapons flashing, Henrik took on another Al Pacii and whirled full circle. A quick flick. A brutal twist, and he sliced the enemy's throat. The bastard's head left his shoulders, spinning end over end.

More black liquid splashed across mosaic tiles. His gaze narrowed on the strange blood. 'Twas unnatural. Inhuman. Not normal at all. Aye, Al Pacii assassins might act demonic, but they always bled red. Always *red*. Like everyone else on earth.

Henrik dodged, avoiding another enemy blade, his eyes on the corpse. Except . . .

The decapitated body moved. Hands flat against the floor, the dead man crawled toward his head. Incredulity rose. Incomprehension circled. With a quick shift, Henrik parried another thrust, body moving, mind mired in the mystery.

"*Merde*," Andrei growled, severing an Al Pacii arm with one slice.

"Jesu." With a sharp twist, Shay snapped his opponent's neck. Body twitching, the assassin hit the floor, then tried to get back up. Wide-eyed in disbelief, Shay watched the body squirm and took a step back. "Hellfire, H . . . they're not dying. The bastards keep getting up. I cannot—"

A hellish hiss slithered from beyond the altar.

Enemy assassins took a breath, pausing mid-fight.

Silence descended. Alive with mystical power, cold air heated and rose. The warm wave rolled up the stairs and slithered around the base of the altar. Stance set, Henrik's focus narrowed on the lip of staircase. Blond head bent, a man mounted the steps, becoming visible a little at a time. As his boot touched down on the top tread, the assassin lifted his chin. Pulling the blade from the center of his throat, he tossed the dagger aside and met Henrik's gaze. Orange irises flickered, bright color moving like fire and—

Henrik bared his teeth. Holy Christ. It couldn't be. Just wasn't possible. But as he shifted to meet the threat, the truth rose to greet him. He'd have recognized the bastard anywhere. Had spent years under his thumb, trying to survive his brutality inside Grey Keep. Halál, leader of the Al Pacii nation . . . the aging assassin who wielded cruelty like a blade. Except . . .

That wasn't true. Not anymore.

The bastard was changed in significant ways. Strong of body. Steady of hand. No longer an old man, but a young one with familiar features cast in demonic lines.

With a snarl, Henrik raised his blades.

His former sensei growled and, taking aim, loosed an arrow. The bolt roared from the bow. Time stalled, slowing perception as instinct sparked. Henrik's heart paused mid-thump. The bowstring twanged. The air warped and realization struck. Halál hadn't aimed at him. The bastard had found a narrow laneway instead. Had taken the shot and now—

On her knees behind him, Cosmina gasped.

The smell of blood infused the air. Her whimper of pain hit him like a body shot. Not wasting a moment, Henrik spun toward her. He needed to reach her—this instant. To assess the damage and pull her out of harm's way. Before the charged pause ended and the enemy regained momentum. Before Halál loosed another arrow in her direction, but . . . Jesus help him. The enemy was so close. And he was still too far away.

Boot soles slipping against the floor, Henrik ramped into a run, trying to close the gap. Twelve feet. Now ten . . . then eight sat between him and Cosmina. No small distance. Not great odds that he'd reach her in time, either. Al Pacii assassins aimed well and always shot to kill. Which meant Halál's skills had grown rusty with disuse. Thank God. Otherwise Cosmina would be dead—done in by an arrow to the heart—instead of injured.

The creak of a bow being drawn sounded behind him.

Henrik pushed himself harder. Goddamn it. She was too vulnerable right now. Sitting out in the open: hunched over on the floor, blood spilling down her side, a black feather-tipped arrow protruding from—

Sweet Christ. He couldn't tell where she'd been hit. Not from this angle.

Sheathing his sword, Henrik lunged toward her. "Andrei . . . Shay . . ."

"Go!" Green eyes flashing, Shay unleashed his throwing stars. Razor-sharp discs whistled through the air as his comrade shifted to protect his back.

Enemy assassins howled in pain.

Moving to intercept Halál, Andrei snarled and magic flexed. A river of blue flame streamed in behind Henrik. Heat blew toward the ceiling as the inferno snaked across mosaic tiles. Shaped like a viper, ravenous tendrils rose from the temple floor, and fangs bared, filled the chamber with venomous fumes. With a sidewinding shift, the fiery serpent struck. Flames blew outward, shooting over the altar, melting solid gold into liquid metal. As yellow rivulets poured onto the marble floor, the Al Pacii assassins closest to the blaze caught fire.

The stench of burning flesh rolled into the rotunda.

Almost at Cosmina's side, Henrik stayed low and listened to the flames hiss. A voracious beast, the magical inferno ate the assassins, devouring the enemy with flaming fangs. He heard Halál curse. Glancing over his shoulder, Henrik watched the Al Pacii leader leap backward, away from the blaze, and retreat down the steps.

Breathing hard, Henrik blinked. What the hell? Where had the fire come from? Someone snarled in French. He shifted focus. His gaze landed on Andrei. Jesus be swift and merciful. Was the inferno coming from his comrade? It sure looked like it. Particularly since fire rose like twin swords in Andrei's hands, the bright blue of the blaze the same color as his eyes.

Startling, but not much of a mystery.

Goddamn the Goddess of All Things. She never stopped meddling. Now she toyed with his comrade, infecting Andrei with magic just as she had him. Not that Henrik felt the need to complain at the moment. With the magical fire burning and Cosmina in trouble, he'd take what he could get and use the inferno for cover. He'd solve the riddle—and unearth the deity's plan—another time. When the enemy wasn't at his back. And the woman he'd sworn to protect wasn't bleeding all over the temple floor.

* * *

Still counting each click of the key, Cosmina sheathed her second dagger. Not the smartest thing to do, considering a battle raged behind her. The clang of steel resonated in the rotunda, along with unholy snarls and the hammer of footfalls. Goddess keep her, it was all upside down and backward. So completely wrong.

She should be moving toward the fight. Should be helping Henrik keep the enemy at bay. Not stowing her blades while she turned her back on the man standing between her and certain death.

Her conscience panged.

Less than a second behind, her sense of fair play thumped on her too.

Cosmina shoved both aside. She didn't have time for guilt and even less for reflection. Desperate times called for desperate measures. She must get inside the chamber. Which meant getting the combination right. She'd tried twice and failed. Palms slick with sweat, her hand slipped on the key again. She cursed under her breath. Finicky flipping lock. She was running out of time—courage too. Now all she wanted to do was run. Make like a ghost and disappear. Wiping the perspiration from her brow, Cosmina clenched her teeth and forced herself to refocus. She could do it. Stay strong. Stand firm. See her duty done, even if it meant death.

The thought made her hesitate. Just a split a second, but . . .

Cosmina drew in a fortifying breath. She held it a moment and, gaze glued to the disc-shaped key, exhaled in a rush. Pressing her ear next to the lock, she started the sequence again. Another howl of pain echoed behind her. Eyes closed, she blocked out the sound, hearing nothing but each individual click of the lock. Tick-tick-click. All right. First number complete. Now for the second. As she hit the second marker, Cosmina reversed course again. One number left. The most difficult in the sequence. The one she kept getting wrong but—

Tick, tick, click . . . pop. The growl of gears ground into motion.

Cosmina blinked. A second later she retreated, pushing away from the lock. Relief spiraled into triumph, making her throat go tight as the vertical slab shifted sideways in front of her. A narrow slice of light appeared between the door edge and the wall, widening by the moment. The gods keep her. She'd done it. Now all she needed to do was—

Something hit her from behind.

The force of the blow threw her forward. Her cheek banged into the stone wall. Liquid splashed over her shoulder, leaving a heated trail on her skin. Shock spiraled into a sidewinding wave. Cosmina sucked in a quick breath and—

Her arm went numb, dragging her hand away from the key.

She glanced down, then blinked. An arrow with something red running along its length. Time stretched and her mind shut down, delaying comprehension. Cosmina frowned. Blood . . . dear God, it looked like *blood*—on her cloak, smeared on the black shaft, dripping from the sharp arrowhead. She stared at it a moment, watching liquid pool and individual droplets fall. Another drop splattered against the top of her thigh. Her brain whirled into action, supplying details. Sensation clawed over her shoulder. Agony stole her ability to breathe, pushing the air from her lungs as understanding struck.

Oh gods. She'd been hit.

Panic punched through. Horror spread like the plague, infecting her with fear as she reached out and grasped the arrow shaft with her good hand. The slight jostle made her cry out. Her skin tore as she jerked in pain. More blood welled, wetting her tunic, coating the back of her arm as reality dragged the truth to the forefront. She was in serious trouble. The kind she couldn't afford. Not right now. Not when she sat so close to success. But even as she tried to deny it, the searing sensation wouldn't let her. God, it stung. But worse? She was weakening. Could feel her body draining, the awful trickle as blood pooled in her elbow joint. Bile rolled up her throat. Cosmina swallowed the burn and shifted on her knees. She must hold the line. Was just seconds away. Mere moments from achieving her goal, so . . .

No panicking allowed. Duty demanded she stay the course.

Supporting her injured arm, she shuffled toward the narrow opening. Patience. Almost there. But gods, she wished the door would open faster. Slower than molasses in winter, the slab retreated to one side, old gears working hard to pull the heavy stone across the floor. Heart beating so hard it hurt to breathe, Cosmina counted the seconds. She bumped the arrow tip by mistake. Pain ripped through her. Clinging to her goal, she watched the door slide open another inch. With a gasp, she grabbed the stone edge and pulled, lending her strength to the slow glide, but . . .

It didn't help.

She had no strength left to give and . . . oh gods. Her arm hurt. And her strength? Nothing but a distant memory. Cosmina groaned as she raised her injured arm and, smearing blood across the wall, pushed at the door again. Her vision dimmed. Combating the blur, Cosmina shook her head. No quitting allowed. No matter how desperate the situation, she refused to give in to the weakness. 'Twould be all right. She would be *all right*. The wound might look bad, but despite the blood loss, it was actually the best kind: a through and through, a clean strike that would no doubt respond to proper tending and—

"Goddamn it," Henrik growled from beside the high altar. The concern in his voice carried, making her want to turn toward him instead of away. A weak reaction, one propelled by foolishness. No matter his willingness to protect her, she must rely on herself, not him. "Cosmina, move to your left."

Nay. No way. She couldn't do as he asked. Moving left would put her out of range—too far away from the door opening. Even so, she wanted to listen. To let Henrik lead while she followed. She quelled the urge and, forcing her limbs into compliance, slid toward the Chamber of Whispers.

The movement gouged at her muscles.

Ignoring the anguish, Cosmina bit down on a groan and glanced toward the pictographs. Her gaze found the key still embedded in the wall. Reaching up, she wrenched it from its mooring and looped the necklace over her head. The key bounced against her breastbone. The arrow caught in her cloak, twisting the shaft. Anguish bit. Tears gathered in her eyes, but she didn't stop. Tucking her elbow against her side, Cosmina wedged her knee against the door edge and, setting her good shoulder against the jamb, tried to squeeze through the opening. The second it opened wide enough—the moment she could slip through—she'd slam the key home on the other side and, with a quick twist, close it behind her.

Ensure the Druinguari stayed out. Keep the faith while doing her duty. Block Henrik so he couldn't—

Heat exploded behind her.

Cosmina sucked in a quick breath. Surprise made her glance over her shoulder. Fear kept her staring as the door widened another inch. Heaven help her—fire. An inferno of blue flame streaked across the floor near the top of the steps. Screams of agony echoed against the high dome. The stench of burning flesh rolled into the open air. She gagged. The slab continued to slide. She followed suit, angling her shoulders, breathing through the pain, pushing through the narrow space and . . . dry heaved again.

Movement flashed to her left.

Halfway through the opening, Cosmina flinched. Distress tightened its grip, snaking around her rib cage. Her heart hopped hard, thumping the inside of her breastbone. Blood dripped from her fingertips, landing beside her on the mosaic tile. Baring her teeth, she reached down with her good arm. Her knife. She needed it in her hand before the enemy arrived on her blindside. Her middle finger brushed the leather-wrapped grip. She stretched harder, twisting in a bid to grab her weapon, but . . . gods. She kept missing the hilt. Couldn't secure a good enough grip to pull the blade free.

Henrik slid to a stop beside her. Hazel-gold eyes met hers. With a quick flick, he sheathed one of his swords and reached for her.

"Don't touch me," she said, wincing as pain knifed through her upper arm. "D-do not—"

"Easy."

"Get back. Stay away."

He shook his head. "I cannot do that, *iubita*."

Stupid endearment. And heaven help her . . . his tone. So soft. Too low. Completely apologetic, as though he felt her pain and would take it away if he could. His obvious regret did her in. Tears rolled over her bottom lashes. Drat the man. He'd bullied her earlier, using his voice and the endearment to get a rise out of her. To pull her off-balance. To taunt and tease while he gauged her reaction and gained the upper hand. Now, though, he sounded concerned . . . and looked the part too. She saw the worry in his eyes, heard the sincerity in his voice and . . . blast and damn.

There she went again, wanting to believe in him.

Under normal circumstances, Cosmina would never have considered it. Strangers were dangerous creatures. Self-serving.

Untrustworthy. More harmful than helpful. The past had taught her that well enough. But as she held Henrik at bay, Cosmina recognized futility when she saw it. Resisting wasn't the smartest move. She needed help and had very little time left. The ritual wouldn't wait, so like it or nay, Henrik had just become her only hope . . . the only way to achieve her goal and end up inside the Chamber of Whispers.

Which meant asking for his help. Before the moon reached its apex and time ran out.

"Henrik, I need to get inside." Elbow still pressed to her side, Cosmina twisted a little. The arrowhead banged against the jamb. Air left her lungs, escaping her throat on a low whimper. "Help me. Please help me inside. I have to—"

He yelled at his comrades, then turned back to her. The inferno blazed into a wall of flame. Heat blasted through the rotunda as Henrik settled next to her. He raised his hands. She tried not to flinch. Avoiding the arrow and her injury, he grabbed the edges of her leather tunic. His fingers curled inward, pressing against her shoulders. He jostled her a bit, seeking a better grip. Another round of pain streaked down her arm. She moaned. He cursed, but didn't apologize. Cosmina didn't expect him to. All she wanted was for him to lift her clear and shove her through.

"On the count of three, all right?"

She nodded.

He started to count. "One."

"Two," she said through clenched teeth.

"Three."

With a grunt, he heaved her upward. Her feet touched down with a thud, but her legs refused to hold her. As her knees buckled, Henrik held on, keeping her upright, and set his shoulder against the stone edge. With a snarl—and more strength than any man ought to have—he pushed the door open another foot. His comrades appeared over his shoulder, blurring into one as Cosmina's vision wavered. Tightening his grip, Henrik lifted and sidestepped, moving them through the half-open door and . . .

She was through the opening. And one step closer to fulfilling her promise to the goddess.

Half-dead on her feet, she clung to Henrik as his friends followed him over the threshold. Fire hissed from beyond the chamber. Heart pounding behind her breastbone, Cosmina clutched the key and tugged on the chain. The silver clasp resisted the effort, refusing to release against the nape of her neck.

"Blast." Out of strength, she sagged against Henrik.

"Tell me."

"Take the key. Lock the door." Her stomach pitched. Bile splashed against the back of her throat. Cosmina swallowed and stayed on task. "One full crank to the left, and it will close again."

"The locking mechanism?"

"Right-hand side. Eye level."

Grabbing the key, he lifted the necklace over her head. A quick shift, and he tossed it to one of his comrades. "Shay."

The warrior caught it mid-volley and spun toward the door. "On it."

Shivering hard, Cosmina glanced toward the center of the chamber. Thank the gods, it was just as she remembered. Round room. Huge megaliths forming a circle around the perimeter. Cut from the Carpathian Mountains, rising twenty feet toward the ancient dome, the stone uprights gleamed in the low light. The Chamber of Whispers. The most holy of places. Birthplace of the Goddess of All Things on earth.

Finally. At last. She'd made it.

Gears ground into motion. Stone scraped across tile as the wall closed, shutting out the glow of blue flame, along with the enemy. Shay locked the door, then turned away from the entrance. His eyes narrowed on Cosmina, he pulled the key from the stone lock. "'Tis done, H."

"Good," Henrik said, his focus steady on Cosmina. "Look for another way out."

As his friends moved to obey, Cosmina switched tack. Safe from the Druinguari, yet only halfway to her goal. Forcing herself to refocus, she stared at the space between two megaliths. Not long now. Ten—mayhap twenty steps at most—and she'd be standing where she needed to be: on the raised stone platform inside the stone henge. Setting her courage, she braced for the pain and shifted toward the dais.

Henrik held on, refusing to let her go.

"Unhand me."

"I do and you'll fall on your face." Leather creaked as his grip on her tunic tightened. "The arrow needs to come out, Cosmina. Now. Before—"

"Later," she whispered, her tone a soft plea for understanding. "Please, Henrik, let me go. My injury can wait, but the rite cannot. It must be done now."

His gaze narrowed a fraction. "What rite?"

She shook her head.

"Christ. *Mica vrăjitoare* . . . stubborn to a fault," he growled. Swaying in his hold, Cosmina huffed. She shouldn't find it funny but for some reason she did. Whether he intended it or not, the statement sounded more like praise than insult. "Where do you need to go?"

"Inside the circle." Her hand shook as she pointed past the megaliths. "Center of the dais."

With another curse, he shifted to her good side and picked her up. She gritted her teeth, smothering a grimace. The gods be swift and merciful, what a tangle. Injured. Weak. Reliant on a man. The trio of faults were not her usual fare. She prided herself on keen eyes, steady hands, never-say-die fortitude, and in her ability to rely on all three. Tonight, though, she'd missed the mark. Now fate forced her to admit that Henrik was all she had . . . here, now, in this moment. And as he cradled her close and strode into the sacred circle, she decided that sometimes asking for a little help went a long way.

"Here?" he asked, stopping at the edge of the dais.

"Here's good."

Pulling his forearm from beneath her knees, he swung her feet to the floor. Her arm squawked. Cosmina winced and smothered a groan. Muscled arms flexing around her, Henrik murmured her name. His tone said it all. He wanted her to be reasonable. Sensible. Rational. Call it whatever the situation warranted, but—

Cosmina shook her head, refusing to acknowledge his plea. Or the underlying current at play between them. No matter how necessary, her reliance on him unsettled her. She didn't like it any more than the motive behind his agenda. She knew what he wanted—for her to acquiesce while he tended her injury. Why he cared, she couldn't understand. He didn't know her. She wasn't his concern. But as her arm throbbed and she started to tremble, temptation circled, urging her to lean on him. To become his responsibility. To allow him to take her pain away.

'Twould be so easy to do.

But she refused to go that way. Forget here and now, 'twas the future that worried her. The precedent must be set. Naught good would come from relying on him. Or making him believe she needed him.

Meeting his gaze, she pressed her palm to his chest and pushed. Henrik didn't budge. She shoved again. As his arms slid from around her, she sank to her knees in the middle of the platform. "Back away. Give me some room."

"Cosmina, let me—"

"Please, Henrik," she whispered. He growled something obscene, and Cosmina started to pray. She needed him off the dais. Couldn't afford the distraction, never mind the time spent arguing with him. "Just . . . *please.*"

Her *please* did him in. With a snarl, he stepped back, leaving her alone on the dais.

And Cosmina didn't hesitate.

Elbows tucked to her side, she drew a deep breath, held it a moment, then exhaled long and smooth. Another lungful. In. Out. Inhale and release. The rise and fall of her chest helped center her. Time to focus. Time to embrace her past and do what needed to be done. Closing her eyes, Cosmina bowed her head, settled into the cradle of her mind, and forced herself to concentrate.

The words—the *words*—she must remember each one.

Recall flashed. Deep-rooted memory rose, serving up the ancient rite.

"Great goddess of the moon, of shadow and light, hear me now. I come to you in this . . . most sacred of places, on a Sabbath blessed by a winter moon. Guide me with your power. Imbue me with your light. Grant me grace so that I may . . . may . . ."

As Cosmina paused, searching for the next phrase, a familiar vibration buzzed in her veins. The hum expanded beneath her skin, pushing the pain aside. Knowledge stepped into the breach, then gained speed, rushing the rest of the incantation along in the goddess' native tongue. Cosmina sighed, her relief instantaneous. Gods, it had been too long. So many months. So many years. Far too long since she'd heard the language of the gods—the one always spoken inside High Temple. Tipping her head back, she became a channel, allowing the divine words to flow off her tongue and meld with musical notes, marrying intent with a melodic chant.

Singing.

She was *singing* again.

After five years of near silence. After overcoming every hardship. After all the heartache. Here she knelt, serving the goddess inside White Temple—righting a wrong, resurrecting her family honor, following in her mother's footsteps. The thought made her voice stronger. Clear as a bell, beautiful as birdsong, she hit each note as her childhood came back to embrace her. Happy years sped past, then turned ugly, reminding her of dark days. Cosmina shoved the memories aside. All faded in the face of renewal and return. Here, now, in this place . . .

She belonged.

Ylenia, the late High Priestess of Orm, couldn't hurt her anymore. And despite her mother's passing, Cosmina knew the goddess was right. All things happened for a reason: all the pain and desolation, every one of her mother's attempts to shield her from Ylenia's savagery, even her mother's death at the hands of the High Priestess. Terrible in every way. Now, though, Cosmina could see the connection. The strife—all the heartache—had served its purpose, preparing her for this moment, helping her understand her gift better and why Ylenia had coveted it.

A powerful oracle was a matchless weapon. Foreknowledge equaled mastery, the kind skilled manipulators wielded without mercy. In the right hands, it shaped countries, shifted the balance of power, and built strong alliances. In the wrong ones, it caused horrific tragedy.

War. Strife. Famine. Once powerful empires reduced to complete ruin.

History told the tale.

Inside the Chamber of Whispers, however, her gift meant something more. Something better. Something pure and full of hope, so Cosmina lifted her voice high, singing the incantation with timeless rhythm. But as the song crested and the spell formed, the air grew thin, warping against the vaulted ceiling. The ancient symbols carved into the megalith's faces started to glow. Bright light exploded above the dais, then rushed toward the floor in a cascade of illumination. Magic engulfed Cosmina in a sickening wave, making her stomach churn as sensation crawled over her skin.

Panic sent her sideways. She must get off the dais. Needed to stop singing before—

Powerful magic bore down—pinning her knees to stone, holding her immobile, forcing the spell from her throat. She fought the mental slide. The pressure increased, tightening its grip inside her mind. Oh gods . . . nay. Not now. Her gift needed to stay locked away. The instant she allowed her Seer's eye to open—and the magic to merge with her own—it would be over. Overload would suck her into a vortex of pain. But even as Cosmina struggled to keep her gift contained, she knew her loss of control was what the spell wanted . . . was what it needed to complete itself.

She cried out in dismay. The goddess expected too much. Giving in would cost her *too much*. Cosmina understood her power all too well. If she gave it free reign, the magic would steal her sight. It had happened once before, leaving her blind and helpless for days. Resistance, however, didn't help. Despite her best effort, the cosmic pressure continued to build and the terrible cascade began.

Sharp and insistent, the beast banged on her mental gates.

Cosmina clenched her teeth and pushed back. Another round of denial spilled through her. Magic snarled and, raising a powerful fist, broke through the barricades she defended. Multiple visions streamed into her head. The steady rush of imagery stretched her mind, pulling at psychological seams.

The song died in her throat.

Henrik cursed from somewhere nearby.

The spell chased its tail inside her head. Burning bright, magical mist rose, shrieking as it revolved in a ring around her. Imprisoned by the ethereal glow, Cosmina's lungs closed. Unable to breath, she watched the strange smoke separate into seven rings. The bands thinned into discs, each spinning just inches above the next—smooth as glass, edges sharp as steel, an impenetrable cage fueled by her life force.

And so it began . . .

The magic was siphoning her strength, slowing her heartbeat, taking her life one breath at a time. Overload blurred her vision. Tears pooled in her eyes and the glow pulsed—once, twice, a third time—showing no mercy, stealing her power as it sent the goddess' message out in a blinding burst of light.

The explosion rocked the chamber.

The megaliths swayed. Stone dust flew into the air as pain ripped through her.

Recall the Blessed to White Temple. The future rests with you.

Aye . . . there it was. Words to live and die by, ones Cosmina now understood. But it was too late. Too late to stop the goddess' signal from being sent. Too late to protect those trapped inside the Chamber of Whispers with her. Too late to prevent the cosmic slide into physical blindness as sorcery tightened its grip and death reached out to touch her.

CHAPTER SIX

Each pulse a rhythmic chant, magic throbbed through the chamber. Henrik recoiled, fighting the onslaught. Almost impossible to do. The cold ate at him and frost slithered over stone, coating the walls and megaliths, forcing its way down his throat, stealing his ability to breathe. The temperature dropped another notch, dipping into bitterness. His throat closed, and he coughed as pressure banded around his rib cage. Christ. He couldn't breathe. Couldn't force himself to move, never mind think straight.

Henrik sucked in a desperate breath. And then another.

The influx of air didn't help. He was in trouble. Serious goddamned *trouble* in a place he'd never wanted to return . . . the Chamber of Whispers. But it was too late. He hadn't remembered in time. Now he was trapped inside the sacred chamber with one of the Blessed—lost to memory and the brutal lash of childhood abuse. Like ghouls from the pit of hell, the past rose to taunt him. Cruel images and savage experience collided, forcing him to remember. God, he despised those rings. Didn't want to be anywhere near the pulsing glow. The awful light leached into everything—the walls, the megaliths, his bloodstream—making him burn from the inside out.

Bile splashed up his throat, bleeding onto the back of his tongue. Boots rooted to the floor, gaze fixed on Cosmina, Henrik swallowed hard. Nay. Not this time. He wouldn't allow himself to throw up. He'd come too far to be dragged back into the past. Wasn't seven years old anymore, but . . . Christ help him. He was losing it, allowing the magic to elevate his pulse and destroy his control.

Henrik snarled. The sound did nothing to steady him.

Horror locked him down instead, feeding him a steady stream of memories. The need to vomit grabbed him by the balls. Henrik shook his head. So much for being stronger. Wiser too. Age didn't matter. Neither did experience or the passing of years, 'cause—Jesus—he'd always thrown up, emptying his belly on the mosaic tiles. Had never been able to handle watching Ylenia—his mother, former High Priestess of Orm—perform the sacred rite. Or abide her voice while she worked the spell and—

The recollection made him gag.

Sweat dripped into his eyes. With a vicious swipe, Henrik wiped the droplets away and, chest pumping, took a step back. He needed to get out. Out of the chamber. Out of his own head. Away from the circle of stones and Cosmina. But even as his feet moved, his mind remained stuck in the past. Goddamn recall. 'Twas a bitch of a thing, resurrecting his pain, forcing him to remember what he worked every day to forget. All the beatings. The anger in Ylenia's eyes. The harshness of her tone. The revulsion on her face every time she looked at him. Born in a place that honored women and abhorred men. Unwanted by the Order of Orm. Unloved by his own mother.

Twisted in so many ways.

The unfairness of it sickened him. Cosmina's song did the rest, making his skin crawl and his heart shrivel. Not enough air. There wasn't enough air in the room. Struggling for breath, he took another step backward. Sweat trickled between his shoulder blades. Henrik followed the trickle down his spine, distracting himself while he continued to retreat. Boot soles brushing over the marble floor, he widened the distance until . . . the swords on his back bumped the megalith behind him. Arse pressed against the solid upright, he doubled over. Both palms planted on his knees, he hung his head, tried to catch his breath and hang on, but . . .

Cosmina's voice rose in a melodic wave. So pure. So beautiful. A total goddamned tragedy. She sang like an angel, each note perfection as she performed the ancient rite.

His stomach clenched again.

Sweet Christ, he wasn't going to make it. Was about to—

A tremor rumbled through the chamber, cutting Cosmina's song short.

"Jesu," Shay said from somewhere to his right. "H, grab her. She's—"

"*Merde!*" Andrei shifted behind the megalith holding Henrik upright. "Move it, Henrik. Get out of—"

Boom. Boom . . . crack!

A sonic blast exploded from around the dais. The violent wind gust hammered him. Henrik cursed as his feet left the floor. His head whiplashed. The magic-driven burst spun him around, then let go, hurling him across the chamber. Wind whistled in his ears. His vision blurred. He heard his comrades shout in alarm. Stone columns whirled past, speeding into streaks. He stopped going up and started to come down. Henrik sighted the ground and—

Oh shit. The landing wasn't going to be pleasant.

Shoulders leading the way, he hit the floor with a thud. His swords clanged, digging twin furrows into his back. With a grunt, Henrik tucked his arms and, working with velocity instead of against it, spun into the skid. Using his boot heels for traction, he dug in and rotated full circle. Mosaic tiles sped past, sliding underneath him. The wall rose to meet him. Gritting his teeth, he pressed his forearms into the floor. Skin squealed against stone, burning twin tracks up his arms. Agony seared him. He barely noticed. Legs poised to absorb the brunt, he slammed feetfirst into the wall.

His knees rebounded, hammering him in the chest. Air left his lungs in a rush. He wheezed, but stayed still and—legs spread, arms splayed wide, senses throbbing—stared up at the vaulted ceiling. Clumps of plaster fell, the fine grains sprinkling him like fairy dust as he struggled to catch his breath. After a moment of extreme concentration, his rib cage unlocked and his chest expanded.

Thank Christ. Good God. What the hell had just happened?

Twin groans echoed across the chamber.

With a grumble of his own, Henrik flipped over. His shoulder squawked in protest as his stomach touched cold tile. Ignoring the chill, his gazed lit on Andrei. Lying belly down, his friend cursed and, pressing his hand to the floor, pushed himself upright. Half-standing, half-bent-over, he wobbled a second, then gave in and fell backward, ass-planting himself on the floor. Head bowed, angry-sounding French peppering the air, Andrei cupped the sides of his head, and Henrik switched tack. Bruised but all right. His friend would survive, but . . . where the hell was Shay?

A nasty curse turned his attention.

Henrik's focus snapped left and . . . well, hell. Talk about bad luck and—he grimaced—an unfortunate position. Shay was tangled up with a statue. Pinned down by stone, his apprentice yanked on his leg, struggling to free himself from the marble clampdown. Which meant . . . two down, one to go. He couldn't see Cosmina. Or the dais. Not from his vantage point behind the megaliths.

Alarm hammered him, making his heart thump harder.

It was too quiet. So still, silence reigned, making concern rise and dread follow. A boatload of self-recrimination whispered through him. He was an idiot for listening to her. For allowing Cosmina to sway him. For respecting her wishes when she'd asked him to back away. God help him. She'd been at the center of the blast. Smack-dab in the kill zone with nowhere to hide. Now she was probably hurt . . .

Or worse.

The thought made Henrik pop to his feet. His brain went sideways, sloshing inside his skull. Off-balance, he stumbled and . . . goddamn it. He should've realized. The slam-bang of the blast—along with the magic—had messed with his equilibrium. Now he struggled to walk a straight line. Not that it mattered. He didn't have time to fool around. Forget the discomfort. Discard the pain—the ringing in his ears too. Cosmina needed him and, despite his aversion to her kind, he wanted to protect her. Give her his all. Become her shield. Do whatever was necessary to get her on her feet again.

The sentiment smacked of serious attachment. Of deep-seated feeling and the sort of sappiness he avoided at all costs. Henrik didn't care. He knew without examining it too closely that she was different. Somehow. Some way. For some reason. Mayhap 'twas her history with White Temple. Mayhap 'twas her skill with a blade and the spunk she showed him. Mayhap 'twas the fact he enjoyed the look of her. Henrik huffed. She surpassed beautiful with her red hair and razor-sharp wit. The reasons for his interest in her didn't matter. Not right now. And as he limped toward the megalith closest to him, Henrik prayed she was all right. That her status as a member of the Blessed had protected her somehow. That despite the force of the shock wave, she'd come through unscathed.

"Cosmina," he said, voice ringing in the silence.

No answer. Not even a rustle of movement from beyond the great stones.

Trepidation swept in, then ricocheted as he tallied the likelihood of her survival. Twenty to one. Mayhap more. The odds weren't good. She was no doubt dead, lying lifeless on the dais: body broken, blood flowing, and spirit crushed. Henrik upped the pace anyway. So witless to hope. So ridiculous to want. More foolish to pray. Even so, Henrik sent a word heavenward, allowing faith to lead the way even as his fear for her burned a hole in the center of his chest.

* * *

The magic loosened its grip one brutal talon at a time. As the band of pressure downgraded, allowing her lungs to expand, Cosmina fell into a sideways slump. Her shoulder touched down on the stone. The chill kicked up, slipped over her skin, then delved deep to reach muscle and bone. Squeezing her eyes closed, she shivered in the quiet and tucked her legs in tight, desperate to hold on to her body heat.

The curl-up-and-stay-quiet routine didn't help.

Not this time.

Usually the position calmed her after suffering an attack. But luck wasn't with her tonight. No matter how hard she tried, she couldn't slow the escalation of sensation—the throb kicking against her temples—never mind get her bearings. She knew she was somewhere inside the Chamber of Whispers, but . . . Cosmina frowned. Was she still on the dais? Blown halfway across the room? Stuck atop one of the megaliths? Her breath rasped on a painful wheeze. Blast it all, she didn't know. With reality blurring into the mist of aftermath, her mind remained foggy and her thoughts jumbled. Now her head not only hurt, but hope drained away, leaving her with one certainty . . .

The blindness had returned.

Cosmina swallowed a sob. So much for the power of her gift. Per usual, it worked against her, leaving her to take the brunt alone. In the black hole of premonitory overload. Tears welled behind her eyes. Refusing to give in, she refused to let them fall. Crying wouldn't help. And the pain? Well, she was accustomed to it—almost immune to the terrible headaches that always accompanied her visions. And yet, even as she reminded herself of the facts, desolation crept in.

Gods, how she hated the darkness.

Releasing a shaky breath, Cosmina cracked her eyes open. Denying the truth never served a person well. No matter how adverse to the blindness, she must assess the extent of the damage and determine the best course of action. Mayhap this time she would get lucky. Mayhap the magic had only taken her peripheral vision. Mayhap some light would seep through. Clinging to hope, she raised her lashes. A whimper escaped her. No luck. Not a sliver of illumination either. The darkness was absolute, so overwhelming she saw nothing but a black void, unending isolation, powerlessness its bitter sidekick.

With a panicked cry, she tucked her knees in tighter. Her arm squawked. Agony ripped over her shoulder, then reached down to squeeze her heart. "Goddess help me, I hate this. I hate this. I—"

"Cosmina!"

The shout made her flinch. Self-preservation made her turn toward it. "Henrik?"

The rush of footfalls echoed, coming closer by the second. Relief struck like a mailed fist. Praise the goddess. She wasn't alone. For the first time in a long while, she had help—a lifeline in the dark and someone to guide her through. Henrik's voice told the truth. He would aid her if she let him. Not that she enjoyed the idea. Stronger than most, she always looked after herself. Self-reliance. Independence. Zero trust in men. All three served her well, ensuring she stayed out of trouble. Well, under normal circumstances anyway. But tonight didn't qualify as ordinary. Which meant she needed to let go of her pride. At least, for the time being. She required protection and a way out.

Henrik had just become both.

"Henrik," she whispered.

"Here. Right here." A callused hand cupped her face. Awareness sparked, thrumming to life as a strange current rose. The contact prickled over her skin, easing her aches, dimming the pain, chasing her chill away. She sighed in gratitude. So good. He felt *so good*, like sinking into the soothing water of the hot spring not far from her home. Turning toward him instead of away, she pressed her cheek into his palm. "Don't move, Cosmina. Lay still. I need to check you. Your arm—"

"I'm cold," she said, her voice whisper thin.

"Understandable. You've lost a lot of blood." With a gentle touch, he examined the gash on the side of her head. "You need stitches. The arrow needs to come out too. Andrei, bring the kit."

Cosmina blinked, a slow up and down. *The arrow?* "What arrow?"

"The one in your arm."

"I don't feel it."

"You're in shock, *iubita*. Hold still. It'll be out soon."

Uh-huh. All right. He would see to it. Wonderful. Especially since she was now floating, adrift in a stream of soft sensation—no pain to speak of, just the gentle rush of his hands on her skin.

Footfalls sounded beside her. The chill in the room stirred, brushing over her temple. Cosmina twitched, reacting to the unexpected rush of cold air.

"'Tis only Andrei, Cosmina," Henrik murmured, reassuring her. "Shay is right behind you."

"Your men?" she asked.

"His brothers," the man behind her said, his tone touched by the shades of youth.

Something flapped open. A satchel, mayhap?

"*Tiens*, Henrik. Hold this." Andrei settled beside her, brushing her boot. "The witch hazel tonic?"

Senses attuned to him, she perceived Henrik's nod. "The wound needs to be cleaned."

Cosmina grimaced. Witch hazel tonic. Gods, that was going to sting. But as Henrik helped her curl onto her side, she didn't resist. He was right. If the wound went untreated, infection would set in. And honestly, more pain was the last thing she needed. So instead of arguing, she followed Henrik's instructions to the letter—refusing to complain, gritting her teeth, and cursing under her breath when he examined her arm and the arrow shaft.

The sound of a knife leaving its sheath broke through the quiet.

Years of mistrust reared, pushing panic to the surface. Unable to fight it, Cosmina squirmed beneath Henrik's hold. She wanted to escape the warriors and return to what she knew. To the familiar stone cottage sheltered inside the Limwoods, the forest not far from White Temple. Safe. Secure. Untouched by the outside world.

Her home for the last five years.

The image settled her, helping her stay still as Henrik's grip tightened. Tone soft, he talked to her, asking her to trust him. Trust. It seemed like an abstract term, one that felt unfamiliar. She sank into it anyway, and exhaling long and slow, surrendered to the moment and the certainty Henrik would keep his word.

Steel cracked against wood.

Her arms jerked. The fletched end of the arrow flew up, feathered edges flicking at her cheek. Cosmina bit down on a scream. A soft cry escaped in its place, expanding through the quiet. Henrik cursed, but didn't relent. Grip firm, he held her down as Andrei grabbed the arrowhead. Someone whispered an apology. Henrik? Andrei? Shay? She didn't know. Didn't care much either. Not while the pain increased and—

"Forgive me," Henrik said, voice edged with regret. "Now, Andrei."

With a smooth draw, the Frenchman pulled on the arrow. Wood dragged through muscle, past bone, tearing her skin. The excruciating slide arched her spine. Clenching her teeth, Cosmina struggled, whimpers clogging the back of her throat. A cacophony of curses rose in the wake of her outburst. She barely noticed. Didn't care about the trio's remorse either. Fighting the lockdown, she scrambled in full retreat, holding tears at bay.

Don't cry. Do not cry.

She couldn't stomach the vulnerability. Her reaction was silly. It shouldn't matter if she wept. But somehow standing strong, proving her toughness in the face of adversity, had taken precedence over circumstance. And as her arm throbbed and pain clawed over her shoulder, pride stepped into the void. She needed to save face. To prove to herself that she could handle anything.

Tough as nails.

She'd always been that way. But even as she clenched her teeth and told herself to hold the line, tears escaped. The droplets rolled over her temples. And in the moment, she knew it was over. She'd failed. Fallen hard. Lost track of herself along with the magic. Now she was more than just vulnerable, she was weak. Something she couldn't abide. Something a man never respected. Which left her more than helpless. It left her alone in a place where Henrik possessed all the power and she held none.

CHAPTER SEVEN

With a muttered curse, Henrik watched the blood well on Cosmina's pale skin. Flowing unchecked now, it soaked her shirt, running down to pool in the V of her elbow joint. The sight tightened his chest. His heart went overboard, splashed down, and hit hard. Sympathy spilled through the cracks in his ultra-thick guard. His eyes on her face, he talked to her, his voice soft, his tone even and sure. The soothing words didn't help. She was too far gone, deep in shock now, shaking so hard her teeth chattered and . . .

He couldn't stand it. Hated to see her suffer, never mind watch her cry.

But as her tears fell, rolling over her temples, regret sank deep. The urge to shove Andrei aside, pick her up, and hold on hard ripped through him. Henrik gritted his teeth. A witless reaction. Not the least bit productive either, but . . . Christ. He didn't like any of it. Not the look of her injury. Not the weakness Cosmina now displayed. Nor her gasps of pain. All necessary, he knew. The arrow needed to come out, and the wound tended. Pain walked hand in hand with the procedure. But God, it was hard not to howl at the unfairness as he held her down and allowed Andrei to do his work.

Goddamn bastards. The Order of Assassins had no shame. No code. Or honor.

The truth shouldn't surprise him, but somehow it did. Al Pacii didn't waste energy on the insignificant. Slip in. Hit hard. Sneak out with leaving a trace. 'Twas always the objective. No need to waste time on those not marked for death. Which prompted a serious question: Why target Cosmina? Halál's arrow had flown straight and true. No mistake about the intent or the bastard's mission. The leader of Al Pacii stood inside White Temple for a reason. A deliberate one. Instinct told him it had everything to do with Cosmina and—

"Andrei. Hurry the hell up." Worry in his eyes, Shay met his gaze, and Henrik understood. The young assassin might be deadly, but the time with Al Pacii hadn't damaged his heart. He didn't like seeing a woman hurt anymore than Henrik. "You're hurting her."

"It cannot be helped." With a scowl, Andrei twisted the arrow shaft, pulling gently.

Cosmina grimaced. More tears fell, streaking over her temple.

Shay growled an obscenity.

"There are small barbs on the arrow shaft, Shay," Henrik said, his throat tight and voice even. How he managed to sound normal, he didn't know. Especially while watching Cosmina suffer. Christ, the sight made him want to unsheathe his blades and maim someone. "If he pulls too fast, he'll damage the muscle."

"Henrik . . ." Lashes spiked by tears, eyes shut tight, Cosmina shifted in his grasp.

"Almost done, Cosmina." His focus strayed back to her face. God, she was pale . . . far too pale. Holding her down with one hand, he cupped her cheek with the other. Desperate to calm her, he caressed her, tracing the rise of her cheekbone with the pad of his thumb. His touch settled her. With a choppy exhale, she turned her face into his touch. Her faith laid him low. Split him wide open. Such acceptance. So much trust. More than he would've been able to give had the circumstances been reversed. "Hold tight, *iubita* . . . just a bit longer."

"Sorry." Her eyelashes fluttered. "I'm sorry."

Sorry? Henrik frowned. For what? "There is no need—"

"Is everyone all right?" She flinched as Andrei pulled on the arrow again. "I didn't mean to hurt anyone. But the spell, it . . . I had no idea it would blow out like that. I would never have . . ."

"'Tis all right," he said as she trailed off. "We're all in one piece."

Well, except for her.

But even as Henrik lamented the fact, he left regret in his wake. No sense dwelling on the past. He couldn't go back and change it. The debacle was where it belonged . . . behind him. Now he must deal in the present. Move forward. Give Cosmina what she needed while he found an alternative route out of White Temple.

A good plan. Particularly since he could still hear them out there.

Tilting his head, Henrik listened harder. Aye, most definitely. He could actually hear the enemy. Strange in more ways than one. By rights—and all human standards—he shouldn't be able to perceive anything outside the sacred chamber. The walls were too thick and the door too solid. Somehow, though, he heard everything. The soft scrape of multiple boot treads on the tiled floor. The quiet draw of a knife being unsheathed. The almost imperceptible murmur of Al Pacii warriors searching for a way inside.

Each minute noise wound him a notch tighter. He glanced at his apprentice. "Let go, Shay. I can handle her from here."

Quick to comprehend, Shay's focus sharpened. "What do you need?"

"Check the walls for hidden doors. Find another way out."

"Halál's still out there?"

Henrik nodded.

"Can you hear them?" Surprise in his expression, Shay pushed to his feet. Turning toward the megaliths ringing the dais, eyes skimming over stone walls, he strode toward the far side of the chamber.

"Clear as a bell."

"Impressive," Andrei said, his attention still on Cosmina and the arrow. "But then, you've always been a beautiful predator. Senses far too keen."

True enough. And even more so now. As much as he hated to admit it, magic upped the ante—along with his prowess. "Andrei, how close—"

"Done."

With a flick, Andrei tossed the broken arrow shaft aside. As it clattered across the stone floor, his comrade pivoted toward the healing kit on the floor beside him. Digging inside, he tossed a cloth over his shoulder. Henrik caught it in midair and, releasing Cosmina's wrist, pressed the wad of linen to her wound. She winced. A puff of air escaped her. And Henrik's heart sank as Andrei turned back toward him with a bone needle and thread in his hands. Intense blue eyes met his over the top of her head.

"Get it done, Andrei."

Picking up a vial of clear liquid, his friend flicked at its top. The stopper popped off the glass.

"Wait," Cosmina said, hearing the cork lid bounce on the floor. "Give me a—"

"No time."

Hating the idea, but knowing it was necessary, Henrik tugged her upright. She settled on the edge of the dais, then swayed, drifting backward. With a gentle shift, he steadied her, but . . . goddamn it. Too late. The movement jarred her. She gagged in reaction. Empathy tugged on his heartstrings. Henrik ignored the pull. Feeling sorry for her wouldn't help. Keeping her mind busy and her moving, however? Aye, that just might. On his knees in front of her, Henrik cupped her nape and raised her chin, forcing her to sit up straight.

"Please don't. I cannot—"

"Aye, you can," he said, interrupting again. "It needs doing, Cosmina. Andrei will be gentle."

She shook her head. "No more."

He held firm. "Open your eyes and look at me."

The hard edge in his voice made her jump. A furrow between her brows, she turned her face away, refusing to obey. Henrik's mouth curved. Stubborn little spitfire. Even injured, she was difficult to handle. Why he enjoyed that about her, he didn't know. Mayhap he was a masochist. Mayhap he got off provoking redheaded hellions. Mayhap he'd lost his mind. Who knew? But whatever the case, he refused to back down. Or allow her to wallow. She needed a distraction—a target, someone to be angry at while Andrei saw to her wound. Like it or nay, he would give her one. Poke. Prod. Put a bull's-eye on his own back in order to give her what she needed to get through the pain.

"Come, *mica vrăjitoare*," he said, using the nickname he knew she hated to get a rise out of her. "Don't be a weakling—look at me."

His insult pushed her brows together. "Don't c-call me that."

"Then open your eyes."

"Bonehead."

"Hellion."

She huffed. "I want my knives."

"Why?"

"So I can stab you with one."

He bit down on a grin. "I'll give you one free shot, but only if you listen to me. Now . . . open."

She winced as Andrei set to work, and his heart went into a free fall. Taking a deep breath, Henrik swallowed another apology and raised his free hand. His fingertips touched her skin. She sighed. He drew a circle on her temple, encouraging her to give him what he wanted. A moment later, she complied. Spiked by tears, her eyelashes fluttered, then rose, and—

Henrik frowned. Something was wrong. Very, very *wrong*.

Pressing his thumb to the corner of her eye, he applied gentle pressure, asking her to open wider. She obeyed. He sucked in a quick breath. Christ. Had he said *wrong*? Well, add bizarre to the mix. Throw in a dash of startling too, because—Jesus. Her eyes were . . . were—hell, how to explain? Almost colorless, the green of her irises had faded, leaving naught but contracted pupils in a sea of white.

Surprise struck, wiping his mental map clean.

Henrik shook his head. "Cosmina . . ."

"I know. It's bad this time," she said, panic in her voice. Her hands trembled as she reached out, looking for something solid to hold on to. Without hesitation, Henrik became her anchor, and shifting closer, gripped her forearms. Blood slickened his palm, making his fingers slide on her skin. "I cannot see anything. I cannot . . ."

"What do you mean . . . *this time*?"

"I hate this." Following his voice, she grabbed a fistful of his cloak. "I hate it."

"'Tis all right," he said, trying to soothe her. But goddamn, it was hard not to become distracted. The lack of color in her eyes surpassed surprising. 'Twas downright strange—magic born . . . something he never liked to dabble in. But as she quivered, each breath coming hard and fast, curiosity took hold. "Has this happened before—the blindness?"

Her chin dipped, relaying her answer.

"How many times?"

"Twice." Shielding her gaze with her lashes, she turned her face away.

Cupping her cheek, he brought her back toward him. Andrei drew another stitch. As she flinched, Henrik smoothed his thumb over her jaw, soothing her with gentle strokes. Back and forth. Over and over. Past experience had taught him well. Women liked to be caressed. Could be soothed with tenderness and a soft touch. He hoped the hellion in his arms would react the same way. He needed to know everything about her. All the finite details. Every aspect of her life along with what had brought her to the brink.

"Explain, Cosmina."

"It's complicated," she said, hedging to avoid the truth.

The dodge was a good one. Most men would've taken the easy way out and headed in the other direction. Not him. Curiosity was a powerful thing. Now he wanted to know. "Humor me."

"I don't know you."

"True, but you can trust me." Another stroke across her skin. God, she was fine. An incomparable beauty with more than her fair share of brains. And surprise, surprise . . . he liked that about her too. Shifting mid-caress, Henrik brushed over the furrow between her brows, then drifted right to trace one of her eyebrows. She sighed, the sound one of relief as though his touch eased her pain. "I'll keep you safe. Trust me with the truth. I cannot help if I do not understand what ails you."

"Why would you want to help?"

Good question. One without an easy answer. So he stayed quiet, allowing the silence to speak for itself. Her mistrust was normal. Necessary even, so . . . nay. Pushing for the truth wouldn't garner the desired results. Not with Cosmina. He recognized her breed: smart, sassy, too stubborn for her own good. So instead of pressing her for the truth, he kept his hands moving—sweeping over her skin with light caresses—and waited.

Andrei murmured and, tying off the last stitch, snipped the thread.

"I cannot tell you," she said. "'Tis a secret."

His mouth curved. Bull's-eye. Silence was definitely the way to go. Success lay moments away, and as Andrei finished securing the bandage, Cosmina broke. Henrik saw the shift, the instant she moved past doubt into partial acceptance . . . into the beginnings of fragile trust.

"I'm not supposed to . . ." She hesitated a beat. Uncertainty lay in the pause. Fear too, the kind that made his gut twist and his heart ache. So unsure. Too vulnerable. Carrying so many secrets, the weight of them bogged her down. "I was told to never tell anyone."

"Things are different now, Cosmina." He dipped his head, getting in close. His cheek a hair's breadth from hers, he used his closeness to breed more confidence. She wanted to trust him. He could feel it with every breath he took. Her need for a confidant— someone who understood and would never judge—infused the air around her. "You can tell me."

A fine tremor rumbled through her. "I'm not safe anywhere."

"You are with me."

She swallowed. "I see things . . . sometimes."

"What kind of things?"

"The future . . . events that have yet to occur."

"Visions?"

"Aye."

Henrik drew a quick breath in surprise. A Seer with the ability to tell the future. One of the most sought-after commodities in all of Christendom. "How often do the visions come?"

"Too often," she said, her voice hushed. He knew that tone. Often used it himself when talking about the magic in his blood. "I don't understand half of it, Henrik. The tumble of images . . . the echo of voices inside my head. 'Tis always such a jumbled mess. I never get the whole picture, just pieces at a time. And the headaches . . ." She frowned, then shook her head. "They are terrible when the visions come. Sometimes the pain is so powerful my eyesight goes blurry. Or I lose my peripheral vision for days. Other times I—"

"Go blind."

She nodded, bumping her cheek against his. "The blindness doesn't happen often. 'Twas the worst when I saw my . . ."

As she trailed off, Henrik stayed silent, employing patience, waiting her out, hoping she would continue. A secret lay inside the charged pause. Something so devastating she turned away, refusing to speak of it. Henrik understood the tactic well. 'Twas a call to arms, a way to protect herself from the past and avoid the pain. Not a bad strategy. He'd used it a time or two himself, enough to know avoiding the truth never made the hurt go away. And as he watched myriad emotions flash across Cosmina's face, he sensed the burden she carried. 'Twas heavy. So cumbersome she struggled beneath its weight.

His throat went tight. Another person in pain. A kindred spirit in need of comfort—the kind he'd never gotten. And as he brushed the hair away from her face, something strange happened. A chasm opened inside him. Tenderness surged through the gap, flooding him with the need to protect her. To give Cosmina what he'd never received. To lighten her load, if only for a little while.

"Who hurt you, Cosmina?"

"It doesn't matter." Fingers flexing in his cloak, she pressed her knuckles against the front of his shoulder. "'Tis naught but ancient history now—over and done."

The strain in her voice told a different tale. It mattered. A whole helluva lot. At least to her. But Henrik refused to push. He understood the nature of secrets and the underbelly of lies. Both took time to dismantle, so . . . aye. He had time and more to gather clues and solve the puzzle—days, mayhap weeks, before her vision returned and he let her go. Until then, he would do his duty, ensure her safety, and—

"I saw you, you know . . . in one of my visions."

His gaze sharpened on her face. *Saw him?* Had she really? "When?"

"As I entered High Temple tonight." Succumbing to fatigue, she swayed. He caught her on the backward glide. With a gentle tug, Henrik drew her in his arms, encouraging her to lean on him. "'Twas just a flash. A mere slice of time. I thought you might hurt me."

"I did." Shifting to sit on the dais, Henrik settled her in his lap. Cheek pressed to his chest, bottom against his groin, she relaxed, letting him hold her, making him feel worthy for once. "I sent you flying, remember?"

"Didn't hurt. Not really," she said, words coming slow. "I was playing possum back there."

"You tried to stab me."

"You deserved it."

Henrik snorted, amusement circling into enchantment. Plucky hellion. Way too adorable. Brash and bold when necessary. Soft and sweet when warranted. 'Twas an alluring combination. A dangerous one he needed to resist before his attraction to her ran wild. Aye, he wanted to know more about her, but that didn't involve losing his head. Getting tangled in her witchy web would only land him neck-deep in trouble . . .

With no way out.

Never a good place for an assassin to find himself.

Sex was all fine and good. But not with someone like Cosmina. She wasn't his usual fare. He liked down and dirty. Fast and furious. No strings attached. The women he slept with never complained. Each understood the rules going in. Wanted the pleasure he provided, not his presence in their lives. But Cosmina didn't qualify. Wasn't in the same category, never mind on his wish list. So nay, no matter how compelling, the woman in his arms needed to remain off-limits.

'Twas quite simply the honorable thing to do.

But even as certainty sank deep, a pang throbbed inside his heart, making his chest hurt. Given half a chance, he would've spent time with her. Pleased her well. Taught her more . . . and enjoyed the doing. Some things, however, weren't meant to be. So, no time like the present. He needed to grab Shay and—

"The Druinguari are still out there, aren't they?"

He frowned. "Who?"

"The men with flames in their eyes." Pressing closer, she burrowed in, seeking more of his heat. Henrik obliged, raising his head to make room beneath his chin. She murmured in thanks. He gathered her up, and cradling her close, pushed to his feet. "The ones who want me dead."

"Druinguari?" Done repacking the kit, Andrei slung the leather satchel over his head. As the wide strap settled across his chest, he stepped alongside Henrik. Bumping shoulders with him, his friend drilled him a look.

Henrik seconded his friend's concern. "Who are they, Cosmina?"

"Creatures." Her eyelashes flickered, playing butterfly against his throat. She shook her head, the movement sluggish and wane. "Servants to the Prince of Shadows."

"Explains a lot," Andrei said from behind him.

Hell, it explained more than *a lot*. Cosmina's claims helped him put the pieces together—the hows and whys of Halál's miraculous return to youth along with the reason Al Pacii assassins didn't die in the usual fashion. All of it led to one inescapable truth. The enemy was no longer human. Henrik bit down on a curse. The Order of Al Pacii, now minions to the Prince of Shadows. Christ. He'd been right to worry. Halál's absence the past month signaled a serious shift in a dark direction.

War on the earthly plane.

Battle lines drawn between two powerful deities fighting for territory and ultimate control.

Which meant he needed answers. Ones that would give a method to the madness and show him how to kill the Druinguari. There must be a way. Some implement of destruction to not only wreak havoc on the enemy but also ensure the bastards stayed dead.

Putting his boots to good use, he pivoted toward the megaliths. "We need to go home."

"To Drachaven?" Footfalls soundless, Andrei followed in his wake.

"Aye. I need to talk to my sister." A good plan. An even better start. Afina might know something about the Druinguari. Or, at least, be able to find out. As new High Priestess to the Order of Orm, she shared a direct link with the Goddess of All Things. Not that Henrik liked it. He loved his little sister but didn't trust the goddess. The deity was selfish. Brutal. Without conscience or mercy. Which made her more than just untrustworthy. It made her as much his enemy as Halál. A fact Henrik never forgot, even though his sister often did. "Afina might—"

"Home." Cosmina hummed, the sound full of longing. "Will you take me?"

"Where is home, *iubita*?"

"The Limwoods," she said, head bobbing against his chest. "Not far from Gorgon Pass."

The news stalled his forward progress. Slowing to a stop between two megaliths, Henrik absorbed the information—the tidbit at the edge of Cosmina's secret. Mind churning, his eyes narrowed on the symbols carved on the face of the stone uprights.

She lived inside the Limwoods. Intriguing.

Rumored to be enchanted, the ancient woodlands frightened people the same way wolves did rabbits. Then again, common folk spooked easily—lords and ladies too—refusing to speak of the dark forest for fear of revenge and warrior fairies. Complete nonsense. Superstitious drivel. But an effective deterrent nonetheless. No one entered the Limwoods, much less followed another soul over its threshold, and returned unscathed. So aye. All things considered, it made for an excellent place to hide.

Especially for someone who didn't want to be found.

More secrets. Another mystery to solve. One with Cosmina's name written all over it. And knowingly or not, she'd just given him another piece of the puzzle.

"Hey, H," Shay said, frustration in his tone.

"Any luck?"

"Nay," A frown on his face, Shay glanced over his shoulder. "I cannot find another passageway. The pictographs hide all trace of another keyhole."

"*Merde.*" With a growl, Andrei strode into the wide aisle ringing the megaliths. "No escape."

Turning sideways to avoid bumping Cosmina's feet, Henrik stepped between two uprights and followed his comrade. Boots brushing over mosaic tiles, he scanned the wall carvings and clenched his teeth. *Escape.* He despised that word. It signaled retreat. Meant evasion, backpedaling instead of facing the enemy head-on, and . . .

Ah hell. He hated to do it.

Didn't want to turn tail and run. Would prefer to fight his way out. But with Cosmina injured and half-conscious in his arms, no better option existed. Not while outnumbered with a pack of undead stalking her. He couldn't keep her safe—never mind alive—if he didn't find another way out. Halál wouldn't miss a second time, so . . . nay, Shay's assessment of the situation wasn't welcome news. Which left him with little choice. Time to trust that Cosmina knew White Temple better than he did.

"Cosmina . . . wake up, *iubita.*" She grumbled in protest. He crouched, lowering to one knee in the middle of the aisle. Ridged stone pressed into his shin. Balancing Cosmina on his thigh, he jostled her, needing her conscious enough to answer his question. "I need your help."

"With what?"

"You know this place." Cupping her nape, he lifted her head from his chest. His gaze on her face, he held her upright, refusing to allow her to fall back asleep. "Is there another way out of here?"

Her brows puckered. "Dragon statue. Beside the pool . . . back of the chamber. Where's my key?"

Henrik regained his feet. "Shay?"

Footfalls quiet, his apprentice turned away from the wall. Reaching into the pouch at the small of his back, he pulled out the round key. The necklace rattled, metal links tinkling as Shay jogged past them. Without a word, Andrei followed, allowing the younger assassin to lead. Eyes scanning the space, Henrik turned and headed for the rear of the room. Three steps down and he stood in a small alcove. Circular in shape, the chamber looked more like a chapel—or mayhap the nave of a church—with high walls arching up to meet the vaulted ceiling.

Water splashed in the silence.

Henrik glanced right. Impressive. Beautiful even. A bathing pool, clear blue water lapping at the stone sides, the golden dome above it reflecting its rippling surface. The smell of stale jasmine in the air, grey ash lay in the incense holder next to the tub's fluted lip. Keepers of time, protectors of White Temple, seven stone dragons looked on, standing sentry at equal intervals around the water, holding up half columns that rose in an impressive sweep against the back wall.

Henrik glanced at the woman he cradled. "Which dragon?"

"Middle one."

"The lock?"

"Inside its mouth." Reacting to the deepening chill, she shivered in his arms. With a curse, Henrik caught his comrade's eye. Andrei nodded and, sidestepping the pool, stopped in front of him. A quick flick. A firm tug, and Andrei loosed the tie of his cloak. Henrik shifted his hold on Cosmina, allowing his friend to tuck the heavy wool around her slight frame. "Henrik?"

"Aye?" Gaze glued to Shay, Henrik watched him peer into the dragon's open mouth.

"Careful with the combination," she said, her voice wavering as sleep threatened to pull her under. "Five clicks to the right, three to the left . . . twelve back the other way."

Shay nodded in acknowledgment. "What's beyond the door . . . a tunnel?"

"Aye. Narrow . . . dark, but good."

Andrei breathed out in relief. "Where does it lead?"

"The mausoleum."

"North end of the cemetery?" Henrik asked.

Closing her eyes, Cosmina dipped her chin.

"Perfect."

And it was—except for one thing. Henrik disliked tight spaces. A throwback to his mother's cruelty and White Temple's burning secret . . . and the Order of Orm's hatred of men. But even as the brutal memories circled—and he remembered being locked in the dungeon—he refused to back down. His aversion to dank passageways didn't matter. The hidden tunnel was the only way out. A better option than heading back into High Temple, where Halál and the Druinguari awaited.

Particularly since the mausoleum sat outside the city walls.

Surrounded by massive trees and row upon row of tombstones, the crypt possessed thick walls, a single entrance, and the possibility of multiple vantage points across rough terrain. His eyes narrowed as he drew a mental map inside his head. Tareek and Kazim stood sentry to the west, watching the mountain passes. He needed to reach the pair. Kazim's sword would be welcome. And Tareek? Hell, a fire-breathing dragon with a bad attitude constituted an excellent asset.

Enough of one to scatter the enemy . . . and buy him time.

A fantastic strategy. Wonderful and brash. Now all he needed to do was stick to the plan. And pray his fear of tight spaces didn't rise up to swallow him whole.

CHAPTER EIGHT

The wall wasn't giving up its secrets. The pictographs hid every sign of entry. All trace. Leaving Halál no trail to follow. Flexing his fists around dual knife hilts, he took a step back. And then several more, retreating until he stood inches from the top step next to the altar. Destroyed by the firestorm, tiny flames still ate its wooden frame. Smoke swirled, rising to meet the vaulted ceiling, sending an acrid smell across the rotunda.

Caught fast by the slow burn, he stared at the fire, then shook his head. Devil take him, the heat had been horrifying. A real flare-up. One that had left scorch marks on the marble tiles and caused the gold altar to liquefy. Upper lip curled off his teeth, he watched a yellow rivulet flow past the tip of his boot. He swallowed the snarl. Frustration served no purpose. Neither did worry, but . . .

He couldn't quell either.

Two of his men lay dead, burned to death by magical blue flame. A serious cause for concern. Particularly since Andrei was responsible for the blaze. Aye, he'd seen the flaming swords rise from the assassin's hands. Hadn't missed the look of surprise in

Andrei's glow-filled gaze either before leaping out of the fire-storm's path, down the stairs to safety. The skill represented a major shift, one—surprise, surprise—Armand hadn't warned him about.

He should've expected it. Somehow, though, he hadn't, trusting his new master to tell him all and prepare him in good faith. A mistake. A costly one. Arrogance and trust walked hand in hand with stupidity. His had just lost him two skilled fighters. Glancing left, he stared at the twin piles of black goo on the temple floor. 'Twas all that remained of the pair he'd chosen to initiate into the Druinguari—those he'd turned in the same way Armand had him.

Disappointment tightened his throat. Indestructible, his arse. Armand had lied. His kind could be killed. And now, Halál knew how. He'd seen the magical capsule behind his soldier's breastbone burst while fire consumed his body and the black fog spill down his chest. Seconds later, the assassin had dissolved, liquefying onto mosaic tiles.

A quick death, but not the least bit painless.

Unease drifted through him. The turn of events—along with the chink in Druinguari armor—worried him. He must find a way around it, a way to protect his budding army. Magical breast-plates mayhap, forged in the pit of hell, touched by Armand's power and imbued with invincibility. As his eyes narrowed on the wall, Halál filed the idea away. Another thing to talk with his new master about, but . . .

Not right now.

First things first. One obstacle at a time.

He refocused on the pictographs. Gaze skimming over the intricate carvings, he searched again for a seam in the stone. Nothing. No break in the design. No obvious keyhole either.

Each symbol flowed into the next, burying secrets amid curving lines and intersecting loops. No chance he would find the hidden entrance and slip inside the chamber beyond. Which was—Halál flexed his fists—unacceptable.

Henrik stood mere feet away. His for the taking. His for the torturing. His for the killing.

Along with the betrayers who now fought alongside him.

He bared his teeth. Oh, how he wanted to eviscerate the bastard. An image flared in his mind's eye—of Henrik strapped to the blue stone inside Grey Keep as his knife drew bloody patterns on the bastard's skin. A mistake. An error that couldn't be forgiven. He should've killed the assassin when he'd held the chance. He'd known Henrik was dangerous—too skilled, too volatile, a wild card in an organization with room for none.

Now he paid the price.

Assassins he'd trained now stood as his enemy.

Halál shook his head. The irony. 'Twas upside down and backward. The exact opposite of what he'd expected. And yet, even as he told himself to let the past go, he held on tight. Smart or nay, he yearned to make Henrik pay. To exact his revenge and send a message to Xavian and the others. To cut deep with his blades, strip flesh from bone, and take his due. An unbecoming reaction. A dangerous one too. Emotion didn't belong in the equation. Neither did personal vendettas. Or holding a grudge.

All posed serious problems. Particularly since his mission had shifted. He no longer served the human world and the requests of its kings. Somehow, though, as he stood in the dim light of High Temple, it didn't matter. The parameters might have changed, but he had not. He still believed in the cause, in the Order of Assassins, and what he'd spent a lifetime building. He'd simply added another dimension, choosing power and youth, deciding to serve two masters: himself and the Prince of Shadows.

And speaking of which . . .

Time to do what his new master expected. He must open a hole in the wall. Or at the very least, find a way around it.

Halál frowned as the thought prompted another. An idea sparked to life. With a quick pivot, he turned toward his men. Lined up behind him, each stood ready, awaiting his orders, eager to serve, the orange flame flickering in their eyes matching his own. The perfect storm. A team of skilled assassins full of dark forces and cruel intent. Satisfaction surged. He'd been proud of his men before, but now . . . Hmm. He reveled in the power each exuded, wallowing in it like a vampire in blood.

So nice to have adequate playmates for a change.

Sheathing his blades, he met Valmont's gaze. Black blood coating his tunic, his lead assassin tipped his chin. The movement smacked of impatience. Valmont wanted a target, awaited his order in the hopes of finding something to hunt and kill. Halál's mouth curved. Wonderful. Far be it from him to deny one of his best hunter-killers his fondest wish . . .

Henrik on a silver platter. Or rather, pinned beneath Al Pacii blades.

"We split up," Halál said, rolling his shoulders. "Three groups. V . . . take five with you. Set up on the northeast portion of White Temple's outer wall."

Gaze roaming over his assassins, Halál's eyes narrowed. 'Twas time, but he must choose wisely. He needed the best candidate, a killer of true skill and supreme intelligence. Valmont was a natural choice. Smart, talented, ruthless, the German-born assassin not only obeyed without question, but could also rally the rest. Which made him an excellent first in command. But not all his men were cut out to be captains. Most were sheep—meant to follow, not initiate. The task at hand, however, required a leader of men. Which meant he couldn't delay his decision any longer. He must set the stage, establish the third pillar in the tripod of power, and propel one of his assassins up the Al Pacii ranks.

He focused on the last man in line. Face wiped clean of expression, the assassin met his gaze head-on. Pure viciousness. Unequaled malice. Perfection wrapped up in a lethal attitude and killer instinct. Halál hummed in appreciation. Aye, he would do.

"Beauvic . . . do the same. Take your contingent and set up on the ramparts to the south." As his newly appointed captain nodded, Halál turned and, footfalls fast, skirted the ruined altar. "The rest of you, come with me."

"Hunting groundhogs, are we?" Beauvic asked, anticipation in his tone.

"Tunnels." Baring his teeth, Valmont checked his weapons, ensuring each dagger slid free of its sheath with ease. "The bastards have found another way out."

"Aye." Rumored to be riddled with hidden passageways, White Temple was a veritable warren, full of entrance and exit points . . . with only one way through the maze. Jogging down the stairs, Halál glanced over his shoulder. He met each captain's gaze in turn. "Henrik holds the Keeper of the Key, and thereby certain knowledge of the maze beneath the city."

"The woman." A twang sounded as Beauvic restrung his bow. "Right hand to the High Priestess of Orm."

Halál nodded, his mouth curving in approval. Trust Beauvic to know that. A bookworm with a real thirst for knowledge, the assassin read everything he could get his hands on, so the comment came as no surprise. Neither did the intelligent gleam in his eyes. Or the fact Beauvic understood the woman's importance to the Order of Orm. As Keeper of the Key, she stood at the top of the hierarchy, helping the High Priestess lead the Blessed. Which meant she knew everything. Every bit of history. All the secrets. Was tasked with performing the ancient rituals as well as guarding the goddess' sacred spells. Throw in the fact she possessed the key—and the combinations—that unlocked every door, hidden and otherwise, inside White Temple and . . .

Aye. Without a doubt. She was an excellent pawn to control.

An even better one to kill.

A frisson of excitement raced beneath his skin. Be damned, but he could hardly wait to get his hands on her. Although, now that he'd discovered her position within the Order, she wouldn't die quickly. With agonizing precision, he would do what he did best—put his knives to good use and wreak maximum damage. Draw her death out. Make it last. Force-feed her pain until she gave him what he wanted: information, every last scrap of knowledge she secreted away inside her mind.

All while making her bleed.

Excellent incentive. An even better plan, but for one rather large wrinkle. Henrik. Taking what the betrayer protected would be no easy task.

One of the most exquisite hunter-assassins he'd ever trained, Henrik stood as a shining example of what was possible. Of Al Pacii prowess and skill. Of Halál's ability to take a boy and turn him into a first-class killer. Although not as skilled as Henrik, fifteen of the same breed filed in behind him, footfalls silent on stone. Halfway across the rotunda, he paused beneath the golden dome, then looked back. His gaze found the pictographs once more.

Secret doorways and hidden passages. So many options. So many places for Henrik to pop his head up. Too many avenues to get the woman to safety.

Unsheathing the sword on his back, Halál strode on, his attention fixed on the high archway that served as High Temple's only entrance. Steel glinted in the moonlight as he swung his blade full circle. "Bring me the woman."

"Dead . . ." Valmont cracked his knuckles. The sharp sound ricocheted, echoing across the vast space.

"Or alive?" Beauvic's voice slithered in like a viper, deadly undertones hissing in warning.

"And kicking." Increasing the pace, Halál bypassed the last pillar and trotted down the shallow staircase. He stepped off the last tread and into the corridor. Denied the light of the moon, the gloom thickened, descending from high ceilings. His senses sharpened, propelling him down the dark passageway. "Get to your positions on the wall. The instant Henrik sticks his head up, blow the horn, then shadow him until the rest of us catch up."

Valmont murmured in assent.

"Strength in numbers." Reaching over his shoulder, Beauvic slipped the bow back into the quiver on his back.

"Precisely," Halál said, body tight, anticipation rising even as experience tempered his eagerness. "Until we know what the bastards are capable of, we fight together."

A sound strategy.

Andrei and the blue fire made him wary. The fact he hadn't seen or sensed Henrik upon entering High Temple doubled his usual caution. Something odd was afoot—the power play of deities chief among them. Armand had altered him, after all, gifting him with eternal youth and powers yet beyond his ken, so aye, little doubt remained. The Goddess of All Things had leveled the playing field, countering the Prince of Shadows' move. Which meant . . .

No room for error. Even less for impatience.

He must proceed with extreme care. Tease out the truth. Assemble all the facts. Find the weakness in Henrik's armor in order to exploit it. But as Halál split from the pack and led his group toward the western wall, the throb in his veins picked up a beat. And then another. As it beat a drum, thrumming inside his head, he admitted the truth. Impartiality wasn't possible tonight. He wanted the Keeper of the Key. Couldn't wait until he held her in his grasp.

Youth presented him with all kinds of possibilities: the power to enforce his will, do as he pleased, and make her his pet the more interesting among them. Halál pursed his lips. Or mayhap he wouldn't do anything of the sort. Mayhap he'd present her as a gift to Armand, just to see what happened. A hum lit off in his veins, gripping his body until muscle tightened over bone.

A plaything inside Grey Keep with one purpose—his master's pleasure.

Infinite possibility. Unending entertainment. Could prove to be very, *very* interesting.

Moving down the deserted corridor, Halál jogged around a blind corner. Deep in shadow, the entry to the corner tower beckoned. Not wasting a moment, he ran beneath the archway, and legs pumping, ascended the spiral staircase. Brisk night air turned frigid, washing over him as he reached the apex. The iron handle chilled his palm. Metal clicked against metal. He shoved the door wide and stepped onto the rampart atop the western wall.

Within seconds, he stood halfway down the narrow walkway. His assassins filed out behind him, taking up positions along the parapet. The wind whistled through the abandoned guardhouse, flicking at the hem of his cloak. Halál ignored the icy rush and scanned the terrain beyond the city walls. He glanced left, then right, and smiled in satisfaction.

The perfect vantage point.

From his position high above the dell, he saw everything—the wide, flat expanse of fields, the main road into White Temple, and the thin line of hedgerows on either side. The cemetery, though, captured and held his interest. North of the road, the grove possessed real possibility. A point of cover. Mayhap even a ready escape. Even stripped of foliage, the large beech trees surrounding the cemetery threw shadows, impeding his view, and—

The moon emerged from behind wispy clouds.

Illumination spilled, painting the terrain in winter white. His mouth curved. Beautiful. Light abounded. No cover in sight. Very little for Henrik to work with if he chose the boneyard as his means of escape. Gaze roaming over tombstones, Halál refocused on the front of the mausoleum and, giving a hand signal to his assassins, settled into a crouch. Nothing to do now but wait. And hope that whatever tunnel Henrik traveled exited on the western front . . .

On Halál's side of the wall.

CHAPTER NINE

The tunnel walls closed in, constricting until Henrik felt the squeeze. The lockdown caused a visceral chain reaction. Nothing new. Being underground did that to him, spinning him in dangerous directions, making it impossible not to relive his history inside White Temple. Like a brutal taskmaster, past experience rose, twisting the screws, building the pressure until his temples throbbed and his mind bled, force-feeding him the first seven years of his life.

All of it spent in hell. Under his mother's thumb.

His arms flexed around Cosmina. She shifted in his embrace, tucking her head beneath his chin. Warm and soft in his arms, the feel of her helped center him. It wouldn't be long now. Just a bit farther. The thought should've calmed him. It didn't. He couldn't ignore the walls. Like a closing vise, stone shifted, narrowing the tunnel with each step he took. Nonsense, he knew. An optical illusion brought on by irrational fear. The passageway wasn't moving. The vertical slabs stood strong and still, as stalwart as ever. And yet . . .

Sweat trickled between his shoulder blades.

Sucking in a shallow breath, Henrik gave himself a pep talk. *Stay steady. Stay true. Be strong.* The words and reassurance didn't help. Neither did the constant pump of his chest. No matter how much air he forced into his lungs, he couldn't get enough. 'Twas too thin. Too musty. Too damp with winter chill and the weighted claw of warning. Henrik drew another lungful anyway and, forcing one foot in front of the other, followed Andrei's lead.

Not that he could see his friend.

Hell, he couldn't see past the end of his own nose, never mind along the length of the narrow passageway. No torches to use. No light to rely upon. Just total darkness, the kind of blackness that consumed everything.

His stomach pitched. Henrik exhaled hard, then drew in another breath. Pressure tightened its grip, banding around his rib cage. More sweat bloomed, wetting the hair at the nape of his neck. Like a snake, the beads slithered down his spine, raising gooseflesh on his damp skin. Gritting his teeth, Henrik stared straight ahead. He needed to stay calm. Refused to break down now. He'd survived far worse than a tight corridor deep underground.

Being stuffed into the murder hole each night qualified as *worse*.

Eyes straining in the darkness, Henrik dragged his mind away from the past. As it settled back on the present, he slowed the pace. Walking now, he listened for his comrades. Andrei was still in front of him . . . up there . . . somewhere. Shay moved behind him, bringing up the rear of their unhappy little procession through the bowels of White Temple. Rhythmic splashes of quick footfalls through the trench of water underfoot offered up clues. Each noise added to the next, amplified in the small space, allowing him to gauge distances.

A thump echoed five feet behind him.

"Jesu," Shay said, sounding set upon. The sound of brisk rubbing ensued as his apprentice tried to soothe whatever part of him had struck stone. "Where the hell are the torches? Anyone with half a brain knows to equip an escape route with torches, for God's sake."

Andrei grunted in agreement.

Wood groaned an ominous warning.

Henrik tensed and . . . oh shit. Not good. The high-pitched creak signaled trouble. The kind no one needed in cramped quarters and a dark corridor. Wood groaned again. Henrik listened harder, waiting for telltale signs and his friend to fill him in. He needed to know what the hell was going on. If Andrei didn't—

Cosmina stirred against him. "What is it?"

Henrik shook his head, then realized the absurdity of the action. She couldn't see him. Not while surrounded by darkness, never mind blind. "Not sure. Give Andrei a moment. He'll—"

"*Merde*," Andrei muttered, sliding on something underfoot. Like a low snarl in the dark, another creak drifted, skimming the stone walls. "Stop. Back up. I just stepped on—"

Crack! Timber snapped, obliterating the quiet.

Andrei cursed. Steel clanged against stone. A loud splash echoed. The harsh rasp of breath and the sound of flailing followed, beating the air around them.

"Son of a—*Mon Dieu*, I'm in a well of some kind." Water slapped against something hard as Andrei swiveled. "Henrik, I fell. Mayhap twenty feet. It's a trap. Full of water. Wide mouth, smooth sides, and—"

"Are you injured?" Shay stepped alongside him, crowding Henrik in the corridor.

"*Non*, but . . ." Nails scraping against the side walls, Andrei paused. "I'm not a strong swimmer."

"Hold on." Heart beating triple time, Henrik tried not to think about the trap. Or the fact he might have to go down to get his friend. "Let me put Cosmina down and—"

"We need light." Eyelashes fluttered against the side of his throat. Cosmina raised her head, bumping the underside of his chin. Henrik flinched. Hell, she was more than just awake. She was coherent—mind focused and voice strong even though her body remained weak, nestled against him, still in need of his support. "Andrei . . . use your fire."

Silence greeted that command, then . . .

"I don't know how. In the temple, when I saw Halál take aim at Henrik, I . . . it just happened," Andrei said, a thread of panic in his voice. "I cannot control it, Cosmina."

"Aye, you can. I can see your ability in my Seer's eye. 'Tis a gift from the goddess, one you can control, so . . ." She trailed off, using the pause for effect. "Concentrate, Andrei . . . make the fire grow in your palm."

"But—"

"Do it, Andrei," she said, her tone soft, yet somehow full of command. "And Shay?"

"Aye, my lady?"

"Use your talent . . . control the water to keep him buoyant."

"You are mistaken." Unease drifted on the denial, calling Shay a liar. "I have no such talent."

"Of course you do, Shay," Cosmina said, pressing the issue, leaving the younger assassin nowhere to hide. "Like all of your brethren, you now control an element. Yours is water . . . the goddess decrees it. The magic has already been set in motion."

Light flickered up ahead, painting the walls in blue light. It glowed bright a moment, making Henrik squint, then petered out. His comrade cursed. A cacophony of splashing joined the colorful litany, as though Andrei punched the surface of the water.

"Shay," Cosmina whispered. "He needs your help."

"Hellfire." Each breath naught more than rasps, Shay shook his head. Henrik tracked the movement, registering the rush of stale air as his apprentice stepped back. His hearing pinpoint sharp, he listened to Shay retreat in the narrow passageway. He didn't go far—mayhap a step or two—before his back collided with the wall behind him. The twin blades Shay wore scraped across stone. "I don't know how. I . . ."

"Try," Henrik said as his apprentice trailed off. He hated to push. Understood the shock that came with the sudden surge of magical ability. 'Twas like being possessed and taken over, free will usurped by the goddess' gift while being thrust into foreign terrain without a weapon or map for guidance. And yet, he knew the territory. Had spent weeks struggling with the slow migration . . . the unnatural shift into magic. So like it or nay, he held a road map. Enough of one, mayhap, to ease his apprentice into acceptance. "Think it. Hold it in your mind's eye to make it happen."

Another burst of blue lit up the darkness. It held a moment, flickering like fire and . . .

Shay bowed his head and, inhaling hard, fisted his hands.

The light went out again. Palms slapping against the well's smooth sides, Andrei swore in French, his panic echoing through the starkness.

Shay exhaled. The water flow underfoot increased. The narrow stream gushed, frothing into a current around their boots.

Henrik's senses sharpened. His magic rolled, honing his perception and heightening awareness.

For once, he didn't fight it.

Instead, he assessed Shay in the dark, searching for signs, weighing the magic to ferret out the truth. Enchantment whispered, floating in on musty air. Shay shifted his weight from one foot to the other. He shuffled sideways, moving with the flow of water. The shift brought him closer to Henrik. As the younger assassin's shoulder bumped his, certain knowledge grabbed hold. Henrik drew a shaky breath. Christ help him, Cosmina was right. The goddess had not only tampered with him, but his comrades as well.

The realization rushed through him. Relief swelled, then bubbled up, relieving the strain while infecting him soul deep. Henrik cringed. But his reaction to the news didn't change the facts.

Or how he felt.

He was glad. So relieved his brothers-in-arms suffered the same affliction, his throat went tight. And as he stood, cradling Cosmina, heart pounding and gratefulness rising, he experienced true shame. What did his reaction say about him? That he was self-centered? An egomaniac beyond the pale of decency for wishing magical misery on another—especially those he considered his friends? Turning his head, Henrik set his cheek atop Cosmina's hair. Soft tendrils brushed his mouth. The sweet scent of her soothed him, opened his lungs, helped him take a full breath as he wrestled with each question.

The truth rose to condemn him.

No question. Without a doubt. Selfish described him to perfection.

And yet, even as he despised himself for it, his gratitude deepened. He wasn't alone. Wasn't the only one . . . the singular freak cursed by the Goddess of All Things. Not anymore. As awful as it seemed, the terrible *gifts* forced upon his friends made hope rise hard and him feel normal.

For once. For the first time in life.

"*Dieu*, it's working," Andrei rasped, the relief in his voice telling. A faint gurgle pushed back the quiet, lapping like waves on a shoreline. "The water level is rising."

"Good." Careful not to knock Shay off-balance, Henrik left his side. Frozen in concentration, his apprentice murmured but didn't move. Sliding his foot along the floor, Henrik turned sideways in the passageway and inched forward in the dark. Bit by bit, he tested the ground, looking for the spot stone stopped and wooden floorboards began. He knew the break couldn't be much farther ahead. Andrei sounded close now, mere feet in front of him. "Andrei, try again. Light the fuse . . . give us some light."

Blue flame shot through an opening in the floor. Light consumed the darkness as fire roared, curling over jagged floorboards to lick along slimy stone walls. Heat exploded through the tunnel. The blast hit Henrik in the face. He spun, turning his back to protect Cosmina from the flare-up. After a moment, the blaze subsided, but continued to burn, filling the underground corridor, and Henrik got his first look at the passageway. Long, narrow, mayhap three feet across. Blackened stone walls. Low ceiling that came dangerously close to the top of his head.

Close quarters. Too tight. Far too constrictive.

Henrik's windpipe closed. God, he couldn't breathe. The walls were closing in again and—

"Almost there." Eyes shut tight, boots planted in the gushing stream underfoot, Shay unfurled his hands, then made twin fists again. Open. Closed. White knuckles to open palms. Over and over . . . and over again. "Can you see him yet? Is he—"

Water bubbled against the top of the well. Andrei shouted and reached for one of the broken board edges. His hand caught hold. Wood crumbled, disintegrating into decay, sending Andrei splashing back into the well. The light sputtered, weakening into a flicker. Damp air sizzled, pop-pop-popping until . . .

Andrei tried and failed again.

Henrik dropped Cosmina's feet to the floor. He needed to move. Right now. His friend was in trouble. The wood refused to hold and Andrei was losing strength.

A quick pivot, a gentle nudge, and he pressed Cosmina's shoulder blades to the wall. "Stay here."

She nodded.

But as he turned, searching for Andrei in the dim light, his senses contracted. The tunnel narrowed, dragging his aversion to the forefront. Real? Imagined? Henrik couldn't tell, but—Christ. Everything seemed smaller all of a sudden, as though the walls and ceiling crept inward, closing with malicious intent.

'Twas too narrow. The passageway was too goddamned tight.

Unease morphed into full-blown panic. He couldn't do it. Couldn't force his feet to obey his mind and move. Chest working like a billows, Henrik shook his head. *Go. Move. Take charge.* His body shut down instead, tying him in a web of nightmares, shoving him back to his childhood. Back into hell. Back to her. Back to a place full of pain and betrayal. As he struggled against the onslaught, fear won, sliding into something more: phobia. His lungs contracted, pushing the air from his chest. Gritting his teeth, Henrik slammed himself into reverse. Boot soles scraped over stone. His quiver of arrows rattled, wooden shafts clicking together as his back collided with the wall.

"Henrik."

Cosmina's quiet tone arrested his flight.

Gripping his cloak, she stepped in front of him. Ignoring her injury, she planted her palm in the center of his chest. She cupped the side of his neck with the other. He twitched. She settled him with a murmur and, rhythm sure, stroked over his pulse point. Back and forth, a soft drift, a warm, whispering weight on his skin. "'Tis all right. You are all right. Breathe. Fill your lungs and . . . breathe."

His muscles obeyed, unlocking on command, allowing his chest to expand.

Thumb pressed to his jugular, she circled, applying steady pressure. For some reason, the gentle touch helped ground him. The panic receded, and she nodded. "Good. Now go. Help your friend."

Her voice added to the soothing effect, heating him through. The past faded, and as reason took hold, he calmed under her hands. His mind cleared, slamming back into his skull. Thank Christ. That was more like it. Much better and more his style. So was the power pumping through his veins. His strength returned in a rush. With a snarl, he broke away from Cosmina and spun toward the well.

Andrei coughed, the hack wet and sloppy.

Three strides, and Henrik leapt the jagged hole. His feet connected with stone on the other side. As he turned back to the well, blue flame sputtered. The light winked out, then came back on, rippling beneath the surface. He slid onto the wooden cantilever. The tips of the rotten floorboards crumbled, hampering his ability to maneuver. Lying belly down, he assessed the seven-foot drop between the boards and the lip of the well. His gaze narrowed on the blue glow beneath the surface of the water.

With a quick shift, Henrik jumped down. His feet found a foothold on slick stone. Legs spread wide, back wedged against rotten wood, he plunged his hand into the icy swirl. He was in it now—in a vulnerable position without the possibility of retreat. Nothing left to do but pray. Well, that, and hope like hell Andrei didn't panic and pull him off-balance—into the hole and under— as Henrik tried to haul him out.

* * *

Letting Henrik go almost killed her. A silly reaction. Yet Cosmina couldn't quell the urge to hold on tight. Nor the need to keep him close. She wanted her hand back on his skin. Craved the warmth and the steady beat of his heart to calm the raging thump of hers. Drawing a shaky breath, Cosmina exhaled in a rush. Frigid air attacked, blowing the chill back into her face as she listened to Henrik run. Shoved to the forefront by blindness, her other senses sharpened. Now she heard everything—the thud of his boots against stone, the harshness of each breath, the splash of water rising against the tunnel walls. Scent picked up, speeding the smell of must and mildew along.

His feet left the floor.

A sharp snap sounded. Material, mayhap? The hem of Henrik's cloak cracking in protest as he made the jump? Cosmina tilted her head and, pressing her back to slick stone, listened harder. A faint whistle rose and—

Bang!

Cosmina released a pent-up breath. Thank the gods. He'd landed on the other side of the hole. Was on task. Ready to pull Andrei out of the water to safety.

The realization should've made her glad. The collection of sounds, however, did little to soothe her. Hampered by injury, her arm throbbed, keeping time with the throb of her heart. Frayed by the ritual, her nerves refused to settle, jangling in warning. Now she bled worry—concern heaped upon concern. So unusual. She never allowed angst to get the better of her. 'Twas weakness, plain and simple. Tonight, though, circumstance sabotaged her, tossing her into an emotional quagmire. Now she sank . . .

Into the morass of overload. And an undeniable fact: she needed Henrik.

Cosmina bit down on her bottom lip to keep it from trembling. Had she said *silly* earlier? Well, she'd meant ridiculous. She shouldn't be feeling anything for him. Not one wit, but . . . goddess be swift and merciful. She couldn't fight the compulsion. The urge to be close to him pushed impulse past unwise into witless. Now it ran hand in hand with stupidity. Particularly since her banishment from White Temple always topped her hurts-like-hell list. Somehow, though, uncurling her fist from his cloak— shoving him away, telling him to go—had brushed the five-year-old hurt out of the way, claiming the number one spot. Now all she wanted to do was abandon all restraint and call him back.

Pride stopped her. Right on its heels, dignity put in an appearance.

Thank the gods.

Despite her fear of the dark, she refused to make a fool of herself. It didn't matter how bad it got. Or that blindness raged, and she still couldn't see a blasted thing. Acting like a brainless ninny didn't appear anywhere on her list of things to do tonight. Neither did the shaky hands, wobbly knees, and stomach-twisting nausea. Not that her body cared. Weak from blood loss, physical chaos took a turn for the worse. Struggling to stay upright, she sagged against the wall behind her. The damp seeped through her cloak and tunic to attack her skin. Goose bumps rose. Cosmina ignored the shivers, closed her eyes and, taking a deep breath, exhaled hard.

Filling her lungs didn't help.

Her stomach pitched. She swayed, listing sideways before jerking to a stop. Resetting her stance, she regained her balance, but knew it wouldn't last long. The harder she fought, the more she suffered. The headache was getting worse, clawing at her temples. As the intense throb hammered the inside of her skull, Cosmina's hands and feet went numb. She shook her head. Oh gods. She was in trouble. Would be facedown in the middle of the tunnel any moment now. End as naught but a crumpled heap while she emptied her belly and surrendered her pride.

Cosmina clenched her teeth and reached for calm, struggling to be patient. All she needed to do was hold on . . . just a little longer. 'Twas mind over matter, a simple case of will versus circumstance. She could stave off disaster and combat the discomfort. Tougher than most, she could combat the discomfort. Lord knew she'd been doing it for years. Alone in the forest. Deep in the wilds. Not a friend in the world. Except . . .

That wasn't quite true, was it?

In the space of a night, she'd found someone. Or rather, he'd found her. The thought should have scared her. Gratitude rose instead. Despite her uncertainty, she knew Henrik somehow— understood his ways, accepted him as a friend while dismissing him as a foe. Strange, really. Baffling by all accounts, but even as intuition warned her to be careful, she recognized his value. Felt his strength. Perceived great honor in him and responded to those truths without question.

He'd promised to come back for her. Had given his word.

She believed him.

He wouldn't abandon her. Even now, she could hear him up there, somewhere ahead of her, talking to Andrei. Leather creaked. Someone cursed as water splashed. The wet, sloppy sound beat against the tunnel walls, feeding her information. He had a hold on his friend. Was hauling the other man out of the water.

Leaning forward a little, Cosmina pressed her bottom to the wall and listened to each snippet of sound. Her eyes narrowed. Aye, definitely.

It wouldn't be long now.

Relief was moments away. The second Henrik returned, she would feel better. The nausea would abate. Her nerves would settle. And her body? The pain would go. Crazy to believe it? Cosmina knew better. As odd as it seemed, Henrik's touch soothed her. His closeness helped. The sound of his voice brought the kind of comfort she didn't want to resist. Each syllable, every word, drew her into his circle, making everything better. So forget denial. Toss aside logic too. Agony had a way of burning both out of a person and, like it or nay, she was beyond fighting the pull of attraction.

Stomach cramps twisted her abdomen.

Desperation took hold, pushing pride out of the way as she doubled over. Tucking her injured arm against her side, she planted her free hand on her knee. The movement threw bile up her throat. The awful taste unbalanced her, weakening her resistance. Cosmina struggled against it, but . . .

Her stomach heaved again.

With a moan, Cosmina cupped her hand over her mouth. Oh gods. She wasn't going to make it. She needed Henrik. Or out—out of the dampness, out of the chill, out of the tunnel and into fresh air—to regain control.

"Henrik."

Her tone said help. Naught more than a croak, her voice didn't carry. She cringed in reaction. Gods, she sounded bad, beyond bruised into broken. Cosmina whispered his name again. Attempt number two didn't go any better and as she hung her head, shame came calling. Blast and damn, she was better than this—stronger, more skilled, a member of the Blessed for pity's sake, able to—

"Let it go, my lady. Vomit . . . you'll feel better."

"Gods!" Surprise sent her sideways. Her knees gave out, buckling beneath her.

A big hand grabbed and hauled her upright. "Sorry. Didn't mean to startle you."

Her breath hitched. "Shay?"

"Aye."

She huffed in relief. "Can you . . ."

"What?"

"I cannot breathe. I need fresh air. Please get me out of here."

"Hang tight, Cosmina. Give H another minute." Shay stepped in close. Bumping against her, he grabbed the back of her cloak and held her upright. "He's got a hold of Andrei, but—"

"Goddamn it."

"Oh shit," Shay said.

Cosmina flinched. "What? Shay, what's—"

A horrific snap rolled into a lethal hiss.

"Jesus Christ," Henrik said, more growl than curse. "Andrei, listen to me. You're all right . . . Calm down, brother. Don't—"

Hot air slithered down the tunnel. Fire snarled and . . .

Snap, pop . . . boom!

"Get down!"

Chunks of stone flew like shrapnel, peppering her chest, stealing her air as her arm squawked. Suspended in surprise, she registered the blast, felt blood well above her eye, smelled the sulfur, but—gods. What in heaven's name had just happened?

Hard hands grabbed hold and spun her full circle.

Her feet left the floor. She landed with a thud. Boot soles sliding, she twisted mid-tumble. The ground bit into her hip, then hammered her shoulder. Shay flipped her belly down and landed on top of her. Dirty water splashed into her face. An instant later, blue flame flared in her periphery. Pain streaked across her temples as the flare disappeared. Shock expanded. Holy gods—the light. She'd seen something. A brief flash of . . . of . . .

Drat it all, she didn't know.

Not exactly. Although she could guess.

Andrei had gone cataclysmic. Deep in panic, his fear of the water ruled, making his magic react in unpredictable ways. Not surprising. Nowhere near advisable either. If Henrik didn't get him under control, the flare-up would kill them all. The tunnel acted like a funnel, channeling heat along with the inferno. Cosmina felt the blaze. Flame roared just above her, singeing Shay on the way by. He cursed and shifted, using his body to shield her as fire licked overhead.

"Shay," she yelled above the din. "Water. You need to—"

Quick to understand, Shay growled a command. The stream flowing beneath them obeyed. Water swirled, curving into a wave. Up. Over. Around them. She sensed the wet curl envelope her. It rose in a rush, meeting in the middle over Shay to create a wet bubble of protective cover.

Another burst of blue seared in her periphery.

Cosmina sucked in a quick breath. Sweet heavens. Thank the gods. 'Twasn't much. Was naught but a barely there glimmer, but oh, how it gave her hope. The blindness wasn't permanent. Not this time. The bright flash—no matter how quickly gone—told her so. Which meant it was only a matter of time before the darkness faded, her body healed from magical overload, and her sight returned.

Good news. At least, she hoped.

Magic was a tricky beast. Here today, gone tomorrow. Just like her sight. Which meant there were no guarantees. But as the inferno blazed overhead and ash flew, Cosmina allowed faith to rule. 'Twas better than desolation. Belief, after all, was a powerful weapon, and hope its catalyst. Now all she needed to do was survive the onslaught. A distinct impossibility as Andrei roared and fire raged, burning so hot stone crumbled, cascading into an avalanche above them.

CHAPTER TEN

Facedown on the stone floor, Henrik elbow-crawled farther up the passageway. He needed to close the gap and strike from behind. The direct approach would get him killed. Or set on fire, so . . . aye. Only one avenue left to take. Attack from the rear position. Grab Andrei by the throat. Cut off his air supply until he collapsed in an unconscious heap and the firestorm stopped. Henrik grimaced. He didn't want to do it. Unfortunately, little choice remained. Andrei had lost his goddamn mind. Now panic ruled and the blue flame rolled in a continuous stream from the center of Andrei's palms, pushing the inferno toward Shay and Cosmina.

He heard Cosmina cough.

The harsh sound pinged off blackened walls, zigzagging in the tight space to reach him. Henrik cursed. That cinched it. No help for it now. Her suffering narrowed his focus. Screw Andrei. His friend could handle the headache in the aftermath. Cosmina couldn't take much more of the smoky air. Gritting his teeth, he maneuvered into position. Hemmed in by stone, his shoulder cracked against the wall. Pain clawed down his bicep. Fingers of blue flame licked over his head. The scent of burnt wool rose and—

Cosmina yelled something.

Shay murmured and his magic rose, shaping the water into a shield overhead. Crumbling stone hit the frothing barrier and bounced off, cracking against the side walls. A pop-pop-pop sounded as fire roared overhead and water hissed. Relief grabbed Henrik by the balls. Thank Christ. Didn't know how, his arse. His apprentice was a quick study. Sorcery warped the air, flowing around him as Shay controlled his gift, combating the flames with the only thing that would put it out . . .

Water. A ton of it too.

Another fireball roared along the corridor.

With a quick shift, Henrik struck, clipping the back of Andrei's head. Teeth bared and blue eyes aglow, his friend swung around. Fire blew sideways and hit the tunnel wall. Rock exploded into shrapnel. His friend stumbled backward. Henrik took advantage, and with fast hands, locked Andrei in a choke hold. Palms pressed against his friend's nape, he pushed his thumbs into the base of his skull, forced him to his knees, and held on hard.

Powerful magic seethed. Andrei bucked, twin fireballs rising in his palms.

Henrik tightened his grip. "Andrei . . . calm down. You're out of the hole. No longer in the water. You're safe, brother. No need to fight."

Chest heaving, Andrei paused mid-punch. "Henrik?"

"That's right."

"I . . ." Andrei twitched. He tried to shake his head. It didn't go well. Immobilized by the choke hold, he couldn't move. "What happened? I cannot . . . what . . ."

"You lost your head for a moment. But you're good now," Henrik said, grip still firm, refusing to let go.

He couldn't. Not yet. Mayhap not for a while.

He needed to be sure. Aye, Andrei recognized him now, but that didn't mean he wouldn't go half-mad again. Panic worked in odd ways. Most of the time it came out of nowhere, blindsiding a man, locking him inside a prison of his own making. Henrik understood the ins and outs. Hell, he was a prime example. Water might not be his trigger, but Lord knew he had one. Tight spaces did it to him every time. No matter how hard he tried, he couldn't quell the unease. Or stop his slide into panic.

Tonight stood as an excellent reminder.

His chest went tight. Henrik swallowed hard. Christ, it had been close. If not for Cosmina . . . if not for her hands on his skin, the stirring rise of her scent, the soothing tone of her voice . . .

He clenched his teeth. Thank God for her quick thinking. Had she not stepped in, he would've lost his composure and, just like Andrei, spiraled out of control. How she'd known, Henrik didn't know. Mayhap she'd read the tension in his body. Mayhap it had been the choppy sound of his breathing. Mayhap the Seer in her picked things out of the ether. Whatever the reason, it didn't matter. Her intervention had saved them all. So forget her connection to White Temple. No matter how uneasy it made him, he accepted her without question now. She deserved his trust, or at the very least, the beginnings of it. He could do that—take a step toward her instead of away, if only to discover more and explore the strange connection he sensed growing between them.

The mental shift made him nervous.

Henrik went with it anyway. Backtracking, after all, wasn't his style.

"How we doing, Andrei?"

"I'm solid . . . in control now."

"Good. Keep it that way." Boots sliding on ash, Henrik pushed to his feet, but kept his grip sure. "I'm going to ease up now."

His friend nodded. Not much, a simple dip of his chin, but it was enough.

"Don't lose the fire. Keep the flame burning. We need the light." Gentling his hold, Henrik slipped one arm free. He held his friend in place with the other for a moment, watching, waiting, gauging the reaction. When Andrei stayed put, and the glow from his palms remained steady, he released the choke hold and pivoted. His gaze skipped over the jagged hole in the floor to find the pair farther up the passageway. "Shay."

His apprentice raised his head. The bubble surrounding the pair burst and water sloshed, pouring over their shoulders to reach the floor. "Is it safe to come out now?"

Henrik's lips twitched. Goddamn Shay and his warped sense of humor. Trust him to use a light tone to diffuse a tense situation. "Aye. Is Cosmina—"

"I'm all right."

Light flickered along the walls, beating back the darkness. Henrik squinted into the gloom, trying to get a read on her. Water pooled on the floor, catching the glint, casting shadows as Cosmina shoved at Shay. His apprentice shifted, untangling their cloaks. Planting her hand on the floor, she pushed herself upright.

Legs curled beneath her, she glanced his way. "Half-drowned, but all right."

The hitch in her voice told a different story.

His heart sank in the center of his chest. She was nowhere near *all right* and . . . Christ. The look on her face—the pain and exhaustion, the vulnerability and fear. Nothing, however, compared to the shock. Weak from blood loss, hampered by injury, she shivered as the heat faded and the cold returned. With a frown, Henrik studied the gaping hole between them, searching for a safe way across the void. The need to soothe her rumbled through him.

Which was, well . . . surprising, actually.

He wasn't the coddling kind. Wasn't the least bit possessive either. He didn't yearn for commitment or anything long-term. Women came and went. Fast, fun, easy to forget in the aftermath of mutual pleasure. No need to hang around, never mind become entangled. But as he watched Cosmina struggle to her knees, his admiration for her grew. So brave. Trying so hard to be strong. Refusing to ask for help.

Innate toughness times a thousand.

The realization tugged at his heartstrings. God, she cracked him wide open. Respect for her stepped through the fissure, breeching his defenses. Now all he wanted to do was bridge the distance and hold her. Henrik shook his head. Ah hell. Not good. He was in big, *big* trouble. The kind a warrior didn't come back from. Henrik knew it well. Recognized the truth because he witnessed it all the time at Drachaven—in the way Xavian looked at Afina, in how the pair touched and talked to each other as well. 'Twas a place no sane man wanted to go. Putting a name to his peril, however, didn't change a thing. The urge to stay with Cosmina dragged him closer to the edge, inch by terrible inch toward what felt an awful lot like fate.

Aye, exactly . . . *fate.*

Unease slithered up his spine. Warning bells went off inside his head. As the clang got going, Henrik tried to deny it, but the facts refused to let him. He was a logical man, able to follow the trail to its conclusion. Chance meeting, his arse. Cosmina hadn't been inside White Temple by accident. Neither had he. Tonight was about more than just his mission and her duty to the Blessed.

It was about collision.

His with Cosmina. A meeting set in motion by the Goddess of All Things.

Henrik bit down on a snarl. Goddamn *her*. She never stopped. Was always meddling, pulling cosmic strings, making others dance to her tune. And right now? Well, it was his turn. A cog in her wheel, the deity spun him round, throwing obstacles in his path, rousing his protective instincts to achieve her own ends. He frowned. Damn it to hell and back. The goddess knew him too well. Had sent the one thing guaranteed to get under his skin . . .

A woman. A redheaded hellion in need of his protection. An alluring combination Henrik couldn't resist. Which meant he couldn't walk away. Not yet. Not while his attraction to her simmered and honor whispered in his ear, telling him Cosmina wouldn't survive long without him.

Swallowing a curse, he dragged his gaze away from her. He glanced at his apprentice. Quick to comprehend what Henrik wanted, Shay fisted his hands in Cosmina's tunic and lifted her off her knees. Her feet landed in the middle of a puddle. The soft splash echoed. One of her legs buckled, refusing to hold her. She gasped and, reaching out, grabbed hold of Shay to keep from stumbling sideways.

Shay steadied her. "Ready, H?"

"For what?" she asked, alarm in her tone.

Henrik didn't answer her. He nodded at Shay instead, knowing silence was the best strategy. The moment he explained, 'twould be over. Cosmina would fight the plan. He would insist on seeing it through. And Shay would end up causing her more pain while he put it into action. So aye, keeping her in the dark might not be nice, but 'twas necessary.

Henrik took a step forward. Boots planted on solid ground a foot from the rotten floorboards, he tipped his chin. "Take a deep breath, Cosmina."

Her brows collided. "Why?"

Her suspicious tone made Henrik tense. Christ, she was a quick study. So smart, he could practically see the wheels turning inside her head as she hunted for the truth.

"What are you—"

"Now, Shay."

Grip tightening on her tunic, Shay lifted her off the floor. She yelped. Henrik blocked out her cry of distress. It couldn't be helped. Neither could what came next. Widening his stance, he flexed his hands and got ready. Movements quick, timing impeccable, Shay whirled full circle and—

"Oh gods . . . nay. Don't—"

At the apex of the turn, Shay let go, launching her through the air.

Cosmina cursed as she went airborne. Up and across. A smooth, well-executed toss. Dark cloak flying around her, she sailed over the jagged floorboards. Andrei shifted, providing support as he controlled the fire and held the light steady. Counting out the seconds, Henrik plotted her trajectory. She stopped going up and started to come down. An instant before her boots connected with stone, he plucked her out of midair.

A quick tug. A controlled pivot, and he spun her into his arms.

Wrapping her up tight, he tucked her close. She didn't fight. Instead, she settled like she belonged—head nestled beneath his chin, body pressed to his, her good arm wrapped around his waist. A violent shiver racked her. She snuggled in, seeking his warmth and, mayhap, the comfort of his embrace.

Henrik huffed. *Cosmina* seeking comfort from *him*. The notion sounded absurd. An idea without substance or mooring. Probably naught but wishful thinking. Still, he couldn't deny the allure. He liked that she depended on him. Enjoyed that she trusted him enough to allow him so close. But even as he chastened himself for the reaction, the need to soothe her rose on a dangerous wave. Ah Christ. Not again. True connection belonged in the category called *bad ideas times ten*. Emotion held no place in his world. Neither did a pretty redhead with a stubborn streak a mile wide.

Another tremor rolled through her. He hugged her tighter.

"'Tis all good, *iubita*," he murmured as she trembled in his arms. Her shivers set off an awful chain reaction, making his heart thump hard and remorse rise in a devastating wave. Goddamn it. She deserved so much better than this . . . better than *him*, a man incapable of true connection. Throat gone tight, he drew circles down her spine, caressing her with a gentle touch. "'Tis all right. The worst is over."

"Liar."

"Probably."

"Blast and damn . . ." Her voice broke. His stomach dipped, clenching hard as she shivered again. "Y-you are . . . are . . ."

"Wonderful?" he said, filling in the blank when she trailed off. Bad plan or excellent strategy, Henrik didn't know. Teasing her might not be the right tack to take, but, well . . . hell, it couldn't hurt. Might even distract her long enough to settle her down. "Brilliant? The best tactician ever?"

She snorted. "Not what I was going to say."

Henrik clenched his teeth to keep from smiling. "What then?"

"You're out of your ever-loving m-mind. A complete m-madman."

"Mayhap." Losing the battle, amusement seeped into his tone. "But I got you over the hole without causing you more pain, now didn't I?"

She scowled against the side of his throat.

His mouth curved. Little hellion. Such a bad attitude. She wouldn't give an inch. A lovely trait, but one best saved for another time. Along with his reaction to her, but . . . Christ help him. He couldn't contain the admiration. His attraction to her grew by the moment, compromising his control, making him ache and yearn and . . .

Want.

A serious problem. One he'd never encountered before now. Before *her.* Anything but ordinary, Cosmina pushed him up against the limits of his control. Which meant he needed to do one of two things: hand her off to Shay or pick up his feet and get a move on. The first option chaffed, rubbing him the wrong way. Stupid as it seemed, he didn't want anyone else touching her. So instead of handing her off, Henrik picked her up—one arm supporting her back, the other cradling her knees, a precious bundle in his arms.

She murmured in protest.

Ignoring her, Henrik glanced over his shoulder. "Make the jump, Shay. Let's get out of here."

"*Oui*, let's." Andrei frowned at his hands. Blue flame flickered, twirling between his fingers without burning him. "What the hell, Henrik?"

"I'll explain," he said, feeling his friend's confusion. Magicless one day, full of power the next. He'd been there, done that . . . over a month ago. "But not here."

Andrei studied him a moment. "But you know."

"Aye."

"Move, H." Boots scraping stone, Shay retreated a few steps. "You're in the way."

With a nod, Henrik backpedaled, giving Shay the room he needed.

Eyes narrowed, Shay unleashed his speed and sprinted for the edge. He found a toehold. His feet left the ground. Black cloak rippling behind him, he leapt over the trap, landing with a thump on the other side.

Andrei met the younger assassin's gaze, opened his mouth, and—

"Do not." Stepping in close, Shay slapped Andrei on the shoulder. The sharp sound rippled, ricocheting down the length of the tunnel. "Naught to worry about, Andrei. I'm singed, but otherwise intact."

"All right, then." Blowing out a breath, Andrei flexed his fingers. The blaze reacted, burning hot and bright, painting the stone walls in a blue wash. Fisting one hand, Andrei snuffed out the flames. Smoke swirled, rising from his fingertips. Using his other palm like a torch, he raised it high and turned to search the tunnel for pitfalls ahead of them. "I'll lead."

"Go." With a gentle shift, Henrik adjusted his grip on Cosmina.

She flinched. "I can walk."

"I know," he said, lying through his teeth. She could no more walk than he could grow wings and fly. But pride was a fragile thing, and for some reason, he wanted to preserve hers. "But we've a ways to go yet. Save your strength, Cosmina. Sleep if you can. 'Twill be a hard ride once we reach the horses."

"We won't make it that far, unless . . ."

"Unless what?"

"It's going to sound crazy."

Her eyelashes flickered, revealing pure white irises. His senses sharpened as her eyes started to shimmer. Dipping his head, he pressed his jaw to her temple and nudged her. She got the message and tipped her chin up, giving him a better view of her face.

"What are you seeing?"

She shook her head, apprehension clouding the air around her.

He bumped her again, then changed course and brushed his mouth over her temple. As she sighed, he prompted her again. "What is it, *iubita*?"

"You'll make fun."

"Nay, I won't," he murmured against her cheek.

Hmm, her skin was so warm. So soft. So goddamn touchable his fingertips tingled, making him want to press the advantage of their proximity. A small sip. A little taste. A gentle kiss—naught more, just enough to satisfy his curiosity and put an end to his craving. Henrik huffed. Talk about base instincts . . . and all-consuming want. Yearning played a part too—one Henrik knew he shouldn't indulge. His desire for her wasn't right. 'Twas, in truth, all wrong. He shouldn't be wondering what she tasted like, never mind contemplating the best way to find out. So aye, no question. He needed to pull himself together. Bury his need six feet under. Right now. Before he did something stupid . . . like lose his head and kiss her senseless.

"I understand magic, Cosmina. I have lived with the knowledge of it all my life. You need to tell me."

She opened her mouth, then closed it again. God grant him patience. She was stuck, mired in mistrust. So afraid to share her ability, she refused to speak of it. Or mayhap, couldn't. Fear did strange things to people. Sometimes it made them run. Other times it shut them down. Like now with Cosmina. Which meant he was about to get his wish . . . and his first taste. A kiss would distract her long enough to help her fall into trust.

The thought made his heart thump harder. Anticipation burned through him.

Henrik rechecked his position. Andrei moved at a steady clip ahead of him, hand raised, blue flame flicking as he checked for more traps. Shay's quick footfalls echoed behind him. Perfect. He had just enough time. Dipping his head, Henrik touched his mouth to the corner of hers. She inhaled in soft surprise. He flicked his tongue over her bottom lip. She hummed. His heart hopped like a jackrabbit, leaping all over the place inside his chest and—

Sweet Christ. Bad move.

Henrik knew it the instant he made contact. One kiss would never be enough. She tasted so good, and he was too needy. He bit down on a groan. Goddamn it. What the hell had just happened? His plan had seemed brilliant moments ago. Misdirection via pleasure. Distraction dressed up in gentleness. Quick. Simple. Effective. An excellent strategy rooted in a noble goal: procuring the answers he needed. But as she whispered his name and opened her mouth wider, inviting him in, Henrik struggled to hold the line, never mind remember the reason he'd kissed her in the first place.

The tip of her tongue touched his.

Henrik delved deeper, giving her more and . . . oh God, 'twas beyond anything. Better than good. The heat scorched him. Her willingness revived him. Desire ignited in his belly, incinerating right, pushing him toward wrong, tempting him to find a private spot and strip her bare. Henrik growled. Just a touch *more*. Another heated taste. A little deeper this time. What could it hurt? With his comrades guarding his back, coherence wasn't an absolute necessity. Not right now. So . . .

To hell with wrong.

He kissed her again. And then again. As he came back a third time, Shay cleared his throat. The sharp sound of disapproval slapped, dragging him back to reality.

With a silent curse, Henrik lifted his mouth from hers. "Sorry."

"Wrong thing to be sorry for." She licked her bottom lip as though seeking more of his taste. Which—God forgive him—cranked him a notch tighter. Now all he wanted to do was kiss her again. "Apologize for having me tossed like a sack of grain, not for the kissing."

Her teasing tone loosened his tension. His mouth curved. "Duly noted."

Her lips twitched a second before her expression smoothed back into serious lines. "Promise you won't scoff . . . or laugh . . . and I'll tell you."

"Cross my heart."

Her throat worked as she swallowed. Henrik stayed silent, trying to be patient. Such a difficult thing to do. Time was running out. Colder now, fresh air blew in on wind gusts, flicking at his wet clothes. The tunnel walls flared too, widening by the moment, telling him they neared a junction. Soon the passageway would either change direction or end. Which meant he needed to know about Cosmina's vision.

Now. Before it ended up being too late.

"Cosmina—"

"A dragon. I saw a dragon. Red scales. Green gaze." Her eyes drifted closed, cutting off the soft glow of white irises. As the shimmer winked out, she turned her face into his shoulder. "He awaits your call."

Henrik blinked. *His call.* Well now, that cinched it. Cosmina wasn't lying. She was a powerful oracle, one able to predict and see what others could not. Naught else explained how she knew of Tareek . . . and the special bond he shared with the dragon-shifter. The magical connection allowed him to relay messages, summoning Tareek when needed. History stood as a painful reminder—of that day, the moment he'd finally understood how much his mother hated him as she handed him to Halál and Al Pacii.

The memory made him cringe. The aftereffects made him hurt.

Not for himself, but for Tareek and the awful price the dragon-shifter had paid. Imprisonment for flying to his rescue. Damned for years for trying to protect him. Taken down by black magic alongside his brethren, Garren and Cruz, for doing his duty to White Temple and the Order of Orm. Only then had his mother delivered him into slavery. Into the hell of Grey Keep and Halál's brutal guardianship.

Until Afina had come along.

His younger sister had changed everything, undoing Ylenia's spells, restoring order to the earthly plane, wielding kindness instead of cruelty to right the wrongs of the past. Each correction continued to bring peace, knitting the fabric of a broken world back together, soothing nature, allowing all living things to grow and thrive. As the fractures created by his mother healed under the force of his sister's hand, so did his relationship with Tareek.

Time and trust. Important commodities. Both of which took effort to rebuild. And even though he and Tareek worked hard to mend it, problems still cropped up. The biggest one of all—at least, right now? He didn't know how to call Tareek. Twenty years was a long time for a skill to go unused. He wasn't a child anymore. His mind was no longer that pliable, and his faith? Hell, it wasn't nearly as strong.

"Henrik, we need him," Cosmina whispered. "Otherwise the Druinguari will—"

"We're here." Andrei stopped short in front of him.

"Where?" Shay asked.

His comrade looked around a blind corner. "Stairs leading up."

"To the mausoleum?" Leather rasped against steel as Shay unsheathed his twin daggers.

"'Tis my guess." Palming his throwing stars, Andrei paused, and boot poised on the bottom step, threw Henrik a questioning look. "You still tuned in, H?"

He nodded.

Andrei raised a brow. "Picking up anything?"

Eyes narrowed, Henrik reached for his magic. He knew what Andrei wanted: clues along with confirmation of the threat outside. Easy enough to do. Thrall allowed him to sense things others did not. His comrades might not be able to perceive the enemy, but he could. Sinking into the swell of his gift, he retuned his senses. A buzz lit off between his temples. The clawing sensation raked the inside of his skull, sending a clear message.

"We're not clear yet," he said, holding his friend's gaze. "The Druinguari lay in wait."

Andrei grunted.

Shay cursed. "How close are they?"

"Close enough." Hitting one knee, he balanced Cosmina on his thigh and, reaching around, gripped the dagger snug against his lower back. Smaller than the rest, the five-inch blade would fit better in Cosmina's hand. He needed her to understand. Things were about to get nasty again. Cupping the back of her hand, he set the hilt in her palm. Her fingers tightened around the grip, accepting the weapon without hesitation. Murmuring in approval, Henrik pulled his favorite knife from a sheath on his chest and, resettling Cosmina, pushed to his feet. "We make a run for it. The sooner we reach the horses, the better."

Turning her head, Cosmina set her mouth to his ear. "Call your dragon."

The whispered words echoed inside his head.

Easy enough to say. Nowhere near as simple to see accomplished.

But as Henrik followed his comrades, taking the stairs two at time, he cleared his mind and tried anyway. Cosmina was right. Three swords against twenty weren't good odds. They were deadly ones. So to hell with his pride. Like it or nay, he needed backup. Tareek would provide the sort his enemy wouldn't see coming, never mind be able to thwart. An excellent plan, but . . .

First things first.

He turned inward and, unleashing his magic, summoned his friend. He hoped like hell Tareek got the message. Otherwise the Druinguari would tear them apart piece by bloody piece.

* * *

Leaping up onto the parapet, Halál sank into a crouch. As he settled on the balls of his feet, using the stone teeth along the city wall for cover, he looked over the terrain again. Jagged mountain peaks rose in the distance, then swept down, rushing into the Limwoods. A long way off. Naught to catch his attention. Even less to worry about. His gaze narrowed on the thick stretch of forest anyway. Dark with shadow, deep with intrigue, ancient trees stood sentry, thick limbs spread, skeletal tops unmoving even though winter ruled and the wind howled.

Haunted, some said. Majestic, others argued. Unnatural, all agreed.

A prickle ghosted down his spine.

His nostrils flared. No doubt in his mind. 'Twas where Henrik would head when he exited the tunnel—straight into the depths of the forbidden forest.

A problem. More than a touch vexing. Particularly since instinct screamed, warning him to stay clear of the Limwoods. The same thing had happened on his trek from Grey Keep to the holy city. Severe aversion. Catastrophic delay as he took the long way around, refusing to traverse the eerie stretch of forest. It had always been that way. Why? Halál shook his head. No rhyme or reason. He couldn't place the feeling. Or put his finger on the cure. But something told him the woodlands disliked him. Then again, mayhap *dislike* was too mild a word. *Despised* was a better one. *Alive with murderous intent* might be a phrase worth using too. Not that the descriptor mattered. Intuition spoke volumes, and Halál remained convinced . . .

The Limwoods would kill him the instant he set one foot inside its lair.

He scanned the edge of the forest again. Revulsion churned in the pit of his stomach. Ridiculous. Completely foolish. Superstitious twaddle believed by dullards and soothsayers, naught more. And yet even from leagues away, he sensed the violence. Felt the unreserved menace as the ancient trees stared back at him, daring him to tempt fate and come within easy reach.

Disquiet rose on a dread-filled wave.

Halál dragged his gaze away. He refocused on the boneyard. Aged by weather, tombstones stood in neat rows, rising like blunt teeth from bleak earth beyond old oaks and bleached beeches. Greyed by the cold, moss feathered the top of each headstone, awaiting the promise of spring and the return of summer sun. Not that anyone would see it. He'd given his word and intended to keep it. The Blessed would die along with the Goddess of All Things. White Temple would never be resurrected. But first, he must see to Henrik. Where the devil was he? What the hell was taking the bastard so long to—

Metal squeaked. Carried by cold air, the soft squeal rolled on the brisk wind.

Halál's attention snapped toward the mausoleum. The groan of iron hinges came again. Senses sharp and focus heavy, he stared at the entrance. The wooden door cracked open an inch. Snow blew through the crack, cascading into a dancing swirl.

"Master."

"I see it." Halál hummed in satisfaction.

Well, well, well . . . 'twas about time. Restless from waiting, his assassins shifted behind him. Blades slid from leather sheaths. The wind picked up the collective scrape, holding it high as Halál raised his arm. He fisted his hand, giving the signal to wait. He needed to be sure. Must see the trio of assassins file out with the woman in tow before he made his move.

Hand engulfed by blue flame, Andrei crept over the threshold. He slid left and, making a quick fist, snuffed out the fire rising from his skin. Shay followed. Halál bared his teeth. Traitor number three. The whelp had betrayed him the moment he set foot outside of Grey Keep. Was the one responsible for a serious setback when he'd disobeyed a direct order and rewritten the incantation. The result had not only released the dragons from their prison deep within the mountain, but also turned The Three against him, binding the beasts to his enemy for all time. Now Xavian held a terrible advantage—the services of the most powerful creatures on earth. Dragons, shape-shifters of incomparable skill. Warriors capable of unequaled violence and . . .

Be damned, he might as well admit it. He coveted the dragons for himself. Wanted the beasts chained in his backyard like pets, awaiting his orders.

Shay would pay for the loss. He would take his time too. Tie the betrayers to trees. Render the enemy assassins helpless as he killed the youngling slowly, cutting him apart a piece at a time . . . while he made Henrik watch.

Ah, and speak of the devil.

Henrik crossed the threshold. Halál's focus sharpened on him. His mouth curved into a smile. Good. He held the woman. No time like the present to get things rolling.

"Blow the horn. Inform the others," he said, planting his palm atop the outer wall. "The hunt is afoot."

As his men moved to obey, Halál pushed off the parapet, propelling himself over its chiseled lip. His boots cleared the highest part of the wall. The horn sounded. Gravity took hold. He dropped like a stone over the side and sighted the ground. The two-hundred-foot drop didn't faze him. Black magic filled his veins, fusing muscle over bone. Which—joy of joys—made him nearly indestructible. A truth Henrik was about to learn . . .

All over again.

CHAPTER ELEVEN

Boots moving at a volatile clip, Tareek completed another circuit around the clearing. Up and down. Back and forth. Pause a moment, pace some more, do it all over again. He finished the next round and roared into another, blowing past ancient trees. Tethered in the shadow of the Blackwood, the horses shied. Glancing sideways, he soothed the warhorse closest to him, but refused to slow. He rolled his shoulders instead, working out the tension, trying to calm down and clear his mind.

It didn't help. Naught did. The constant buzz at his temples was driving him daft.

Out of his christing mind.

Now he stewed in sensation, trying to place it. What the hell did it mean? Was it a warning? A signal? Naught but interference, the sizzle and pull of being so close to the origin of all magic? Hristos, he hoped not. But as Tareek wore a deep track in frozen earth, instinct prickled, shoving him toward worry an inch at a time. Muscles twitching, he stomped past a low-lying shrub. Bare of foliage, thin branches bobbed in protest. He snarled at the plant, taking his displeasure out on undeserving vegetation.

Curse and rot the lad. Troublesome wee whelp.

Henrik was late. Again.

Never a good sign. The breach in protocol didn't bode well. Something was off. Not by much. Just by hair, but . . . *Dumnezeu*, skin him alive and call it a night. He had a bad, *bad* feeling. The kind that poked at instinct and warned of foul play. Unquantifiable. No proof in sight, and yet, he knew—just *knew*— he should be on the move . . . in dragon form, wings spread in flight, flying fast toward the holy city.

Urgent need jabbed at him. Tareek flexed his hands, then shook his head. Silfer forgive him, but . . .

He couldn't do it. Couldn't go there, back into the belly of the beast.

Too many memories lay in the Valley of the Blessed. His throat went tight as the past rose to claim him. So much disappointment. So much hurt. Way too much rage. All of it originating from one place . . .

White Temple. Wretched, godforsaken city.

Spinning on his heel, Tareek reversed course and headed in the opposite direction. Senses humming, his night vision sparked, allowing him to see everything. Every frostbitten blade of grass. The ridges of rough bark gracing the heavy-limbed trees at the edge of the dell. Each individual crystal in the snowflakes that fell. Like rain, the frosty collection landed on his face, then melted, evaporating into thin air. To be expected. As a fire dragon his internal temperature always ran hot, swallowing the cold, thawing the puddles in his vicinity, ensuring the chill never reached him.

A good thing most of the time. But not tonight.

He needed the cooldown. Enough of one to help him keep a level head. Mayhap give him some perspective too. God knew pacing wasn't working.

Disgusted with himself, Tareek stopped short. Tipping his head back, he looked up through the snowy swirl to focus on the night sky. No stars tonight. Ripe with heavy clouds, the heavens hid behind thick, grey tumble, violent winds pushing the storm toward White Temple. His heart thumped against his breastbone.

Goddamn the lad and his obstinate nature.

"Call me, H," he murmured under his breath. "Let me know you are all right."

The quiet plea drifted. A rustle of movement rose on frosty air. His focus snapped to the right.

"Relax, Tareek." Dark eyes serious, Kazim stopped at the edge of the clearing. Stance wide, body ready, he raised his hands and flipped both palms up. The move sent a clear message: I come in peace. An excellent preventative measure. Particularly since Tareek wanted to kill something. "'Tis only me."

"Anything?"

"Not yet."

Tareek bared his teeth on a growl. "Something is wrong."

"Something is always wrong," Kazim said, stepping over a rotten log. Ice crunched beneath his feet. The soft sound drifted up before escaping through the leafless limbs stretched high above the assassin's head. "Have you yet to learn this, *fratele*?"

Brother. Acceptance and support wrapped up in one word.

The reminder should've settled him. It cranked him a notch tighter instead. Not that he didn't appreciate the sentiment. He did, but that didn't solve the problem. No matter what he tried, the buzz between his temples refused to abate and worry turned the screw, making him bleed concern. The boy he'd vowed to protect wasn't back yet—might even now be in harm's way. The situation smacked of another time and place. Of deep trouble and endless pain. Of White Temple and the permanent pinch of the past.

Tareek swallowed a curse. Talk about a ballbuster. Even after all this time, he couldn't forget, never mind forgive. Couldn't dismiss a history bound in magic or his mistake the night he'd flown to Henrik's rescue. So arrogant in his skills. So secure in his position as one of the Guardians of Orm. Foolish in the extreme. He'd trusted too quickly, given the former High Priestess her due, and been betrayed for his trouble. The price had been high: imprisonment without hope, twenty years trapped in dragon form, forced to serve a master without conscience or mercy.

A brutal tangle with unending ties. And epic proportions.

An experience Tareek refused to endure again. And yet, despite all the savage violence, the bond he shared with Henrik remained strong. So powerful, he'd retaken the vows, pledging to shield Henrik as he had in boyhood.

Which explained a lot, didn't it? Like why he stood in a field less than three leagues from a place he never wanted to see again.

Curse and rot the lad. For the umpteenth time.

Unfurling his fists, he tore his gaze from Kazim and resumed pacing. He kicked at a rock in his path. The stone tumbled, cracking the quiet as it splashed through a slushy puddle. On the final turn of another circuit, he changed direction. Striding across the middle of the dell, he stopped a foot from Kazim and met his gaze.

Back pressed to a stout oak, the Persian raised a brow.

Tareek frowned. "I should have gone with him."

"Aye, you should have." Crossing his arms, Kazim leveled him with a look.

Tareek glared back. Christing Kazim. Always so unflappable. The warrior had to be the calmest son of a bitch on earth. Annoying as hell most of the time, but useful upon occasion. Like now, when Kazim called it as he saw it, telling the truth even when the message proved unpopular.

Bowing his head, Tareek fisted both hands in his hair. "Hristos, something is wrong."

"Has Henrik called?"

The question throbbed between his temples. No, he hadn't *called*. That was the problem. But then, in all honesty, Tareek didn't know whether Henrik could connect with him anymore. Aye, he'd mastered the skill as a boy, reaching out with his mind to tell him all was well or to hurry if he needed help. Sometimes the whelp had just wanted to say good night. His mouth curved as he remembered Henrik's audacity as a child. Boundless courage. Imp to the next level. So full of piss and vinegar, he'd kept Tareek hopping, trying to outsmart a lad who feared naught and liked trouble.

But that lad was gone now.

In his place stood a man. A skilled assassin full of caution and mistrust.

Tareek understood the parameters. He suffered from both himself. Which meant naught came easy. Not for him. Nor for Henrik. Trust required effort. Brotherhood was earned, not given without proof, and a broken relationship took time to rebuild. Aye, it might be frustrating, but slow and steady always won the race. The groundwork must be laid—and the foundation set—before the bond of true friendship returned.

"Kazim . . ."

"Bad feeling?"

"Aye." Unease tightened its grip, making his stomach turn. Releasing the death grip on his hair, Tareek raised his chin. "My temples are throbbing. The infernal buzz won't go away and— Silfer's balls. I'm not sure . . . I can't tell if—"

"Go Tareek. Call forth the dragon and fly for White Temple."

Boots rooted to the ground, Tareek didn't move.

Kazim sighed. An instant later, he pushed away from the great oak and, footfalls silent, walked straight toward him. No hesitation. No fear of the dragon. Just straight courage as he strolled within striking distance. Black gaze steady on his, the assassin halted beside him and raised his hand. Tareek tensed, but stayed true, refusing to bolt. Or shy away. He wasn't a coward. No matter how much he disliked physical contact, he must stay the course. Kazim was now his brother-in-arms, which meant . . .

'Twas time.

He needed to start somewhere. Trust a little further and put himself on the line. A simple touch—no matter how vexing— seemed as good a place as any to begin.

A knowing glint in his eyes, the assassin slapped the back of his shoulder. Skin cracked against leather. The contact made Tareek flinch.

One corner of Kazim's mouth tipped up. "Do not worry so, *fratele*. I will see to the horses as planned."

Tareek released the breath he'd been holding. "Where will you be?"

"West of the holy city." Another solid slap to his back. The love tap rocked him forward. Tareek widened his stance to keep from losing his balance. Kazim nodded in approval, then pivoted, returning the trust by turning his back on Tareek. Twin sword hilts flashed in the gloom, rising over the Persian's shoulders as he strode toward the horses. "If there is trouble, Henrik will head for cover. The Limwoods provide the best."

True enough.

Although, it might prove troublesome. The forest wasn't exactly hospitable. Getting in never presented a problem. Getting out, however? Well now, that would be tricky. Alive with magic, the trees liked to keep what they found. He should know. As a fledgling, he'd gotten caught inside the Limwoods. Or rather gotten his wings tangled up in it and the thick vines that snaked across the turf without warning.

Tareek gritted his teeth. Wonderful. Just terrific. Another experience he'd rather forget.

Not that he could avoid it. Not with Henrik out there—somewhere—doing his usual thing. The thought made him move as Kazim untethered the horses. Standing too close to the forest's edge wasn't advisable. Greater space equaled more wingspan and a better launchpad. Backpedaling into the middle of the dell, Tareek unleashed his magic. Muscle expanded and bone grew. With a hum, he transformed into dragon form, hands and feet turning into talons, bloodred scales flashing in the gloom, spiked tail rattling in warning. Loving the stretch, he unfurled his wings. Black webbing slid into interlocking dragon skin, becoming one as cold air flowed, swirling over the horns atop his head.

Baring his fangs, Tareek snarled at the night sky. The poison-tipped spikes along his spine rippled, sounding like wind chimes. Mmm, mmm good. Music to his ears. Better than—

The horses screamed. Multiple hooves left the ground.

Kazim cursed. Hands wrapped in the long tether, the assassin bore down as the small herd bolted, dragging him across the turf toward the trees. More cursing ensued. Tareek sighed. Well, hell. There they went again. Same story, different night. Finicky beasts. It wasn't as though he planned to eat them or anything. Scales clicked as he shook his head. A smarter bunch would've caught on by now.

Resigned to the chaos, Tareek sent magic rolling on a soothing wave. The horses calmed, settling into a sideway prance.

Kazim threw him a dirty look. "Do you mind? Get your scaly arse out of here before I skewer you like a—"

"At River's Bend, edge of the Limwoods."

Still pissed off, Kazim's gaze narrowed on him. "Meet you there."

Tareek nodded and leapt skyward. Snow whirled, billowing from his wing as he climbed above the treetops. He heard Kazim curse his name, but he didn't care. The assassin could handle the wind gust along with a bunch of unruly horses. Henrik wouldn't survive long without him. How did he know? No clue, except . . .

The unpleasant prickle intensified, raising his radar.

His sonar pinged. Locked into the signal, Tareek cast the cosmic net wide. As it settled over rough terrain, he banked hard, coming down out of the mountains as he gathered information. He growled. Aye. Definitely. No doubt in his mind. Something dangerous was afoot. Something dark and unpredictable. Something that smelled far too familiar.

Dread congealed in the pit of his stomach.

His gaze narrowed on the treetops. Naught yet, but soon. Whatever was out there would show itself *soon*. He sensed it in the air. Felt it rise upon the wind. Knew trouble when he found it. Fine-tuning his radar, he increased his wing speed and swung wide. More of the unholy stench blew into his face. Tareek bared his fangs on a curse.

Oh so not good. He recognized the smell now.

Alarm thrummed through him. Tareek inhaled again, filtering the sensory burn, wanting to be sure. Silfer be merciful, let him be wrong. Let him be—

Acrid air washed over his scales. An awful taste rushed into his mouth.

Tareek flinched and, wobbling, lost altitude. With a growl, he tucked his wings and flipped in midair. The twist took him up, then over. Muscles stretched. His body screamed. He ignored the discomfort and, gritting his teeth, rotated into another body-torqueing spin.

Better. Less volatile. Much more even.

A necessary thing. Losing control wouldn't help matters. But even as his brain relayed the message, his body rebelled, kicking his heartbeat up a notch. Boom-boom-thump. Bang-bang-throb. Tareek shook his head. The sound of catastrophic failure if he didn't control it. And fast. Necessity dictated the path. He must push aside the past—forget what the terrible smell signaled—and calm down.

Otherwise he wouldn't be able to get the ball rolling.

Or stay steady enough to warn the others.

Centering himself, Tareek reached out with his mind. Magic writhed around him. His eyes started to glow, washing out in front of him, painting black treetops bright-green. The cosmic cable unwound, bridging the distance to find a connection. Static slithered through the void. The mental hook grabbed hold. A snick echoed inside his head and . . .

The bond snapped into place. One moment fell into the next, then—

"You all right?" The deep voice slammed into his head, cracking through mind-speak like a battering ram. Tareek winced, but went with it anyway. 'Twas forever the same. Quick on the

trigger, Garren linked in fast and always talked first. *"What is going on?"*

"Naught good."

"Shit." His commander paused. Meaning coalesced in the silence, thumping the inside of his skull. Tareek didn't say a thing. Words weren't necessary. Not while Garren cherry-picked the problem off the front of his brain. *"It's back."*

"Aye."

"How bad?"

"Bad. More lethal. Stronger than before," Tareek said, feeling his commander's unease rise along with his own. *"The stench of black magic is thickening."*

Garren growled. *"Christ. 'Tis as we feared. It has begun."*

Little doubt.

The Goddess of All Things was right. Armand, Prince of Shadows, was out, exerting his influence, already wreaking havoc and spreading his stink. Tareek knew the scent well. Had lived with it for twenty years while trapped in dragon form and imprisoned deep in the mountain near Grey Keep. God, how he wished for something different. A new memory to replace the old. A way to right the wrong and erase the past. Wipe it clean by going back to that cursed day and slaying Ylenia when he'd had the chance.

But time didn't bend for just anyone. He couldn't go back. Or undo his mistake.

Shame grabbed him by the throat, making his chest ache. *"Garren . . ."*

"I know." A thump echoed. The scrape of rapid footfalls followed, coming through mind-speak. *"But 'tis over and done,* zi kamir. *You need to let it go."*

If only it were that easy. If only guilt would loosen its grip. *"The smell is getting stronger."*

"Back off. You need backup. Don't go in until I reach you."

"I cannot wait." Angling his wings, Tareek banked into a tight turn. *"Henrik didn't show at the rendezvous point."*

"Troublesome brat," Garren said, tone full of affection.

No kidding. Tareek couldn't disagree. Didn't want to either. Aye, he might be a pain in the arse, but it was hard to find fault with Henrik. The lad always landed in the most interesting situations. Ones that started with a good fight and ended in a lot of bloodshed. Right up his alley. Exactly the way Tareek liked it. At least, under normal circumstances. These, however, didn't qualify as *normal.* Messed up with a healthy helping of *oh Jesus.* Aye. Absolutely. And as black magic seethed and the north wind howled, Tareek's instincts screamed, urging him to fly faster.

"Garren . . . I think he's in trouble."

"Nothing new about that."

Tareek huffed.

His commander growled. A moment later, metal clicked and hinges creaked. Something slammed against stone. A door, mayhap? Tareek tilted his head, listening to the sound of heavy footfall through the cosmic link. Aye. Definitely. Garren was on the move.

"Hold tight." A thud sounded as Garren jumped from somewhere high. *"Don't do anything stupid. I will gather the others and come for you."*

"I'm going in now."

"Tareek—"

"No choice," he said, refusing to back down. No easy task. One of the oldest of their kind, his commander sat at the top of the food chain. Hard. Strong. Cold and merciless when needed.

The kind of warrior another wanted at his back. Few disobeyed Garren on a good day. And no one tangled with the male and lived to tell of it. *"I have to go. You would do the same for Xavian."*

Garren cursed. Not much else the male could do. His commander understood his dilemma. The bond he shared with Xavian, after all, rivaled his with Henrik. *"Go after him, then get out. No fooling around. Until we know exactly what we're dealing with, we err on the side of caution."*

"Agreed." The wind picked up. The stench of decay grew stronger. Another round of unease rolled through him, making muscles tighten and his scales itch. Tareek shook off the discomfort. 'Twas no time for distraction. He neared the apex . . . was less than three miles from the outer marker buried beneath White Temple. Mere minutes from the Valley of the Blessed. *"Come when you can. I'm just west of—"*

"I know where you are," Garren said, mining the unique energy signature Tareek carried like a scent to pinpoint his location. *"Fucking White Temple. I hate that place."*

Didn't they all?

Without a doubt. But hatred didn't change the facts.

Or what he must do.

His aversion didn't matter. Neither did the history. Or that he wanted to turn tail and fly in the opposite direction—avoid the fortress of the Order of Orm at all costs. Tareek snorted. Sparks flew from his nostrils, glowing like fireflies as he shook his head. Talk about an understatement. He'd gone to great lengths to do that very thing—refusing to venture into White Temple with Henrik—and yet, here he was, flying into the teeth of his past anyway.

"Later, Garren."

"Make sure of it," his commander said, concern melding with menace.

Tareek's mouth curved. Flipping male. No one else could show love and threaten him at the same time . . . from over a hundred miles away.

With a quick twist, Tareek severed mind-speak and went wings vertical, slicing between two high cliffs. Rock rumbled. Shale rolled, cascading into an avalanche of jagged stone. The Limwoods rose, stretching into a black carpet beneath him. Eyes narrowed and night vision sharp, he mapped the terrain. His sonar pinged, gathering details, sifting through facts, fueling his flight. Banking right, he rose hard, then dropped low, swooping in over the lip of the dell. The valley dipped, then spread, opening up into a large web. The holy city rose at its center, pale stone walls shining in the gloom, the golden dome of High Temple a beacon in the dark and . . .

Black magic frothed in a wave of orange energy.

The impure aura throbbed, seething across the ground. Dragon senses alight, Tareek tracked the glow. His focus snapped to the right. He snarled, baring his fangs. There. On the main road. A lethal fighting force composed of . . .

His gaze narrowed. Nay. Not men at all.

The large pack was something else. Something more. A *something* he'd never encountered before. Still too far away to strike, he watched them move across the frozen landscape. Too fast to be human, the group ran like a pack of wolves, closing the distance between the outer wall and the cemetery with uncanny speed. Tareek exhaled on a growl. Creatures of immense power fueled by unnatural forces. Minions to the Prince of Shadows. An army to do his bidding. Servants sent to kill them all.

Rage rose in a ravenous wave.

As it bubbled up through the cracks in his guard, the buzz between his temples morphed into something more concrete. The signal lit off inside his head. Tareek sucked in a quick breath. Henrik. His friend was calling, laying down a cosmic trail for him to follow. Magic tightened its grip, narrowing his focus. His gaze swung toward the graveyard north of the high walls. Aboveground crypts and tombstones stood at odd angles, sharing the terrain with huge oaks and towering beeches, creating visual interference and a plethora of places to hide.

Good lad.

Henrik knew what he was doing. The stone monuments would not only provide cover but also buy them both time. Mayhap enough for him to intervene—to become Henrik's shield before the pack reached him and the assassin Tareek loved like a son died an excruciating death.

* * *

Senses pinpoint sharp, Henrik sprinted beneath the canopy of a huge oak. Leafless and cold, brittle limbs swayed overhead, gnarled branches creaking in the quiet. The eerie rattle joined the throb inside his head. Painful now, the sting jabbed at his temples, killing hope along with comfort.

Gritting his teeth, Henrik flipped a mental switch and tried again.

The distress call spiraled out.

Nothing came back. No static swirl. No hint of connection. Just silence on the other end of a cosmic line.

Goddamn Tareek. Where the hell was he?

The question thumped against the inside of his skull. Henrik ignored the pain and leapt over a downed tree trunk. Slung over his shoulder, bottom up and head down, Cosmina bounced, then slid sideways in his hold. He shrugged, heaved her back into place, and upped the pace. She gasped, the sound of distress coming through clenched teeth. God bless her. No matter how hard he ran—or how rough the treatment—she refused to complain. A marvelous trait. Particularly since he couldn't slow down. Or stop to make her comfortable. His speed meant continued safety, so . . .

No help for it. Much as it pained him, he had to keep running. And Cosmina needed to hold on. Bear down and stay strong . . . just a little longer.

Boots churning over icy ground, he took a tight turn into a narrow aisle. Thin skiffs of snow slithered underfoot. Twin crypts rose in the distance, blocking his view and—

He lost his footing and slid sideways.

Cosmina whimpered. He cursed and, fighting for balance, tightened his grip on the backs of her thighs. One moment shifted into the next. His feet found traction. Henrik sprang forward, slicing between two high tombstones. Almost there. Just a few more twists and turns. The instant he found a safe spot, he'd stop. See to Cosmina while he took stock and plotted his next move. The square crypts at the north end of the cemetery were the best bet. Good cover. Lots of alleyways and high walls to hide behind. Eyes scanning the terrain, he judged the distance, then glanced over his free shoulder. No Druinguari yet. No Halál either. Just violent wind gusts blowing snow into a white wall behind him. Thank Christ. Everything else might be wrong, but at least the weather cooperated, raging in his wake, helping to cover his tracks.

"Henrik . . ."

"Almost there," he said, trying to ignore her discomfort, but . . . hell. It was hard. He didn't like the weakness in her voice. Or the pain that drove it. "Not much farther."

Cheek pressed to his back, a shiver rippled through her. "I don't feel well."

"I know."

"Can we rest for a moment? Just a moment . . . please."

"In a while. Hang on a bit longer."

"How c-close . . ." Another shiver racked her, making her teeth chatter. "How c-close are they?"

Excellent question. One he didn't want to answer. He mined the signal anyway, hunting for black magic, following the trace Halál threw into the air. The buzz inside his head intensified. Goddamn it. Not good news. The bastard was less than a mile away and closing fast.

Henrik swallowed a snarl. "We'll make it."

A half-truth. One with a fifty-fifty chance of being right.

Henrik knew it, but refused to take the lie back. Frightening her wouldn't help. Misdirection, however, might. He needed her calm and thinking—able to run, hide, escape into the Limwoods while he protected her back—not terrified. Dwelling on what might happen never solved a problem. Or helped formulate a plan. His mind didn't care, churning his mental wheels, burying him under an avalanche of what-ifs as he sprinted for the aboveground crypts. What if Halál caught up? What if Cosmina's strength gave out and she couldn't run? What if he failed to shield her?

Torture. Rape. Murder. In that order too.

Halál would show no mercy. The bastard never did. His former sensei always struck fast, finding a man's weakness to inflict maximum damage. Physical. Mental. Emotional. Nothing was off-limits. And like it or nay, Halál knew exactly how to hurt him. Fear for Cosmina wound him tight. Dread joined the party, serving up a memory he longed to forget. But even as he shut recall down, blue eyes full of terror—full of tears—came back to haunt him.

Ah God. Not *her*. Again.

He hated when she invaded his thoughts. Shit, he didn't even know her name, and yet, she refused to leave him in peace. To be expected. He didn't deserve any. Not after what he'd done and she'd endured. The girl had been so young . . . so very innocent. A small slip of a thing who'd never hurt a soul and hadn't deserved to die. Halál hadn't cared. An order given was one meant to be followed . . . without question. Henrik had understood too late. Halál had made him pay for his hesitation, stripping the girl of dignity, ensuring she died hard to make a point, punishing Henrik for refusing to kill her.

It had been a test. One he'd failed. On his twelfth birthday.

His age shouldn't have mattered. Youth was no excuse. Five years at Grey Keep had taught him well. He'd understood how to kill—quick and clean—even then. But by refusing his first kill, he'd made things worse. For himself certainly. But especially for her. Had he done as instructed and used his knife, she would've died with dignity. Instead she'd suffered . . .

Endless torment. Needless violence. Terrible pain.

All things at which Halál excelled.

But not tonight. This time would be different. What little honor he had left dictated the course. He would not fail Cosmina as he had the girl.

His boots crunched over an icy patch. Sound rippled, pinging off stone, rising beneath weak moonlight in the frosty air. Veering right, Henrik ducked behind a massive tombstone and slid to a halt. With a huff, he swung Cosmina off his shoulder.

She clung to him for a moment, then let go. The second her feet touched down, her knees buckled. Quick reflexes allowed him to catch her. Cupping her shoulders, he helped her sit down. White puffs escaped between her lips, joining his, frosting the air between them as she struggled to catch her breath.

He cupped her cheek, anchoring himself, trying to comfort her. "All right?"

"A little seasick."

Henrik huffed at the analogy. 'Twas an apt description. Especially since she'd just suffered a serious bout of bob-and-weave atop his shoulder. "We'll rest here a moment. 'Twill help settle your stomach."

"Gods, I hope so." Auburn lashes flickered a moment before she looked right at him.

He frowned. "Cosmina . . . your eyes."

"Is the color returning?"

Brushing his thumb over her eyebrow, he leaned closer. Thin fissures of dark green bled in from the outer edge of each iris, eating at the white, reaching for her pupils. It wasn't much. Barely anything at all, but it gave him hope. If she could see, she could run. "Can you see anything?"

"Naught much. Just shadows, but 'tis a good sign." Pushing her arms through the front fold of her cloak, she set his knife in her lap and cupped her hands. Both shook as she blew on her cold fingers. "A day, mayhap two, and my vision will return."

"Good news."

"'Twould be better if it happened faster."

No question. But beggars couldn't be choosers. He needed to work with what he had, not what she hoped would happen.

"How far away are we?" she asked, flexing her fingers to work blood back into the tips, making him wish he had gloves to give her.

"A league from the edge of the Limwoods."

"Your dragon?"

"Not answering."

"Try again, Henrik." Sightless gaze fixed on him, she reached out and found his face. She fumbled a moment, fingertips sliding over his jaw before her palm settled against his cheek. "You can do it. Even while imprisoned, he was never far from you. A bond like that never dies."

True enough. He'd felt it all his life. "Christ, 'tis eerie how much you know."

"The curse of my gift," she whispered, raising her other hand. Cold fingers touched the side of his throat a second before she pressed her thumb to his pulse point. "Try again."

The north wind howled, pushing against his back.

Henrik didn't fight it. Instead, he leaned in, feeling the warmth as her skin heated against his, and touched his forehead to hers. She murmured. He took the encouragement and opened his mind wide. She thought he could do it. He was willing to try—again and again—if only to keep her safe, far from harm's way. Filling his lungs to capacity, he exhaled long and slow. Her thumb drifted over his jugular. Back and forth. A soft glide coupled with a smooth return. 'Twas hypnotic, a rare drift that helped him go with the flow. He sank deeper into her embrace.

Magic sparked.

The gloom gathered, enclosing them in a cloak of invisibility.

Hidden from view, safe for the moment, Henrik relaxed into the stream that housed enchantment and rose whenever he fought. A blast of frigid air shoved at him again, tearing at his hair, pulling the hood from Cosmina's head. A riot of curls, her hair tumbled, brushing his temples, and—

The signal whiplashed, reaching across distance and mental space.

Henrik bared his teeth, and holding the message in his mind, threw it like a dagger. It whirled end over end, then struck home. Static hissed, slithering in, then out, as it gathered speed inside his head. A growl came through the cosmic weave.

His breath hitched. *"Tareek."*

"Airborne. On my way."

Henrik flinched as the voice punched through, raking the inside of his skull. Cosmina shifted, pressing her cheek to his, helping ground him, but . . . sweet Christ. Talk about bizarre. It was working. He could *hear* his friend. Was communicating through—

Well hell, he didn't know what to call it.

"How close?" he asked, testing the link, struggling to stay connected.

"Five minutes out."

"Too long. We're under attack."

"I know." Scales rattled as wind whistled through the connection. *"Hold tight. I'm circling around. Head for high ground."*

Henrik frowned. High ground meant he needed to move west, not toward the northern rim as planned. *"Where's Kazim?"*

"Riding hard for River's Bend. Edge of the—"

Heavy static washed in as the storm moaned overhead. Snow blew in, swirling thick and white around him. Fisting his hands in Cosmina's cloak, he dipped his head and pressed his forehead to the top of her shoulder, desperate to hang on to Tareek's voice. The cosmic tether whiplashed, then snapped, whirling out into empty space, severing the connection.

"Goddamn it."

"Did you reach him?" Cosmina asked, the urgency in her voice telling. Her palm slid across the nape of his neck and into his hair. Fingers buried in the short strands, she flexed her hand. "Did you—"

"Aye." Lifting his head, he broke her hold. "We need to move."

She nodded and, injured arm tucked to her side, rolled to her knees. "Let's go. I can run for a while if you need me to."

The offer leveled him. Christ, she was something. Far too brave for her own good. Brushing tendrils of hair from her face, he caressed her cheek. She shivered and leaned in, turning into his touch instead of away, making his chest go tight and his heart pound hard. "You'll only slow me down. Conserve your strength, Cosmina. 'Twill be better for you in the—"

The scrape of footfalls rose from the other side of the tombstone.

Henrik glanced right. Blown clean by the wind, a sheet of ice reflected a flash of movement. With a snarl, he palmed his sword hilt and drew hard. Steel whined against leather as he shoved Cosmina backward. Her back thumped against stone. Air left her lungs in a rush. Ignoring her gasp of surprise, he leveled his blade and pivoted on the balls of his feet. Magic crackled, attacking the chill around him. Tightening his grip, he strengthened the cloak of invisibility, deepening the shadows and—

Andrei skidded around the edge of the tombstone.

Shay spun around the other side, sliding to a stop in the narrow aisle. Brows drawn tight, he scanned the terrain, gaze skipping over Henrik without registering his presence. Henrik's mouth curved. Excellent. A good sign. As much as he disliked the magic, the invisibility shield worked for him. Particularly if it ensured he stayed hidden . . . from everyone, brothers-in-arms included. Gaze narrowed on Shay, Henrik dropped his sword tip and, with a murmur, widened the scope of his spell. Both warriors slid inside his web, disappearing into thin air alongside him.

Shay jumped backward. "Jesu!"

"*Merde.*" Andrei threw him a startled look. "I knew you were over here somewhere. I could feel you, but . . ."

"Couldn't see me?"

Low flames flickered, cascading over Andrei's shoulders. "Nifty trick."

"Only if it keeps us alive." Reaching up and over, Henrik re-sheathed his sword. He crouched in front of Cosmina. His gaze slid over her face. Goddamn, she was pale. Far too cold— sliding fast into fatigue too. With a quick flick, he unbuckled his cloak. Wool snapped as he threw the fur-lined mantle around her shoulders. "Here, love."

"Nay, Henrik." Lashes shielding her eyes, she shoved at his hands. "'Tis too cold. You need it."

"Not as much as you."

"I'm all right. Don't—"

"No arguing."

Finished bundling her into his cloak, he threaded the clasp and pulled it tight. Eyes riveted to her face, he debated a moment. Should he or shouldn't he? Getting any closer was no doubt a bad idea. Still temptation called and he couldn't deny the urge to touch her. Just a bit more. What could it possibly hurt? Not much, considering he already stood neck-deep in infatuation. Past the point of no return—responsible for her care, in charge of keeping her safe, yearning to provide comfort even as he called himself a first-class fool. So . . .

Forget about doing the right thing. Wrong sounded a helluva lot better.

Hand shaking a little, he reached out again. Her hair caressed his palm, then tangled between his fingertips, whispering over his skin as he sank into her curls. He breathed deep, playing in the thick strands, gathering up the tendrils, twisting until the mass settled against the nape of her neck, and . . .

Desire burned a heated trail south. His body tightened. His heart throbbed. His mind went sideways inside his head, and Henrik swallowed. So inappropriate. Not even close to advisable, but . . . holy God. She had gorgeous hair. So soft and thick. So rich a red he wanted to get lost for a while and just . . .

Linger.

In her warmth. In her beauty. In the trust she showed by allowing him so close. *Him.* An assassin with little honor and even less worth.

The thought set him straight. Regret hit hard. He withdrew, untangling his hand from her tresses, distancing himself even as he mourned the separation. 'Twas stupid. Abject idiocy to want something more. Something pure and right. Something untouched by violence and the harsh reality he lived every day. She wasn't his. He didn't want her to be.

Case closed. Slam the lid, block it out, and let it lie.

Releasing a pent-up breath, he dragged his gaze from her face. Intense blue eyes met his, then ping-ponged, moving from him to Cosmina, then back again. Andrei raised a brow. Henrik almost cringed. He caught himself at the last moment. Smart son of a bitch. His comrade didn't miss much and understood even more.

Henrik nailed his friend with a warning look. "Don't say it."

"Not even thinking it," Andrei said, a glint of amusement in his gaze. Henrik gritted his teeth. Andrei's lips twitched, then smoothed into serious lines. Unclipping his bladed boomerang from his belt, he tested its weight. As the weapon bobbed in his hand, he peeked around the edge of the tombstone. "Game plan?"

"Need one fast." Crouched to his left, Shay threw him a sidelong look. "How much time before they reach us?"

"Minutes." His eyes narrowed, Henrik tuned back into the unique signature Halál emitted. The signal sizzled, helping him estimate time and distance. "The bastards have split into three packs."

Andrei grunted. "Multiple points of attack."

"Even more ways to hem us in." Expression grave, Shay sheathed twin daggers in favor of throwing stars. As the razor-sharp discs settled in his hands, he scanned the aisle opposite him. "They'll have trouble finding us, though."

"Not much," Henrik said. "We left footprints in the snow."

"Nay, we haven't."

Gaze steady on Shay's, Henrik raised a brow, asking without words.

His apprentice shrugged. "Snow is made of water."

Cosmina drew a soft breath. "You're covering our tracks."

"One snow drift at a time."

"Good. Keep it up," Henrik said. "Time to go."

Pushing to his feet, Andrei circled around behind him. "Any chance you can hide our movements?"

If only. He wished. Too bad wishing and wanting never counted. He'd spent the last month fighting the magic in his blood, not exploring it. An unwise decision. Practice, after all, made perfect. "I cannot gather the gloom while on the run yet, so as soon as we move . . ."

Shay cursed. "The bastards will see us."

"Aye."

"*Merde.*"

"Head for the crypts on the west side. Higher ground." Focus narrowed, Henrik reached for Cosmina. As she settled in his arms, he sent out another ping. Magic spiraled outward. Nothing came back. No answer from Tareek. No cosmic signal of any kind. Tension crawled along his spine. He brushed it aside. It couldn't be helped, and he couldn't wait any longer. "If we get separated, rendezvous at River's Bend."

His comrades nodded.

He glanced at Andrei. "On my mark . . ."

Andrei tensed, preparing to break cover.

"And Shay?"

"Aye."

"Rear flank. Watch our backs." Giving Cosmina a gentle squeeze, Henrik tightened his grip and dipped his head. She nodded, telling him to go. Muscles flexing around her, he lifted her off the ground. The curve of her belly connected with his shoulder as he flipped her upside down. She settled with a gasp. He pushed to his feet and got ready to move. "Go."

Boot treads scraping over ice, Andrei lunged into the aisle between tidy rows of tombstones. The air expanded, then contracted, slamming into the cloak he held with his mind. Magic snapped, then recoiled. Henrik bore down, struggled to hold on, but . . .

A sharp pop exploded through the silence.

The invisibility shield shattered. Andrei materialized out of thin air. Henrik leapt after his friend, racing across the narrow laneway. A shout rang out, rising on the midnight air. An answering yell echoed across the cemetery as the call went up. Henrik cursed under his breath. Enemy message sent and received. So much for covert movement and silent escape.

He'd been spotted. Now the Druinguari converged on his position.

Senses screaming, he listened to the clamor. Chaotic sound rippled—the hammer of multiple footfalls, the demonic snarls, and the zing of weapons being drawn—painting a clear picture. Goddamn it. He needed more time. Was just moments away from the iron gate and high stone wall. The west side and aboveground crypts lay just beyond. A mere fifty feet from slipping into labyrinth-like streets that would provide cover, but . . .

The bastards were already too close.

Three, mayhap four, aisles away, running parallel tracks, trying to get ahead of them.

Tombstones sliced past as he pushed himself harder, sprinting for the end of the laneway. Shay cursed behind him. Henrik veered right and slid on slippery ice. Fighting the fall, using his momentum, he skidded sideways. Cosmina yelped, grappling for purchase as she bounced on his shoulder. He strengthened his hold, swung into the next aisle, and—

Fire streamed into view, streaking across the night sky.

Heat went cataclysmic. Snow melted into pools. Water evaporated, throwing mist into the air. Eyes on the unholy blaze, Henrik dropped and rolled. Tucking Cosmina close, he pressed her head beneath his chin and tumbled across the turf. Right on target, the fireball struck the ground. Dirt and ash erupted, blowing sky-high. Enemy assassins shouted as the blast picked Henrik up and threw him sideways. Cosmina screamed. Limbs tangled with hers, Henrik held on tight, trying to control the spin midflip. He landed with a thump and slid, smashing into a cemetery wall. He heard a curse, felt the secondary heat wave hit, and—

Shay slammed into stone next to him. His apprentice groaned. "Hellfire."

Uh-huh. Literally, 'cause Jesus knew Tareek wasn't fooling around.

Thankfulness split Henrik wide open. He took it back a moment later when another fireball roared across the night sky. More deadly than the first, flames spilled, splashing up and out like lava flow. Trees caught fire, throwing ash into the air as tombstones whirled end over end, taking enemy assassins out at the knees. Breathing hard, Henrik searched the trail of smoke overhead. Any moment now. Another few seconds and . . .

Green eyes aglow, Tareek shot through the acrid swirl.

Spotting Henrik on the ground, his friend tucked his wings. He dropped out of the sky like a stone. Huge talons thumped down. Bloodred scales rattled, glinting in the blaze as Tareek slid sideways on scorched earth. Time slowed, warping perception. Ignoring Cosmina's "Oh gods!" Henrik watched in awe as Tareek's razor-sharp claws tore into the ground, ripping wide trenches in the dirt. Goddamn, the male was huge and all kinds of vicious. Thank Christ. He couldn't ask for a better self-appointed protector, but . . .

Henrik shook his head. No matter how many times he witnessed the transformation, the shift startled him. How Tareek went from a man to, well . . . *that*. 'Twas downright amazing.

Coming to a sudden halt in front of him, Tareek glanced over his shoulder. Shimmering eyes met his. The dragon bared his fangs. *"Run."*

The snarl slammed into his mind. Henrik didn't hesitate. Scooping Cosmina off the ground, he spun around the high wall and made for River's Bend. He hated to do it. Would rather stand and fight alongside Tareek, but that wouldn't work. Not tonight. Cosmina had endured enough. The faster he got her to safety, the better. The quicker he'd acquire answers too, 'cause . . . no question. 'Twas time to do the unthinkable. No matter how much it chaffed him, he must shelve his grudge and summon the Goddess of All Things. Otherwise he wouldn't get what he needed . . .

The secret to killing Halál and the band of unnatural bastards he led.

CHAPTER TWELVE

Perched atop the high wall overlooking the Jiu River, Cristobal Torres watched the ripple from eleven hundred feet up. Winter winds dove deep, then rose hard, tugging at his shirttail, caressing him like a lover as starry skies tossed brilliance like well-honed dice. Illumination tumbled, glimmering across the surface of the Jiu. His gaze on the ebb and flow, he shook his head. He shouldn't be here, outside in the cold, atop the parapet that protected Drachaven, the mountain fortress he now shared with his brothers-in-arms.

Not that it wasn't a pretty sight. Far from it.

The view was magnificent, the brutal drop to the river's edge even more so. 'Twas almost enough to tempt him. A quick spin. An even faster fall, and he'd be hanging off the outer wall by his fingertips, moments from feeling the rush as he free-climbed the icy stone face to reach the sheer cliffs upon which Drachaven sat. A dangerous endeavor—one that required supreme skill to achieve and most would call insane. Cristobal huffed. Call him mad, then, and get it over with, 'cause . . . hell. He'd already made the climb . . . twice. Once from the river's edge up. The second time from the high wall down alongside Xavian.

A race to the bottom.

A fun one that had ended with bragging rights and a lot of backslapping. Which was why he shouldn't be here. Xavian—his best friend and commander of The Seven—would kick his arse if he knew. Would tell him to go back to bed and get some rest, but . . .

He couldn't sleep. For the fifth moonrise in a row.

'Twas the damnedest thing. Most nights he slept like the dead. But times changed, and now he suffered the effects. Tension ate at him, pricking along his spine, pulling worry to the surface. He needed to sleep. Felt the draw and tug of fatigue even now—while brisk winds bit and the moon shone bright—but everything he tried failed. Warm milk with honey before bedtime? Nothing. A ball-busting training session after supper? No results. Reading ancient texts until his eyes grew gritty and his mind numbed from boredom? A big fat zero on the sliding slumber scale. 'Twas beyond frustrating.

Particularly since he knew the cause. Or at least, thought he did. And still couldn't do a thing about it.

Flexing his fingers, Cristobal glanced down at the back of his hand. His knuckle points stared back at him. He debated a moment, then gave into the urge, and shoved at his shirtsleeve. Butter-soft linen slid up his forearm and . . . *rahat*. No change. The lines were still there. Weren't getting any better either. Fine and precise, an invisible hand drew on his skin, weaving black lines in and out, creating a pattern that, as of yet, remained incomplete. A conclusion based in presumption? Probably. He couldn't be certain, after all, the tattoo lay unfinished. But then, he didn't need to be sure.

Instinct never lied. Neither did the truth. Or the fact he hadn't asked for the black ink.

He'd woken from a deep sleep six nights ago, the sting almost unbearable, to discover the tattoo starting on the backs of both hands. Now it crawled like creeping vines, staining his skin, burning deep into flesh until he felt it in his bones.

Strange. Painful. Scary as hell.

And clearly not done yet.

His lip curled as the lines slid over his right forearm. With a rough yank, he checked his left arm. Same design. Identical marks forming twin patterns. No deviation in contour as each headed for his elbows. Cristobal blew out a shaky breath. Not normal. Hell, no wonder he couldn't sleep. Forget the agony—the constant sting of the unnatural tattoos. Put aside his resistance to, well . . . whatever the hell was happening to him. He'd already buried the fear six feet under. 'Twas the voice inside his head he couldn't stand. Like a gong being struck, the witchy whisper beat against his temples. Over and over. Again and again. Always the same words . . .

Find her. Find her. She needs you . . . find her.

Cristobal yanked his shirt cuff back down. The rough movement raked along his forearm. Anguish scraped across his skin. Balanced on the balls of his feet, he snarled at the mountain peaks rising in the distance.

"*Ma rahat*," he said through clenched teeth.

None of it made any sense. Not the burn of creeping tattoos. Not the words shredding the inside of his skull. Not the urgency he felt either. He didn't even know *her* name. Who the hell was she? And why in God's name did she need him? The annoying chant came again. *Find her. Find her. She needs you . . . find her.* More questions circled. Per usual, answers refused to follow.

He snorted. Like he should expect anything less? Nothing ever came easy. Solutions to problems enjoyed playing coy and never arrived out of the blue. The world didn't work that way. A mystery required legwork and razor-sharp intellect to solve. So . . .

Time to stop stewing and step up his game.

Avoiding the inevitable wasn't his thing. Neither was panic. And honestly, he'd never been the idle sort. Trained to kill, the most talented tracker in an order full of elite assassins, he preferred to be on the move—hunting, shadow walking, taking down his prey. Which meant he needed to tell someone. His gaze on the snaking current of the river, Cristobal frowned. Mayhap he should talk to Xavian and reach out to Afina. A magic wielder and High Priestess to the Order of Orm, she possessed a direct line to the Goddess of All Things, the deity he now served. Mayhap if he shared the problem—showed her the ink and incomplete tattoos—she would know what to do. Or at the very least, explain what the hell was happening to him.

Nerves got the better of him.

He shoved the angst aside. Hiding the ink was foolhardy. He needed help. Could no longer deny the pain or contain his worry, so . . . aye, despite the need to solve his own problems, 'twas past time he sought aide from his best friend. With a quick shift, Cristobal pivoted atop the wall. His boots brushed against stone. Sound whispered, drifting on frigid air as he—

A door slammed open. Wood banged against stone, shredding the silence.

Cristobal's focus snapped toward the main entrance.

Eyes aglow, Garren roared over the threshold, then down the stairs, heading for the wide-open space of the inner bailey. Hot on his heels, Cruz, the youngest of the dragon-shifters, made tracks in his commander's wake. Cristobal went on high alert.

Rahat. Not good. Calm, cool, and collected most of the time, not much upset the dragon-shifter. But as he scanned Garren's face and read his expression, he knew—just *knew*—the warrior carried bad news. Taut muscle rippling, Cristobal leapt from his perch. His feet touched down on the rampart. Garren looked up from the bottom step and nailed him with shimmering violet eyes.

Cristobal tipped his chin. "What?"

"Trouble." His deep voice rose on a wave of magic, making Cristobal's skin prickle in warning. Massive shoulders rolling, Garren broke eye contact and jogged across the inner bailey. His destination: the blacksmith's shop. Or more precisely, the bed-chamber hidden behind it. "I will rouse Xavian. Find Razvan. We fly for White Temple as soon as all are assembled in the courtyard."

Ah hell. White Temple.

The location could only mean one thing. Henrik and the others were in danger. Which meant Tareek was in the thick of it. Jesus, Mary, and Joseph. No wonder Garren smelled of unease and moved like the wind.

Urgency pumped through him.

Putting his boots to good use, Cristobal ran the length of the walkway. Footfalls hammering stone, he reached the door at his end, yanked it open, and crossed into a large chamber. Sprinting across Afina's healing room, he skirted the huge table at its center and made for the double doors on the other side. The keep proper lay beyond, and his comrade's chamber along the first corridor. He must move fast. No time to waste. The quicker he hauled Razvan out of bed, the sooner Henrik would have the help he needed.

* * *

Candlelight flickered, casting odd patterns across the white walls. Alone in the weaving room, sitting in front of her favorite loom, Nairobi Brue watched the eerie shadows dance and listened for the telltale creak of wooden floorboards. Naught yet. No low rumble of male voices. No scrape of footfalls or the soft rattle of weaponry. Naught but the chill of midnight and blessed silence. Thank goodness. She needed the extra time. Enough to find her courage and settle her nerves. She couldn't afford any mistakes. Not tonight. Everything rested on the next few minutes.

On her ability to forge ahead and make something out of nothing.

Hands moving at a furious pace, she tied another knot in the makeshift cloth rope. Another few lengths of wool, and she would be on her way. A hop, skip, and a jump from tying one end to the window frame, climbing down to the pathway below, and running hard for the garden gate, but . . . not yet. She needed every advantage. Must wait a while longer even though fear circled, making her palms sweat and her want to flee now.

Sooner than *now* would be better.

Nairobi shook her head and finished knotting the last woolen strip.

"Patience," she murmured. "'Tis a virtue for a reason."

The whispered words made her lips twitch. Such sentiment. So much old-fashioned faith. Kind of ridiculous when she thought about it, but for some reason, hope didn't seem out of place tonight. She'd made it this far, hadn't she? Was due for some good luck, wasn't she? Nairobi nodded. Without a doubt. 'Twas her turn, but as chance rolled the dice and she tugged on the cloth, testing the rope, nerves got the best of her. Shoving the makeshift cord beneath a pile of yarn, she glanced toward the arched entryway into the room. With the double doors folded open, she had a clear view into the hallway.

Usually her favorite spot. Too bad it afforded little comfort tonight. Any moment now, the whisper of footsteps would fall and the quiet creak would come, heralding the guard's approach and . . .

Her eviction from the weaving room.

Not that she didn't belong. She did. More than most, anyway. But the owner of Saul's Silk Emporium liked rules as much as she enjoyed breaking them. Which meant it wouldn't be long now. Hardly any time at all before Adam, head guard and colossal pain in her backside, rounded the corner and saw her sitting where she wasn't allowed to be at night. In front of her loom. Colorful yarn bobbing on multiple spools along the top crosspiece.

Inhaling a calming breath, Nairobi exhaled in a rush, then reached out and picked up the threads. Under. Over. Weave, knot, cut, brush it down—start all over again. The familiar rhythm settled her, untangling tight muscles as she fell into the tried and true. Fingers working as hard as her mind, furious in the fray, one weaving a Persian rug, the other searching for an adequate excuse. She needed one in order to remain in front of her loom. And by extension, next to the long run of windows that made a home along one side chamber.

A lie spiked with the truth would work best.

It always did. And she should know. She'd spent the last two years lying . . . about everything. Who she was. Where she'd come from. Why she was alone in the world. Lies, lies, and more lies. Untruth stacked upon untruth. Curious thing, though, no one ever called her on it. Or investigated her sudden appearance in the town of Ismal. Fortuitous or disastrous? Nairobi couldn't tell. Being found out—called a fraud and made to pay—would be easier than maintaining the front. And as moonlight spilled into the chamber, casting shadows across piles of yarn and tables littered with embroidery tools, she almost wished someone would grow a brain and get a clue.

Almost, but not quite.

Danger, after all, lived inside her truth. The kind of knowledge others coveted. A secret so profound she would go to her grave to protect it. Knotting another thread, Nairobi bit down on her bottom lip. *Death* . . . a distinct possibility tonight. Especially if she escaped as planned. Not that anyone would agree she was a prisoner. She was paid, after all—given room and board along with a few coins each month for her efforts inside the silk house. Most would call that employment, not prison.

The truth was far more sinister.

She'd been trapped the moment she stepped inside the Emporium. Now she played the pawn in a ruthless game enjoyed by the rich and greedy.

Nairobi shook her head. Goddess be swift and merciful. Creativity could be a curse sometimes. Combine it, however, with supreme talent and the effect multiplied, setting her apart from the others. Her employer—or rather *jailer*—loved her for it. The other women she worked alongside each day? Not so much. Like venomous green thread, jealousy ran deep inside the silk house, individual weavers in constant competition to win the master's favor. A pity, really, particularly since she didn't want the distinction.

Or to be noticed by Saul.

Nairobi huffed. Good luck with that. 'Twas far too late to change course and go unnoticed. Her designs ensured his attention. Her skill at the loom cinched it. More fool her. She never should've shown her true colors . . . or revealed the extent of her talent. Now she couldn't move without drawing notice.

Guarded by day. Watched at night. Followed everywhere.

A steep price to pay for the skills she possessed.

Brows drawn together, Nairobi shifted on the low stool. Wooden legs scraped over greying floorboards. The ragged sound echoed inside the empty chamber, knotting the muscles between her shoulder blades as she fingered the wool threads, testing her loom for tension. Taut. Strong. Evenly spaced. Sheer perfection to a master weaver with a love of design and an eye for detail. Half-done, the Persian rug took shape and form, individual knots, each color, the repetitive motion of her hands carrying the one-of-a-kind motif ever upward, toward the wooden rail anchoring the whole. Another month and she would finish. Would lay the enormous carpet flat and see it in its entirety for the first time. After weeks of planning. After months of toiling. After years spent dreaming.

Her creation would be called a masterpiece.

Those who called Ismal—the marketplace nestled at the foot of the Carpathian Mountain Range—home would gather, hoping for a chance to see it. Wealthy merchants and celebrated noblemen would bid for the privilege of taking it home. The other weavers would sneer behind her back while Saul boasted of her talent . . . then locked her away. Put her under heavy guard. Again. Like always. For fear another silk house would view her work and attempt to steal her.

Just like the last time.

Which meant the Persian would never see completion.

Regret invaded her heart. As it tugged at her artist's soul, Nairobi sighed and paused mid-knot. Hands hovering above the weft, she debated a moment, then gave in, and traced the colorful pattern with her fingertip. Soft wool brushed against her calloused skin. An ache bloomed in the center of her chest. 'Twas a crying shame. A terrible tragedy to leave something so beautiful unfinished. But no matter how difficult, she would leave the rug behind and never look back.

The Goddess of All Things commanded it.

Aye, she'd heard the call. The cosmic thread held on hard, tugging at her heart, collecting in her soul, relaying the message . . . loud and clear. Now all she wanted to do was go home to White Temple. Tears stung the corners of her eyes. Goddess, she could hardly believe it. She'd prayed every day for so long— from the moment she'd been forced to flee the holy city. Two years spent struggling. Two years of uncertainty, of not knowing who to trust or where to turn. Two years adrift in the wilds of mankind, awaiting the day the goddess recalled the Blessed and reclaimed her own.

Two years.

And now—finally, after all this time—'twas safe to return home.

The mark between her shoulder blades tingled. Burned into her skin, the moon-star gave her strength. Enough to believe she could do it. Gods, she had done it. Or at least, started down the path to freedom.

Along with the rope, she'd spent an hour sneaking from room to room, gathering what she needed, preparing her getaway bag one item at a time. Her gaze cut to the wooden box beside her loom. Piled high with yarn, no one would ever guess her satchel lay hidden beneath the colorful wool. Tying another knot, she wove another line of thread and took inventory of her supplies. Two knives. A tin cup. Wire for setting rabbit snarls. A flint for starting a fire. Enough food for three days . . . if she rationed and was careful. A warm cloak, good boots, and fur-lined gloves. Nairobi frowned. It wasn't enough. Five days' worth of food would've been better. But with time ticking down, she couldn't delay to gather more.

She must leave. Now. Tonight.

Before the buyers arrived to view her design. Before Saul locked her behind closed doors. Before she lost all hope of escape and—

Floorboards creaked in the hallway.

Nairobi flinched, then forced herself to settle down. 'Twas all right. She needed the guard to show up. Her plan hinged on her catch and release. All knew she loved to work late, when the night grew quiet and the other weavers slept. Even though Saul forbade it, Nairobi still slipped out of bed to sneak into the weaving room after hours. The guards had caught her often enough to know 'twas a running theme with her.

All part of her plan. Familiarity, after all, lessened vigilance.

Pretending absorption in her work, Nairobi bent over the threads. Any moment now, Adam would—

Footfalls thudded to a stop on the threshold. "For the love of God, Nairobi."

She jerked, feigning surprise as she looked his way. Dark eyes met hers. She blinked like an astonished owl. He sighed, the heavy sound full of exasperation. The urge to laugh bubbled up, tightening her chest. Nairobi quelled the inclination. Finding his expression amusing was all fine and good. Showing it, however, was not.

"Oh, good eve, Adam."

"Good eve," he grumbled, throwing her a look of extreme irritation. "'Tis the middle of the night, Nairobi. All are abed, and well you know it. You are not to be here at this hour."

Uh-oh. Grumpier than usual. Not a good sign, but . . . no help for it. Time to play the innocent card. She bit down on her bottom lip and shrugged. "I know, but—"

"But naught." His eyes narrowed on her. "Go on with ye. Back to bed."

"Just a bit longer?"

He scowled at her.

"An hour . . . not a moment more, I promise."

"Nairobi, you cannot continue—"

"Please?" Placing her hands in a prayer position, she pleaded with her eyes. His expression softened a second before he huffed. Thank God. Both were excellent signs. Adam might be a stickler for the rules, but he wasn't heartless. A good thing too. A soft heart would give her the added leverage she needed to get him to agree. "I won't cause trouble. You know I won't. 'Tis just . . . I'm almost done, so very close to finishing and . . ."

As she trailed off, Adam shook his head. She made another pleading sound. He treated her to another sigh, then held up a finger. "One more round. I'll walk one more, Nairobi. When I get back, I want you gone. Back in bed . . . understood?"

"Aye." Relief made her smile at him. His lips twitched in response and . . . oh bother. Just what she didn't need: her conscience rearing its ugly head. Lord love her, it wasn't fair. She didn't want to get Adam in trouble, but that was exactly what would happen the instant Saul realized she was missing. Awful in every way. Especially since Adam had always been, well . . . all right. Not *kind* to her. That was stretching it a bit. The guard, after all, worked for the silk house. One of his duties included ensuring she stayed put. But that didn't change the facts. Adam, for all his gruffness, had always been halfway decent to her. "Thank you, Adam."

He made a rough sound, gave her another stern look, then turned into the corridor. A second before he disappeared from view, he glanced over his shoulder and wagged his finger at her. "One more round."

"Right. Got it."

And she did. Had *gotten* precisely what she needed—what she'd waited beside her loom in the hopes of acquiring: time. A whole quarter of an hour's worth if Adam stuck to his usual route and his pace stayed true. Which meant . . .

Time to go.

Senses keen, Nairobi listened hard, tracking Adam as he walked away. The second he reached the end of the corridor, she grabbed the cloth rope and spun off her stool. The work of seconds, she unearthed her satchel from beneath the yarn pile. Leather strap in her hand, she dipped her chin, and with a quick toss, looped the bag over her shoulder. As it settled, she turned toward the closest window. Heart beating triple time, she glanced at the door one last time, then forced herself to move.

One guard distracted. A not-so-easy fifty-foot drop left to accomplish.

'Twas now or never. Do or die. Two options that offered no comfort and little choice. But as she wove the cloth rope through the ironwork next to the window and pushed the coiled bundle off the ledge, Nairobi refused to turn back. Or remain frozen in fear. No matter the risk, she must break free and leave the silk house behind. Opportunity knocked. Providence provided the key, gifting her with a narrow slice of time. Now all she needed to do was stick to the plan and stay alive long enough to disappear for good.

CHAPTER THIRTEEN

It was official. The whole being carried thing stunk . . . in serious ways.

Still slung over Henrik's shoulder, Cosmina lifted her head and cracked her eyes open. Dense shadow expanded, then contracted, leaving naught but shades of grey. She squinted, trying to force her eyes into focus. Henrik dodged right, then pivoted around a corner. The visual grey-out lengthened into a blur. She bit back a groan. Terrific. Just her luck. Little to no improvement. So much for believing her vision was returning. Or that self-reliance rested a blink away. Goddess, she couldn't stand it—the weakness along with the vulnerability that fostered it. Such inadequacy. So much insecurity. Way too much guilt. If she were as strong as she thought, she wouldn't be here.

Again. Like always. Prey to circumstance and her stupid gift.

The realization pushed tears into her eyes. Cosmina blinked them away. No way. Not happening. No matter how deficient, she refused to give in and tumble into the death trap of self-pity. Feeing sorry for herself wouldn't help. It never did, which meant she needed to buck up and hold on hard. Cosmina huffed. Such a lovely thought. An even tougher sell to her battered senses. Blind as a bat. Sick to her stomach. Hurting like the devil and—oh right, let's not forget bottom up and head down over Henrik's shoulder while he navigated what felt like a steep slope, feet moving at a fast clip.

The word *undignified* came to mind.

She could hardly argue the point. Thank God pragmatism saved her from it, dragging pride into the rescue effort and sending folly spinning into the background. It could be so much worse. The Druinguari could've killed her—aimed well and shot true, putting the arrow through her heart instead of her arm. She could've failed in her mission, disappointing the goddess, but had succeeded instead. Henrik could've left her to die—cold and alone in the place of her birth. He hadn't, and despite everything, she was grateful. So, complain about her position? Not on her life. Whining about the rough hold and rapid pace wouldn't change anything. Neither would throwing up, but . . .

Blast and damn, that didn't mean she wasn't thinking about it.

Henrik swung around a tight bend. Rock crunched beneath his feet. Her stomach sloshed, throwing bile up her throat as her hips bounced on his shoulder. His grip on her legs slipped. She lurched sideways a second before he caught her, big hand settling on the curve of her bottom. Modesty murmured, but Cosmina ignored it. She didn't care where his hands wandered. Touch her. Don't touch her. It didn't matter anymore. He could do whatever he wanted—strip her bare, lay her down, kiss her with as much heat as before. She wouldn't complain, just as long as her head stopped spinning.

Wishful thinking?

Absolutely.

From their pace, she surmised the Druinguari were down, but not out. Which meant Henrik couldn't stop. Not until he knew for certain. Not until he received the *all clear* from Tareek. Knowing it, however, brought little solace and no relief. Desperate now, trying to hang on, Cosmina sent a prayer heavenward, asking for deliverance. From everything: chilly wind gusts, the mind-torque of fatigue, and . . . ah hell. Who was she kidding? She was beyond asking. Now she begged in silence, pleading to whatever god wanted to listen. But as the litany of *please make it stop* lit off inside her head, she didn't hold out much hope.

Despite Tareek's interference, the Druinguari wouldn't stay down long. The second the dragon took flight, the enemy would be back on their feet—hunting, tracking, chasing them across the frozen landscape. So aye, as far as luck went, she was plum out. No reprieve in sight. No rest either. At least, not for a while. Except . . .

Cosmina frowned. What was that noise?

Both hands gripping Henrik's tunic, she squeezed her eyes closed, shutting out the chaotic throb of her heartbeat. The mental whirl settled. A familiar sound registered. Cosmina listened harder, isolating the source and—aye, definitely. Horses. What sounded like a whole herd, hooves hammering in thunderous rhythm. Relief hit her with a round of *thank you God* a second before prudence took hold. Dear goddess, she'd lost what little remained of her mind. Approaching horses didn't mean safety. Most of the time the occurrence equaled serious trouble. The kind she avoided, usually by finding a safe place to hide until the intruders passed on whatever trail they traveled. Always the better bet out here . . . in the middle of nowhere, surrounded by rough terrain and no help.

Unease licked deep, raising alarm bells.

"Henrik."

"Quiet, Cosmina."

The sternness of his voice startled her. Especially since he didn't sound the least bit out of breath. Her hold on his tunic tightened. How could that be? He'd been running flat out while carrying her. He ought to be tired by now. Despite her condition, the realization raised serious questions—the who, what, and why of Henrik. All the things she'd failed to ask when she'd had the chance. The lapse in judgment wasn't like her. Mistrust was more her style and inquiry her weapon of choice. Cautious by nature, she fed on facts. Enjoyed information the way noble ladies did sweets. Knowledge equaled power. Or, at least, the ability to protect herself and deal with whatever came her way.

Henrik included.

"Here we go," Shay said from behind her on the path.

"Andrei." Henrik slowed the pace and sidestepped. Cheek resting against his spine, Cosmina opened her eyes. An indistinct shadow wavered just inches away. Frigid air burned across her cheeks. Pain pressed against her temples, throbbing into a full-blown headache as she reached out. Rough bark scraped her chilled fingertips. She exhaled in a rush. Trees. The thunder of horses' hooves. Both meant one thing. Henrik stood at the bottom of the ravine, just feet from the main road. "Got an angle?"

"All clear," Andrei said, voice playing in wind gusts. Boots whispered over snow, coming from above and behind her. A whistle rushed through the air. A second later, Andrei landed beside Henrik. "Kazim with the horses."

"About time," Shay said.

"Shay . . . flag him down." Shifting his hold, Henrik pulled Cosmina off his shoulder.

Her feet touched the ground. Nausea threw bile up her throat as agony clawed her shoulder. Desperate to stay upright, Cosmina locked her knees. With a quick dip, Henrik swung her back into his arms. The jarring movement made her wince.

"Sorry," Henrik said, regret in his tone. "I know you're hurting. I don't mean to be rough."

"'Tis nothing," she said, even though it wasn't true. "Naught to worry about."

Cradling her close, Henrik skirted the trees and followed his friends. "Liar."

"Better than the alternative."

"Which is?"

"Crying."

He grinned against the top of her head. "Just a bit longer, *mica vrăjitoare*."

"Nice try." Understanding his game, she ignored the provocation and pressed her cheek to his chest. Heat radiated off him in waves, curling around her. So nice. His strength. His warmth. His willingness to share them both. Unable to resist, she snuggled closer, taking all he gave her. "But I'm too tired to care what you call me."

"You'll get me back later, though, right?"

She snorted. Score one for Henrik. The man never said quit. "Hammer you, for sure."

"I'm relieved."

"You're an idiot." He chuckled. Her mouth curved in appreciation. For some reason, his teasing revived her, helping her change tack. *Tough as nails, remember?* She needed to hold on to the truth of who and what she was and . . . *remember*. Despite her injuries, she wasn't a weakling. Never had been. Never would be either. "You forget how good I am with a blade."

"Not for a moment. I'm looking forward to sparring with you."

"Like I said . . . an idiot."

He laughed again, then dipped his chin and kissed the top of her head. He lingered a moment, mouth pressed to her hair, making surprise rise and confusion surface. Cosmina frowned. He shouldn't be doing that—kissing her. The show of affection seemed misplaced and yet somehow, it felt right too.

Meant to be.

The phrase whispered inside her head, stirring her Seer's instinct, unearthing questions best left unasked. Cosmina knew it marrow deep. Allowing curiosity free reign—becoming entangled with Henrik—was a bad idea. 'Twould be better to ignore the tug of attraction. Safer still to turn away. Some things, after all, were meant to stay buried. But even as her senses prickled, warning her to stand down and stay clear, she couldn't deny the truth. He intrigued her. A hardened warrior one moment, gentle the next. The ability to kill without conscience coupled with a need to protect. Polar opposites tucked inside one man. A complete mystery, one far too alluring for the sleuth in her to pass up. Which meant she couldn't back away. Not yet. She wanted to explore a little further. Needed to know more . . . about everything, all he hid from the world.

Even if she grew to regret it in the end.

A shout went up. The thundering echo of hooves slowed on the trail. Henrik strode out from beneath the sway of tree limbs. The wind picked up, telling her he'd walked into an open space. Cosmina titled her head, pressing her forehead to Henrik's collarbone, gathering sound, gauging distance, plotting the trajectory of approach. Horses snorted, blowing hard somewhere to her right. Seconds lengthened into more as multiple harnesses jangled. Ten feet away, mayhap a bit less. Henrik tensed. Muscles flexed around her and . . . oh gods. She knew what his shift in tension signaled. He planned to—

"Get ready."

"Henrik, wait. Don't—"

He heaved her upward. She landed with a bump. Cosmina moaned. The horse shied, sidestepping beneath her. She reached out with her good hand, latching onto the soft strands of the long mane a moment before Henrik swung into the saddle behind her. Strong arms closed around her. With a quick tug, he pulled her against his chest and put his heels to his steed's sides. The horse lunged forward. Others followed, hooves hammering in Henrik's wake as he took the lead.

"Tuck in, Cosmina," Henrik said, voice rising above the howl of winter wind. "Hold tight. 'Tis going to be a rough ride."

Heart beating triple time, Cosmina didn't argue. She did what he asked instead, hooking both legs over one of his thighs. One shoulder nestled beneath his arm, she hung on hard, moving with him, watching dense shadows flash past from her position in his lap. Deft hands on the reins, Henrik galloped around a bend on the trail. A burst of light perforated her periphery, slicing through her mind before splintering into imagery.

Her breath caught.

Gods. 'Twasn't much. Barely anything at all, but the flash gifted her with a brief glimpse of the terrain. Now she knew what trail they traveled. She'd spotted the marker—the jagged boulder signaling the last turn—amid the soaring trunks and leafless tree limbs. Add that to the rumble of water and—aye, no question—she neared River's Bend. Was naught more than half a mile from the edge of the Limwoods.

Which meant she needed to warn Henrik.

Ritual must be followed and etiquette observed. Otherwise the ancient forest would react . . . and not in welcoming ways. Most people scoffed, mocking the magic even as they gave the woodlands a wide berth. But she'd seen it at work and respected its power, feeling privileged enough to call the mystical force friend most days. At first, she'd thought it odd the forest spirit liked her—had opened its borders and invited her in, allowing her to make a home under its watchful eye. Now she knew the truth. The goddess had ensured her welcome, sending a protector to see to her in exile. Praise be. Without the Limwoods, she might've died. Instead she'd found friendship, one that would last a lifetime. But as much as she loved the forest spirit—and it her—Cosmina understood its limitations.

The forest's benevolence didn't extend to anyone else.

A problem. Particularly right now.

If Henrik crossed the river before she introduced him and asked for safe passage, violence would ensue. The kind no one—least of all her—wanted to see.

"Henrik," she said, her voice a low rasp. Drat and damn, she sounded awful, like an old woman on her deathbed, so frail her words didn't carry. Which wouldn't do. She needed him to stop. Otherwise she wouldn't be able to explain. A circumstance that would get Henrik and his friends killed. "Slow down. Wait before—"

"Later."

"Nay. Now." Fighting her injury, Cosmina pushed herself upright. He tightened his grip, keeping her flush against him. She thumped on his chest with the side of her fist. "You don't understand. The Limwoods won't—"

The horse's front hooves left the ground.

With a growl, Henrik locked her down, keeping her contained in his arms. Thigh muscles flexing, he controlled the jump and landed on the other side of the embankment. Water roared, flowing along the banks of the Mureş River. Smooth stones tumbled, cracking into the next as Henrik raced for the river's edge. The stallion's hooves kicked high, spraying cold water into her face. Panic struck. Cosmina shoved at Henrik, desperate to stall his forward progress.

"Henrik, stop! Turn around—stop!"

Her desperate shout rang out. Too little, too late.

The scent of hollyhocks rose as the Limwoods awakened. She heard the lethal hiss. Sensed the ancient presence coil and powerful magic rise. Throwing both hands out in front of her, she yelled the forest spirit's name, hoping to stave off the attack. To no effect. Already on the defensive, the woodlands sent thick creepers slithering toward them like snakes. Under. Over. A writhing symphony of sound driven by deadly intent. Cosmina cringed. Henrik cursed and hauled hard on the reins. The warriors behind him shouted. Horses screamed, water arcing as each reared, hooves clawing thin air. Venomous vines struck, reached out like tentacles, then yanked hard, plucking her from the saddle, breaking Henrik's hold, dragging her along with the others deep into the recesses of the forbidden forest.

* * *

Henrik came to, shooting into awareness like a bottle thrown into rushing water. He bobbed on the surface a moment, heart beating an unnatural rhythm as he shifted. Sore muscles squawked, sending sensation prickling along his spine. He frowned and took stock. Hands bound behind his back. Check. Feet pulled together, a tight tether around both. Double check. He cracked his eyes open and . . . oh goody. Hanging upside down inside a dark plant-infested alcove too. Lovely. Just terrific. He'd just cornered the market on a triple threat called *absolutely screwed*.

Not that it meant anything. He'd been in tight spots before. A lot of them. All kinds of life-threatening situations, but, well . . .

Being attacked by a giant plant ranked as the most bizarre. One of the worst situations he'd encountered in a while. A close second to being strapped to the blue stone inside Grey Keep. The memory sliced deep, elevating his pulse. His heart punched the inside of his chest. Sucking in a deep breath, Henrik shook his head. Not good. Nowhere near fair either. He didn't need reminding. His mind didn't care, reacting to the bondage, serving up the memory on a mental platter.

Tied down. Spread eagle on cold stone. Helpless in the face of Halál and his knives.

A shiver rolled through him. Refusing to give in, he shut it down. 'Twas rank insanity. The height of stupidity. No way should he be comparing incidents. Or dwelling on the past when the present stared him in the face. Christ, he had enough to worry about right here. So forget the awful lash of remembered torture. The bitter memory needed to stay where he put it . . . locked in the dark pit at the back of his brain.

Flexing his hands, Henrik tested his bonds. Thick tentacles reacted, coiling higher, slithering up his forearms to brush the insides of his elbows. The cold, leathery slide gave him a bad case of the creeps. He hated being bound. Despised the weakness along with the vulnerability. Which meant he needed to figure a way out fast. Henrik wasn't alone. He could feel the sway and bump of the body hanging next to him as wind swirled on a gentle updraft. One of his friends? Some other sorry shmuck who'd been punished for getting too close to the Limwoods? Cosmina? Henrik's chest went tight, closing his throat. God, he hoped not. Prayed she'd gotten away. Was even now headed for safety, but . . .

Jesus help him. He couldn't tell. The darkness was too thick, impeding his ability to see, never mind assess the situation. Guess now he knew how Cosmina felt, didn't he? Blind. Vulnerable. Hemmed in by the reality of weakness and reliance on another. Not fun—any of it. Particularly since—

"Goddess help me." Full of vexation, the mutter came somewhere off to his right. Henrik's head snapped in that direction. Gaze narrowed, he searched the darkness and listened hard. A rustle of sound. A rasp of harsh exhales, almost as though she couldn't catch her breath. The coil and hiss of unfriendly vines. "Thea, for the love of God, 'tis me . . . Cosmina. Please let go."

Relief hit Henrik like a runaway horse. Oh Jesus. Thank Christ. She was unharmed. Sounded all right too—voice hushed but strong.

Cosmina cursed again. The low grumble rolled through the quiet, cluing him in to her mood. She wasn't scared. Her tone said angry instead. A good sign. One that gave him hope as thick creepers tightened their grip, writhing around him.

"Cozs-meeena." More hiss than voice, the whisper shivered through the trees, rolling on long-drawn s's, raising the hair on the nape of Henrik's neck.

"Aye." She huffed. "'Tis me. Now, let go."

The forest hummed, the slither and slide full of warning.

The body next to him jerked. "*Merde.* What the—"

"Jesu," Shay said, coming awake on his other side.

Kazim stirred with a groan. "Allah be merciful."

"Quiet." Rocking sideways, Henrik bumped Andrei, then used the momentum to swing in the opposite direction. He touched shoulders with Shay. The gentle collision made his apprentice flinch, knocking him into Kazim. Steel rattled as blade hilts kissed. Shay sucked in a quick breath. Henrik snapped his fingers. The soft sound triggered a reaction. His friends took the cue and buttoned up, staying silent while vines creaked in the swaying to and fro. Excellent. Necessary too. The last thing he wanted was Cosmina distracted. Particularly when she appeared to be making headway, conversing with, well . . . he didn't know. An enchanted plant named *Thea*? "Let Cosmina work."

A thump echoed through the quiet. "Ouch! Jeepers . . . watch it, would you?"

Henrik's lips twitched. Probably not the smartest reaction, but hell . . . he couldn't help it. Cosmina didn't sound happy, and the fact she directed her displeasure at Thea tickled his funny bone. Somehow, though, he wasn't surprised. Unafraid to speak her mind, Cosmina packed a wallop when she wanted to . . .

Man-eating plants included.

"Blast and damn, Thea." A slap reverberated in the alcove as Cosmina swatted vines away. "Be careful of my arm."

The air stilled, growing colder. Thea growled. "Hurt."

"Naught time won't heal," Cosmina said, tone switching from annoyed to soothing. "Now . . . where did you put them?"

"Bad men."

"Nay, Thea. Good men. They protected me at White Temple and mean you no harm." A scrape, then the shuffle of boots on frozen earth drifted in the dark. Henrik tilted his head, listening, interpreting each noise and . . . aye, definitely. Cosmina was now on her feet. "I'm sorry I did not ask for safe passage. You know I always do, but we are being hunted by—"

"Halál of Grey Keep." Violence shivered through the forest. Roping vines twisted, reaching up to brush Henrik's cheek. "Bad man."

"Very bad man."

"No like."

"Me neither. But Henrik and his friends are not like that."

A pause. The darkness expanded, stealing his breath, tightening its hold, enclosing him inside his own head. Pressure built between his temples. Henrik clenched his teeth. His comrades twitched, reacting to the mind-bending pulse as the forest took a breath. An ominous rattle followed. Baring invisible fangs, Thea turned to stare at him. Pure conjecture, considering he couldn't see anything? Mayhap, but Henrik didn't think so. The magic in the air told the tale. And as she hissed his name, Henrik held his breath and stayed very still. No sense provoking the thing. Thea oozed potent power and the menace of predatory intent. Otherworldly. A force to be reckoned with . . . an intelligence rooted deep in the earth. The kind he'd only felt once and knew could only mean one thing.

Thea belonged to the Goddess of All Things.

Supposition? Or fact? Henrik bet on the latter. The theory made a certain amount of sense. Cosmina, after all, lived inside the Limwoods. Not something just anyone could do. As a member of the Blessed, Thea recognized her for what she was: a servant of the goddess. Someone who played on the same side. A woman to be protected and cared for as the deity decreed.

Henrik cleared his throat. "Cosmina?"

"Oh thank the goddess." A rustle sounded as Cosmina turned in his direction. Still somewhere to his right, she paused mid-step. He didn't blame her. 'Twas too dark to see anything. "Henrik . . . are you all right?"

In a manner of speaking. Strung up like fresh kill, his position didn't exactly inspire confidence. "All in one piece, but 'tis too dark. I cannot—"

"Thea . . . some light, if you please," Cosmina said, providing what he needed before he asked.

Henrik frowned. *Some* light? Any at all would be good. The thought echoed, bouncing around inside his head an instant before a low hum cut through the quiet. Pinpricks of light blinked on, illuminating the darkness. He squinted, vision adjusting to the sudden glare, and . . . good Christ. An army of lightning bugs, the drone of tiny wings buzzing above the roll of writhing vines. Blood rushing in his ears, hanging upside down six, mayhap seven, feet from the ground, his gaze swept the enclave. Surrounded by dense forest. Hemmed in by creeping vines. Deep in the heart of the Limwoods. A place most had never seen, never mind survived.

A soft whinny pushed through, capturing his attention.

Henrik glanced left. He breathed out in relief. Clustered together, the horses stood to one side, spooked and still, acting like living statuary, frosty air puffing from their nostrils. Alive with movement, vines slithered around the edges of the large den, blocking any chance of escape. And Cosmina? His gaze landed on her. Just feet away, she stood in the center of the dell, one arm cradling the other, looking pale but so beautiful his throat went tight.

The lightning bugs' glow grew more intense.

Her brow furrowed. Her lashes flickered, and she turned her head away from the radiance, almost as though the light hurt her eyes. Which meant one thing. Her vision continued to improve. Was returning little by little. Now full recovery was just a day or two away. At least, he hoped so—for her sake and his too.

He liked the woman he'd met inside High Temple, the hellion who'd held him at knifepoint and threatened him with supreme skill. Odd, he knew. But no matter how strange his reaction, he couldn't deny the tug . . . the need to know her better and see just how good she was with a blade.

"Hey," he said, his focus fixed on her.

She glanced his way. No longer white but pale green, her eyes met his. She squinted as though unable to focus, then blinked. The flutter of movement drew him tight. Made her even more appealing—if that were even possible. With her hair tumbling in disarray, she looked like a siren, making him surrender to the libidinous pull.

Breaking eye contact, she glared over her shoulder. "Release him. The others too."

The vine closest to Cosmina snapped its tip. The quick flick reminded Henrik of a disobedient child turning up its nose.

Cosmina pursed her lips. "I mean it, Thea."

A soft snarl gathered speed until it throbbed in the enclave. An instant later, the creepers loosened, and with a flick, sent him spinning arse over heels. Cold air slapped against his face. Henrik cursed, and twisting in midair, fought to get his feet under him. No chance of that. He hit the ground with a thud. Pain streaked over his shoulder. His teeth clenched on a curse, he flinched as his comrades thumped down beside him, but didn't hesitate. With a quick flip, he jumped to his feet and, ignoring the threat of creeping vines, strode across the clearing. Cosmina met him halfway, limping into his open arms. Settling like a gift, she nestled in as though she belonged against him.

Blowing out a pent-up breath, he enveloped her in his embrace and set his chin atop her head. "Are you unhurt?"

She nodded. "Are you? Thea can be a touch rough and—"

"A touch?" Henrik snorted. Christ. If that was only a *touch*, he didn't want to be around when Thea unleashed the true extent of her power. "How far to your cottage?"

"From here?"

"Aye."

"A day and a half on foot. Mayhap less. I wasn't in a hurry when I walked it."

Well, he was now. Hurrying seemed like an excellent idea. A secure place to rest and recoup. Time enough to regroup and come up with a game plan. The strategy ticked all his boxes. The sooner he found a safe haven, the better off he—and everyone else—would be. But as he turned toward the horses and told the others to mount up, he sensed Thea following him. Green tentacles slithered around his feet. He froze mid-stride.

"Ignore her." Cold nose pressed to the hollow of his throat, Cosmina shivered. "She's all show."

Not quite. In fact, not even close. "Not going to happen."

"Ever," Shay said.

"Fascinating," Kazim murmured, watching the vines slip across the ground. He held his hand out to one of the tentacles. Magic thrummed, heating the air. The creeper rose like a cobra from a basket, coiling around his arm. Kazim hummed in welcome as Thea stroked his skin, then reached up to caress the side of his throat. Dark eyes alive with pleasure, Kazim's mouth curved. "Fantastic. She's beautiful."

"*Es-tu malade?*" Andrei said, accent thicker than usual, boots rooted to the ground. He shook his head. "You like her so much, you go first."

Shaking loose of the creeper's hold, Kazim nodded and started toward the horses. Henrik tensed. Shifting Cosmina, he got ready to move—to intervene and protect Kazim. Funny thing, though: naught happened. Thea didn't attack. She purred instead and followed Kazim, acting like a lovesick cub, the pleasant scent of hollyhocks rising in her wake.

Cosmina smiled. "She likes him."

"Good."

He hoped it stayed that way. The last thing he needed was more trouble. A smooth trail and a fast gallop, however? Both sounded good. More than necessary. Especially while surrounded by the Goddess of All Thing's creation. That alone rendered Thea untrustworthy. Too bad little choice remained. To avoid Halál and keep Cosmina safe he needed to traverse the ancient forest. His unease meant little and mattered even less. Only his goal remained: keep the magical plant happy while he planned an attack that would not only take the enemy down, but ensure the bastards stayed dead.

CHAPTER FOURTEEN

The trail dead-ended at the river's edge. Just like he knew it would.

Crouched on the lip of the ravine, Halál pivoted on the balls of his feet and looked down on failure. On the tumbling rush of water. On the break in the trees. On hoofprints left in the narrow strip of sand flanking the Mureş River. Aye, he could see the trail. His vision was pinpoint sharp, the dark and distance no impediment to his enhanced eyesight. Black magic afforded him all sorts of interesting tricks.

A perk of leading Armand's budding army.

Eyes narrowed, he searched the smooth stretch of pebbled beach and sandy bank flanking the Mureş again. He bared his teeth on a snarl. Clever bastard. Henrik had done it again. Evaded him. Thwarted him. Mucked up his plans. The assassin was more trouble than he was worth. His former pupil never said quit or gave in easy. Admirable traits most days. Halál had enjoyed that about him at Grey Keep. His stubborn nature and ironclad will had made torturing him a joy.

Now the bastard wore the stain of Al Pacii on his skin . . . the mark of ownership.

Halál huffed, acknowledging the lie. *Ownership.* Ha. Right. A nice, if somewhat foolish, thought. Even so, he would've liked that—to own Henrik. Somehow, though, it hadn't happened. Aye, he'd marked him well enough, cutting into him, leaving scars with well-used knives. In the end, the trail of physical damage hadn't been enough. Or proved anything. No matter how many times he'd strapped Henrik to the blue stone and made him bleed, the bold bastard had defied him, refusing to beg like his other assassins.

Something to be respected. Mayhap even celebrated.

But not tonight.

Particularly since he couldn't follow Henrik across the river. Not without entering the Limwoods. A place he refused to get anywhere near. Which explained a lot, didn't it? Like why he crouched on the ridge, three hundred yards upslope instead of making his way down to track the traitor into the forest.

Halál pursed his lips. Time for a new plan. One that bagged him his quarry and ensured success. Another failure, and his window of opportunity would close. He knew it well enough. Henrik wasn't stupid. The bastard would regroup inside the Limwoods. Which would make him harder to kill and the woman less accessible. Not acceptable by any means. He needed the Keeper of the Key along with the information she possessed. His mouth curved as his imagination took flight. Be damned, he couldn't wait to get his hands on her.

So many possibilities. Untold pleasure. An equal amount of satisfaction.

She'd provide it all before he handed her over to Armand.

Anticipation grabbed hold as Halál pushed to his feet. A gift. His master would no doubt be pleased to receive a member of the Order of Orm.

Turning away from the ridge, he surveyed his soldiers. As his gaze skimmed each one, he swallowed a curse. His assassins looked a touch worse for wear. Soot marred their skin, smudging faces and bare arms. The smell of burnt hair and leather drifted, clouding the air around them as he glanced down at his chest. Halál shook his head. He looked just as bad. Scorched by fire, burn marks dotted the front of his jerkin. And his trews? Holes peppered the leather, leaving raw patches of skin exposed.

Halál scowled. Damned dragon.

The beast had taken its pound of flesh, unleashing hell, ripping tombstones from the ground, setting trees alight with his nasty exhale before flying off again . . . denying Halál a clear shot. Another failure to add to the growing pile. The kind that tweaked his temper. He despised the disadvantage along with the weakness. Two more Druinguari lay dead, burned alive by magical fire. Halál snarled, the low sound more hiss than growl. His assassins shuffled, unease rising like perfume from their skin. Good. He wanted them on edge. Sharp. Hostile. Willing to do anything for revenge. Comfort of any kind wasn't part of the plan. It wouldn't be, either, until he found a way to even the score.

Incapacitated. Maimed. Dead and gone.

The method didn't matter. Not with his target list widening to include Henrik, those who fought alongside him, and now . . . a dragon. So aye, some in-depth research was now in order. Well, that and a serious chat with Armand. If anyone knew how to kill dragons, it would be the Prince of Shadows.

Unfurling his fists, Halál glanced at his first in command. "V."

"Aye, master?"

"New plan." Mind churning over multiple avenues of attack, Halál frowned. "Take your men back to the holy city. Set up out of sight and wait. The call has gone out. The Blessed will return to White Temple."

Valmont hummed. "Capture or kill?"

"Catch and keep if you like," he said, giving his assassin some leeway. Loyal and stout of heart, Valmont deserved the reward. Gifting him with a Blessed or two would serve well enough. "But when you are done, kill them all."

"Their blood will blacken the earth," Valmont said, anticipation in his low tone.

"Excellent." Stepping alongside his assassin, he treated Valmont to a slap of affection. His palm cracked against leather. Harsh sound echoed as he nodded to his second in command. "Beauvic . . . you and I will travel west to Gorgon Pass."

Beauvic's mouth tipped up at the corners. "The high cliffs at the foot of the Carpathians. A good place for Henrik to escape into the mountains."

He nodded. "Exactly. I want him cut off from all help."

In other words . . . Drachaven and Xavian.

He didn't want the entire group of traitors together. The bastards fought too well as a unit. 'Twould be easier to pick them off one at a time. Which meant he must keep Henrik contained. The longer his quarry stayed isolated, the more vulnerable he would be.

CHAPTER FIFTEEN

The dirt trail narrowed on the downward slope, fishhooking into a tight curve. Another blind corner. Another potential pitfall. One of many over the last few hours.

Eyes scanning the foliage on either side of the path, Henrik slowed his mount to a walk and adjusted his hold on Cosmina. Snug in his lap, fast asleep in his arms, the gentle bobble 'n' sway didn't bother her. She resettled with a sigh, then snuggled in as though she belonged against him. A perfect fit in every way. He blew out a pent-up breath as insight reared its ugly head. So tempting to indulge. So dangerous to want. So foolish to dream. All perilous endeavors, ones that would bring him low if he allowed it.

Naught good would come from encouraging the fantasy.

Henrik knew it. He'd witnessed the aftermath—the trauma too—time and again when a man overreached, longing for a woman he held no right to hold. But accepting the truth and putting it into play were two very different things. Point in fact? He couldn't set Cosmina aside. Oh, he'd tried. Had toyed with the idea of handing her over to one of the others and riding on ahead. But each time he opened his mouth to call Shay forward, he lost his voice . . . and then his nerve.

Henrik huffed. Goddamn need. Stupid yearning. Miles ahead of common sense, both ruled at the moment, setting him up for a hard fall. Knowing it, however, didn't change a thing. Or set him straight. He wanted her too much. So he cuddled Cosmina close instead of pushing her away, condemning himself with action and a cartload of compelling what-ifs: What if she liked him back? What if she desired him as much as he did her? What if she accepted him for who and what he was—an elite assassin with too much blood on his hands?

Excellent questions. None of which he had any right to ask.

He'd given up the possibility of closeness eons ago . . . the instant he'd chosen a killer's path. So nay, he didn't deserve happiness or a second chance. And Cosmina? Hell, she represented everything he refused to entertain—love, acceptance, a chance at normalcy.

Mayhap even a family of his own.

A little boy with her eyes. A little girl with her spirit. Henrik's throat went tight. God, the image had the power to slay him where he sat. Shifting in the saddle, he shook his head as his gaze strayed to her face. Unable to help himself, he watched her sleep. The shadows thickened around him, painting the Limwoods with a black brush. Lightning bugs lit up the path, showing the way, dancing against the darkness, making him wish he could be as carefree. But then, easy wasn't his style.

He preferred hard to wholesome, so . . . no question in his mind. Cosmina didn't belong in his world. He didn't want to live in hers—a place where the goddess ruled and old wounds festered. Which left him with little choice. He needed to do the right thing and walk away. Take her home, leave her behind, and never look back.

'Twas a solid plan. The best, really, but for one thing . . .

He hadn't even done it yet, and it hurt like hell.

Dragging his gaze from her face, he refocused on the road, and with a flick of his reins, guided his warhorse around the next bend. Ancient trees stood sentry on either side of the lane, acting like soldiers, creating a tunnel through the forest. Most would've called it beautiful. Enchanting. Symbiotic even, the way massive oaks leaned in and stretched, closing the distance to create a tangled canopy over the trail. Too bad all he saw was danger. A warren full of dark shadows and ominous intent.

Paranoid much? Absolutely. He had every right to be.

The Goddess of All Things never let up. And the magic? Christ, it never went away. Or got any more amenable. Thea and the vines roaming the underbrush proved that well enough. So did the awful prickle of unease. With each mile, it slid over his skin, winding him tight, raising the hair on his nape, telling him to get the hell out of the Limwoods. An excellent strategy. Brilliant by all accounts, except . . .

'Twas easier thought than done. Naught but wishful thinking.

Turning back now wasn't an option. Deep in the forest, the chime and rattle of enchantment closed rank, hemming him in. Now he was surrounded on all sides by supernatural forces. The kind he tried hard to avoid, but somehow never managed to escape. Tied down. Locked up. Nowhere to go. The feelings of isolation were ever present. To be expected, he guessed. Especially with the goddess breathing down his neck. It was eerie. His resistance to her plan didn't matter. Not to her. She pursued with purpose, refused to leave him alone when anyone else would've given up by now and given him his way.

Which was what, exactly?

Peace. Soul solace. A chance at self-fulfillment.

And yet, destiny wouldn't allow it. Henrik sighed. Mayhap 'twas his fault. Mayhap his refusal to fall into line made him selfish. Mayhap all the uncertainty and pain was a side effect—punishment for his aversion to magic. Henrik didn't know. Particularly since he'd never been given a choice. Or seen the other side of the equation.

Born of a High Priestess, magic ran in his veins. It didn't matter whether he liked it or not—or that he longed for something different. Something better. Something *more*. Freedom to choose his own path, perhaps? The belief that he could control his own life? Without a doubt. Not that any of it mattered. It was what it *was*. No negotiating with it. No circumventing what he was or who the goddess wanted him to be. Lord knew he'd tried . . . over and over, time and again.

Yet nothing changed.

Fate fought on, placing a target on his back.

Disquiet itched along his spine. Rolling his shoulders, Henrik shrugged off the discomfort and tightened his arms around Cosmina. Ah, and there it was again . . . the urge to turn toward her instead of away. A strange reaction. Stupid in so many ways, and yet he brushed a kiss to the top of her head anyway. He couldn't fight the awful tug of attraction.

Or his need to get closer.

Hmm, she was something. So relaxed against him. Such a sweet fit in his arms—head on his shoulder, body snug against his, each breath deep and even—trusting him enough to sleep in his presence. 'Twas a gift, an incredible source of comfort too, helping him stay steady as the Limwoods breathed around him. Alive with magic, the sizzle writhed in the chilly air and his restlessness shuffled into full-on dread. Like dice, uncertainty rolled in and instinct piped up.

Mayhap it was time.

Time to stop fighting and accept his legacy more fully. Blame and hatred only got a man so far. Aye, he could go on despising the Goddess of All Things—for abandoning him as a child, for all the torture and pain . . . for the death of his twin sister.

Most days, he tried not to think about it. Usually, he failed. It was his fault, after all. If he'd been there—instead of in Poland, seeing to Halál's greed and Al Pacii business—he might have been able to shield her. Not that anyone else agreed with him— Afina, in particular. She'd been present during their sister's illness—when the blood disease had taken hold, decimating Bianca after the birth of her daughter. His chest went tight. Beautiful Sabine, his niece and pride and joy. The two-year-old was a lot like his twin—gentle, full of grace and a keen wonder for the world. He wouldn't trade her for anything. Loved her more than he did himself. And yet, he mourned Bianca, even though wishing his twin were still alive meant Sabine would never have existed.

He shook his head. God, what a tangle. But even as Henrik recognized the dichotomy in his thinking, he acknowledged the truth. The past couldn't be changed. And honestly, it took too much effort to hate someone. Even more to resist what Afina already embraced: the truth of their history. The purpose bred into his bloodline.

Henrik frowned. It seemed counterintuitive. A classic case of insanity. Nothing else explained his willingness to accept his connection to the goddess. He'd never acknowledged it before, not even when he pledged allegiance to her. The vow had been made for his brothers-in-arms, not her. Never *her*. But curiosity called and knowledge equaled power. Accurate information kept a man alive. How many times had he said that? Too many to count or remember, so the hell with it. He'd made his decision. Was now headed straight into the belly of the beast. Into an unwise—and no doubt deadly—confrontation with the Goddess of All Things. He wanted answers. Needed closure. Planned to get both, but . . .

Not yet.

First things first.

Cosmina needed care, and the rest of them required a reprieve. From constant threat. From all the fighting. A day or two of lying low was a necessity now. Halál wouldn't quit. The bastard never did, so after being denied entrance into the Limwoods, the Druinguari would circle around. Set up somewhere north of Gorgon Pass, wait until he entered the Carpathian foothills, then move in to cut him off.

A sound strategy. No guesswork involved.

He knew his former sensei. Understood his methods and had studied his ways. Certain knowledge coupled with brutal experience. So now he must decide. Henrik shifted in the saddle, adjusting Cosmina in his lap as two options played tug-of-war. What to do . . . what to do? Which route should he take? Avoid his former sensei, make for Drachaven, and gather the others? Or scout Halál's position and attack in the hopes of killing the Druinguari leader?

Cut off the head of the snake. Watch the body die.

Seemed like the best plan. Hunting and killing, after all, suited him better than running and hiding. He'd done enough of the latter tonight. Way more than he ever wanted to do again, but that didn't solve the problem. Two options: attack or evade. Different strategies dependent on the same things—his ability to ensure Cosmina's safety and the Goddess of All Things' cooperation.

Neither of which were sure bets.

Nudging his warhorse into a canter, Henrik upped the pace. Halfway down the laneway, a ping echoed inside his head. The prickle ghosted over the nape of his neck, then skittered down his spine. His gaze narrowed on the trail end where the trees thinned and branches lifted, funneling into what looked like a clearing. Wind blew in, rattling low-lying shrubbery. Old leaves tumbled over frozen dirt, kicking the smell of must into the air. The scent and brittle crackle joined the rustle of slithering vines as he sensed Thea rise.

Habit made him reach for his knife.

Sliding one arm from around Cosmina, his palm settled on the hilt strapped to the outside of his thigh. Ears tuned, eyes narrowed, he adjusted his grip. Leather creaked, and the warriors riding behind him shuffled, the thump of horses' hooves loud in the silence.

Steel zinged, leaving multiple sheaths at the same time.

"H?" Sword in hand, Shay came alongside him.

"What is it?" Kazim asked, deep voice full of menace.

Andrei rode up on his other side, bumping him with his knee. "Trouble."

Henrik shook his head. He didn't know yet. The vibration seemed familiar, and yet felt foreign too. More than out of line. A touch left of center as though the buzz played jackrabbit inside his head, jumping all over the place. As it spun into a death skid between his temples, he bared his teeth and bore down. Something was off. By a lot? By a little? He couldn't tell. Not with his magic skipping from one mental node to another, defying his ability to get a read on the approaching threat.

"Something's headed our way," he said. "Something big."

"*Merde.*"

Kazim palmed his throwing stars. "Not good."

Not even a little, but—

Vibration erupted into a roar inside his head. Henrik frowned and, using a hand signal, told his comrades to settle. All went quiet as he unleashed his magic, trying to get a hold of the signal, hunting for trouble as moonlight broke through the thicket of branches overhead. Illumination spilled between the cracks, joining the glow of fireflies. Iced-over evergreens sparkled in the burst of moonglow. His focus narrowed on the trail's end. Aye. Definitely. Trouble. The kind that carried static and—

A dark shadow flew over, staining the ground black.

Henrik glanced up. "Tareek?"

Blowing out a ragged breath, Andrei sheathed his weapons.

Kazim grunted. "About time."

"Thank God," Shay murmured.

"*Finally,*" his friend growled through mind-speak. "*I've been searching all over for your sorry arse. Flipping Limwoods. There's too much magical interference. Couldn't connect or track you from a distance.*"

"*Likewise. Been trying to reach you for hours. Are you all right?*"

"*Better now that I found you.*" Wings spread wide, Tareek banked into a tight turn overhead. Moonlight bounced off blood-red scales. Squinting to combat the glare, Henrik watched his friend circle back around. "*We need to talk. Got some information. You stopping soon?*"

"*What's up ahead?*"

"*Naught. A small clearing, no more.*"

"*We'll rest there.*"

"Good," Tareek said. *"I'll find a spot to land."*

"Not the best idea." Henrik glanced left. Thea stared out of the shadows, unearthly gaze fixed on him, snakelike tentacles slithering alongside the path. She wanted blood. Then again, mayhap that was simply paranoia talking. Not a bad way to lean. He had every right to be leery. The thing loved Cosmina. One false move, and Thea would act. Tear him apart. Scatter his remains from one end of the Limwoods to the other. But not before causing him a serious amount of pain. *"We're not alone down here."*

"Vines?"

"Aye. Nowhere near friendly either."

"Hell."

An understatement. A dangerous one considering Thea's violent disposition and nasty skill set. She wouldn't welcome Tareek, never mind permit him to land. At least, not without attacking. The Limwoods liked to keep what it found and kill what it caught. Instinct raised the warning. Knowledge clanged the bell, presenting him with two options. One . . . wake Cosmina. Or two . . . put Kazim's gift to the test.

The second alternative appealed to him more than the first. No way did he want to place Cosmina back in danger. She'd endured enough. And after hours of discomfort—of shivering against him, twisting in the saddle, and hiding the pain—she was finally asleep, so exhausted no amount of jostling disturbed her. Add that to the fact the forest struck without mercy or looking to see who it hit and—aye, no question. The farther he kept Cosmina from the fray, the better he would feel.

Tareek banked overhead. *"Henrik . . ."*

"Hold on. I might have a solution." Twisting in the saddle, Henrik glanced over his shoulder. "Kazim."

Serious dark eyes met his. "What?"

"Tareek needs to land. Do you think—"

"I can handle Thea."

"Are you certain?" Henrik asked, eying his friend. "No room for error."

"Trust me. I'm not sure what is happening, but I can feel the forest breathe. The vibration is in my veins. I am connected to the earth, Henrik . . . able to make things grow and call upon the trees." Dark gaze narrowed, Kazim searched the vegetation on the north side of the trial. "Even the wolf pack tracking us acknowledges my dominion."

"Wolves?" Shay asked, looking nervous as he glanced around.

"Don't worry. The pack is now under my control. And Thea?" Kazim raised his hand. Magic rose, swirling in the center of his palm. Wolves howled somewhere nearby, making Shay twitch in his saddle. Henrik grinned. All right then, point proved and well taken. Kazim knew what he was doing. Was 100 percent in command as he murmured, coaxing Thea out of the shadows. The forest spirit purred, the sound one of bliss as vines stroked over his friend's hand. "She's half in love with me already."

Andrei snorted.

Shay shook his head. "Too confident."

"Simple fact," Kazim said, spurring his mount forward. The scent of hollyhocks rolled as Thea followed. At the lip of the path, Kazim met his gaze and tipped his chin. "Tell him to wait for my signal."

"Already done."

"Relax, H," Kazim said, disappearing into the dell.

Relax? Kazim had clearly lost his mind, 'cause—no chance in hell. Much as he wanted to believe in Kazim's gift, logic shoved faith out of the way. Thea wasn't a puppet. She possessed a mind of her own, which meant his guard needed to stay where he always kept it. Up very, *very* high. Tension raised it even higher, making his muscles flicker in protest as he set his heels to his warhorse's sides. His steed leapt forward, moving from walk to gallop in less than a heartbeat. So did his mind, charging ahead, finding all kinds of flaws in the strategy. Magic never cooperated. Not in his experience anyway, so . . .

Little room for doubt. The plan was already doomed. And Tareek was headed for a fall.

* * *

Wings spread wide, Tareek banked into a holding pattern. Around and around. Back and forth. Pacing Dragonkind-style, revolving into continuous circles in full flight. Hristos, he seemed to be doing a lot of that tonight—waiting, watching, hoping. At least now, though, the endless source of trouble was in his sights. Five hundred yards below, riding hell-bent into the clearing. His eyes narrowed on Henrik. Huh. Strange, but . . .

His friend looked all right and yet not quite himself either.

Something had shifted. Not by much, but enough to raise some alarm bells.

Tareek growled as unease surfaced. Unleashing his magic, he tapped into Henrik's bioenergy. Overkill? Probably. Unwelcome? Certainly. His friend wouldn't appreciate the shakedown. Nor the coddling. The male wasn't a lad anymore or in need of paternal protection. Tareek huffed. His dragon reacted, spilling magma into his throat as he registered the ridiculousness of the thought. *Paternal protection.* What a farce. Henrik needed a sire like he needed another hole in his head. The warrior was all kinds of vicious. So talented with his blades and bow, most refused to tangle with him.

Too bad the realization didn't stop instinct.

Old habits died hard. And warranted or nay, so did his desire to shield Henrik.

So instead of reeling it in, he let his magic roll. Henrik's physical grid went up on his mental screen. Banged up. Some scrapes. A few bruises . . . naught more. Relief banged around inside his chest, making his heart flip-flop. Thank Silfer. His charge was none the worse for wear . . .

No thanks to him and his bonehead move in the cemetery.

He'd nearly killed his comrades. Tareek grimaced. Not his finest hour. Nowhere near a well-executed plan either. He'd flown in quick and struck too fast, unleashing the first fireball before assessing the situation—before dipping below the cloud cover to get the lay of the land and all the players in it. He snorted. Lava-infused sparks flew from his nostrils, then blew back, whirling over his horns as he shook his head. A complete understatement. He'd allowed emotion to cloud his judgment and nearly taken Henrik out in the process.

Lucky. He'd gotten so damned lucky.

Not something that would likely happen again, so . . .

No question. He needed to pull his head out of his arse and even out. Right now, before he ended up hurting someone he didn't want to. A distinct possibility, one Garren had warned him about when they'd been freed from prison. Captured and tortured. Twenty years spent locked behind bars—condemned to cramped conditions and little food—did strange things to a male. Some went crazy. Others' minds stayed strong as their bodies gave out. In his case, the inactivity had mucked up his timing.

Hence his less-than-stellar performance tonight.

Eyes on the ground, Tareek angled his wings, gliding into another turn as Kazim dismounted. The warrior's feet thumped down. He glanced skyward. Tareek went on high alert. Any moment now, the Persian would give the signal and—

A shiver rippled through him.

His scales clicked together, making the spikes along his spine rattle. The sound wound him a notch tighter. And no wonder. He really didn't want to go down there. Not while the Limwoods hissed and creepers streamed around the edge of the dell, weaving between large blackwoods and hundred-year-old oaks. Stripped of foliage, the treetops swayed, parting to give him a bird's-eye view of the ground. Thick vines intertwined with thinner ones, slithering in and around until the mass looked like a writhing nest of vipers. Unforgiving ones with sharp fangs and a venomous strike. Recall slammed through him. He swallowed a growl. Four days. *Four wretched days* spent tangled up in the Limwoods.

Not exactly an experience he wanted to undergo again.

"Tareek." Eyes on the sky, Kazim leapt onto a rocky outcropping in the middle of the clearing. "Almost ready."

"You better know what you're doing," he said. "I get strangled, I'm coming after you."

Kazim huffed. "You get strangled, you'll be dead and no longer my concern."

Good point. Tareek's lips twitched. Arrogant little pissant. "I'll haunt you from the grave."

"Bring tea when you visit. I prefer chamomile."

"Pansy."

"Scaly ingrate."

"Stow it . . . both of you." Authority rang inside the growl. Tipping his head back, Henrik glared at him, treating his comrade to a warning look. "Kazim, move your arse. Get him on the ground."

The Persian nodded, then met each assassin's gaze in turn. "Weapons stay sheathed. No one draws unless I say so and . . ."

The male trailed off. Tareek banked left, completing another circuit above the clearing.

"Back off," Kazim said, finishing his thought. "I don't want to upset her."

"Good plan." With a quick tug, Shay walked his warhorse backward.

Gaze riveted to the creepers, Andrei sheathed his boomerang. "Better advice."

Tareek glanced at Henrik. His mouth curved and . . . surprise, surprise. His friend stayed still, refusing to back his steed away. Typical. The male personified stubborn, bringing the character flaw to life without effort. Tareek shook his head as Henrik shifted in the saddle. The move spoke volumes, and his friend's body language even more. He was preparing, getting ready to jump into the fray if Kazim failed and violence became necessary.

The realization made his heart beat harder. Hristos help him. Henrik was too loyal for his own good. Not that Tareek minded. He was cut from the same cloth and suffered the same fault: the overwhelming need to protect. Which meant . . .

No sense asking Henrik to back away.

Or trying to temper the concern he sensed in the assassin.

Neither approach would work.

'Twas heartwarming in many ways. To be so well loved. To be valued and needed. To have a friend willing to risk everything to keep him safe. A strange thought, one with sharp teeth and a startling bite. And as awareness struck, cutting him to the bone, faith roared into view. 'Twould be all right. All of it. The hard grip of the past would eventually loosen and fade. The present would smooth out and friendship would return. Despite the rocky start, he and Henrik would find a way to make it right.

Drawing a deep breath, Kazim rolled his shoulders and bowed his head. He held the lungful a moment, then let it go. A gentle breeze tousled the treetops as the assassin flexed his hands. Magic rose, streaming off the Persian in cresting waves. The scent of evergreens blew in and the Limwoods murmured. Thick vines changed course, slithering out of the shadows to surround Kazim. His voice dropped an octave and, tone low, the male spoke like a lover, praising, cajoling, caressing the creepers with his fingertips. The forest sighed, the soft sound rising to a steady hum of pleasure.

Tareek blinked. Holy hell. Kazim was . . . was . . .

Hristos, color him surprised. The Persian was wielding magic with skill and a serious amount of attitude. His brows collided. When in Silfer's name had that happened? Dumb question. Irrelevant too. The *when* didn't matter. The *how*, though? Well now, that needed answering. Particularly since, as far as he knew, Henrik was the only gifted one—the sole male out of seven to be afflicted by magic and the discomfort that went along with it.

"I'm ready," Kazim said, vines writhing around his feet. "Tareek . . . land as close to me as you can. I'll try to keep her from dragging you out of the sky."

Try. Not the most inspiring word.

Tareek nodded anyway. Despite past experience and his disquiet, cowardice wasn't an option. Ever. So instead of banking hard and flying away, he sliced through the thin clouds, descending another hundred feet to set up his approach. The Limwoods hissed in warning. Kazim murmured his reassurance. Tareek held his breath and, painting an invisible target on the rocky ground at the assassin's feet, tucked his winds in tight. Gravity took hold, yanking him out of the night sky. The ground rose to meet him. Deadly vines snapped skyward, shooting above the treetops. Frigid air burning across his scales, Tareek counted off the seconds. Three . . . two . . .

One!

Tareek shifted from dragon to human form and tucked into a somersault. Smaller equaled better right now. And creating a diversion? Well now, that equaled an excellent plan. If the Limwoods couldn't find him in the chilly swirl, the greater his chances of reaching the ground in one piece. Free-falling fast, he conjured clothes and flipped into another revolution. The forest hissed. Vines whiplashed, slicing above and below him. One mind-torqueing turn spun into more and—

Slam-bang. His feet rammed into stone.

The hard landing sent his knees rebounding into the wall of his chest. Bone cracked against bone. Air rushed from his lungs and pain struck, decimating rational thought as he doubled over. As he wheezed, struggling to breathe, the Limwoods rose with predatory intent. Crouched in a ball, Tareek listed to one side, knocking into Kazim's legs.

Creepers curled around his forearms, Kazim widened his stance, supporting his sideways slide. "Stay still, Tareek."

Excellent advice. Music to his ears. Especially since he couldn't catch his breath, never mind move. Which meant Kazim better think fast and work smart. Otherwise the Limwoods would strike and he wouldn't stand a chance. But as the thought circled and worry expanded, something miraculous happened. The vines withdrew, releasing the assassin one tendril at a time before retreating toward the edge of the dell.

Exhaling long and slow, Kazim raised his head. Eyes as dark as midnight met Tareek's. A moment later, the Persian's mouth curved. "One beast tamed. One scaly arse saved."

Levity lived in the words. The kind of teasing designed to do one thing: lessen the tension and break the stranglehold of unease. Normally, Tareek would've appreciated the effort. But not right now. The frivolity didn't belong. Hristos, that had been close. Far too close. And as the wind picked up and storm clouds rolled in to hide the moon, deepening the night shadow, Tareek fisted his hands to keep them from shaking.

God-awful memory. It refused to let him go.

"My thanks, Kazim," he whispered, forcing air into his lungs, giving the assassin his due. 'Twas only fair. The male deserved the praise. As much as Tareek could throw his way. Sure, Kazim might like to tease, but the assassin was solid when it counted. "I owe you a—"

"Nay, do not." Kazim shook his head and held out his hand. Tareek hesitated a moment, then took it, allowing the male to pull him to his feet. "We're family now, remember? Brothers look after one another, *fratele*."

Unable to find his voice, Tareek nodded.

Kazim slapped him on the shoulder. "Better?"

"All good," he said, even though it wasn't true. At least, not yet. Mayhap in a minute or two when the tension cramping his muscles loosened. Night vision pinpoint sharp, Tareek glanced toward the forest's edge. Magic coalesced into an entity, staring out of the darkness. Revulsion shivered through him. He swallowed the bad taste in his mouth. Well, so much for hoping for a moment of relaxation. Loosening up wasn't possible inside the enchanted forest. "How long do we need to be here?"

"A while." Frozen leaves crackled as Henrik walked his warhorse forward. Hazel-gold eyes met Tareek's a moment before his friend tipped his chin, sending a silent inquiry. One that asked "you all right?" without him saying a word. "Enough time to rest and regroup."

The undertone put Tareek on high alert. His gaze narrowed on Henrik as suspicion rose out of experience. He swallowed a snort. Wee whelp. *Rest and regroup*, his arse. The male was up to something. Something important. Something he wanted to hide from the others. Tareek could tell. Aye, Henrik looked calm enough, but Tareek knew he churned beneath the surface. He detected the upheaval in his emotional grid. Understood the doubt, dread, and pain that drove his friend.

Even as a lad, he'd been that way—reckless and volatile. Passionate as well, far too intense for his own good.

Which meant Tareek had work to do. Cracking through the male's guard wouldn't be easy. Nor could he do it here, in plain view of his fellow assassins. Respect deserved its day, and caring equal measure. No way would he challenge Henrik in front of the others. If he tried, the whelp would dig in and he wouldn't learn a thing.

Certainly not enough to help with whatever Henrik had planned.

Rolling his shoulders to combat the tension, Tareek strode across the low bluff. With a hop, he leapt off the edge. Icy turf crunched beneath his soles as he touched down in front of Henrik. "Got a spot to rest in mind?"

Henrik nodded. "A cottage. Three, mayhap four, hours from here."

Interesting. The information, sure, but mostly Henrik's knowledge of the Limwoods. How the hell had his friend come by it? Good question. Particularly since he knew Henrik had never been inside the forest before. Hmm . . . another mystery to solve. One that fed into an even larger one. Sidestepping, Tareek came alongside his friend and—

Jesus.

He blinked, realizing two things at once. The first? Henrik wasn't alone atop his horse. And the second? He really needed to pay more attention. No way he should've missed the small form in Henrik's arms. Or the strong female energy surrounding his friend. Leaning right, he peered around the curve of the hood covering her head. A ringlet of red hair peeked out, looking lush and thick against her smooth skin. Fast asleep, auburn lashes made half-moons against her pale cheeks and . . . ah hell. Here they went again. Despite his rough beginning—and the fact he'd never been accepted by the fairer sex inside White Temple— Henrik loved women.

Evidence of it pervaded the male's life.

Especially while visiting Ismal, the marketplace nestled at the foot of the Carpathians.

Females threw themselves at Henrik. Not surprising. Most women coveted a strong male. And Henrik? Hell, he had it all— good looks, a menacing vibe, and more charisma than any male ought to possess. But 'twas his reputation more than anything that made him so popular. Generous to a fault, skilled in the sexual arena, he liked to take his time with a female. His renown preceded him wherever he went. Females talked and word spread quickly, giving rise to the rumors . . .

Go to bed with Henrik. Never leave unsatisfied.

Normally the axiom wasn't a problem for Tareek. The lad deserved his fun, after all. But as suspicion opened the door to possibility, his instincts served up the facts. His friend wanted the female sharing his saddle. Tareek smelled it on him—the yearning, the need, the desire for closeness that brought most males low. Unprecedented. Unsettling. Troublesome too. Henrik wasn't prone to entanglements of any kind. He liked to play, not commit. But as his gaze met and held his friend's, the truth couldn't be denied. Henrik was wildly attracted to her. Was already invested in her well-being. Which meant he was going to get burned in a big way, 'cause . . .

Tareek huffed. Aye, without a doubt. She represented a huge problem.

For him as well as Henrik.

The Druinguari wouldn't quit. Were even now sniffing around the edge of the Limwoods, tracking, hunting, searching for the best way to bring them down. How did he know? His sonar kept pinging—bringing back traces of magic, gauging distances, assessing the danger. Even from deep inside the enchanted forest, tendrils of black magic teased, making his skin crawl and his dragon senses scream.

All of which pointed to one inescapable truth. Her close proximity would distract his friend. Not good. Or anywhere near advisable. With the battle lines drawn and war coming, no mistakes could be made. He needed Henrik focused and battle ready, not distracted by a redheaded dove with a pretty face and a curvy body.

Dropping his hand, Tareek tipped his chin. "Picked up a passenger, I see."

"'Tisn't what you think."

"Really." He raised a brow. "Where have I heard that before?"

A muscle twitched along Henrik's jaw. "I couldn't leave her there. She—"

"Of course you couldn't." Made perfect sense. When, after all, had Henrik ever been able to deny a female anything?

"Is one of the Blessed."

Tareek blinked. He frowned as the new detail sank in. "Confirmed?"

"Aye."

"Shit."

"Exactly."

One word. Big impact. Tareek sighed. No need to explain further.

Message received and accepted.

The female couldn't be left behind. More's the pity. Terrible, in fact.

Ditching her somewhere along the way would've made things easier in the long run. Particularly since *true believers*—those who served the Goddess of All Things—tended to be fanatics. But no matter his aversion to all things White Temple, Tareek refused to walk away. No way would he abandon his vow along with his principles. Henrik was right. She was too valuable, an asset to the goddess, a member of the Order both he and others had promised to protect. So only one thing left to do: mount up and get moving . . .

While he filled Henrik in on the way.

Dragging his focus from his friend, Tareek glanced at Andrei. Quick to react, the warrior tugged on the lead in his hand. Horse hooves cracked against the brittle leaves. Twin streams of air puffing from its nostrils, the enormous roan tossed his head and stepped forward. As the beast came abreast of him, Tareek murmured, reached out, and stroked his muzzle with a gentle hand. The second the roan accepted his touch, he took the reins and swung into the saddle.

Leather creaked. Tareek settled in, making himself at home. "I reached out to Garren."

Shay glanced his way. "Is he en route with Xavian?"

"And the others."

"Good. I have an idea of where Halál will try to intercept us. We'll need the others to help set the trap and lure him in," Henrik said, nudging his warhorse into a walk.

The forest reacted to the movement, rustling the underbrush and . . . Tareek flinched. Hristos, talk about eerie, and, well, mayhap the tiniest bit alluring too. The Limwoods might be a violent anomaly, but as the vines parted—opening to reveal a trail across the clearing, one that reached deep into the forest, showing Henrik the way—Tareek realized something important. As an enemy, the magical entity was a brutal force to be avoided at all costs, but as an ally? The possibilities became not only infinite, but interesting as well.

As though able to read his mind, Henrik met his gaze. "Impressive, isn't she?"

Tareek frowned. *Impressive?* Well that was one way of looking at it. Terrifying might be another. "She?"

"Thea," Kazim said, a hint of awe in his tone. "Beautiful creature."

"Yet to be determined," Tareek said, clinging to prejudice.

A good grudge, after all, never went out of style. Neither did caution. Both kept a male alive longer. But as Henrik galloped onto the trail, disappearing into shadowed recesses of the forest, Tareek followed in his wake. No sense being a pansy about it. Or denying his curiosity now that he was on the ground. He wanted to know more about the Limwoods. Press up against her boundaries and see where it led him. Had the forest truly accepted them or was she playing a game of wait and see? Would she allow them to leave when the time came or imprison them instead? Forever friend or cunning foe? All excellent questions, ones that needed to be explored and answered . . . in a hurry. Otherwise he and his comrades wouldn't make it out of the Limwoods alive.

CHAPTER SIXTEEN

Blood rushing in her ears, Nairobi sped past the garden's T-shaped wading pool. Iced over, skiffs of snow gathered along its edges as the slap of her footfalls echoed out to reach the fountain at its center. Devoid of water, bare-breasted mermaids stood frozen in time, unable to lure sailors to their doom without the usual sea of blue surrounding them. She scowled at the marble statues on the way by.

Stupid Persian design.

Beautiful, symmetrical, annoying mess. At least, right now. The fountain along with the garden layout provided almost no cover. No hedgerows or high walls in the middle. Just colorful mosaic tiles on wide pathways and barren flowerbeds set in geometric patterns. Not even the multitude of trees helped. Planted at equal intervals next to the outer wall, the tall, thin cypress threw little shadow, leaving her exposed as the moon bathed the garden in winter-borne light.

Stars above, she was in trouble.

One false move, a touch of bad luck, and she'd be done. Lost to circumstance and consequence. Panic clogged her throat.

Sucking in a desperate breath, feet flying over slippery stone, she descended the shallow steps next to the sunken pool. The heavy satchel she carried bounced against her lower back, throwing her off-balance. As she stumbled forward, fighting to stay upright, moonlight mocked her, growing brighter by the moment. A figment of her overstimulated senses? Pure imagination? Fear-induced paranoia? Nairobi didn't know, but . . .

Call her foolhardy and be done with it.

She should've taken the clear sky into account while planning her escape. A cloudy night would've lessened the risk and increased her chances of reaching the iron gate at the far end of the first courtyard. Not that it mattered now. 'Twas far too late to lament her lack of foresight. She was neck-deep in it. No room for doubt. Little chance of going back either.

Nairobi glanced over her shoulder anyway. The former palace turned silk house loomed large behind her. Arabic archways and dark windows stared out from behind a wide balcony. So far, so good. No one stood watching her flight. Which meant Adam had yet to discover her missing from the weaving room.

Making a tight turn, she skirted a star-shaped flowerbed. Her conscience panged. Silly to feel bad. Ridiculous to allow guilt to win. She had naught to feel contrite about and even less choice. Freedom didn't exist in the grey areas. It lived in black and white; a person either possessed it or not. And yet, even knowing no other recourse remained, remorse found a home inside her heart. The guard didn't deserve what she was about to give him—derision, punishment, or worse from the owner of the silk house.

A nasty outcome. One no one in his right mind wanted to face, never mind endure.

Her sense of fair play nudged her. Regret dug its claws in, cutting through, elevating her self-reproach to new levels. An ache bloomed behind her breastbone. Nairobi ignored it, and arms pumping, sprinted toward freedom. It stood just ahead, a quick jump and hard climb up the garden gate. Designed to keep others out, and the weavers in, 'twas a thing of beauty, intricate ironwork melding into immaculate design. The result? Impenetrable twin panels that ascended twelve feet, falling just shy of the outer wall's upper lip. Anxiety made her heart pound harder. Climbing in icy conditions would be challenging—no question. But the true worry lay at the top of the gate. Steel thorns crowned the crosspiece, ruling with timeless efficiency, setting the tone as each spike lorded over the entrance.

By no means optimal. Even less encouraging.

Hurrying between two low-lying shrubs, Nairobi descended the last set of stairs and entered the courtyard. Her footfalls slowed as she approached the high gate and, eying the thorny deterrents at its top, reached into the front pocket of her satchel. With a tug, she pulled out a pair of leather gloves. Tearing her gaze from the spikes, she studied the ironwork and plotted her course—handholds, footholds, the best places to find a good grip, the smaller spaces to avoid. Up one side. Down the other. No problem. She could do it. Keep the fear at bay long enough to win her freedom and find her way home.

Each breath naught but a harsh rasp, she pulled on the protective hand-wear and approached on silent feet. Almost there. One more obstacle. A fast climb, a quicker descent, and she'd be standing outside the outer wall, running for her life, looking over her shoulder, navigating the streets of Ismal to reach the forest's edge. From there, she knew the way: due north to White Temple. The only place she'd ever truly belonged.

With a yank, she tugged the hem of her short jacket down, then tightened the leather strap across her chest. All good. Despite its weight against her back, the bag would hold. Now so must she. Flexing her fingers, she reached out, grabbed her first handhold, and searched for the next. Slow and steady, calm and sure, she started to climb. Nairobi huffed and wiggled her foot, wedging the toe of her boot into a small crevice. *Calm.* Right. 'Twas all an illusion. She was nowhere near steady. Shaky, full of panic, about to lose her grip on the icy ironwork—goddess, all true, but she refused to stop now.

Inhaling hard, she forced her lungs to expand. Hanging four feet off the ground, she exhaled in a rush, then repeated the process. White puffs pushed from her mouth, painting the metal with frost. In. Out. Catch her breath, then release it. The influx of air helped, allowing her to look for the next handhold, helping her go on, soothing her nerves even as her muscles trembled and her courage shook. Just a bit farther. Six feet to her goal. Now three. So close. All she needed to do was hold the line, make it to the top, pick a path over the spikes, and—

"Nairobi!"

The shout echoed across the garden. Her focus snapped to the right, then traveled up the path next to the outer wall. Oh nay. Oh gods . . . Adam. He'd spotted her the moment he'd rounded the blind corner next to the row of cypress trees. Time lengthened and stilled as she met his gaze. Her grip tightened on the finger holds. The astonished look on his face vanished as his brows collided. The second he shifted to the balls of his feet, Nairobi reacted, finding another handhold, peddling her feet, climbing upward faster than was prudent, and . . .

Her toe slipped off metal.

One boot knocked into the next. Her right foot joined the left, dangling in the air as she swung sideways. With a cry, she dug in and held on hard, fighting to get her feet back under her. She heard heavy footfalls rush across the courtyard behind her. Fear roared through her, infusing her muscles with strength. Gritting her teeth, she found a foothold and clambered higher, eyes glued to the multi-headed spikes. Adam yelled, raising the alarm, shattering all hope of a clean getaway as he called for more guards and the keys to the gate.

"Nairobi . . ." More growl than word, her name swirled on the cold air. Adam slid to a stop below her. "For the love of God, woman . . . get down. You've nowhere to go."

Untrue. She had a home. One that beckoned. A place unlike any other where she would be loved, accepted, and safe—just like before.

Heart pounding so hard her chest hurt, Nairobi grabbed the base of an iron thorn cluster. Feet planted against steel, dangling by a single handhold twelve feet from the ground, she lifted the leather strap over her head. With a huff, she tossed the satchel over. Leather groaned in protest before landing with a thud in the deserted laneway.

"I mean it, girl. Come down. Right now or I—"

"You'll what?" Indignation surged. Determination picked up the gauntlet, accepting the challenge. So what. She'd been discovered. Adam didn't have the keys. Not yet anyway. Which meant she still had a chance. Still possessed some time. Enough, mayhap, to save herself and stay true to her purpose. Adam— along with everyone else inside the silk house—could go to the devil. She would not lie down. Or crumble beneath the pressure. Her eyes narrowed, she grabbed a second handhold and heaved herself upright. Lifting one leg over the spikes, she planted her foot on the thin lip on the other side. Crouched like a cat atop the high gate, she looked down at the guard. "Take away my freedom? Punish me by locking me away? Too late for that, Adam. You've done that from the start."

Surprise winged across his face. A moment later, his brows furrowed. He opened his mouth—no doubt to threaten her again.

She cut him off. "I'm sorry, Adam. I've no wish to cause you trouble, but I cannot stay. I am going home. I need to go home."

"Your place is here."

"You're wrong," she whispered, navigating the thorny barbs. "I never belonged here. My calling has always been much greater."

The truth of it gave her added courage. Saying it aloud granted her power. Treating the guard to a defiant look, Nairobi slid her second foot over. Adam cursed. She kept climbing, descending the opposite side of the gate as he yelled again, demanding the keys. The rapid beat of footfalls scrambled the quiet, rushing toward her as the moon winked in the clear sky. Halfway down, she let go and jumped to the ground. Her boots slammed into the cobblestones, making her teeth rattle. Pain stung her temples. Ignoring the discomfort, she spun, grabbed the satchel strap, and slung it over her shoulder.

The guard snarled at her from behind the swirling ironwork.

"Fair thee well, Adam."

"God's grace, Nairobi," he said, the threat of violence in this voice. "You will need it when I find you."

More promise than threat, his words sent a chill down her spine.

Feet churning through the thin skin of snow, she ran for the end of the alleyway. Another of the guards shouted, organizing the others. Keys jingled, sound rising on a rapid gust of frosty air. Skidding into the next laneway, Nairobi sprinted for the mouth of another, making certain each footfall landed on a clear patch of cobblestone and stayed out of the snow. Leaving a trail for Adam amounted to a bad idea. The guard wasn't stupid. He knew how to hunt women. Had proved it on more than one occasion when he returned an escapee to the less reputable section of the silk house—a place created for one purpose: a client's comfort and pleasure.

Disgusting practice. Especially considering many in the harem didn't want to be there.

Revulsion moved behind her breastbone. Goddess forgive her, she hated to leave all those women behind. Ought to be helping each one find a way out of hellish circumstances. A noble intention. A task in desperate need of doing. But not right now. Tonight belonged to her own freedom. Liberation would come for those inside Saul's Silk Emporium, but first she must evade Adam and get out of Ismal. Otherwise she wouldn't be able to save anyone, least of all herself.

* * *

Surrounded by thick cloud and frosty air, Cristobal looped the leather strap tethering him to Cruz around his fist. A wise move. A dragon shifted fast in flight. His comrade was no exception, angling his wings, slicing between steep cliffs as condensation beaded his chilled skin and his friend's black, bronze-tipped scales. Banking into another tight turn, Cruz dipped low and ducked his horned head. Tucked in tight, the wall of his chest against the back of the dragon's neck, Cristobal watched a weathered stone arch sail overhead.

Eying the rocky ridge on the flyby, he grinned. Jesus. Talk about close—less than a foot—solid stone mere inches above his head. To be expected. Cruz loved to fly and wasn't careful in its execution. Each turn the dragon-warrior made was insane—wing tips inches from jagged outcroppings, velocity muscle-clenching brutal, little light to see or fly by. And the wind? Mother of God. Nature howled, picking up speed, throwing snow like fistfuls of confetti as they hopscotched across the Carpathians, leaving one mountain pass only to blast into another.

Not that he was complaining.

Cristobal loved the wildness, the elemental fuck-you of a clenched fist and raised middle finger. So aye, shrug off the chill. Forget the mind-bending speed. Dragon flight was the absolute best—fast, furious, efficient. Right up his alley, a method of travel he embraced with relish . . . even if his flying companion was a touch nuts and boatloads of brave.

Gritting his teeth, he hung on hard as Cruz flipped in mid-air, avoiding a lopsided stone tower in the center of the gorge. Cold air burned across his cheeks, blowing the hair off his face. His mouth curved as pleasure thrummed through him. Astride a dragon's back, fast and free in flight. Who would've thought it possible? He huffed. Not him. Not until a month ago, anyway. But oh how quickly things changed—in both good and bad ways. Good equated to a midnight flight and his bird's-eye view. And bad? Well now, that came with a smell, an acrid one that rose on winter-borne wind, leaving a trail along with a terrible taste in his mouth.

Not a good sign, considering he and his comrades flew toward it.

With a frown, Cristobal leaned into another turn as his mind raced ahead, over landscapes he'd yet to cross to settle in the Valley of the Blessed. He shook his head. White Temple—the holy city shrouded in mystery and steeped in unfortunate history. A place he'd never visited, yet disliked already. No rhyme. Even less reason, but something about approaching the goddess' domain put him on edge. Cristobal snorted. Right. He should probably rephrase the statement. *On edge* didn't begin to describe what he felt. 'Twas more dangerous than that. Far more volatile too. Even from a distance, he sensed the magic. Smelled the discord as well, the bitter smell of—

Rahat. He didn't know. But God, the scent wouldn't leave him alone. No matter how deeply he inhaled, he couldn't acclimate. Or lessen the sensory burn.

'Twas as though something foreign had entered his body, triggering a primal reaction. An animalistic one that amplified everything—sight, sound, smell, taste, and touch. Now his skin crawled and instinct hissed, overloading him on all fronts. Tightening his grip on Cruz, he examined his reaction and new abilities. The uptick in visceral perception made little sense. He sensed the fracture between normal and what he experienced now—a great divide that widened by the moment, branding him an entity he didn't recognize. Now he grappled with the changes, fighting to understand. To put the shattered pieces of himself back together like a potter might the broken shards of a clay pot.

More than worrisome. 'Twas downright alarming.

Reaching out, he grabbed one of the prongs that rose behind Cruz's horns with his free hand. Heat rolled off his friend and into his palm. The protective cocoon deflected the windchill, enclosing him in a warm bubble.

The temperature shift didn't help.

Naught did. He couldn't control the influx of awareness. Or shut down the bombardment of sensation. God be merciful, the smell. The awful ceaseless stench. It overpowered him even as his vision sharpened. Cristobal winced. Another unsettling change.

No way should he be able to see in the dark, never mind the individual crystals inside the snowflakes. Or the ridged lines on each evergreen needle as Cruz left the foothills and leveled out over the forest.

Total mind-twist territory.

One heightened by the fact his forearms still throbbed.

Cristobal fisted one of his hands. He stared at the white points of his knuckles a moment, then shook his head. Jesus help him. He didn't understand. Couldn't begin to sort it out, never mind put a name to the oddity. Not that it mattered. An explanation wasn't in the offing. The invisible hand didn't talk—or offer an ounce of solace—as it continued to draw, elevating pain to new heights, marking his skin with black ink beneath the steel sleeves he wore. Swallowing a curse, he glanced down at the hardware encasing his arms from wrist to elbow. Crafted by the blacksmith at Drachaven, the clever cuffs sported three bladed fins along the outer edges, allowing him to block a blade thrust while turning his forearms into weapons.

A nice pair, but for one thing.

Cristobal wasn't wearing the cuffs to help him fight. He was wearing the pair to hide the unfinished tattoos. From Xavian. From Cruz. From anyone who would ask the questions he held no answers to, which—Jesus grant him grace—made him a first-class fool, considering he'd already decided he needed help. Well either that or to be put down. Planted six feet under. Covered in topsoil and left to rot. Too bad every time he opened his mouth, he clammed up, then shut down. A normal reaction? Not really. Xavian was his best friend, for Christ's sake. An elite assassin with supreme skill, a keen mind and solid heart, so . . .

He needed to come clean soon. Before the others discovered the change in him on their own. Before Xavian kicked his arse for hiding the truth.

Nervousness rattled his cage. Cristobal shoved his angst aside. Desirable or nay, he couldn't deny the changes in his body any longer. Honor dictated the way forward and set him on the right path. Xavian deserved the truth. His comrades needed to know—just in case. The ink and heightened awareness might not be a good thing. It could land them all in a world of trouble instead. Which meant 'twas time to buck up and lay his fears on the table. Before the malevolent force he felt growing inside him usurped his will and spiraled out of control. Otherwise he might end up harming those he considered his brothers instead of aiding the cause.

The thought sent a chill through him.

Fighting the internal deep freeze, Cristobal glanced over his shoulder. His gaze landed on Xavian, then bounced over to Razvan. Both astride Garren, just off Cruz's left wing, the pair seemed none the worse for wear. Excellent in every way, but for one. The awful smell didn't appear to be bothering either of his comrades while he . . .

Cristobal's stomach rolled. He swallowed, fighting the urge to gag. "*Rahat.*"

"What's wrong?" Cruz turned his head. Wind changed direction, curling over his horns, causing white streaks to stream from the jagged tips. Dark eyes with vertical pupils met his a moment before his friend raised a scaly brow. "You sense something?"

Sense something? Jesus. A total understatement. The perfect opening too—a clever segue that invited him to disclose the truth. To talk about the tattoos and changes in sensory perception.

Cristobal hesitated. Should he? Or shouldn't he? He'd thought to discuss the problem with Xavian first, but . . .

He frowned. Mayhap Cruz was the better choice.

Despite being the youngest dragon-shifter, Cruz understood magic. Hell, the male lived with it every day—dealt in the fantastical each time he shifted into dragon form. Toss in the fact the warrior was whipcord smart, more observant than most, and, well aye, it could work. Might even be prudent considering Cruz watched him like a hawk, shadowing him everywhere he went, refusing to allow him to leave Drachaven unescorted.

A surprising turn of events. One Cristobal appreciated, even if he found it a touch strange. He was, after all, a breed apart, a trained assassin accustomed to his own company. A man who shunned emotional attachment along with constant companionship. Something about Cruz, though, put him at ease. He didn't mind having the warrior around. 'Twas a comfortable relationship based in mutual respect and similar skill. Acceptance rooted in brotherhood; no judgment or burden of expectation.

Not unlike the one Garren shared with Xavian.

"Cristobal, do not hide from me. I sense the difference in you," Cruz said. "Tell me what ails you."

No doubt the best plan. Better to get it out in the open now, before things went from bad to worse. The thought made his heart pound harder. Cristobal struggled past his unease, forcing himself to think straight, 'cause, aye, no question. If Cruz felt the shift in him, it wouldn't be long until the others picked up on it too. "I'm undergoing a few . . . ah, changes."

"Heightened senses—sight, sound, smell?" Cruz asked. "Trouble sleeping?"

"Aye. All those."

"What else?"

"Twin tattoos. The first line appeared five nights ago."

His friend glanced at one of the finned cuffs. "Forearms?"

Cristobal dipped his chin, answering without words.

Wings spread wide, Cruz settled into a fast glide. Stars winked through the cloud cover, taking turns playing peekaboo with the moon. "You will show me when we are on the ground."

"If there is time," he said, his eyes on the horizon. He had a bad feeling. Something wasn't right. An odd vibration hung in the air, the unfriendly kind that packed a punch, then came back for more. Which meant time was of the essence and Cruz would have to wait. His problem would be solved—sooner or later. The one he approached, however? Cristobal breathed in through his nose, filling his lungs, filtering the assortment of scents. The stench remained front and center as other odors rose—smoke, charred wood, the scent of spilled blood. *Rahat* . . . not good. Particularly since the forest was set to drop away and toss them into the unknown—into the valley that cradled the holy city. "How close are we?"

"Three miles out. White Temple lies just ahead."

Shifting on his seat of scales, Cristobal palmed one of the hilts rising over the tops of his shoulders. With a smooth draw, he unsheathed the curved blade. Steel glinted in weak light, slicing through the cold air. "Cruz . . ."

"I feel it. Hold on, but be ready."

One hand wrapped in the tether, the other gripping his sword, Cristobal leaned in as his friend banked left, then dipped low, catapulting them over the rim of the treetops. The forest dropped away. Barren fields surrounded by crooked fences took its place, rushing to meet the deep ditches abutting the main road. Wings spread, Cruz hung in midair a moment, the glow of a golden dome in the distance, then shot over the frozen landscape toward soaring stone walls. Eyes narrowed, Cristobal scanned the terrain. Naught so far. No one on the ground. Nothing to consider a threat, but . . .

A black plume of smoke rose beyond the walled city.

Twisting into a sidewinding flip, Cruz roared over White Temple. Snow blew up and out, streaming into a frosty swirl behind him. The ground blurred, making building outposts indistinguishable from narrow thoroughfares. Wind whistled in his ears as they came up over the west wall. Cristobal's attention snapped north and—bingo. Ground zero. The site of the fight, once a cemetery now a bloody mess. Jesus, it looked as though an army of monsters had torn through the boneyard. Tombstones and statues lay askew—shattered, ripped from the ground, granite faces blown to bits. Huge trees stood ablaze, throwing flame and smoke into the air. Two massive craters dove into scorched earth, shallow pools of lava steaming at the north end of the cemetery.

"*La dracu*," Xavian said, voice pushed forward by a gust of wind. "Tareek?"

"Aye," Garren growled as he flew alongside Cruz. "His exhale packs a helluva wallop."

Evidently. The damage was beyond vicious. 'Twas downright impressive.

"Cruz . . ." Gaze riveted to the carnage, Cristobal trailed off as his vision warped into colorful multi-dimensional arrays. The variant hues stained the ground, expanding, contracting, each shifting like a living net, helping him assess the danger and read heat signatures. He blinked, trying to clear the color away. His focus sharpened instead, intensifying perception. Talk about eerie. Not the least bit normal either. But even as unease pricked his skin, he wielded the ability as though he'd been born doing it.

Now he knew what each pigment represented. Hot spots, fire and flame: red. Residual heat left by bodies and in footprints: orange and yellow. Cold, inanimate objects: blue, green, and grey. He shook his head, hoping to knock a few wits together, trying to understand.

Hell and a half. Another change. This one more unwelcome than the last.

Swallowing a snarl, he tapped his friend with the butt of his sword hilt. Steel thunked against hard scales. Still circling above the scene, Cruz glanced over his shoulder.

He met the dragon-shifter's gaze. "Land. Time to take a closer look."

With a nod, Cruz swooped over a huge oak engulfed by flame. Smoke billowed up, swirling around them. Heat joined the rush, devouring snowflakes, wetting the air as he tucked his wings. His back paws thumped down. Razor-sharp dragon claws scraped over granite, turning tombstones into rubble. The second Cruz settled, Cristobal threw his leg over and leapt to the ground. Stepping around his friend, he walked between two headstones. Or, what was left of them. Stone stubs sticking out of the ground, a felled tree burned a few feet away. Magic joined the scent of burning grass as Cruz shifted into human form.

With a growl, Garren landed behind them. "No one here. Any sign of Henrik and the others?"

Cristobal shook his head. "Not yet."

Jumping from the dragon's back, Xavian cursed.

Ignoring the outburst, Cristobal tipped his chin up and inhaled. Senses seething, he sifted through the stench to unearth an underlying fragrance. His nose twitched. He breathed in again, drawing on the scent, and—

Ah, right there. Right on time too.

Faint, but familiar, the scent rose, turning him north toward the square crypts and a stone half wall. His eyes narrowed. Aye, definitely. Henrik and the others had been here, but not for long. And not alone either. A light perfume clung to Henrik. Wanting to be sure, he inhaled again, then exhaled on a huff. A woman. It figured. Everywhere Henrik went, the fairer sex followed, hoping for an hour—or five—of the assassin's time.

Something about *her* scent, though, drew him tight.

The muscles bracketing his spine flickered. *Her scent . . . that scent.* Where had he smelled it before? With a frown, Cristobal tracked it and, with a quick pivot, strode toward two tall statues. Sword at the ready, he heard his comrades follow, boots crunching through snow and slush in his wake. The fragrance grew stronger. He stopped short and glanced left. Stone dragons glared down from their perch atop twin tombstones as he crouched next to boot impressions that glowed yellow. Ignoring the strange color shift, he reached out and touched one. Here . . . right here. Henrik had rested against the granite face beneath twin dragons while protecting the woman with his body.

More of her scent drifted. Sweet. Sultry. Touched by wildflowers and . . .

Something else. Something more.

A *something* he'd not smelled before, a kind of—*rahat*. He didn't know. Couldn't place it either. Odd considering his new talents. But one thing for certain? Henrik had taken her with him. Which meant she must be important . . .

Somehow. Some way. For some reason.

"They've picked up a passenger." Pushing to his feet, Cristobal met his best friend's gaze. Pale eyes narrowed, Xavian came alongside him and raised a brow, asking without words. He pointed to the impressions in the snow. "A woman."

"How do you know that?" Blond brows furrowed, Razvan stared down at him from Garren's back.

Focusing on footprints in the narrow alleyway, Cristobal shrugged. "I can smell her."

"You can . . ." Razvan's mouth opened, then closed. A second later, he jumped down from his perch. His feet hit the ground with a crunch. Boots planted beside Garren's huge talons, his comrade threw him an incredulous look. "What the hell, Cristobal? All I smell is smoke."

"*Smell* her?" Xavian said, speculation in his pale eyes. "Care to explain that?"

Not really. And certainly not here. "Later."

Stepping in close, Xavian thumped him on the chest. "How long has it been going on, brother?"

He sighed. Wonderful. Just great. Trust Xavian to catch on more quickly than most. Not surprising. His best friend didn't miss much and never dropped the ball. Which meant he needed to take the time and explain now . . . or find a way to stall. Putting it off sounded better than baring all. At least, for the moment. He wasn't ready. Didn't know how to talk about the changes, never mind explain them. Each step away from normal made him feel like a freak—one who stood outside nature's law and his comrade's fold. A stupid reaction? Probably, but admitting it didn't change how he felt. And honestly, he didn't want an audience for the unveiling. Cruz and Xavian would be the only ones invited when he unburdened himself and revealed the truth.

"It's complicated," he murmured, skin itching beneath the steel cuffs. "I'll explain, but not—"

"Five days," Cruz said, giving him a verbal shove.

Son of a bitch. He glared at the dragon-shifter. "Traitor."

"Pansy." Refusing to back down, Cruz drilled him with a look. "Take the hardware off, Cristobal. Let's have a look."

Gaze steady on his, Xavian tipped his chin. "The sooner you do, the faster we can start tracking Henrik."

"*Ma rahat*," he growled through clenched teeth.

Talk about unwanted attention and bad timing. All right, so no one was in immediate danger. The graveyard stood empty. Extrasensory perception and his messed-up vision told him that much, tracking the unique heat signatures before tucking each one into the nonthreatening category. Still he never should have opened his big mouth. Too bad Xavian was right. Avoidance never helped. Naught but facing a problem head-on ever did, so . . .

Time to come clean. In front of way too many witnesses.

Damn Cruz to hell and back.

With a flick, Cristobal undid the clips holding one of his cuffs in place. Tiny hinges squeaked. Cold air seeped through the steel crack. Goose bumps spread across his forearm, making the ink react and pain pinch as he drew the protective gear off. Fisting his hand, he held his arm up for inspection and waited. For the horror. For the revulsion. For his friends to back away as the tattoo undulated across his forearm, thin lines becoming thicker, an invisible quill drawing in black on his skin.

"Jesu," Xavian said, leaning closer to examine the tattoo. "What is that?"

Feeling like a mutant, Cristobal shifted in discomfort. "Your guess is as good as mine."

"Holy hell. 'Tis incredible." Reaching out, Cruz grabbed his wrist. With a gentle tug, he tilted his arm this way, then that. Dark eyes shimmering, he studied the incomplete pattern. "Garren . . . come look at this. Is it what I think?"

Magic flared as Garren shifted into human form and stepped alongside him. Cristobal tensed. Garren exhaled in a rush, wonder in his expression. "Hellhounds."

Cristobal blinked. "What?"

Violent eyes met his. "Do you have similar marks on your other arm?"

"Aye."

"Twin hellhounds," Garren said, awe in his tone. His mouth curved a second before he nodded. "You've been given a great gift, Cristobal. I thought Xavian and Henrik were the only ones affected by magic, but . . . the marks on your skin tell a different tale. The tattoos are incomplete, but once finished, you will be able to call on the beasts."

He frowned. "*Call* on them?"

"'Tis the Goddess of All Things at work. She has bound the hellhounds to you."

Eyes trained on the ink, Garren reached out. Cristobal tensed, but stayed still. The dragon-shifter might be lethal, but well . . . hell. The warrior was now on his side, a brother-in-arms, not an enemy that needed guarding against. So no need to over-react, never mind freak out.

Watching him, Garren touched a fingertip to the ink. The tattoo reacted, shimmering on his skin. "Hristos, that is amazing."

"Amazing." Cristobal frowned. Really? Not exactly what he liked to call it.

"Embrace the change, *fratele*. Can you not see the beast taking shape and form?" His touch featherlight, Garren traced the design. "The eyes . . . here. And gods, the fangs and teeth . . . there. Incredible."

Incredible. Huh. Another word he wouldn't use to describe it.

Cristobal angled his forearm anyway and studied the incomplete tattoo, struggling to see what the dragon-shifter did. After a moment of staring, a pattern started to immerge and—

Holy God. He saw it—the slanted eyes with vertical pupils, the razor-sharp fangs and claws, the shaggy coat, spiked spine, and bladed tail. Jesus. No wonder he felt out of sorts. All the radical changes. All the worry. Each prickle of unease over the last few days. He understood his new abilities now, along with his aversion. 'Twas instinctual, a natural reaction to the magic invading his body. The kind that came with beasts, an animalistic nature, and enhanced capabilities.

"How does it work?" Tearing his gaze from the tattoo, Cristobal refocused on Garren. All of a sudden, he needed to know. Curiosity was a powerful force, awakening the first thrum of excitement. A pair of hellhounds. Twin killing machines under his control. The possibilities surpassed interesting, roaring into open territory called *fascinating*. "How do I call them?"

"When the ink is complete, they will make themselves known," Garren said. "Be prepared. The first meeting is the most important."

First impressions usually were, but that didn't answer his question. Needing more information, Cristobal opened his mouth and—

"You'll figure it out." Garren slapped him on the shoulder. The harsh sound echoed, drifting on smoke and across the cemetery as his comrade pivoted. Violet eyes narrowed, he eyed Razvan, then raised a brow. "Xavian's gift I know about. You, however, remain a mystery. Got something to tell me, assassin?"

Razvan flinched and backed up a step.

Quick to back up his commander, Cruz stepped around Cristobal. Footfalls silent, he walked between the tombstones toward Razvan. "Show us."

"There is naught to—"

"Now, Razvan," Garren said, hemming his comrade in from the opposite side.

"Bloody hell." The growl drifted. Razvan's gaze bounced from Garren to Xavian, then back again.

Cristobal nodded, encouraging his brother-in-arms. He understood the hesitation—the unwillingness to bare all and expose a perceived flaw. He huffed. Hell, another understatement. He'd just suffered the same reaction. But Garren was right. Secrets were dangerous things. Especially among warriors who fought side by side . . . day after day, night after night. Trust wasn't optional. Understanding the warrior who stood at your back—both his strengths and weaknesses—was more than just advisable. 'Twas an absolute must.

"Come on, brother," Xavian said.

Razvan sighed and raised his hand. Tombstones groaned, broken edges scraping together. His comrade flicked his fingers. Stone levitated, rising off the turf. With a murmur, Razvan made them fly. As they whirled through the air, spinning into a circle ten feet off the ground, his friend shrugged. "I can move things just by thinking it. A kind of mind control."

Cristobal grinned. "Nice."

"Better than nice," Xavian said, returning his smile.

Cruz chimed in. "Downright fantastic."

"Tremendously useful, but I sense something else in you. Another skill just as powerful." Taking a step closer, Garren bumped Razvan with his elbow. "What is it?"

Razvan hesitated a beat, then gave up the information. "When I am still of body and calm of mind—like while in meditation—I can travel across great distances with my mind."

Surprise winged across Garren's face. "Astral projection?"

"All I need to do is hold the place in my mind's eye. Once I've fixed upon it, I can will myself there and . . ." Razvan paused, shifting his weight from one foot to the other. Tombstones followed suit, wobbling in midair. "Sometimes 'tisn't just my mind that travels."

"You've appeared in the places you envisioned?" Cristobal asked.

"Once."

Shock rippled through each warrior as he stared at Razvan. The ability to move across time and space with naught more than a thought. How . . . incredible. Unprecedented. More than just *useful* too. Why? If Razvan could harness his power—wield it to maximum effect—he could go anywhere he wanted with both mind and body. Be the inside man, one capable of providing them with information before they reached the point of no return and walked into an ambush.

Cristobal tipped his chin. "You will show me sometime."

"If you like," Razvan said, still looking wary as stone whirled overhead.

"Count me in. I wish to be there when you mind travel." Xavian waited until Razvan nodded, then flexed his fingers. Magic swelled, crackling through the cold. Pale eyes shimmering, Xavian smiled as a ball of lightning appeared in the center of his palm. Cristobal's mouth fell open. His best friend didn't bother to explain. He cranked his arm back and hurled the sphere instead. Heat sizzled through the air. Blue lightning streaked into a long tail behind the orb and—

Boom!

Light flared. One of the levitating tombstones exploded. Dust blew sky-high. Chunks of granite flew, raining down on those still embedded in the ground. Razvan flinched. The remaining headstones he held aloft with his mind tipped, then tumbled. Each slammed into the ground, cracking the silence wide open.

Xavian grunted in satisfaction. "I can conjure force fields as well."

"Seems we all have our talents." Glancing at the sky, Garren inhaled, filling his lungs. His brow creased a moment before he switched focus. Alarm bells clanged inside Cristobal's head as the warrior met each of their gazes in turn. "But playtime is over. Time to go. Black magic . . . unnatural forces are afoot."

Re-buckling the steel cuff, Cristobal sheathed his sword. Flexing his hands, he reached for his daggers. "Black magic . . . is that the awful stench I smell?"

Garren nodded.

Xavian palmed his favorite knifes. "Anything from Tareek?"

"Nay. I cannot reach him through mind-speak. There is too much interference."

Pivoting toward the north end of the cemetery, Cristobal scanned the aisles between tombstones and statues. "I can track Henrik. The woman's scent is strong."

"Go." Retreating ten feet, Cruz transformed into dragon form. Black, bronze-tipped scales glinting in the firelight, the dragon-shifter unfurled his wings. Webbing stretched wide, he leapt skyward. Scales rattling, Garren followed suit and shifted in a flash of dark blue. "Garren and I will scout the terrain from above."

Good plan.

A bird's-eye view was always helpful. Especially while on the trail of God only knew what. Black magic? A malevolent force full of bad intentions? The latter seemed like the better guess, 'cause . . . aye, whatever had gone down in the cemetery hadn't been pretty. More than just the physical devastation told him so. The hellhounds—animal instincts writhing—chimed in too, allowing him to see the whole picture. Unnatural black blood on the ground and splashed across stone. Abnormal heat signatures in the snow. Multiple footprints following Henrik and the others. It all pointed to one thing . . .

Unholy pursuit. Escape and evade.

An unusual tack for his comrades to take. Which meant one thing. Whatever hunted Henrik was powerful. Cristobal smelled it on the wind. Felt it gut deep as the tattoos on his skin throbbed in warning. So . . .

Time to put his tracking skills to the test. Find Henrik along with the others before death came calling, and he lost his friends in the fray.

CHAPTER SEVENTEEN

Cosmina surfaced on a slow glide, skimming through layers of slumber, enjoying its fluffy confines and cocooning heat. Hmm, it felt so good to be warm. Comfortable too, as though she lay cushioned and safe, far from the dangers of the world. A strange thought. Yet one that made perfect sense too. Polar opposites attached to the same situation—difficult to understand, particularly when she didn't want to come up for air . . .

Or be bothered by the thornier side of reality.

Not right now.

Remaining adrift and warm, mind fuzzy in the fog of relaxation, seemed like a better plan. Eyes still closed, curled on her side, she burrowed deeper beneath a weighted warmth. Something soft brushed across her cheek. Rabbit's fur, mayhap? Sure felt like it. And she should know. She'd spent all summer gathering rabbit pelts to make the warm throw that now graced the bed inside her cottage. 'Twas a luxury. An undeniable boon. One she was lucky to have, never mind slide beneath each night. The winter months would be more comfortable for it. Her mouth curved at the thought. The movement tweaked her temples and—huh. Another oddity to add to the pile.

For the first time in a long while, her head didn't hurt.

No ache. No persistent sting. No sign at all of the god-awful throb that often plagued her. She frowned. The shift pulled her brows together and . . . naught. Still nothing. The pain really was gone. 'Twas more than odd. Its absence signaled a new day. Something other than the continuous barrage of the unwelcome. Confusion circled a moment before acceptance sank deep. Her chest went tight, pulling at her heartstrings. Gods, it had been so long. Eons since she'd woken without a headache. Or felt so well rested.

Usually she tossed and turned, fighting the ever-present pressure inside her skull. All the imagery. The slither of whispered words spoken by strange voices inside her head. The coil and pang of premonition that never left her alone.

But not today.

Or was it night? Good question . . . and probably something she should know. Which meant she needed to open her eyes and get her bearings. The realization made her grimace. Of all the rotten luck. She didn't want to leave the comfort of her cozy haven. Given her druthers, she'd ignore the call to action and stay put. Preference, however, had little to do with it. Necessity dictated the course, shoving the sticky cobwebs of sleep aside, piling on mental acuity, forcing her to pay attention. Without moving a muscle, Cosmina fine-tuned her senses and assessed the situation.

No movement. No one talking. All quiet, but for the crackling of a well-laid fire.

Cracking her eyes open, Cosmina stared out into an open space. Soft light filtered in. Pain lanced her temples. Her eyelashes flickered as her vision warped. Blurry shapes expanded, then contracted, making objects dance in her line of sight. She blinked. Once. Twice. The third time brought everything into focus. Relief snaked through her, banding around her rib cage. Thank the gods. She could see again . . .

Everything in stunning clarity.

The low table situated across the room. The trio of rickety stools gathered around it. The compact dirt floor and rough handwoven rug in front of the lopsided stone fireplace. Each finger of flame as fire licked between the logs, throwing heat into the room. Turning her head on the pillow, she glanced up at the ceiling. A mobile made from falcon feathers hung from the thatched ceiling, its bob and sway all too familiar.

Tears tightened her throat. Everything just as she had left it. So grateful she could hardly breathe, Cosmina allowed her eyes to drift closed again. Home. Praise the goddess. She'd somehow found her way home. To safety and solace. To her tiny cottage inside the Limwoods.

The realization gathered inside her head and unearthed another. A picture rose in her mind's eye, one of hazel eyes and a too-handsome face. She sighed, the soft exhale half appreciation, half apprehension. Henrik . . . the warrior with unequalled strength and a gentle touch. No other explanation fit. Especially since she remembered falling asleep in his arms—head tucked beneath his chin, body curled around his, desperately seeking his warmth as her chill ran marrow deep.

The memory should've embarrassed her. Made her squirm in discomfort and want to forget her need for him in the wee hours. Helplessness, after all, was not a girl's best friend. More often than not, it landed a woman in trouble—the kind from which many never recovered. She'd seen it time and again. Had crept through the streets of Ismal on her yearly visits, ghosting in, stealing supplies, then getting out without anyone being the wiser. So aye, she knew all about men. About sex too, and the ways they procured it. Men preyed on the vulnerable. Experience and a lifetime spent watching told her that much, but . . .

Focused on the mobile bobbing on its thin string, Cosmina shook her head. 'Twas odd, but she didn't feel that way about Henrik. She couldn't put her finger on the reason, but despite her natural caution—the mistrust she carried around like a blade—she trusted him not to hurt her. Or take undue advantage. Wishful thinking? A by-product of her infatuation with him? The stir of attraction she felt for him, her need to explore it and know more? She pursed her lips. Mayhap. Mayhap not. But one thing for certain, she refused to be embarrassed for relying on him. Despite her helplessness, she knew Henrik didn't perceive her as weak. Like recognized like . . . and the strong welcomed strength. She acknowledged his, and intuition told her he saw hers.

Something to celebrate, not ignore.

So forget the vulnerability. Never mind the embarrassment.

Cosmina refused to entertain either notion. Or allow shame to grow. She flexed her hand, tweaking her sore muscles, feeling her injured arm throb, and indulged in gratitude instead. She'd needed him. He'd provided all she required without hesitation—holding her, warming her, enduring discomfort so she wouldn't suffer. Add that to the fact he'd saved her life and—aye, pride could go hang itself. Courage deserved equal measure. His had ensured her survival and safety, so no other way to look at it. The situation held no room for humiliation, just heartfelt thankfulness.

Which meant she needed to find and thank Henrik before he left her for good.

Bracing herself, Cosmina gripped the edge of the fur-lined throw. Time to leave the warm comfort of her bed, face the chilly room, and the rest of the day. Not that there was much left of it to conquer. The lone window across the cottage told the tale. Covered by shutters she'd woven from small saplings and leather strips, light crept around its edges and over the sill, allowing her to gauge the time. The end of the day, early evening in all probability. She cringed. Goodness, she'd been asleep for hours. Much longer than usual after suffering a vision.

Or dealing with magic.

A point of concern? Or normal after performing the goddess' ritual? Excellent questions. Ones best left for another day. She needed to stay focused and on task. Job one equated to finding the man who'd risked his life to keep her safe. After that, there would be plenty of time to figure out what the goddess expected from her next. Once Henrik was gone. Once things returned to normal, and she found herself alone in the Limwoods once more.

The thought sent a pang straight to her heart.

Regret followed. Cosmina swallowed the lump in her throat. *Alone.* Forever on her own. In the world, but not of it. Strong. Tough. Self-reliant to the point of isolation. She'd played that role for five years, stayed on the fringes, and embraced obscurity. It had seemed fine to her—a true necessity—until last night. Until Henrik. Meeting him inside White Temple had done something strange to her. Poked at her soul. Awakened a yearning. Dragged need to the forefront, forcing her to acknowledge the deprivation she lived with day in and day out. Now her life no longer seemed good enough. It felt bland and colorless, making her long for more. Something better. Something only boldness and a wild sense of adventure would cure.

With a quick flick, she flipped the covers back and pushed herself upright. Cold air rushed in, chasing goose bumps across her skin. She stared down at her bare legs for a moment. Her brows collided. Oh dear. Great heavens. A complete surprise too considering she was half-dressed—no stockings or trews, no sign of her leather tunic or the binding she always wrapped over her breasts either. Just her short braes beneath a too-big linen shirt that didn't belong to her and . . .

She blinked. Good goddess. Henrik. He'd undressed her while she slept.

The realization should've set her back a step. Or, at the very least, lit the fuse on her temper. Somehow, though, it didn't. Ire remained suspiciously absent. In its place, curiosity bloomed. Had he liked what he'd seen? Did he find her beautiful? Silly questions. Ones that meant naught in the grand scheme of things. He'd been kind and gentle, nothing more—removing damp clothing, seeing to her comfort, tucking her in without waking her . . . caring for her when most men wouldn't have bothered.

All lovely gestures that didn't mean a thing.

Anyone with two wits to rub together would realize it. Naught good would come from romanticizing Henrik. Or reading anything into the way he cared for her. Honorable men treated women with respect. 'Twas protocol, a rule among warriors or something, so . . . aye, fantasy needed to stay where it belonged, in the realm of impossibility. Pragmatism owned the here and now. Was as much a part of her life as eating and sleeping. But even as she reminded herself of that, Cosmina pressed her nose to the collar of Henrik's shirt and took a deep breath.

His scent invaded her scenes.

Pleasure prickled through her. She hummed in reaction. Goddess, he smelled good, like man and musk—of decadence, heat, and perfect summer afternoons. She inhaled again, filling her lungs with him, and called herself a fool as a chasm opened deep inside her. Yearning stepped into the breech, spilling through her until she could no longer deny the truth. She desired him. Wanted to spend a night—hell, strike that, make it a few days—coming to know him as a woman did a man. No holds barred. No shyness. No regret in the aftermath. Just him, her, and an avalanche of satisfaction before they went their separate ways.

Unable to help herself, she drew in his scent again.

"Hmm . . ." She hummed, the sound all kinds of wrong. 'Twas madness. The claw and pull of attraction. Her cresting arousal. The ludicrous way she breathed him in, needing some part of him—any part of him—deep inside her, feeling foolish even as her enjoyment grew. "Henrik."

Something moved beside her bed. "Here, *iubita*."

Cosmina yelped in surprise and skittered backward. The web of ropes beneath her mattress swayed. Her bottom collided with the crooked log posing as a footboard. Rough wood scraped the side of her leg. "Ouch!"

"Christ."

Arm muscles flexing, Henrik sat up. Sleepy eyes met hers a moment before he tossed a wool blanket aside. Firelight bounced off his leather tunic as he rolled off the floor and shifted to sit on the edge of her bed. The mattress dipped. She peered over the side and around him, focusing on the thin pallet spread out on the dirt floor. Good goddess. He'd been asleep beside her the whole time. Just a few feet away while she'd fantasized about touching him . . .

About *being* with him.

Running a hand through his messy hair, he stared at her. "Are you hurt?"

"Nay." Stroking the outside of her thigh, Cosmina rubbed the sting away. "You startled me, 'tis all."

"Seems to be a running theme with me."

"Scaring people?"

"Aye."

"There are worse things." Like lust. And overwhelming need and crazy, ridiculous desire for the man seated a few feet away. Take your pick. No matter how she sliced it, each one signaled disaster. The kind good girls didn't come back from in one piece. Another excellent observation. One big problem. Cosmina didn't give a wit about the danger surrounding him. She wanted to be brave instead—to explore, claim new territory, and conquer it. Or mayhap she should say . . . *conquer him.* "You don't scare me."

He raised a brow. "Nay?"

Holding his gaze, she shook her head. The corners of his mouth tipped up in the beginnings of a smile. 'Twasn't much, the twitch of his lips, a mere hint of amusement, but it unleashed something inside her. Now she wanted to reach out, bridge the distance and touch him. Run her fingers through the messy strands of his hair. Smooth each lock back into place, discover its softness, and mayhap even—goddess strike her dead for lustful thoughts—revisit his kiss and come to know his taste.

Wicked in so many ways. But oh so tempting too.

Heat bloomed in her cheeks. "Sorry I woke you."

"You didn't." Eyes steady on her, he raised his hand. Flipping it palm up, he invited her to take it and come closer. Her breath caught as she accepted his invitation and slid her hand into his. With a murmur, he laced their fingers together and tugged. She didn't resist the pull and, knees skimming over the sheet, settled alongside him. "I woke the instant you moved."

"Oh," she whispered, warming under his touch, enjoying his scrutiny.

Not hard to do. She liked his gaze on her. Enjoyed the attention and the way he looked at her, with eyes full of appreciation, but . . . gods. As much as she relished his nearness, the weight of his regard made her nervous too. The worst kind of needy, a condition she found difficult to explain. 'Twas unholy and delicious, curious and complex, bedeviling yet oh so compelling. The intensity of it picked her up, swept her along, tightening the muscles over her bones until her skin felt two sizes too small and . . .

Panic prickled through her.

Drat it all. Desire came with all kinds of complications. Not the least of which was instigation. Some sort of action, after all, was required. Let angst win and back away, or be brave and forge ahead. Option two appealed much more. She wanted him. Despite the craziness. Despite her nervousness. Despite everything. Her need for him wasn't based in logic. Common sense had naught to do with it. 'Twas more of a feeling, the claw and rip of her Seer's eye. Which begged a question, didn't it? Was it premonition driven by her gift? Or instincts gone awry? Cosmina didn't know. But as the silence expanded and she held his gaze, the pressure built inside her head, urging her forward into the uncertain, toward Henrik instead of away.

Butterflies lit off, taking flight across her abdomen. She shifted on her knees, pressing both to the side of Henrik's thigh. The linen sheet rustled, joining the quiet crackle of the hearth. "You're a light sleeper."

"Very."

"Probably a good thing and, ah . . . necessary. I mean, you can never be too careful, because you know, well . . ." Desperate to gain control of her nerves, she paused.

Patient as ever, Henrik raised a brow and waited for her to continue.

Which—blast it all—made her want to die of embarrassment. Or crawl under the nearest doormat and never come out. Cosmina smothered a grimace. Way to go. Brilliantly played . . . or not. Nothing like acting like a ninny. One who didn't know what to say to the man she desired in her bed.

"Someone might . . . umm, you know . . . sneak up on you." Nibbling on the inside of her lip, she forced herself to stay the course. But gods, it was hard not to squirm as his fingers slid between hers. Goose bumps snaked up her arm, making her shiver. "Or something."

He stroked his thumb across her palm. "You can sneak up on me anytime, Cosmina."

She frowned. Was that an invitation? Sounded like it, and yet, she couldn't be sure. Had no way of knowing what he intended. Or how she ought to proceed. Be straightforward and hope for the best? Let the silence stretch until he took the lead? She didn't know. And Henrik didn't help her decide. Like a patient predator, he watched and waited for her next move.

Which needed to happen now—before she lost all sense of herself.

Mouth gone dry, she reached for courage. "Can I sneak up on you now?"

Interest sparked in his gaze. "Depends."

"On what?"

"What you intend."

Be brave, her mind whispered. *Touch him now*, desire urged.

Heeding both, Cosmina shook free of his hold and cupped his cheek. He made a gruff sound, one full of surprise as her fingers stroked along his jaw. Rough whiskers rasped against her skin. Prickles of pleasure ghosted up her arm, then turned tail, and cascaded over the tops of her shoulders. She murmured his name, the yearning hard to deny. She heard it in her voice. Felt it as he turned his face into her palm, seeking more of her touch. Her heart hopscotched, rebounding inside her chest as her other hand slid across his nape. Wonderment swirled. Goddess, his hair was soft. So thick. So incredibly dark against her pale skin.

His dark. Her light. A fair comparison.

In truth, it made perfect sense. He'd suffered. Had been caught in something terrible. Instinct and facts gathered by her unnatural talent told her so. She might not understand the extent of it, but as she caressed him—loving him with her hands, finding a place for him in her heart—certain knowledge wielded a heavy weight. Henrik was damaged, just like her. Abandoned. Cast out. Left for dead.

Which made them a sad but perfect fit. Two ruined halves making whole.

Empathy sank deep. Cosmina understood. She really did. He needed softness in his life in the same way she needed companionship and acceptance. She craved true freedom, the right to be herself without the heavy hand of judgment. The idea he might give her all of that made her bold. She wanted to be something other than cautious and afraid. Needed more than mistrust and distance. No worries for the future. No care for the consequences. No time for second-guessing either. Just commitment coupled with a passion so powerful it couldn't be denied.

Tunneling through his hair, she turned his face toward her. His eyes met hers. She leaned in and touched her lips to the corner of his.

He groaned. "Cosmina."

"I want to make love with you, Henrik," she said, laying it on the line, letting honesty lead the way. "I want to know your touch before you leave me."

"Sweet love." Eyes dark with desire, he kissed her back. A gentle touch. The merest brush of his mouth against hers—so soft, so sweet, so filled with longing he made her want to cry. "Have you ever been with a man?"

"Aye."

Surprise made him pause. Raising his head, he brushed the tangle of curls from her temple and retreated enough to look at her. Apprehension lit off, making her heart pound harder. Did her honesty bother him? Did he expect her to be a virgin? Most men would. She'd never been married, after all . . . or even close to betrothed. Another misstep in a whole string of them. She'd lost her innocence years ago. Had made mistake after mistake, trusting the wrong boy, believing the lies he told. And yet as she held Henrik's gaze, she refused to lie.

Or pretend to be someone she wasn't.

"I was fifteen and foolish," she said, memories rising from the ashes.

Gods, she'd been so naive. So very wrong, but then the former High Priestess of Orm had driven her to it—keeping her sequestered inside the tower room, locking her away, allowing no one to visit. The reason for her imprisonment had been simple. The old witch had wanted to keep Cosmina's gift a secret—all to herself, so that she might profit while others floundered. Her mother had fought long and hard for Cosmina's freedom. To no end. Ruthless, without conscience, Ylenia had removed her mother from the equation. A deadly poison splashed into her wine goblet and . . .

Grief tightened Cosmina's throat. Goddess . . . five years. *Five long years* had passed, and yet the pain never lessened. The loss of her mother still hurt. If only she'd seen Ylenia's plan in advance. If only she'd understood the jagged pieces of premonition. If only she'd put enough clues together and warned her mother in time. *If only . . . if only . . . if only.* Two words that would forever haunt her. Along with the aftermath of her mother's murder and her rebellion against the Order of Orm. Had she been smarter, she could have wielded her gift like a weapon. Made Ylenia and those in her inner circle dance to her tune. Instead she'd rebelled, refusing to share her visions, getting involved with the wrong boy, making the High Priestess believe the loss of her virginity meant the end of her gift.

A huge bluff. One Ylenia had called the day she evicted Cosmina from White Temple. And a history she had every right to hide. Something about Henrik, though, made her want to let it go and lay herself bare.

"I was young. Too trusting," she said. "I thought I was in love, and he—"

"Took advantage."

"Not really. I was willing and . . . curious." Sad, but true. She'd craved a friend, a companion outside her tower prison and the kitchen staff who brought her meals. The smithy's son had provided that and, well—Cosmina grimaced—a whole lot more. Tracing the shell of Henrik's ear, she pressed her cheek to his. A gentle shift. A quick adjustment, and she kissed him again. He drew a sharp breath. Daring to be bold, she licked into his mouth. He responded, delving in, deepening the contact, and pulled her toward him. Her knees slid on the sheet. His hand settled on her back as she touched the tip of her tongue to his. "My cross to bear, I guess."

"What is, *iubita*?"

"Curiosity . . . The need to experience things."

"Understandable," he said, kissing her back. "Did he give you pleasure?"

She frowned. "What do you mean?"

"I'll take that as nay," he growled, disgust for her onetime lover in his tone.

"I only slept with him once, but . . ." She shrugged, then shivered as Henrik's fingertips played along her spine. Up. Down. Around and around. He drew circles on her skin, watching her, descending until he stroked the curve of her bottom. Pleasure rippled through her, making her muscles twitch as she moaned against his mouth.

With a hum, he nipped her bottom lip. His fingers stroked up, slipping beneath the hem of her braes. "But?"

Cosmina blinked. But *what*? Good Lord, she couldn't remember what they'd been talking about, never mind follow the conversation. Not with his hands on her, caressing, exploring, trailing across her bare back.

Henrik helped, prompting her memory. "You slept with him once, but . . ."

Oh, right. *That* conversation. "I don't think he knew what he was doing."

"Imbecile."

"Probably."

Henrik smiled against her throat. A second later, he flicked her pulse point with his tongue. "You deserve better, *iubita* . . . to know joy, every ounce of pleasure."

"So show me better."

"Cosmina . . ." Regret in his tone, he raised his head. "Sweet love, 'tisn't a good idea. I shouldn't be touching you like this, never mind—"

"Please?"

Caressing her bottom lip with the pad of his thumb, he held her gaze. Longing reflected in his eyes, mirroring her own, providing what she wanted most: all his desire, every ounce of his yearning centered on her. But even as she rejoiced in his need, remorse stole into his expression, and he shook his head.

She tightened her grip in his hair. "Do you want me, Henrik?"

"More than I want my next breath."

"Well, I want you back," she said, a plea in her tone, strength in her hands.

She couldn't let him go. Not while pressure mounted between her temples and premonition threatened. 'Twas strange, her need for him. Naught about it made sense. Then again, naught about her gift ever did. She never received the whole story, just bits and pieces. Broken shards that didn't amount to much. Still, she refused to ignore the coil and strike of second sight. Somehow . . . some way . . . Cosmina knew being with him was right. Was good. Would make a difference down the line and change the course of her life. So nay, no going back. Or shying away. In this moment, he belonged to her. And she needed to claim him, even if it meant she must let him go in the end.

"Henrik, I need to know you. I cannot explain it. 'Tisn't based in rough urges or right and wrong," she said, holding his gaze. "'Tis a necessary thing . . . pure instinct. I need this from you. Please . . . do not leave me wanting."

He growled, the rough purr so low she barely heard it. A denial? Unabashed acceptance? It didn't matter. Her course was set, and fate turned the dial, pushing her into his arms. So she kissed him again, sinking into his mouth, holding on to his taste, hope rising hard as she waited to see what he would do . . .

Push her away. Or do as she asked and lay her down.

CHAPTER EIGHTEEN

He shouldn't be touching her. Shouldn't be enjoying the feel of her so much either. Giving into need. Doing what he wanted. Making love to Cosmina. All bad ideas. Worse than terrible, actually. Henrik knew it. Every instinct he owned told him it wouldn't end well. He'd do what he always did and leave. She'd end up with a handful of memories and a heart full of hurt. Not good for either of them. But even as he told himself to do the right thing, ease up and back away, he couldn't force his hands from her, never mind deny her kiss. Not with her small hands buried in his hair and her lush body up against his.

Henrik groaned. God forgive him but . . .

She tasted so damned good.

Better than decadent. A delicious temptress who twisted intention, making him yearn in ways he never had before. Now he longed for her. For the softness of her skin. For the taste of her tongue and heat of her mouth. For the acceptance she gave. No judgment. No second-guessing. Not an ounce of hesitation, just full-on welcome wrapped up in all-consuming need.

Please do not leave me wanting.

Captivating words. Desperate desire. Such a powerful plea. All of it hers.

She whispered his name like a benediction. The need in her tone throbbed between his temples. Tore into his heart. Left him grasping at straws, searching for self-control, a way to hold the line as she kissed him again. Her tongue flicked along his teeth, burning a path into his mouth. Passion flamed into a wall of heat, licking through his veins, making his balls fist up tight and his heart pound the inside of his chest. Thump-thump-throb. Boom-boom-slam. The sound echoed, roaring into a lust-filled chant, tempting him and . . . oh God. He wanted to do it—continue, lose all restraint, and be the first to show her pleasure. Be the only man to lay her down and teach her true abandon.

It would be so easy to do. To let go, lose control, and give Cosmina her way.

She wanted him. And honestly, he yearned to please her. Was driven to provide all she asked, so . . . no harm, no foul. The situation held all he insisted upon—willingness, a bed, and explosive desire. All incredible components. A great combination heading into a brief interlude. One that benefited both parties. Except for one thing . . .

It wasn't that simple.

Particularly since *brief interlude* would never apply to Cosmina. 'Twould be more of a love affair, a complicated one in which he lost his mind and got burned in the process. Logic pointed out the flaws in the plan. Instinct backed up the theory. One night—afternoon, evening, whatever; he didn't know what time it was—would never be enough. Not with her. It was a simple fact wrapped up in unshakable certainty that led to an inescapable conclusion. All based on how he felt about her—hot, needy, proud, invested, so goddamn possessive he understood the implications.

Laying her down and loving her amounted to self-annihilation.

He wouldn't survive the experience unscathed. Not with his heart intact. She wasn't like the other women he'd bedded. She was infinitely more precious. Special in ways he found difficult to describe, but knew to be true. Which meant his *love 'em hard, leave 'em fast* maxim wouldn't work with her. For the first time in his life, Henrik wanted to stay. To stick around long enough to make a play for another's heart. To see if, by some miracle, she came to value him in return. Xavian had done it, risked all, been brave, and held on to Afina. It defied logic—and the code of their kind—but somehow their relationship, the love the pair shared, worked. His sister was happy, and his best friend full of the kind of contentment most men never found.

Odd. Baffling. So very tempting. Almost irrepressible, but for one thing.

Cosmina deserved so much better than him.

Heart heavy with regret, Henrik retreated a little, lifting his mouth from hers. He needed to end it now. Set her aside and walk away this instant. Before he forgot restraint and—

"Nay," she said, her lips brushing over his. Her hands flexed in his hair. She leaned in, bridging the distance, and bit down on his bottom lip. A gentle nip. A sweet tug, and bliss swirled, taking him on a passion-fueled ride. "Stay. Kiss me again."

Another whispered plea. More soul-stirring need. Enough to drag him closer to edge. "Cosmina."

"Now, Henrik."

Her tone brooked no argument. Her command of the kiss fueled his fire, forcing him to respond even as he tried to resist her. But Christ, it was hard. He wanted what she offered. Needed to touch, taste, and discover. And as she took control, Henrik lost his will—his mind too—and opened wider, encouraging her to explore and take and tease.

Which—goddamn it—scared the hell out of him.

For good reason. His need for her was unsettling, beyond anything he'd ever experienced, which left him at her mercy. A problem, particularly since she didn't appear to have any—kissing him as though starving, sending her tongue deep, eating at his mouth the way he yearned to feast upon her body. And as she stoked his flames higher, ramping him into dangerous territory, Henrik felt himself crack and give ground.

Something he never did.

Always dominant in bed, he dictated the play. 'Twas a hard and fast rule. One he lived by. Too bad it wasn't working for him right now. Her touch. The soft sounds she made. The feel of her pressed against him. Temptation personified. Beautiful wanton. Gorgeous hellion. She sent him soaring. Each caress compounded the effect, multiplying until the word *no* disappeared from his vocabulary. Not a good sign. The ground rules must be laid in advance. He needed her to understand and accept before they went any further. Believe him when he told her they had no future together. She was a member of the Blessed, a valuable asset to the Goddess of All Things. He was an assassin assigned to protect her, one with a tainted past and too much blood on his hands.

It wouldn't end well. Was doomed to fail. He knew it, even if she didn't.

Reaching for some small measure of restraint, he turned his head and broke the kiss. She protested and, with a tug, tried to bring him back. He almost gave in. Almost said to hell with honor, took control, and tangled his tongue with hers. *Almost,* but not quite. Despite rampant need, he couldn't do it. Couldn't go on without telling her the truth.

Warning her was the right thing to do.

"Cosmina . . . *iubita,* slow down. Ease up a moment. We need to . . ." Chest pumping, he fought to draw a full breath. A useless endeavor. Cosmina was too quick. Denied his kiss, she dipped her head and set her mouth to the side of his throat. The sharp edge of her teeth scraped his skin. His muscles flexed, tightening in alarm as she shifted to her knees. One moment, she sat beside him on the mattress. The next, she sat astride him, the insides of her thighs pressed to the outside of his as she settled her exquisite bottom in his lap. Heat bled through her thin braes, scorching him through his leather trews, making him twitch. "Christ, don't—"

"What, Henrik?"

Playing the seductress, she undulated against him, riding the hard ridge of his erection. He cursed and rolled his hips, meeting her downward thrust, encouraging her ride as he flicked at the hem of her shirt. Soft skin met his palms and . . . ah hell. Oh Jesus. He was in trouble. He couldn't stop touching her, never mind breathe when she rode him that way. His hands traveled of their own volition, refusing to listen to him, caressing her bare back, loving the feel of her.

She hummed against the side of his neck. "Make you desire me? Take what I want instead of waiting for it to happen?" With a quick shift, she licked over his pulse point, lashing him with bliss, then raised her head. Bright-green eyes met his. "I'm tired of waiting. You're here. I want you. Give me what I need."

He longed to . . . over and over, again and again. "Sweet love, 'tisn't that simple."

"Aye, it is . . . just that simple. You. Me. Desire. Simplest thing in the world."

"Cosmina," he said, his heart aching so hard his whole chest hurt. "I cannot stay."

"How long do we have together?"

"Two, mayhap three, days."

"Well then . . ." Gaze steady, she brushed her mouth against his. So gentle. So sweet. Way too accepting. "We'd best make the most of it, don't you think?"

Think? Christ, 'twas too much to hope for. His brain—along with every ounce of good sense—was gone.

"Make love to me, Henrik. Show me true pleasure," she whispered. "No regrets."

And just like that, he was done. Finished. Beyond the limits of smart, plunging headlong off desire's cliff into the stupidest form of wrong.

* * *

Triumph tasted sweet, and Henrik even better.

Gods, he was something. So hard-bodied. So strong. The sweep of his hands over her bare back so gentle it took her breath away. Now all she wanted was more. More of his taste. More of his heat. More of his skin against hers. A startling thought. She'd never imagined thinking it, never mind having the opportunity to explore the tight tug of arousal. But the slow burn of desire— 'twas incredible, alluring, seductive . . .

So damned good, she yearned to settle in, stay a while, and prolong the pleasure.

Another odd thought. One that wrestled with the first. Aye, she wanted to linger, relish each touch, every tantalizing sound he made and yet, impatience shoved at her too, urging her to rush headlong into bliss and experience all the pleasure Henrik promised. Polar opposites. Two conflicting approaches. Both of equal merit. Pile on her inexperience and—aye, the entire affair held the possibility to send her tumbling into dangerous territory.

A place labeled *true, unadulterated love.*

The realization should've set Cosmina back a step. Or at least caused her to pause, take stock, mayhap even revise her game plan. A good girl, after all, didn't beg a man to make love to her. Or plop herself in his lap, bury her hands in his hair, and press her advantage. A respectable woman demurred, waited, expected a ceremony and commitment before giving herself to a man. She huffed. *Commitment.* 'Twas a lovely concept. An interesting convention and . . .

One best left out of the equation.

Building a fantasy life around Henrik wouldn't end well. He didn't want anything permanent or long-term. And honestly, she wasn't sure she did either. Men were fickle creatures, ones who enjoyed variety and adventure. She'd learned that truth the hard way, five years ago when she'd become entangled with the blacksmith's son. Love did strange things to people—made women stupid, circumstances turn, and heartbreak inevitable. Something about Henrik urged her to risk it. Brave all, tuck in, pull him close, and keep him for as long as fate allowed.

Such a bad idea.

No way should she be dreaming of a future with him. She should be planning the best way to let him go after the loving. Before meeting him, she never would've believed herself capable of loving and then leaving a man. Or rather, allowing him to leave in the aftermath of physical conquest. With Henrik, though, clarity crystallized, dragging awareness to the surface.

She couldn't push him away. Or guard her heart. The strong pull of premonition refused to let her. Denying her gift wouldn't work. Here, now, this moment was about listening—for opening her Seer's eye and allowing intuition to flow.

Which meant . . . no walking away.

Regardless of the fated heartbreak and upheaval in the aftermath, she intended to take everything he gave her. Give as much as she could in return as well. Burn herself into his brain so he never, ever, forgot her. Days, weeks . . . years. Time wouldn't touch what they shared here. No matter the distance, it would endure, rest safe in his heart, mind, and soul in the same way it would hers. Even after Henrik left her and never looked back.

Henrik deepened the kiss, taking charge of her. She let him, loving his taste, reveling in his touch as his warm hands ghosted up her spine. He groaned against her mouth. Bliss swirled in a heated curl. Satisfaction roared in its wake. He wanted her— badly. She could feel it in his touch, in the urgent flex and shift of his body against hers, in the tangle of their tongues, in his need for more. *More.* Oh gods, she loved that word. Couldn't get enough of Henrik's *more.* Wanted to give him all and offered it as he deepened the kiss, making her moan. He growled in return, gripping her hips, teaching her rhythm as she moved in his lap. Denying her nothing, he provided what she wanted, then offered her more. Cosmina took it all. Every soft caress. Each heated stroke, passion urging her to follow his lead. She undulated against him, rolling her hips, riding the hard length pressed between her thighs.

Henrik's breath hitched. "Christ, Cosmina, aye . . . just like that. Take control. Find your rhythm and ride. Ride me, *iubita.*"

Sensation spiraled deep. Pleasure broke through, cresting through her on a wave of ecstasy. She gasped his name. Nipping the underside of her chin, he cupped her bottom with one hand, then sent the other exploring. He fisted the back of her shirt. With a slow draw, he raised the linen and tugged it over her head. Cool air washed over her skin. Awareness bloomed and Cosmina hesitated, feeling exposed, surprised when shyness rose and uncertainty threatened. The urge to cross her arms and cover her breasts nudged her.

Such a silly reaction. Particularly since she desired him. Wanted to be unclothed and skin to skin with him, which, aye, necessitated him stripping her bare, but—blast and damn. 'Twas difficult not to flinch. Harder still to quash her shimmer of anxiety. Nervous tension lashed her, stilling her in his lap. Breathing hard, her chest rose and fell, accentuating the fact she was naked from the waist up. Gaze fixed to his face, she waited for his reaction, for a flicker of disappointment, for him to push her away. Cosmina bit down on her bottom lip. *Oh please, don't let that happen.* She wanted him so much and needed him to want her with the same intensity, but . . .

The inevitable questions circled, destroying her confidence.

Did he find her beautiful? Was her lack of a busty bosom unpleasing? A worry based in complete witlessness. She couldn't, after all, change the way she was made. Strong and slight. She'd always been that way. Henrik would either find her beautiful . . . or not. But even as she settled into the reality, her heart throbbed and uncertainty rose. She longed for his praise. For admiration to ignite in his eyes. For him to look at her with heat and awe and . . . aye, mayhap with awe and the merest hint of love.

A lump formed in her throat. She squirmed in his lap, loving the feel of his hands on her, even as she dreaded his reaction. Goddess strike her dead and be done with it. She'd fallen straight into ridiculousness. It shouldn't matter whether he liked the look of her. Having him in her arms ought to be enough. And yet, it wasn't. She wanted more. So instead of covering up, she held the line and leveled her chin.

Big hands slid from her waist up her sides. As her breath hitched, Henrik held her gaze. Grip firm yet gentle, he cupped her rib cage, thumbs brushing the undersides of her breasts. His fingers flexed. Her breath caught as he broke eye contact. His gaze traveled over her throat, across her collarbone, down . . .

Down.

Down until . . .

She shivered as he skimmed over her breasts.

"Sweet love," he said, tone low, the look in his eyes so hot her nipples reacted, furling tight. He groaned and, breathing hard, dragged his gaze up to meet hers once more. "God, Cosmina. You're beautiful. So goddamn perfect. I knew you would be. I imagined you like this so many times, but—Christ. Nothing compares to the reality."

The praise sank deep, infecting her heart, heating her soul, making relief rise. "Thank you. I was worried you would . . ."

As she trailed off, he raised a brow. "What? Find you lacking?"

She nodded, acknowledging the insecurity. "Most men like women with more up top."

"What idiot told you that?"

Gripping the edge of his leather tunic, Cosmina shrugged.

"Don't believe a word of it," he said. "You're incredible. So pretty and . . ."

With a slow shift, he switched focus. His hands left her rib cage. Heat engulfed her as he cupped her in both palms. Calloused fingertips rasped over her nipples. "Pink—Jesus, high, tight, pretty pink nipples."

Her breath caught on the compliment. Bliss roared at his touch, scorching her, and she arched her spine in supplication. The move begged him for more. He delivered, watching her as he caressed her with gentle strokes, teasing her with each tug and flick. His mouth drifted across her collarbone. Ecstasy sizzled across her skin, shooting straight to her core. As she pulsed deep inside, Cosmina rolled her hips. He met her halfway, then shifted from the edge of the mattress. Hard muscles flexed around her as he picked her up. A quick pivot, and her back touched the sheet. Henrik followed her down, settling a thigh between her legs as he dipped his head. His mouth settled at her breast. Cosmina bucked, arching up, and . . .

Oh gods.

Scorching heat on her skin. A wet stroke over her nipple. Instant, devastating pleasure.

With a groan, he suckled her, each pull gentle and sure, yet somehow rough too.

The throb between her thighs intensified. "Henrik!"

"Hmm, you're sensitive." Stroking her with his tongue, he tugged at the lace holding her braes in place. Nestled just below her belly button, the bow let go. The leather tie loosened, widening by the moment, revealing her skin an inch at a time. He nipped the tip of her nipple. Her back arched. Her breath hitched. Suspended in pleasure, she bit down on her bottom lip as his hand slid over her bare belly, then slipped between her legs. Eager for him, she spread her thighs wider. Separating her folds with gentle fingertips, he slid into her heat and groaned against her breast. "Oh God. You're perfect here too. Gorgeous, *iubita*. You're gorgeous. So hot and tight, so slick . . . almost ready to come for me."

His voice—the deep stroke of it—unraveled her control, leaving her at his mercy. A very nice place to be, particularly since he didn't have any. Stroking the top of her sex, he drenched her in bliss, pumping the pleasure so high she couldn't tell where he ended and she began. And all the while he talked to her, whispering naughty things in her ear, praising her with words and— goddess, she enjoyed the sound of him. Loved the way he spoke to her, tone full of enchantment and awe and oh so much need.

Head thrown back, she listened to his voice, yet barely heard him. She was too busy chasing the sensation to pay attention. Illusive and thick, it gripped her body, strumming a chord while he played between her thighs, teasing her with the promise of . . . something. A something she wanted. Now. This instant. Hmm, she was close. So very close, yet still too far away.

"Henrik . . . I cannot . . . I need—"

"To come. I know." Nipping the underside of her chin, he withdrew. She protested the loss. Kissing her gently, he knelt beside her. Still dressed, knees sinking into the mattress, he fisted his hands in her braes. He tugged. She raised her hips, allowing him to draw the pair down her legs. Chest pumping, gaze riveted to the red curls between her thighs, he tossed her underwear over the side of the bed. "I cannot wait to feel you come."

"Come?"

"The pleasure I promised you."

"Is that what I'm chasing?"

"Aye," he murmured. "Do you want it?"

"Yes."

"Fast or slow?" he asked, unlacing his leather tunic.

"Which is better?"

"Depends. Both are good, but this time . . . your first time . . . I think I'll give it to you fast."

"Fast works." Was the best, really. An excellent plan in every way. She squirmed against the mattress. "I need—gods, Henrik. Do something."

He grinned, the quick flash of white teeth all wolf. "With pleasure, my beautiful wanton. I'll give you all you want ... everything you need."

Eyes locked on her, Henrik drew his tunic over his head and sent it flying. As the leather went the way of her braes, he unlaced and shucked his trews. Cosmina's mouth fell open. By the gods, he was incredible. Long limbs. Hard-bodied. Broad, strong, so beautifully made he stole her breath, then gave it back, kissing her deep, filling her lungs with his scent as he settled solid and warm against her. Opening wide to appease him, she tangled her tongue with his. He groaned. She hummed, welcoming him, cradling him in her arms, stroking her hand down the wide expanse of his back. Raised ridges ghosted against her fingertips and ...

Scars. Many of them crisscrossing his back. Except ...

'Twasn't lash marks made by a whip. 'Twas a pattern. A distinct one rooted in pain and suffering, as though someone had cut into his skin with deliberate precision. The realization startled her, dimming pleasure, raising questions, her concern for him paramount. Backing off a little, she gentled the kiss and skimmed his scars, a silent question in her touch. Cracking his eyes open, he met her gaze.

"Henrik."

"Nay, Cosmina." Mouth brushing hers, he shook his head. "No thinking allowed."

"Later then," she said, caressing his back, tracing the awful lines carved into his skin. He'd been hurt ... badly, in the worst way. Someone had done this to him. A someone he despised. She saw the truth in his gaze, felt the sudden tension in his muscles even as he shrugged, denying the abuse without words. Raising her head off the pillow, she brushed her lips against the corner of his. "You know I'll ask later."

"But not right now."

"Not right now," she whispered, bowing to his wishes, allowing him his way.

Relief sparked a moment before the heat returned to his eyes. Powerful. Enthralling. He devastated her, using his hands and mouth to stroke her into submission. All thought, questions and curiosity included, left her head. Mindless for him, she spread her thighs when he asked, watched him slide down her body and lick his way across her abdomen. Need swirled into an incendiary whirlpool. Bliss rose on a ravenous wave, dragging her under as he kissed the curls atop her mound. She blinked and held her breath. He wasn't going to . . . couldn't be planning on—

Mouth hot, he licked into her folds.

"Henrik!"

Using his shoulders, he pressed her knees wider, sank between her thighs, and laved her again. A delicious stroke right where she wanted him. A delicate flick of his tongue to the bud atop her sex. A hard swirl followed by a gentle suck and—oh aye, that was delicious, unlike anything, better than . . . than—good goddess, Cosmina didn't know. She couldn't breathe, much less string two thoughts together. Could only listen to her body, heed Henrik and feel . . . everything, all he gave, wave after glorious wave of sensation. Deep in the eddy, pleasure slammed through her, making her toes curl. She keened, throbbing hard, tittering on the edge of something magnificent as he settled in, took his time, and bathed her in delight.

"You like that," he growled, finding a rhythm, tongue stroking deeper, "don't you, *iubita*?"

On the cusp of ecstasy, she didn't answer. She allowed herself to feel instead, bowing off the bed, moving with him, begging for release. Relief. Anything. All of him, just as long as he made her come. Right now.

"Henrik, please . . . *please*."

"Hard and fast," he said, stroking her again. "Hard and fast, love."

One hand pressed flat to her abdomen, he lapped at the nubbin atop her sex and slipped one finger inside her. Beautiful withdrawal. Devastating advance. Thrust and retreat. Again and again as he prepared her, stretching her gently. He sent a second finger deep. 'Twas too much, yet not enough. It was incredible, diabolical, the sweetest kind of torture. And as she lost her mind beneath him, he made her work. Made her writhe and fight for each gasp, controlling her so completely she felt nothing but him. Naught but his heat and the shocking pleasure he lavished on her. The advance and retreat, each stroke, every stunning suck and flick, and she undulated, raising her hips, fisting her hands in the sheets, begging without words.

"Scream for me, Cosmina." Watching her from between the spread of her thighs, he nipped her gently. "Now, love. Scream for me."

His deep voice washed over her. Bliss detonated, and she exploded into delight. Ecstasy tore his name from her throat. His grip on her tightened. Muscles flexed as he pushed her knees up and out. With a rough sound, he surged between her thighs, settled deep, set himself to her entrance, and—

Thrust hard to her center.

She screamed again, the pleasure so intense she lost herself all over again. He started to move, his hips driving against her own. Stretched to the limit, overwhelmed, deep in a maelstrom of sensation, rapture spun her around the lip of wonder. Tears rolled from the corners of her eyes. She wrapped her arms around him and held on hard, amazed by the man, ambushed by emotion, matching him stroke for incredible stroke. On the verge. Teetering on the edge of another orgasm, she moaned as passion cracked the hard shell protecting her heart. Awe and need combined, shattering her control, rising hard inside her, allowing reverence and more to bubble between the cracks of her crumbling guard.

Dangerous emotion. Inescapable weakness. Beautiful, catastrophic disaster.

Cosmina didn't care. In that moment, she loved him true. Needed him deep. Wanted him hot and hard against her—inside her—always. A foolish hope. A dreamer's dream, more ridiculous than real. But as he pushed her to new heights, and she listened to him shout her name, felt him tense and throb deep inside her, Cosmina held him close and made a promise to herself, vowing to fight. For him. For her. For a chance at a real future together. Henrik belonged in her arms. She knew it, felt it . . . believed it. So aye, she would fight, defy destiny, and hang on to Henrik for as long as the fates allowed.

CHAPTER NINETEEN

Nestled against Henrik's side with her head on his shoulder, Cosmina slid her hand across his chest. Muscle rippled beneath her palm, and she sighed, letting her pleasure show. Being held was pure heaven. Absolute bliss brought on by the fact Henrik hadn't pushed her away. He wanted her right where she lay—snug in his arms, surrounded by his strength and her rabbit fur throw, skin pressed to warm skin. Oh she'd tried to save face after the first loving. Had made for the edge of the bed, a little unsure, a lot embarrassed by her reaction to him, by how she'd moaned and pleaded for his possession . . .

For the pleasure he'd given her.

But Henrik hadn't let her escape in the aftermath. He'd drawn her close instead, wrapped her in his embrace and held on, coaxing her into relaxation, tempting her to trust him, stealing another piece of her heart. How many that made, Cosmina didn't know. Too many to count or was wise, but—gods—she couldn't help herself. Hadn't said no when he'd made love to her a second time. Nor would she object to a third. Strange. More than a touch disconcerting. Neediness didn't suit her. She didn't moon over men or yearn for connection. Ever.

Independent. Capable. Able to look after herself without *needing* anyone.

Well, at least, under normal circumstances.

Making love with Henrik, though, didn't qualify as ordinary. Hot. Erotic. Fierce. Pleasure-bound exotic. Henrik epitomized each one. Which catapulted him into a category all his own—one named *things she couldn't resist*. She wanted to deny it. Longed to bypass the realization without examining it, but couldn't. So only one thing left to do: admit it. She was in trouble, way past the point of no return, standing in uncharted territory . . . in danger of losing her heart to the hazel-eyed, hard-bodied warrior cradling her as though she were precious to him.

Precious. She huffed. Such a frivolous thought, yet one she wished would come true. The hope made her a first-class fool. Hanging on to him—fighting to spend every moment with him, waking or otherwise, before he left—was one thing. Yearning for something more, however, was quite another. Cosmina knew it like she now knew his body.

Which was to say . . . very, very well.

He'd allowed her exploration during their second loving. Sated by the first round, he'd slowed them down, encouraging her to touch and taste, whispering naughty instructions, giving her free reign before rolling her beneath him again. She'd taken complete advantage, reveled in the power, in her ability to tease and please him as he did her. Now, though, in the body-drain of bone-melting afterglow, with the fire crackling and his chest rising and falling beneath her cheek, all kinds of questions cropped up.

Each one centered on him. His scars, and how he'd come by them, occupied her mind. But more than anything, she wanted to ask about the birthmark on his chest. Stamped over his heart, she understood what the mark represented. Unlike hers, the moonstar hadn't been burned into his skin. He'd been born with it. Solid proof of his relationship to White Temple, and more precisely, to the royal family that ruled the Order of Orm.

Henrik was the son of the former High Priestess. A prince with magic in his blood, one anointed by the Goddess of All Things while in his mother's womb.

An occurrence that had never happened before.

She knew the history. Had studied the tomes inside White Temple's library as part of her training as a member of the Blessed. And yet, as she shifted against him, slipping her thigh over one of his and staring at the flames flickering in the hearth, she struggled to understand . . . to put two and two together and come up with four. Naught added up. No neat columns filled with numbers recorded by the precise strokes of a quill. Everything felt skewed, out of order, as though history had shifted sometime during the last few hours, calling into question all she knew to be true.

A mystery. One at least twenty years old.

Not that the time frame mattered. 'Twas the circumstances—the trail of misinformation—that tweaked her curiosity. Eyes narrowed, she shuffled through all she knew of White Temple, the former High Priestess, and the resulting history. Huh. Interesting. She didn't possess all the facts. Henrik was living proof of that. Particularly since a crypt with his name on it sat inside the holy city's cemetery.

Raising her head, she pressed a kiss to his shoulder. He murmured her name. Her mouth curved as she glanced at his face.

Replete, body relaxed and eyes closed, his thick lashes formed half-moons on his skin, making him seem almost boyish. She knew better. Henrik was all man. He'd spent the better part of the afternoon proving it to her, so . . .

She scanned his face again. Her heart kicked behind her breastbone. Heat pooled in her belly. Muscles deep inside her coiled in abject appreciation. By the gods, he was beautiful, every muscled, masculine inch of him.

"Hey, Henrik?"

Turning his head on the pillow, he cracked his eyes open. Hazel-gold glinting from behind dark lashes, the corners of his mouth tilted up. Holding her gaze, he trailed his fingertips up her arm. As she shivered in pleasure, he brushed over the bandage circling her bicep. "How is your arm, Cosmina? Not too tender?"

"A little sore, but all right," she said, wondering how to ask about his past.

She wanted to know everything about him. Longed to be the one he talked to like she needed her next breath. And yet, fear stilled her tongue even as curiosity urged her to ask. Nerves getting the better of her, she chewed on the inside of her lip, searching for the best way to start the conversation. Should she just plunge in and let the first question fly? Or would he be more receptive to a gentler approach? Cosmina frowned. She didn't know. Couldn't begin to guess, but one thing for certain? His history with the Order hinted at a rough beginning and a painful past.

The empty tomb with his name on it told her that much.

Which meant she should probably leave well enough alone.

Most men didn't tolerate prying. Some became violent. Others attacked without using their fists, maiming with cruel words or, more often than not, harsh silence. She didn't believe

Henrik would do any of those things. Not to her. Not after all that had happened. No doubt a foolish conclusion, but one she held close nonetheless. She wanted to believe she meant something to him. That the way he treated her—with respect, affection, and passionate need—would pave the way to sharing. The true kind in which physical intimacy reached across boundaries, sliding into emotional connection.

A pang tightened her chest.

'Twas probably idiotic. Naught but a silly feminine urge, and yet, she refused to discount it. Or back away. She needed to know him. Wanted every scrap of his trust and interest focused on her, and her alone. True closeness arrived that way, minting memories that would last her a lifetime. Which meant she couldn't turn from the truth. Deduction and common sense combined, telling her something more than just bad had happened to him. Her Seer's eye expanded, calling upon her instincts. Abuse. Abandonment. Agonizing betrayal. He'd suffered all three. Its cruel delivery perpetrated by the one woman who should have protected instead of hurt him . . .

His mother. The former High Priestess of Orm.

Not surprising when she thought about it. Ylenia hadn't been a saint. She'd been closer to the devil, possessing a terrible temper, wielding cruelty the way most women did love: with unconditional aplomb.

Watching her closely, Henrik cupped her cheek. She leaned into his touch. He hummed, caressing her skin before reversing course to tuck an errant strand of hair behind her ear. "What is it, *iubita*?"

She swallowed and reached for courage. Here went nothing. "I was wrong before."

He raised a brow, asking without words.

"Remember when we met and—"

"Collided, you mean?"

She pursed her lips. "Probably more accurate."

Amusement sparked in his eyes. "I have a slice in my favorite trews to prove it."

"You are fortunate you have very fast reflexes," she said, mischief in her tone as she slid her hand across his abdomen. Taut muscles tensed beneath her touch. Without mercy, she cupped him, taking liberties beneath the covers. "If you hadn't been, I might have ruined something other than your trews."

His breath caught as his hips curled, lifting off the mattress. She stroked him again, watched his gaze grow dark with desire, loving the feel of him hardening in her hand.

"Sweet Christ, Cosmina." Breathing hard, he gripped her wrist and tugged, his message clear: talk first, another round of loving after. "What about how we met?"

Excellent question. An even better segue. Especially since it led exactly where she wanted to go . . . toward answers and the truth.

Drawing in a fortifying breath, Cosmina untangled her hand from his and pushed up onto one elbow. The bed creaked beneath her. The soft sound broke through the quiet as she reached out. Her palm touched down on the center of his chest. His heat bled into her fingertips, making need rise and her want more of him. The notion tugged at her, challenging her will, then whispered in her ear, urging her to forget the truth and turn toward desire. Tempting. Oh so much easier too, but she refused to be distracted. He had a secret. She needed to know, so . . . 'twas now or never. Here or not at all. So instead of shying away, she set the course, sealed her fate, and, holding his gaze, drew a gentle circle around his birthmark.

Henrik tensed beneath her hand.

She swallowed hard, but held the line. "I was wrong, Henrik . . . when I said you didn't belong at White Temple . . . *I was wrong*. 'Tis your home as much as mine."

His gaze went flat. The dangerous undercurrent swirled in his eyes a moment before he looked away.

"Please don't," she said.

A muscle twitched along his jaw. "Don't what?"

"Shut me out. I'm sorry if I'm overstepping. I know I've no right to ask, but . . ." Chilled by his shuttered expression, Cosmina suppressed a shiver, fighting to stay calm. Emotion wouldn't impress him. Neither would backing down now that she was neck-deep in it. He valued strength. She needed to show him some. Mayhap if she did, he would open up and let her in. Mayhap talk would lead to trust. And mayhap, just mayhap, if she got very lucky . . . he'd put the past to bed, accept the solace she offered, and gift her with the truth. "We share history. You understand my world, were a part of my home and—gods, Henrik—I remember the funeral . . . *your funeral*. The small white casket, the procession from High Temple, the burial at the stone crypt and . . . all the crying. It's one of my earliest memories."

"Christ . . . *crying*." Baring his teeth, he sat up so fast Cosmina flinched.

The covers went flying. With a quick pivot, Henrik swung his legs over the side of the bed. Afraid he intended to leave, she rolled onto her knees behind him, reached out, then stopped mid-motion. She hovered a moment, her palm a hair's breadth from him, eyes riveted to the terrible scars marring his skin, indecision rising. What should she do? Touch him or respect the stay-away message he threw off like heat and leave him alone?

'Twas a toss-up. In every way that counted.

No one worth their salt provoked Henrik. Cosmina knew it. She'd seen him in action. Had witnessed his skills in battle firsthand. Yet, for all his strength—and ability to inflict damage and dole out death—he didn't frighten her. He made her feel safe instead. Protected. Accepted. Valued and, aye, cherished too. An odd combination, one that bridged the distance, pushing her toward him instead of away.

Her hand settled against his back. His muscles flexed as her fingertips slid, tracing the patterns that had been cut into his skin. "Henrik, you've naught to fear from me. I understand loss. I feel your pain. Please talk to me."

Planting his elbows on his bent knees, he stared at the floor between his feet. After a moment, he shook his head and, eyes haunted by unwanted memories, glanced over his shoulder at her. "The crying. It's so much bullshit, Cosmina. No one mourned for me. No one cared."

"Not true. I mourned you. Many of the others too."

All the Blessed had grieved the loss. Except, perhaps, the one woman who should have: his mother.

With a growled curse, he dragged his gaze from hers and faced the hearthstone once more. Flames hissed between the logs. The mobile swayed above her head, wooden pegs clicking together in the quiet, and Cosmina held her breath, waiting for him to shrug off her touch, stand up, and stride for the door. An awful twinge streaked across her chest. It felt like empathy and presented itself as pain, tightening her throat with the threat of tears.

Poor Henrik. Blast and damn the Goddess of All Things.

She'd placed the sacred mark upon Henrik's chest, then abandoned him to a woman without a maternal bone in her body. 'Twas the worst sort of betrayal. One Cosmina didn't understand. The goddess had been naught but generous with her—providing protection, seeing her through the tough times, visiting her in dreams to bring her comfort—so why not do the same for Henrik? A man branded with the symbol of the Order of Orm. It didn't make sense, but even as she acknowledged the dichotomy in the deity's actions, Cosmina knew there must be a good reason. The goddess was nothing if not precise. All things happened for a reason. The maxim was the Blessed's motto, one she accepted wholeheartedly. And yet as she bore witness to Henrik's pain, Cosmina wondered . . .

Was she was capable of believing it anymore?

His suffering brought the question home. It all seemed so unfair. The goddess had protected her, yet abandoned him. *All things happen for a reason.* The words throbbed inside her head, making certainty rise along with something else . . . the need to soothe him. Mayhap their meeting inside High Temple had been fated. Mayhap the goddess had put her in his path to atone—to make right a wrong by sending her to help him heal the wounds of the past. Mayhap she was the only one he would allow to make a difference in his life. Stranger things happened every day, so instead of pushing for answers, Cosmina stayed still and let silence speak. Rushing him wouldn't work. Nor would pushing him toward resolution. She waited instead, heart in hand, hope rising like a specter inside her.

He cleared his throat. "How old were you?"

"At the funeral?"

He nodded.

"Not very." She frowned, thinking back, searching for details as she shuffled closer and settled at his side. Unable to help herself, her hand roamed over his shoulder. The caress made him sigh. Tense muscle relaxed behind her questing fingertips, and

Cosmina exhaled long and slow. Gods, she loved that about him. He never shied away, always welcomed her touch, allowing her close, trusting her to be gentle with him. Gaze glued to his profile, she cupped his nape, then slid up to play in the soft strands of his hair. "Almost four, I think."

"So young."

"You were too."

"I was seven," he said, tone low and tight. A muscle twitched along his jaw as he shook his head. "When she . . ."

He trailed off. She picked up the thread, guessing at the rest. "She abandoned you, didn't she? Gave you away, faked your death to save face and—"

"Thrust me into hell. Paid Al Pacii to take me off her hands."

Shock made her flinch. The Order of Assassins . . . now the Druinguari. "So the creatures in the temple?"

"Former comrades. Their master . . . my old sensei," he said, flexing his hands. "I defected from the Order along with six others months ago."

"And now you hunt them." It made perfect sense. Held the kind of symmetry Henrik no doubt enjoyed . . . the hunters becoming the hunted. "'Tis the reason you were at White Temple . . . tracking them."

"Aye."

"Did he do this to you?" Leaning forward, she set her mouth to the back of his shoulder. He winced. She kissed him again, and then again, following the raised lines across his skin. "He is responsible for your scars?"

Henrik nodded. "'Tis the crest of Al Pacii."

"The bastard," she said, her outrage catastrophic. "An animal in need of killing."

"Now more than ever." He turned to look at her, the tiniest spark of amusement in his eyes. As quick as his humor arrived, however, it faded. Shifting on the mattress, Henrik half turned, bumping her with his bent knee. As he settled sideways in front of her, he raised his hand and cupped the side of her throat. "She never wanted me, Cosmina. I was an abomination in her eyes . . . a boy in a place where males held no value. She loathed me from the moment I was born."

"Ylenia was a fool. A cruel witch without conscience or merit," she whispered. "I should know. She hurt me too."

His brows collided. "How?"

"She murdered my mother to gain control of me."

"Jesus."

"I know." With a shrug, she gestured to her small cottage. "As you can see, it didn't end well."

"What happened?"

"I saw my mother's death before it happened, but the vision was jumbled, broken into so many pieces, I couldn't . . . I didn't understand." Sad, but true. The story of her life. Always too little, too late. "By the time I figured out what it meant, 'twas over. My mother lay dead and I was locked inside the north tower."

"She coveted your gift."

"Aye."

"So you escaped and found your way here?"

She shook her head. "I wish I had thought of that, but . . . nay. White Temple was my home. It was the only thing I knew, so I did the only thing I could. I rebelled and shut her out, refusing to share my visions. She meted out punishments, kept me locked in that god-awful room, forbidding me friends and visitors. What she didn't know, however, is that I am a very good climber."

Henrik raised a brow, asking without words.

"I left the tower room every day, climbing down from the window. Sometimes I would visit the Limwoods. Other times I would meet Simon outside the city walls."

"The boy you thought you loved."

"And made the mistake of bedding."

"There are worse mistakes, Cosmina."

"Not many. It got me banished from White Temple."

Surprised winged across his face. "She threw you out?"

"With naught but the clothes on my back." Henrik's grip tightened on her as he drew a quick breath. Registering his disbelief, she shrugged, knowing her eviction from the Order had been her fault. Pure and simple. Close the book, no need to look further. Had she told Ylenia the truth instead of lying, insisting the loss of her maidenhead equaled the end of her gift, she wouldn't have been thrown out. She'd have remained locked behind a closed door instead. "In the dead of winter."

"Goddamned witch." Rage gathered in Henrik's eyes. A muscle twitched along his jaw an instant before his expression smoothed out. "I am sorry, Cosmina."

She blinked. "Why? 'Tisn't your fault."

"Her blood runs in my veins." Leaning away, his hand slid against her neck, then left her completely. "I am part of her and—"

"Don't." Eyes narrowed, she leveled her finger at him. "Don't you dare compare yourself to her."

He went stone-still, stalling mid-retreat to stare at her.

And she saw it all. His hope. His doubt. All the confusion along with his need to believe he could be something other than what blood and destiny dictated. Empathy stole through her. Outrage shoved it aside. She wouldn't allow it. Not the comparison. Nor the hint of self-loathing she sensed in him.

"You are nothing like her," she said, sounding fierce, feeling protective. Such a strange inclination. Henrik didn't need her protection. He was warrior strong, a man born and bred for battle. And yet, as she held his gaze, her desire to shield him overcame her. 'Twas undeniable. Inescapable too. He needed someone on his side, and—even knowing it was unwise, naught but a temporary thing—Cosmina wanted to reassure him. "Blood is never thicker than intention. You share a lineage with her—so what? The heart and mind determine your path in life, not the blood in your veins. You are who you choose to be, Henrik. She has naught to do with that."

"Christ, Cosmina," he said, something akin to awe in his eyes. Reaching for her, he pulled her into his lap. She settled astride him and nestled in—breasts to chest, the inside of her thighs pressed to the outside of his, his heat snug against hers. Enthralled by the feel of him, loving his strength, she hummed as he wound her hair around his fist. A gentle tug tipped her head back. A rough nip on the underside of her chin set her ablaze, making her body throb. "You say the damnedest things."

"All part of my charm."

He grinned against the side of her throat.

Both hands in his hair, she kissed him softly. "Henrik?"

"Uh-huh?"

"Again please."

Powerful arms flexing around her, Henrik reversed their positions. Her back touched down on the mattress. He flicked over her pulse point, wetting her skin with his tongue, hips settling between her thighs. "With pleasure, *iubita* . . . with a great deal of pleasure."

Gods, she hoped so.

Now that the talking was done and the truth told, she wanted the pleasure. Lots of it. All he could give her and more than she could handle. 'Twas only fair. He belonged to her now, but not for long. So forget tomorrow. Never mind the worry. Ignore the impending doom. She needed to stay rooted in the present. In the here and now. With him. Far away from thoughts of heartbreak and the threat of loss. The future would look after itself. It always did . . . without any help from her.

* * *

Crouched in front of the hearth, Henrik laid another log on the fire. Not that the conflagration needed it. Already ablaze, flames licked upward, throwing heat into the room. 'Twas busywork more than anything else. A way to distract himself, something to keep him occupied while Cosmina dressed. Looking at her wasn't a good idea. Every time he did, need reared its ugly head, making him want her again. Ravenous gluttony. Unquenchable thirst. Wicked, delicious desire. He couldn't get enough . . . of her lithe curves, of her soft skin, of the slick heat between her thighs and his mouth on hers.

Christ, her taste . . .

The goddamned taste of her.

A tremor rippled through him. Muscles tightened across his abdomen, pulling at his hip bones, awakening the traitor inside his trews. Henrik sighed and, staring at the flames, shook his head. Stupid prick. He needed to get a handle on it . . . and his reaction to her. 'Twas becoming embarrassing. He was a grown man, for the love of God, not some green lad. Yet everything she did aroused him. His fixation was absurd. A real eye-opener considering he'd never experienced it before. Women didn't hold his interest for long. Sure, any number caught his eye, and he enjoyed each one's company while it lasted. But he never stayed. He gave the pleasure expected of him, took some in return, and then got the hell out.

Every single time.

Cosmina didn't fall into that category. She wasn't the usual— a fast lay followed by a quick getaway. Why? Henrik didn't have a clue. All he knew was that he wanted her more with every breath he took. Disconcerting to say the least. Dangerous to say the most. Particularly since duty and honor dictated that he let her go.

She deserved better than him. He kept hammering that truth home, repeating it over and over, telling himself she was his for now, but not forever. But even as decency urged him to do the right thing—push to his feet, turn, gather the others waiting outside, and leave—his senses remained riveted to her. Each rustle of clothing. Every move she made. Her sighs of contentment behind him. He cataloged it all from his position in front of the fire. Without looking, he knew she drew on her trews, dragging the leather up her beautiful thighs, over her gorgeous bottom and . . . ah, there it was. The rasp and tug of lacing against the sweet stretch of skin below her navel.

Henrik swallowed a groan.

Goddamn, he loved that spot. She was so sensitive there, always raised her hips, spread her legs, undulated against him while he kissed his way—

"Henrik?"

Low and husky, her voice stroked over him. A tingle raced along his spine, raising goose bumps on his skin, sending pleasure spinning through him. Bracing for impact, he glanced over his shoulder. Jewel-green eyes met his. His heart kicked, stealing his breath as his gaze clung to hers. Shirtsleeves bunched along each arm, a smile playing at the corners of her mouth, she drew the collar over her head. He clenched his teeth, mouthwatering as he watched her pretty pink nipples disappear behind the linen.

Exhaling in a rush, he pushed to his feet. "Aye?"

"Do you swim?"

"Like a fish."

"There is a hot spring not far from here," she said, tucking her shirttail into her trews. Which—goddamn it to hell and back—made him want to close the distance between them and rip it back out again. "Will you come swimming with me?"

Unable to find his voice, he nodded.

"Good." Mischief sparked in her eyes. "I'm looking forward to washing your back."

Jesus help him, Lord knew he couldn't help himself. "Turnabout is fair play, Cosmina."

Grabbing the satchel hanging from the bedpost, she grinned at him. "I'm counting on it."

Infected by her playfulness, he shook his head. "Insatiable."

"I have to be," she said, bypassing the table in the middle of the room. Boots scraping over the dirt floor, she stopped in front of a tall armoire. With a tug, she opened a door that had seen better days. Old, rickety, way past its prime, the cabinet listed to one side, its frame bent by weather and time. His gaze drifted over sagging wooden shelves. Not much to speak of piled atop each: a couple of linen towels, three or four bars of soap, an extra pair of trews neatly folded beside a stack of shirts. Reaching up, she snagged two drying clothes off the top shelf. After stuffing the stash into her satchel, she glanced over her shoulder at him. "I only have you so long. I need to make the most of it."

So long. Translation . . . limited time, not long enough.

The reminder should've backed him up a step. Made him retreat and seek distance. Thankfulness rose to infect him instead. God, she was incredible. A woman of rare fortitude and unequaled glory. Her beauty surpassed the physical. It went soul deep, shaming him with the knowledge that his carried the stink of death. Was stained, blackened by his crimes, all those he'd killed, maimed, and hurt over the years. Yet, she wanted him anyway—despite the circumstances, regardless of reality. Even knowing he couldn't stay hadn't deterred her. She wasn't angry. Didn't expect anything she did or said to change his mind. Wouldn't be bitter in the aftermath either. He could see it in her eyes when she looked at him. Cosmina accepted him for who and what he was . . . an assassin on a mission that didn't include her.

'Twas a magnificent gift. One he longed to return.

In another life, he would've plunged in without hesitation. Taken what he wanted and committed to Cosmina, heart and soul. But he wasn't that man. He was a killer—ruined, disgraced, unfit for love, and unworthy of her. That he wanted something long lasting with her didn't matter. Shouldn't matter. He knew it with a clarity that startled him. Holding on to her would be a mistake rooted in the worst kind of selfishness. And yet, temptation rolled, urging him to set aside his scruples, close his fist around what fate handed him like a greedy two-year-old, and hang on tight.

Henrik shook his head even as his chest went tight. He refused to let it happen. Or allow himself such leeway. No matter how painful—or how much his heart yearned for her—he'd collect the moments, soak up every minute he spent with her, then do the honorable thing and let her go.

"Uh-oh."

A death grip on the need to claim her, he cleared his throat. "What?"

"You've that look about you."

"Which one is that?"

"The remorse-filled one, but . . ." Stuffing a bar of soap inside, she flipped the satchel closed. Rusty hinges creaked as she swung the lopsided door shut. Soft, yet startling in the silence, the gentle bang made him flinch. Facing him now, she leveled him with a no-nonsense look. "We agreed, Henrik. No regrets, remember?"

"I remember," he said, regrets already circling . . . the kind that whispered: *take a chance, stay for once, tell her how you feel*.

"All right, then," she said, tone quiet yet somehow all business. Slinging the strap over her shoulder, she stepped around the edge of the table and stopped in front of him. Unable to stop himself, his hands found her waist. Her mouth curved a second before she popped onto her tiptoes and kissed him. "Let's go."

"Cosmina . . ." he murmured, drawing her closer, his mouth brushing hers. "You are the most extraordinary person I've ever met."

Pleasure lit in her eyes. She kissed him again, teasing him with her taste. "I'm an even better swimmer, so . . . bring it on. Let's see what you've got."

His lips twitched. "Way too confident, *iubita*."

"You won't think so when I drown you."

He laughed, the unexpected threat lightening his mood.

Eyes sparkling with mischief, she grabbed his hand and, with a solid tug, drew him toward the door. He went without a fight, allowing her to lead, enjoying the easy banter and the promise of a playful swim. It wouldn't last long. The moment she shed her clothes, it would be over. He wouldn't be able to resist her. Would want to be deep inside her again while warm water swirled around him, and she moaned his name.

Over and over. Again and again.

Anticipation picked him up, making his heart thump and his muscles twitch. Not surprising. She had a way about her. Everything she did cranked him tight—her laugh, her imprudence, the way she challenged and amused him. The thing he liked the best, though, was her acceptance. Without even trying, Cosmina made him feel valued, needed, and best of all, wanted. A potent combination when it came to an impertinent redhead with a mind of her own and the skill set to back it up.

"I want you again."

Glancing over her shoulder, she unlatched the door and raised a brow. "And you call me insatiable?"

"Can't be helped," he said as she pulled the door wide. Winter air rolled in on a cold tide, helping to cool his ardor. "You're irresistible."

She huffed. "Smooth talker."

"Beautiful temptress." Turning his hand, Henrik laced their fingers together.

She drew a quick breath. Her expression shifted, moving from playful to . . . Henrik frowned. He didn't know exactly. She'd gone from teasing to serious in a heartbeat. And as she stared at him, he read the subtle tension in her frame, felt the air thicken, and something weighty settle between them. He opened his mouth to ask. She shook her head, lightheartedness returning, the strain in her eyes fading so fast Henrik wondered whether he'd imagined it . . . and what it meant. Not giving him a moment to reflect, Cosmina squeezed his hand, pulled him over the threshold and into the open air. Dusk descended, frosting the treetops with silver strokes. Faint, but growing brighter by the moment, stars dotted a cloudless sky as the moon awoke and—

Cosmina stopped short in front of him.

As he bumped into her, her tension registered. Henrik reacted. Shoving her behind him, he palmed one of his daggers and, scanning the clearing in front of the cottage, pulled the blade free.

"No need, H." The deep voice slithered through his mind. Magic flared, throbbing between his temples as static washed in, then out, and the connection strengthened. *"'Tis just me."*

Knifepoint raised, Henrik's focus snapped left. His eyes narrowed. *"Christ, Tareek."*

"Hello to you too." Arms crossed, one shoulder propped against the cottage cornerstone, Tareek raised a brow, a look of censure in his eyes. *"Nice of you to finally come up for air."*

"Don't."

"What?"

"Disrespect her."

Tareek snorted. *"'Tis no failing of hers, fratele. 'Tis you I'm admonishing. You've been in there for nearly two days."*

Henrik frowned. *Two days.* Really? The time span seemed a stretch but, well . . . hell, 'twas possible. The cottage was well supplied—lots of food, an ample water supply, two long stacks of wood against the long wall—and honestly, he'd been so wrapped up in Cosmina, the sky could've fallen and he might not have noticed. *"Jesus."*

Tareek's mouth curved. *"Lost track of time, did you?"*

"I'm not apologizing."

"Did I ask you to?"

Nay. But then, Tareek never did. He accepted his faults instead, supporting him unconditionally, backing him up, hammering some sense into him when necessary. An excellent friend in every way, even if it meant enduring the occasional scolding.

This time, though, Henrik was hard-pressed to feel bad about leaving his friend out in the cold. *"She needed me."*

Amusement sparked in his friend's eyes. *"I'm sure."*

Henrik sighed.

Cosmina nudged him from behind. "Henrik, is everything all right?"

He wanted to say no. Not far from the truth considering Tareek was a meddlesome prick. Henrik glanced over his shoulder instead. His chest went tight as he met her gaze. Worry swam in its depths, the kind he didn't like and wanted to shield her from. An absurd reaction considering he wouldn't be around much longer. But the compulsion refused to leave him alone. So forget denial. For as long as he was around, he would protect her. From worry. From fear. From idiot dragon-shifters who enjoyed teasing and never let anything go.

"All good, Cosmina." Sheathing his blade, he tugged her out from behind him. "'Tis just Tareek."

"Just?" Tareek scoffed, the sound of derision echoing through mind-speak. Slapping a hand over his heart, his friend went the dramatic route. *"You wound me."*

"Not yet." Flexing his fists, Henrik glared at his friend. *"But it's coming to that."*

Grinning like an idiot, Tareek pushed away from his perch. Boots rasping over the frozen turf, he focused on Cosmina and tipped his chin. "My lady."

"Nay, please . . . call me Cosmina," she said, shifting closer to Henrik as Tareek approached. Eying his friend, she tilted her head. The soft strands of her hair brushed against Henrik's upper arm. Goose bumps rose on his skin as something unexpected moved behind her eyes. Henrik tensed, recognizing her expression. 'Twas a look he'd seen before, one that heralded insight and spoke of premonition. She blinked, thick lashes flickering before her focus sharpened on Tareek once more. "You're the dragon."

Tareek's mouth curved. "Guilty as charged."

"Well then, thank you," she said, tone soft, words sure.

"For what?" his friend asked.

She glanced at Henrik, then back at Tareek. "For getting us out of the cemetery alive."

The gratitude threw Tareek. Henrik could see it in his eyes, which—God help him—was fun to watch. Not much surprised his friend, never mind made him squirm. But as Cosmina held Tareek's gaze, pulling information about him out of the ether, the dragon-shifter flinched, unease rising like a cloud around him.

"*Hristos, H,*" Tareek said, switching to mind-speak. As though unable to handle her intensity, he rolled his shoulders and broke eye contact, dragging his gaze from Cosmina. Expression shuttered, he drilled Henrik with a look. "*She's powerful.*"

"*I know.*"

Brows furrowed, Tareek cleared his throat. "Henrik, a word?"

Quick to comprehend, Cosmina took the cue. Adjusting the satchel on her shoulder, she bumped his shoulder, and stepping around him, pointed to a trail across the clearing. "Meet you at the hot spring?"

He nodded. "Meet you there."

With a good-bye to Tareek, she skirted him and started across the clearing. Tree limbs creaked as silence swelled in her wake. She didn't look back. Didn't slow one iota in the hopes of eaves-dropping either. Pace steady, she hopped over a fallen log halfway across the dell. Her feet landed with a crunch. The satchel flapped against her back. The soft slap echoed, drifting through the quiet as she stepped onto the trailhead. The second she disappeared from view, Henrik scanned the open space, picking up details he'd neglected earlier. Embers aglow in the round pit in the center of the clearing, fire banked beneath a roasting spit. Bedrolls piled to the right of the fire pit. Horses tethered and half-asleep in a small pen to the right of the cottage.

No one in sight. No movement anywhere near the dell.

His attention drifted back to Tareek. "Where are the others?"

"Hunting. We've no wish to deplete Cosmina's winter stores."

Good plan. Particularly since he couldn't stand the thought of Cosmina suffering. He wanted her hale and whole, with enough to eat after he left, not hungry in the dead of winter. "And Thea?"

"So besotted with Kazim, she's allowed us free reign." Henrik snorted in amusement. Tareek's lips twitched. "The Persian is handy to have around. I've no wish to be held prisoner by the Limwoods again."

The tidbit tweaked his curiosity. Henrik raised a brow. "Again?"

"Long story. Not important." With a shrug, Tareek waved a hand in dismissal, then frowned, and glanced toward the trailhead. "'Tis a dangerous game you are playing, *fratele*."

No question. Without a doubt. "I know what I am doing."

"Be sure, Henrik. The Blessed is not your usual fare. You like her . . ."

Henrik snorted. Right. *Like.* 'Twas too mild a word for what he felt for Cosmina. Obsessive. Possessive. Consumed. Neck-deep in trouble without the necessary tools to pull himself free. Pick one. Apply them all. No matter how hard he fought, the truth couldn't be denied. He craved her to the point of witlessness.

"She has her claws in you. You enjoy her company too much." Tareek palmed his shoulder and squeezed. The gentle pump put him on edge. He didn't want to talk about it, but resistance always proved futile when Tareek latched on. His friend loved him. Wanted to protect him and, like it or nay, Henrik returned the sentiment. So forget telling Tareek to shut his mouth and mind his own business. It wouldn't happen. "'Twill be hard for you to leave her when 'tis time to go."

"Not even a little," he said, lying through his teeth.

His friend treated him to a sharp look. "Cosmina knows she cannot come with us, aye?"

"She knows."

"Good." Nodding in approval, Tareek shifted gears, changing the subject. "Any progress with the Goddess of All Things?"

Henrik shook his head. "She is not answering my summons."

"Huh." Tareek pursed his lips. A thoughtful look in his eyes, he glanced across the clearing. His gaze narrowed on the trail to the hot spring. "Mayhap you've no need of the goddess."

His thoughtful tone got Henrik's attention. Tareek was always full of ways to get around a problem. "Lay it out."

"Who told you the bastards are called the Druinguari?"

"Cosmina, after the attack in High Temple."

"So . . ."

"Shit," he muttered, following his friend's train of thought. "You think Cosmina knows how to kill them."

"Stands to reason. She is an oracle, H . . . a Seer of unprecedented power."

"She would have told me, Tareek. Cosmina isn't the sort to hold back. She knows I need that information. She wouldn't . . ." He trailed off as an idea sparked to life. Tareek raised a brow. Henrik exhaled in a rush, the epiphany hitting him like a lightning bolt. "Unless she has no idea that she knows."

"Exactly."

Made sense. On so many levels.

He understood Cosmina's struggle. Her frustration too. She didn't receive all the information at once. That, however, didn't mean she didn't possess all the pieces. It simply meant she couldn't fit enough of them together at any one time, which made it difficult for her to interpret the whole.

And that left him with no out . . . and only one option. "Goddamn it."

"You were given the gift of Thrall for a reason, Henrik. 'Tis time to put your talent to good use." Tareek slapped his shoulder, his palm cracked against his leather tunic, shredding the quiet, echoing across the clearing. "Read her mind, my friend. Control the mental scope to find the truth, and we will—"

"Discover the bastards' weakness," he said, finishing his friend's sentence while hating the implications.

The last thing he wanted to do was to use Thrall and invade Cosmina's mind. 'Twas the worse sort of betrayal, a terrible breach of trust. But as he shrugged off Tareek's hold, Henrik knew his friend was right. He couldn't obtain the information he needed any other way. The goddess refused to answer. Cosmina didn't know that she knew, so . . . no way around, through, or over it. He must face reality head-on and come to terms with necessity.

No matter how much he disliked it.

His comrades were counting on him. Life or death. Love and loyalty. His mission's success or failure depended on his ability to discover the enemy's weakness. Which left him nowhere to hide and even less room to run. It needed to be done, and he must be the one to do it. But as Tareek left his side and retreated to the middle of the dell, Henrik's sense of fair play squawked. Goddamn the goddess and her selfish ways. Her neglect had brought him here . . . to the point of no return, a place that made his heart ache and his soul burn. And yet he stood still and silent, without a counterargument as he watched Tareek shift into dragon form and take to the sky—wings spread wide, red scales flashing in the gloom, snowflakes awhirl in his wake.

Christ, what a choice. What a terrible, indefensible choice.

Betray the woman he cared about or watch his brothers-in-arms die at the hands of Halál and the Druinguari. The magnitude of it weighed on him, but that didn't stop him. He turned toward the trailhead instead and, conscience in tatters, walked across the clearing, toward the hot spring and Cosmina, his heart growing heavier with every step he took.

CHAPTER TWENTY

Twilight descended like a prayer, quiet and sure of itself as Cosmina watched clear skies give way to wispy clouds and the coming night. The magic hour. Not yet dark, still enough light to see by—a place in time where enchantment lived and anything was possible. Chest deep in the hot spring, warm water lapping at her shoulders, she hummed. Such a fanciful thought. Laughable in many ways, but accurate nonetheless. She'd always felt the most grounded at dusk. 'Twas as though the world opened up, revealing the chasm between light and dark, where contrasts ruled and contradictions blended, becoming compatible for a time.

Just like her and Henrik.

Tipping her head back, Cosmina dipped her hair beneath the surface, wetting the thick strands, her gaze on the smooth stones surrounding the small pool. Body calm, her mind drifted, but remained tethered to one thing. Or rather, one man. Henrik. He was like twilight, a study in contradictions—dark and dangerous one moment, gentle and caring the next. It would've confused her had she not understood him so well. She knew what drove him. Had spent enough time with him talking and touching—loving him while trying not to lose her heart—to know his mission was important . . . and in no way included her.

She'd picked that tidbit up from Tareek. Easy enough to do. Derision had been written all over the dragon-warrior's face. He disapproved of her liaison with Henrik. A wise man with the proper sentiment, no doubt. Too bad she didn't care. She wanted Henrik too much to do the smart thing. Cosmina sighed. The right thing . . . the best thing . . . the safest thing. She knew what each of those entailed: her walking away from Henrik . . . this instant. But even as intellect set out the path and realization dawned, she refused to heed it. She possessed limited time with him. Not nearly enough to suit her, so . . .

Forget Tareek.

For once, she would take what she wanted . . . even if it hurt her in the end.

Closing her eyes, Cosmina lay back and, with a sigh, allowed herself to float. The gentle ebb and flow rocked her, pulling residual tension from her muscles as tendrils of steam curled from the surface of the hot spring. Night sounds murmured, the familiar creak of tree limbs beyond the rocks drifted on the winter wind, breaking through the stillness, holding an owl's call high. Each noise brought her comfort, but 'twas the whisper of footfalls by the pool's edge that made her smile.

Hmm . . . 'twas about time. Tareek had finally let him go.

With a throb of anticipation, Cosmina lifted her head and, treading water in the middle of the pond, turned full circle. Hazel-gold eyes riveted to her, Henrik stood beyond the stone lip ringing the shoreline. Without looking away, he unlaced his tunic and tugged it over his head. Her breath caught as he bared his chest. Goddess, he was beautiful. So strong and able.

So gloriously made sometimes she wondered whether he was real. Another fanciful thought. One that vanished the instant he tossed one boot, then the other, over his shoulder, and started on his trews. Arousal rolled through her as she watched him strip. Despite the heat and need, her lips twitched.

Goodness, he was shameless. Without a modicum of modesty. Not an ounce of decency in sight. But, try as she might, Cosmina couldn't stifle her hum of appreciation. The purr rolled from her throat, then across the water, welcoming him with unequaled measure. Henrik growled in reaction, and laces undone, played the tease, hooking his thumbs in his waistband, making her wait, driving her mad. Feasting on the sight of him, she licked her bottom lip and swallowed, reliving his taste, wanting his mouth on hers, so ready for him it embarrassed her.

Not that it mattered.

Shame had no place between them. Her need for him came with the territory. Was part and parcel of her surrender to him. Something she'd done willingly, without an ounce of hesitation or remorse. But as he drew the leather down his thighs, stepped over the rocks, and into the water, a pang expanded inside her chest. As it squeezed around her heart, Cosmina battled the awful rise of emotion. Despite her intentions and best-laid plans, she knew it would get messy. Letting him go. Saying good-bye. Allowing him to walk away—without begging him to stay— was going to be so damned difficult. Almost impossible now that she'd opened her heart and pulled him in, permitting true intimacy.

A mistake of terrible magnitude.

What she and Henrik shared went beyond the pleasure. She felt it, believed it . . . accepted it without question. It was about closeness and acceptance, and, aye . . . love. At least for her. Her affinity for him surpassed the physical, spreading into areas she should have guarded much more closely. Which meant she'd lied. To him as well as herself.

No regrets, indeed.

Such a stupid statement. A miscalculation that would bring her naught but pain in the end. Henrik hadn't lied to her. Or hidden his intentions. He was a man bred for war, one who didn't mince words. He would leave, just as he said he would. No use disputing the truth, never mind trying to change it. So only one thing left to do . . . come to terms with the fact she must let him go and that he would take her heart with him when he went.

A splash echoed, bouncing off the high rocks behind her as Henrik dove in.

Water rippled, rolling into her chest, dragging her focus back to the present and away from the future. Searching beneath the surface, Cosmina bobbed in the gentle eddy, kicking her feet, arms undulating beneath warm water—desperate for him to reach her. She huffed. It figured. Her reaction to him bordered on insanity. She was beyond need. Far too enamored with him. Foolish in every way. She ought to be retreating. Setting up emotional roadblocks with an eye to self-preservation. Instead she waited for him, torment and anticipation cascading into a sordid tangle that simply made her want him more.

Henrik surfaced behind her.

Setting his mouth to the top of her shoulder, he wrapped his arms around her and tugged her into him. Her shoulder blades bumped his chest. Hard muscle flexed around her. Sighing his name, loving the feel of him, she tipped her head back. He accepted her weight, holding her close, supporting her in the water, making her heart pang as she yearned for something more.

Something pure and unmeasured. Something driven by love instead of passion alone. But *more* wasn't part of the agreement.

She'd seen to that when she'd settled for far, *far* less.

Fighting the tight knot of emotion, Cosmina swiped her expression clean and turned in his embrace. Water swirled, moving around and between them. She murmured in need. He understood the plea and, dipping his head, brushed his mouth against hers. Unable to resist, she opened wide, inviting him in, and buried her hands into his hair. The wet strands clung to her fingertips, pushed between, enthralling her as he deepened the kiss and she got her first taste. So good. Decadent. Indecent. Beyond the pale of proper behavior. Not that Cosmina cared. She licked into his mouth instead, refusing to heed reason. Henrik was here. She wanted him as much and as many times as he allowed it.

End of story. To hell with the consequences.

Caressing her beneath the water, Henrik tangled his tongue with hers. Desire flared higher, licking beneath her skin. Cosmina moaned in delight, asking for more, forgetting restraint and the looming devastation in her future. Naught mattered but him— his taste, his scent, the feel of his hands on her body. Right. Wrong. Neither factored in anymore. In that moment, he became the center of her universe, the sun, the moon, all the stars, and . . .

Gods, it wasn't fair.

He tasted so good and felt even better, as though he belonged in her arms, and she, in his. *Meant to be.* The phrase tickled her senses and played with her mind. All an illusion, she knew. A ruse designed with one purpose in mind—to break her heart. But blast and damn, it seemed real, felt right, making her believe even as her more practical side scoffed. Henrik wasn't hers. She wasn't meant to be his. A quirk of fate had brought them here.

Naught more. Nothing less.

"Cosmina. Sweet love, I need—"

"Me too." Holding him close, she kissed him again.

"Nay, *iubita*, don't. I have to . . ." His denial lit the fuse on defiance. Baring her teeth, Cosmina nipped his bottom lip. He groaned against her mouth. "Goddamn it, Cosmina. I need to explain something. You're not . . . oh God. You taste good. I cannot get enough of you."

"Feeling's mutual." An understatement of epic proportions. 'Twas so much more than that. The attraction was delicious, heated, practically flammable. "Can we make love in the water?"

"Aye, but—"

"But nothing." One hand flat against the nape of his neck, she sent the other exploring. Over his wide shoulders. Down his gorgeous chest. Across the taut muscles roping his abdomen. A little lower, and she curled her hand around him. He sucked in a quick breath. Cosmina smiled and, showing no mercy, stroked him from root to tip. "So hard, Henrik. Smooth as silk and hot in hand. You're ready to please me."

"I can't. Not yet. Not until I—oh Jesus." Breathing hard, he rolled his hips into her next stroke, but shook his head. She caressed him again. He cursed between clenched teeth. "Mercy, love. Mercy."

"Nay." Pressing her advantage, she licked over his bottom lip. "I want you, Henrik . . . right now."

"After, Cosmina," he said. "If you still want me after, then I'll give you whatever you want, however you want it. Gladly. Without hesitation, but . . ."

The edge in his voice slowed her down. Her hand stilled its intimate play. Retreating a little, she met his gaze. "After what?"

Brows drawn tight, he drew a deep breath.

"Henrik?" Seeing the regret in his eyes, alarm streaked through her.

Oh dear. Not good. She didn't like that look.

Remorse lived in his expression, the kind she didn't want to see, never mind have directed at her. Something was wrong . . . terribly *wrong*. Treading water with him, she held him close, caressed the tops of his shoulders, hoping to alleviate his tension. It didn't help. Her touch cranked him tighter instead, and as his arms flexed around her, she hooked onto his emotional turmoil. Worry. Remorse. Guilt. All took a turn in his expression and—gods. He was uncertain about something. Completely conflicted. Uncomfortable in his own skin. Not like the Henrik she'd come to know at all.

Desperate to soothe him, Cosmina raised her hand and cupped his cheek. Whiskers scraped her palm, teased the pads of her fingertips as he bowed his head and pressed his face to the side of her throat. His torment tugged at her heartstrings. "What is wrong?"

"Naught."

"You're a terrible liar."

One corner of his mouth tipped up. "I am an excellent liar."

"Probably," she said against his temple. "But not with me, so . . . out with it. Tell me what is troubling you. You know I will needle you until you do."

Her teasing tone was meant to make him laugh. A tremor rolled through him instead.

"Cosmina." He whispered her name like a benediction, with yearning, as though asking for forgiveness for something he hadn't yet done. Raising his head, he met her gaze. Gentle and sure, he brushed wet tendrils of hair away from her face. "Do you trust me?"

She hesitated a heartbeat. 'Twas a loaded question. One she'd hoped to leave unexplored. But as she held his gaze, Cosmina faltered. She should say no . . . no way. No chance in hell. Trust was a big step, but going all in and admitting it? Cosmina knew that might prove fatal. Men talked of trust all the time, but rarely, if ever, proved worthy of it. And yet, as the silence expanded and Henrik waited for her to answer, the truth struck home and . . .

Goddess help her. She didn't want to lie. Not to him.

"Aye, Henrik," she whispered, knowing she shouldn't, telling herself not to, plunging headlong into trouble anyway. "I trust you."

A mistake. Cosmina knew it the second the words left her mouth.

Still she refused to take them back, even when Henrik drew her closer. Warm water swirled between them. Cosmina barely noticed. Locked against him, his gaze bored into hers, making her forget the here and now. A tingle circled her temples, then stroked along each side of her head. She tensed. Something wasn't right. But even as the realization registered, the strange vibration coalesced at the base of her skull, then tugged, pulling her sideways inside her own mind. Pure seduction, the tilting pitch urged her to give in and go along, but . . .

Wrong. All *wrong*. The prickle, the mental fog . . . the drift of sensation.

Clinging to Henrik, Cosmina blinked and, fighting to clear her mind, reached for clarity. None came. Instead the brain fog thickened as, gaze steady on hers, Henrik's eyes started to shimmer. Alarm slithered through her, making instinct rise. She shook her head. His grip on her tightened. Gasping his name, she tried to retreat, struggling in his arms, battling sensory overload as a vortex opened deep inside her. Whispering reassurances,

Henrik cupped the sides of her face, pressed his thumbs beneath her chin, forcing eye contact.

Her breath hitched. Her muscles twitched. Her brain shut down.

In that order. Even as she fought the slow slide into enchantment. Even as she called his name, asking him to stop. Even as the pressure built between her temples and the cerebral burn took hold, making her fall into him instead of away. Panic kicked her heart against her breastbone, but she couldn't move. Couldn't resist or pull away. Lost in the swirling gold of his gaze, a snick echoed inside her head. She whimpered. Henrik murmured, telling her to relax, that he wouldn't hurt her, soothing her with his voice as he pushed past reason and invaded her mind.

* * *

Heart so heavy his chest hurt, Henrik finished lacing his tunic. Boot soles rasping against the dirt floor, he left his knives on the table, picked up Cosmina's necklace, and turned toward the bed. The ancient disc that doubled as a key swung from a delicate chain made of silver links. Back and forth. To and fro. A pendulum of movement that sent him back to White Temple and the instant he'd first laid eyes on her.

So feisty. So full of life.

So goddamned beautiful, clothed in boy's trews and a bad attitude.

His mouth curved. Remorse killed his amusement, filling his chest, squeezing around his heart, making it difficult to breathe as he tumbled back into the present. The necklace came back into focus. Delicate yet strong . . . just like Cosmina. And unlike him at the moment. Bowing his head, Henrik fought the claw of emotion—the need, the want, the god-awful yearning. Firelight flickered against the timber beam walls and off the silver links coiled in his palm, throwing light into the room, mocking him with a warmth he didn't feel and in no way deserved. Comfort didn't belong in his corner. Not anymore.

Not after what he'd done.

Raising his arms, Henrik cupped the back of his neck and pressed down. Taut muscles squawked. Pain streaked down his spine, then clawed across his lower back. He barely noticed. Was too busy telling himself to put his feet to good use and go. To head for the door, 'cause—God. He sure as hell shouldn't be standing inside Cosmina's cottage, occupying the same space, defiling her with his presence while longing to hold her close. Just as he had during the night when her nightmares arrived, and she'd fought demons he couldn't see, never mind vanquish, for her.

His fault. Every terrible moment of it.

Putting her in Thrall had opened mental doors she'd shut long ago. Probing her mind to find what he needed had made it worse, unearthing memories, releasing her monsters—all the things Cosmina kept tucked away and struggled to forget. Things she no doubt didn't want him to know. But it was too late. He'd seen her past, felt her fear in the wee hours, and held her close while she cried out in her sleep. Henrik closed his eyes as recall spun him around the lip of self-loathing. He shook his head, trying to banish the abhorrence, consoling himself with the fact he'd tried to help. Had done his utmost to banish the ghosts and ease her suffering. It hadn't worked, so he'd wrapped his arms around her instead, whispered nonsense, stroked her hair and . . .

Hated himself the whole time for causing her pain.

Which meant he needed to leave. Right now. Before she woke to find him mooning over her like a lovesick lad. A clean break. A quick getaway. Both would be best—safer for her, more advisable for him to cut his losses and walk away while he could, but . . .

Deep-seated longing wouldn't let him.

He needed to touch Cosmina one last time.

Drawn to her against his will, his feet took him to the side of her bed. Fast asleep now, red hair a tangled web around her head, she lay on her side, curled beneath the coverlet, face pale, body relaxed, and mind exhausted. Guilt tightened its grip. Henrik cleared his throat and, unable to help himself, reached for a lock of her hair. The soft strands clung to his fingertips, making his heart throb as he remembered. Her struggle. The gentle insistence he'd wielded to subdue her at the hot spring. Her slide into terrible dreams and restless slumber in the aftermath of mental conquest. Goddamn it, he was a first-rate bastard. The lowest of the low for using his magic against her. It didn't matter he'd had little choice. The facts spoke for themselves and couldn't be refuted—he'd entered her mind, gone against her wishes to retrieve information.

To save himself. To protect his comrades. For the goddess and the greater good.

He flexed his fingers, fisting his hand around the key. The metal dug into his palm, and Henrik swallowed a snarl. *The greater good.* Jesus. If only it were that simple. The end didn't always justify the means. He knew that. And yet he'd done it anyway, cornering Cosmina, pulling the information he needed from her mind, cursing himself as she whispered his name, asking him to stop. He hadn't listened, and that, more than anything, laid him low. Made him recoil inside even as he yearned for her forgiveness.

Another thing that would never come.

Aye, he'd been gentle. So what. Big deal. The manner of it didn't matter. Leaving her unharmed wasn't the point. Hurt took on many different forms, the physical kind just one of them. So nay, he didn't deserve absolution. He had no right to ask for it and knew, beyond a shadow of doubt, Cosmina would never grant it. He'd wronged her. She would hold him accountable. But only if he braved her wrath and . . .

Stayed for the reckoning.

Surprisingly enough, the idea appealed to him. An angry Cosmina, after all, seemed better than the alternative: no Cosmina at all. But even as the thought chased its tail inside his head, tempting him to a dangerous degree, Henrik dismissed it. He couldn't stay. She couldn't come where he was going—into battle with the Druinguari—so he traced her cheek with his fingertip instead, memorizing every detail—the softness of her skin, the beauty of her face, the way she tasted along with the incredible way she fit in his arms. He lingered a moment longer, then turned away, and strode toward the table. And his weapons.

Time to go. Even less of it to waste.

The wildlife was getting restless outside.

He could tell by the pitch of his brothers-in-arms' voices. The heavy stamp and claw of the horses' hooves on the snowy ground too. His comrades awaited him in the clearing. Each was ready to ride, eager to fight, just five strides and one closed door away. But as Henrik strapped on the twin swords he favored and sheathed his knifes, he paused, his gaze on the piece of parchment he'd left on the tabletop. Small. Neatly folded. Ragged on one edge from being torn from the journal he liked to carry. Naught but crisp white corners and messy handwriting, an inadequate good-bye to the woman who now held his heart.

Henrik stared at the note a moment, wondering if he'd lost his mind. He shouldn't leave it there. Should crumple the wretched thing into a ball and feed it to the fire. 'Twould be wiser, the kindest choice for Cosmina in the long run. She didn't need to know how he felt. 'Twas the height of selfishness to leave her with the knowledge, never mind the burden.

Somehow, though, logic didn't hold sway.

Right. Wrong. Neither mattered anymore.

In the end, it came down to one thing. An unforgivable, irrefutable fact. He didn't want her to forget him. Needed to know she thought of him often—as often as he would her. So instead of picking up the missive and throwing it away, he unsheathed his favorite dagger—the one he carried next to his heart—set the weapon atop the parchment, then laid her necklace over both. An inadequate explanation anchored by a gift—a blade, expertly designed and exquisitely wrought, the only thing of worth he had to give. Leaving the offerings in the center of the table, he made for the exit. Flicking the handle, Henrik opened the door, and without looking back, latched it tightly behind him.

CHAPTER TWENTY-ONE

Standing in front of the fireplace wearing nothing but her rabbit-fur throw, Cosmina pulled the coverlet tighter around her. Flames licked between the logs, throwing heat into the room, warming her bare feet as the pelt settled against the nape of her neck. Soft fur against her skin—undeniable luxury, unerring comfort inside her cottage, a safe haven far from the dangers of the world. And yet, the idea of safety—of hearth and home, and all material goods she used to define it—didn't soothe her in the usual ways. No pride for her sanctuary. No satisfaction at its warmth. Naught to ease her mind or calm the raging beat of her heart.

Unusual in and of itself.

She took great pride in her home. Loved the security it offered inside the Limwoods. The dawn of a new day, however, had changed everything, banishing neat and tidy in favor of messy and morose. And solace? Cosmina huffed. It wasn't in the offing. Had disappeared somewhere between here and there . . . that mystical place between absolute certainty and unequaled doubt. Now safe—all things ordinary—felt thin, without their usual weight, like fine comfort cloaked in empty promises. Not surprising. Particularly since she couldn't turn off her brain. She was too far-gone, deep in a space where it would be better to forget, but she couldn't let go of the memories, of heart-wrenching loss, and the fact . . .

Henrik was gone.

Cosmina had known it the instant she opened her eyes. No proof to speak of. No need to look further. No reason to rouse her gift to corroborate the truth. Call it woman's intuition. Or perhaps, a lover's disappointment. Whatever the case, she'd just *known*. In the same way she knew she shouldn't accept the dagger.

Or read the note he'd left on the table alongside it.

Unable to resist, Cosmina glanced over her shoulder. Again. For what seemed like the thousandth time. Surprise, surprise. Nothing new there. She'd been doing the same dance for the better part of an hour. Stare at the folded piece of parchment, talk herself out of picking it up, then look away. Back and forth. Yank, heave, drag—a tug-of-war without end. And yet, she hadn't moved a muscle. Still hadn't snatched the blasted thing off the table and hurled it into the fire. Instead she stood stock-still, gaze locked to the blaze Henrik had built before he left, while trying to ignore his damned note.

Without a great deal of success.

In truth, she was failing. Resolve slipping by the second. The treacherous need to know—to accept one last part of him—dragging her closer to the precipice and her doom.

All part of Henrik's evil plan, no doubt.

A cunning strategist, he'd set the trap, baiting the lure with the one thing he knew she couldn't resist . . . a blade. And not just any knife either. 'Twas his dagger. She recognized the hilt.

Remembered admiring its beauty while lounging in bed with him. Most men would've called her interest unnatural. Not Henrik. He hadn't balked. Had simply handed her the weapon instead—allowed her to test its weight, listened to her praise the design, and smiled when she'd balanced the blade between her fingertips and taken aim, pretending to throw it. The memory tightened her throat. Cosmina shook her head, trying not to appreciate his gift even as she itched to feel the hilt in her hand.

Treacherous, diabolical, beautiful man.

He knew just how to play her. And like it or nay, she was falling right into his trap . . . into the memories and her need to touch something of his. To hold it close. To own it so she didn't forget, remembered him always even though he'd left her wanting, slipping out her door, walking out of her life, all without saying good-bye.

Or looking back.

"Arrogant ass," she rasped, the hurt so thick her chest ached. "Double-damned fool."

The name-calling should've helped. It didn't. Not in the slightest. In truth, it made her feel worse. Made her feel small and restless and . . . wrong. Henrik wasn't a fool. Wasn't much for arrogance either. He'd been good to her, right up until the end. Cosmina swallowed past the lump in her throat, refusing to let heartache win. But it was hard. So blasted difficult. She wanted to scream at the unfairness. Let loose, release the pressure building behind her breastbone and—

Gods, she didn't know what to do. What to say. Or how to feel.

She couldn't get a handle on the emotion, never mind hold it down. But she needed to . . . right now. Before she abandoned all restraint, folded beneath the onslaught, and let her love for him win.

She reached for anger instead. Grabbed hold, held on tight, and let it burn.

'Twas the better choice. She needed fury to sustain her—to help her survive the emotional lash of betrayal and the impact of what he'd done. Bowing her head, Cosmina squeezed her eyes shut and relived the sensation. The terrible throb between her temples. The absolute loss of control. The mind-bending torque of his magic, the ferocity of his gift as he dragged her deep into Thrall.

The memory of it stung.

Her ineptitude made her cringe.

Gods. 'Twas unbelievable. She should have seen it coming. That she hadn't made her question her own skills. Cosmina pursed her lips. A rare lapse in judgment. Aye, that was what it amounted to . . . one she blamed on her feelings for him. Call her a lovesick fool. Chalk it up to inexperience and let it lie. The surprise, though, couldn't be dismissed. His ability to ambush her mattered. 'Twas too big a puzzle. As mysterious as it was difficult to explain, because—drat it all. She should've sensed the raw talent in him.

Her gift should have recognized his.

Too bad clarity hadn't come to the party. She'd understood too late. After all was said. After everything was done. Not soon enough to protect herself. Now her heart lay in tatters, and all she had left was a beautiful dagger and Henrik's note.

The stupid, wretched note.

Eyes narrowed, Cosmina glared over her shoulder at it. Crisp and white, the perfect folds mocked her. With a grumble, she spun away from the fire. The fast whirl pushed air into the hearth. Logs shifted and flames snapped, protesting the sudden movement. Cosmina ignored the fierce crackle and pop and, stomping around the edge of the tabletop, snatched her necklace from atop the small pile. Quick hands looped the silver links over her head. The key swung wide, then landed, bumping against her breastbone. The gentle tap unleashed her temper. Reaching out, she curled her hand around the knife hilt.

Leather settled in her palm. One fast rotation. Another quick shift, and the blade sat perched between her fingertips. Baring her teeth, Cosmina drew her arm back, took aim, and threw it hard. In perfect balance, the blade obeyed, hurtling end over end toward the opposite wall. She watched it fly. Felt satisfaction rise and—

Thunk!

The knifepoint hit the timber beam dead center and sank deep. Violent sound echoed, throbbing through the quiet as the hilt quivered from the force of impact. Perfect precision. Unerring aim. X marked the intended spot, wounding the undeserving wood.

"Take that," she said into the stillness.

"Do you feel better now?" someone asked, the magic-filled whisper frothing into the room.

The voice made her jump a foot and yelp in surprise. Fists raised in defense, Cosmina spun away from the table and set her stance. Radiance spilled from the opposite corner of the cottage. Driven by magic, illumination gathered, taking shape and form until a woman stepped from the sparkling light. Cosmina's mouth fell open. Surprise circled into awe. By the gods—holy mother, the keeper of light and shadow—the Goddess of All Things now stood in her home. Robed in power, majesty folded the deity in an ethereal glow, making her aura burn bright white.

Stunned into stupidity, Cosmina stood stock-still, not knowing what to do. Or how to respond. Some sort of greeting was no doubt in order, but disbelief stole her brain, leaving her standing slack-jawed without a thing to say. The goddess, after all, had only ever visited her inside the dreamscape, where things made sense and seemed less real. But this—the glory of her presence inside her small cottage—surpassed surreal, catapulting her into astonishment and the beginnings of unease.

Had she done something wrong? Did the goddess' arrival signal—

"You've naught to fear, child. I come in peace," the goddess said, soothing the worry before glancing at the dagger still vibrating in the wall. She stared at it a moment, then returned her focus to Cosmina. Speculation in her eyes, the goddess raised a brow. "Well . . . do you?"

"Feel better?" she asked, swimming past shock to regain mental equilibrium.

The goddess nodded.

Cosmina sighed. "Not really."

"You are suffering."

"I am angry."

"To be expected. Men are ofttimes difficult, Cosmina," the goddess said, stepping around the foot of the bed. "They are a mystery unto the ages. Most cause more harm than good."

"Mayhap, but not—"

"Henrik?" Slipping her hands inside the wide sleeves of her gown, the goddess approached with silent steps. A million secrets in her eyes, she stopped at the edge of the table, leaving the stained surface between them. "If you believe that, child, why did you let him go?"

"I had no choice."

"Didn't you?"

The question took her by surprise. The goddess' expectant expression took her the rest of the way. Both hands fisted in rabbit fur, Cosmina pulled the throw tight across her shoulders and frowned. *No choice.* Powerful words with incredible impact. Now she wondered whether they were true. She hadn't tried to make Henrik stay. Hadn't voiced how she felt or encouraged him to come back. Hadn't done much of anything at all, so—

Cosmina frowned. Drat and damn. She'd simply let him leave . . . without a fight.

More fool her. The goddess knew it. Now she did too.

Regret whispered through her, making her heart ache. "Is it too late, Majesty? Have I lost all hope?"

"Time turns and things change, Cosmina, and so must we, but . . ." Understanding in her eyes, her mouth curved. "Love is forever. Do not lose faith in that, child. In the end, 'tis all we have or will ever hope to leave behind."

The advice lit a fire inside her. No matter how angry with Henrik, she wanted the truth. Had she made a terrible mistake? Could she forge a real future with him? Was he worth fighting for? The questions jabbed at her. She couldn't deny the appeal. Or her need to know . . . once and for all. Spinning on her heel, Cosmina strode toward her cabinet. She needed to get dressed . . . right now. Intuition gathered, pulling up stakes inside her mind. She couldn't stay here. Not an instant longer.

"Thank you for your visit, Majesty, but I must go." Reaching the armoire door, Cosmina flipped it open. A list streamed into her head as she stared at the shelves—extra clothes, lots of food, all her weapons. She would need every bit of it to survive her journey to Drachaven. "I need to find him."

"Nay, Cosmina." Raising an invisible hand, the goddess halted her forward progress. Magic swirled, scenting the air with hollyhocks as she spun Cosmina back to face her. Heart locked in her throat, frozen in place, she met the deity's gaze. Expression set in serious lines, the goddess shook her head. "I cannot allow you to travel the mountain passes to Drachaven. Not while evil looms and the Blessed return to White Temple."

"But—"

"Be patient, child. I set the wheel in motion, atoning for my mistakes by placing Henrik in your path. If it is meant to be, Henrik will come back to you. For now, remember your duty to the Order of Orm and do as I command," the goddess said. "You completed the ancient rite and have heard the call. You feel the tug toward home. Heed it, Cosmina. Return to the temple. Welcome your sisters and make ready for the High Priestess' return to holy ground."

The words filled her with purpose. "It will be done, Majesty."

"Then go, child, and know you are not alone." White light glimmering in her aura, the goddess released her. Able to move again, Cosmina breathed a sigh of relief and watched spellbound as the deity faded before her eyes. "I will be with you. Oh, and Cosmina . . ."

The all-powerful voice drifted on a whisper, wavering in thin air. A moment later, the Goddess of All Things disappeared in a ripple of sparkling light.

"Read the note, child," the goddess breathed from beyond the earthly realm. "Read his note."

Wonder made her heart skip a beat. As it resumed pounding, Cosmina heeded the call and, stepping up to the table edge, reached for the note. Fear almost made her stop, trying to convince her that—despite the goddess' insistence—Henrik's message wasn't worth reading. That she didn't need to know. That 'twas the height of foolishness to hope. But her hand refused to listen, picking up the parchment, unfolding the creases, opening the note for her eyes to see . . . and her heart to read.

Cosmina,
I am sorry. Please forgive me.
I love you.
H

Three sentences. Simple, no nonsense . . . direct and to the point, devastating as the message sank in and the truth struck home. He loved her. The impact of it made her knees wobble. Wonder bubbled up, splashed through her, spilling over the edge of reason, obliterating doubt as it scored a direct hit to her heart. Tears filled her eyes. Oh nay . . . oh blast . . . damn Henrik to hell and back. Of all the things to say, or rather, write and—

Goddess help her.

She was going to lose control. Become messy. Cry like a weak-willed ninny—or whatever a girl did when dealing with a man who touched her heart. One hand cupped over her mouth, Cosmina shook her head and retreated a step. And then another. The table edge bumped her bottom. Gaze still riveted to the missive, she reached out and searched for a stool. Smooth wood met her palm. She sank into the seat, shock making it hard to draw a full breath. Filling her lungs, she forced her chest to expand and stared at the messy scrawl. Moments ticked past, falling into more as she struggled to process the message and find fault. But she couldn't. It wasn't possible. The flaw didn't exist. And fury? 'Twas naught but ancient history now.

The gods bless and keep her. She'd never imagined . . . hadn't thought . . .

Cradling the note with both hands, she read the words again. *I love you.*

She lost the battle. Tears fell, tumbling over her bottom lashes.

"Oh, Henrik." Another tear escaped, rolling down her cheek. "I love you too."

Foolish to admit, never mind say out loud.

Cosmina knew it the moment the words left her mouth. Giving them a voice only granted love more power. The kind that often hurt, and she could never take back. Not that it mattered. Love didn't negotiate. Or allow its victims time to dodge. It aimed true, hit hard, and never backed down. So . . . no help for it. 'Twas done, her heart given and her mind set on the man who'd kept her safe and taught her pleasure. On a warrior with a restless spirit, good heart, and gentle soul. No sense trying to fight it. She would forever be fixed on Henrik. Regardless of the manner of their parting.

Or the fact he'd been the one to walk away.

Ironic in a way. Symbolic to be sure. Especially since she planned to do the same.

This very day.

Shifting on the stool, Cosmina glanced around her cottage. It wasn't much to look at it. Naught more than a bunch of sticks and stones, a collection of lopsided furniture scavenged from unwanted piles. More of a temporary way station than a real home. And yet, she'd found solace inside these walls. At least for a time. But that was behind her now. The goddess' visit along with her decree couldn't be ignored.

She must do her duty. Was a member the Blessed and belonged at White Temple. But as Cosmina pushed to her feet, pulled Henrik's knife from the wall, and went about gathering her things, she longed for something more. Something better. Something richer than love words scrawled on parchment. She wanted the man who had written them returned to her.

Solid and strong in her arms. Less than a heartbeat away.

No doubt a foolish dream. And yet, it didn't stop her. The goddess had given her hope. So aye, mayhap if she wished hard enough. If she proved strong enough. If she prayed often enough . . .

Fate would heed the call and bring Henrik back to her.

CHAPTER TWENTY-TWO

Golden rays broke through thick mist, warming the tops of Cristobal's shoulders as the sun rose, welcoming him into the light of a new day. His mouth curved. A rare reprieve. The gift of heat after hours spent crouched behind rock and amid shadow. Not that he suffered any discomfort. The north winds and the brisk cold didn't bother him. The cramped conditions didn't either, nor that he'd taken three watches in a row. Nearly six hours spent atop the cliff edge . . .

Watching. Waiting. Searching for the enemy and movement on the trail below.

He didn't mind the long stretch of time. Or the fact his comrades slept while he remained awake. Xavian and the others needed rest. By some quirk of fate, he didn't. Couldn't close his eyes, never mind relax enough to fall asleep. How many days he'd gone without, he didn't know. Eight . . . or was it nine now? Hard to tell. He'd lost track after the fifth sleepless night. Balanced on the balls of his feet, Cristobal shifted position. Shuffling along the plateau three hundred feet above the valley floor, he stayed low, hidden behind jagged rock, improving his vantage point, concern rising along with the winter wind. His inability to sleep made little sense. He should be exhausted, but for some reason, didn't feel the least bit fatigued.

Scanning the rolling foothills opposite him, Cristobal clenched his teeth. *For some reason.* Right. Try again. He knew what plagued him: the stupid chant. The words spilled through his mind, pushing annoyance to new heights and making rest impossible. It wouldn't leave him alone—always poking, forever prodding, the thrum of urgency unending. Now he throbbed with it, his heart keeping time to the command banging around inside his skull.

Find her, find her. She needs you . . . find her.

Damned frustrating. Particularly since he still didn't know who the hell *she* was. No image to go by. Not a single clue to guide him. Just the words, the awful incessant stream of words. Oh and, aye, the twin tattoos. He couldn't forget about those. The markings—along with the pain burning across his forearms— were as much a part of him now as breathing. An all-day, every night sort of thing, although . . .

For the first time in days, the sting was gone.

Cristobal frowned, then flexed both hands. Odd, but . . . nay, no discomfort whatsoever.

With a flick, he undid the bladed arm cuffs and drew both off. Cold air washed over his skin. Sensation followed, slithering up his arms and over his shoulders before changing course, drag-ging icy fingers down his back. Cristobal shook off the shiver. The ghosting swirl settled, looping into a circle, spinning like a top, chasing its tail against the nape of his neck. Round and round. Back and forth. He frowned, tracking the pinpricks across his skin. It didn't hurt. Not exactly. In truth, 'twas almost pleasant.

Soothing even, a gentle touch delivered by unseen hands.

Brow drawn tight, Cristobal unfurled his fists. Open. Close. Flex and release. Taut muscle moved, making the tattoo dance across his skin. He stared at the pattern, examining the fine lines and all the detail. All done, naught left to complete . . . the last line drawn in black ink. And as the invisible hand fell away, taking the magical quill with it, his gaze bounced from one tattoo to the next. *Rahat*, would you look at that? He could see the hellhounds now—coarse fur, sawtooth spikes rising like jagged fins along each spine, sharp fangs bared beneath slanted eyes. Mesmerized by the design, he traced the thickest line, stroking a fingertip over the bridge of the beast's nose, then behind its blunt ear.

A growl echoed inside his head.

Pain clawed at his temples. Cristobal shook his head, but it was too late. The pressure built and his mind unhinged, opening a fissure into the unknown. Into something greater. Into a vast space filled with majesty and magic. As the chasm grew, twin entities stepped through the breech, one behind the other, huge claw-tipped paws leading the way as—

"Cristobal." Familiar and deep, the voice drifted from the trail behind a rock face.

Ah hell. Xavian. Talk about bad timing.

Choking on magic, Cristobal coughed, fighting to find his voice. He needed to warn Xavian. Tell him . . . he frowned . . . what exactly? Stay away? Put his arse in gear and get him help? Jesus, he couldn't decide. Not while the beasts circled inside his head and his muscles screamed. Absorbing the agony, insight struck. Oh God. The pair was trying to get out—to leave the confines of his mind and take physical form.

Razor-sharp teeth bared, the pair paced—back and forth, round and round—urging him to set them free. The click of claws tapped against his eardrums. Soft snarls pressed in, amplifying the sound, making his skull throb as the two grew in size, lethal presence expanding by the second. The pain increased. The pressure swelled into cerebral burn, threatening to geyser and . . . *rahat*, here it came . . .

His stomach heaved.

Bile touched the back of his throat. Swallowing the bad taste, Cristobal retreated and, head bowed, slid backward onto one knee. Away from the cliff's edge. Toward the trailhead and his best friend. Probably not the best move. Cristobal didn't care. He needed help. Right now. Couldn't contain the hellhounds much longer, much less—

The tattoos shifted.

One moment, the ink sat on his forearms. The next, the pair came alive, leaping off his skin, streaking into black blurs. The duo took physical form mid-jump. Huge paws thumped down on the plateau in front of him, kicking up stone dust. Cristobal froze, becoming a living statue as the twin hellhounds—each movement in perfect accord—pivoted toward him. Heads low, ears back, glossy pelts and bladed spines glinting in the sunlight, the beasts roared at him. The shrieks obliterated the quiet, rising in a deafening wave, bombarding the sheer cliff face behind him. Chips of shale came loose and tumbled, cascading down to slam into the base of the stone wall.

"*La dracu,*" Xavian said as he stepped off the narrow trail, onto the plateau.

Huge fangs bared, the beasts' focus snapped toward his best friend.

"Don't move." Still on one knee, his gaze locked on the hellhounds, Cristobal raised his hand, backing up word with deed. The second Xavian moved—drew his weapons or tried to back away—the beasts would give chase. Stood to reason. Predators, after all, enjoyed the thrill of the hunt. "Stay perfectly still."

Hands gripping his knife hilts, Xavian froze, obeying without question.

Cristobal shifted to the balls of his feet, drawing the hellhounds' ire. Two sets of eyes settled back on him. The pair sidestepped, huge paws padding softly in stone dust. Covered by black fur, interlocking scales clicked as they moved, the body armor sending an ominous message through the quiet. Lethal accord. Duel purpose. The beasts shared common intent—one grounded in a prospect called unfriendly. Bladed tails twitching, the duo met his gaze. Cristobal drew a deep breath, then exhaled long and slow. Calm. Cool. And collected. He must epitomize all three. Otherwise his attempt to tame the twins wouldn't end well, never mind . . .

Nay, scratch that. Not twins. Not exactly.

His eyes narrowed. The twosome looked alike—almost identical—but not quite. Slight though the differences might be, he identified individual characteristics. Without moving a muscle, he looked them over again. The hellhound on his right stared at him through unblinking yellow eyes. The beast on the left, however, possessed a unique pair—one yellow eye, the other bright blue. The variance didn't stop there either. Blue Eyes sported a single snow-white paw while her sibling was black from head to the tip of her tail. Both female. Both huge, standing at least five hands at the withers . . . species not of this world. Razor-sharp teeth set alongside jagged fangs. Lethal claws tipping enormous paws. Blunt ears rising from enormous heads that resembled a cat's with some wolf thrown in for good measure.

He should be afraid. Or, at the very least, wary.

Cristobal was neither. Instead something akin to pride surfaced, urging him to explore the bond he sensed between him and them. One that became stronger by the moment, infusing him with a power not his own. Magic flowed. His senses sharpened and came alive, allowing him to hear, see, and smell everything—just like he had at the cemetery. He hummed, the sound half purr, half snarl. The hellhounds responded, returning the hostile sound. Which made perfect sense. Felt right too. The twins had come from somewhere inside him, leaping off his skin to take physical form. So aye, as lethal and angry as the pair appeared, the hellhounds belonged to him.

Instinct his guide, Cristobal pushed to his feet.

The hellhounds tensed, growling in unison.

"Ah, Cristobal?"

"Relax, Xavian," he said, reassuring his friend. No reason to be alarmed. Well, at least, not yet. Raising his arms, Cristobal turned his hands, palms up, and approached the hellhounds on silent feet. "I've got them under control."

"Jesu, I hope so. I've no wish to be eaten by . . ." Hands gripping the hilts, but blades still sheathed, Xavian dragged his focus from the twins. Pale eyes full of unease, his commander threw him a meaningful look. "Well, whatever the hell they are."

"Hellhounds."

"If you say so."

His lips twitched. "Trust me."

"Uh-huh."

Ignoring the skepticism, Cristobal continued to advance. Blue Eyes bared her fangs and, white paw crossing over black, sidestepped, readying for attack. The show of aggression didn't faze him. He reached for her instead, holding his hand out, encouraging her to catch his scent, while Yellow Eyes circled around behind him. Enchantment rose. The wind died down. He murmured, using his voice to soothe her. The hellhound at his back came in close and . . .

Bumped him from behind.

Her touch unlocked a floodgate inside his mind. Knowledge washed in, bringing insight and understanding. Wrought by magic, the bond between them snapped into place. A name streamed into his head. Lowering his arm, he laid his hand atop her large head—felt the hard scales beneath soft fur—and stroked his palm over the back of her neck.

Allowing his touch, Yellow Eyes nudged him again.

His mouth curved. "Hello, Thrax."

Acknowledging his greeting, Thrax purred. The loud rumble made him smile as she pushed her snout into his hand, asking for more. Cristobal gave it to her, petting Thrax without hesitation while he waited for her sister to come forward and receive the same. It took a while. Moments tipped into more, but he didn't push her. He waited instead, allowing the hellhound the time she needed. After what seemed like forever, but was no more than a minute, she bridged the distance, set her chin in his palm, allowing the bond to take shape and form.

"Vicars," he said, calling her by name, scratching behind one of her ears. She growled and, tipping her head to one side, leaned into his touch. Giving her what she wanted, he rubbed a little harder, then glanced over his shoulder. "We've some new playmates, Xavian."

His friend huffed. "Helluva pair to own. Lethal one moment, naught but kittens the next."

Cristobal grinned. True enough. But in the best possible way. Aye, the hellhounds were dangerous, but they could be controlled and leashed . . . by him. Proof positive lay in the fact they obeyed him on command. Hell, Thrax even rolled over, exposing her belly when he asked. Praising her with his touch, he held her in place—back pressed to the ground, four legs up in the air—and, pivoting toward Vicars, asked for her paw. Mismatched eyes full of trust, she set it in his hand and . . . huh. Interesting. Seven claws instead of the usual five—razor-sharp, bladelike, at least five inches long, with a hooked tip.

Incredibly lethal. Death with one forceful swipe.

"Hey, Xavian?"

"Aye?"

"Come here a moment."

"No way in hell."

Still holding Vicar's paw, Cristobal eyed his best friend. "You want to get eaten?"

Releasing the death grip on his weapons, Xavian grimaced.

"Then come here. I need to introduce you. Otherwise they won't accept you." Murmuring to his new pets, he issued a command. Both hellhounds leapt to obey, sitting on their haunches in front of him as Cristobal pushed to his feet. His face wiped of expression, Xavian stopped alongside him and, making a fist, offered his hand to the pair. The instant the hellhounds caught and accepted Xavian's scent, Cristobal dismissed them both. As the twins went exploring, noses to the ground, he glanced sideways at his friend. "Anything from Henrik?"

Xavian nodded. "'Tis what I came to tell you. Tareek brought word."

Cristobal tipped his chin, asking without words.

"'Tisn't good." Rolling his shoulders, his friend cracked his knuckles. Sound ricocheted, bouncing off rock, bringing the hellhounds' heads around. Two sets of eyes narrowed on him. Seeing naught amiss, each went back to exploring. "Halál and Al Pacii have turned."

"Into what? Magic wielders?"

"Not quite, but close. Druinguari . . . minions to the Prince of Shadows," Xavian said. "We need to get up trail. Henrik's got a plan."

"Always interesting."

"You don't know the half of it."

"Fill me in." With a quick pivot, Cristobal strode for the mouth of the mountain trail. With a low whistle, he called Thrax and Vicars to attention. Twin snarls echoed in answer. He murmured a command. The pair transformed, dematerializing into black blurs, each leaping the distance to reach his forearms. Sharp pinpricks licked across his skin as the hellhounds became one with the tattoos. Shaking off the sting, he rounded a boulder and headed for camp. "I want details."

Keeping pace alongside him, Xavian laid out the plan, providing Cristobal with the timeline. Less than an hour to get into position and ambush a pack of Druinguari. Excellent. A bold strategy that necessitated acting fast and being smarter. Not a problem under normal circumstances. The information relayed, however, didn't inspire confidence. It felt thin, smacked of the unknown and all kinds of challenge.

Particularly if the enemy proved almost impossible to kill.

Then again, he now held an interesting advantage. Something as dangerous as the sorcery Xavian and his other comrades wielded. Two hellhounds. Monsters rooted in magic, packing a whole lot of vicious and even more lethal. A handy pair to own. An even better weapon to unleash when Henrik lit the fuse and the battle got under way.

* * *

Hidden within a copse of spruce overlooking the Carpathian foothills, Henrik rechecked his blades and studied the terrain. The winter wind blustered, blowing against his back. Granular snow whipped around tree trunks, leaving bare patches in some spots and piles in others. Not a problem. The day provided all he needed. Sunny afternoon, clear skies, no new snowfall, and all the high ground he needed to set the trap. Scanning the terrain through the spread of branches, he slid his last dagger into its sheath, then tested the tautness of his bow and slung it over his shoulder. Weapons at the ready—check, check, and triple check.

Optimal conditions heading into battle.

Excellent in every way.

The advantage should've made him happy. Halál and the Druinguari, after all, lay within striking distance. The buzz between his temples told the tale, helping him pinpoint the enemy's location—a thousand yards downhill, lying in wait on either side of the narrow trail just over the next rise. Knowing he held the high ground and upper hand, however, didn't improve his mood. Discontent circled instead, picking him apart, making him ache with the need to go back instead of move forward. Henrik clenched his teeth. 'Twas the height of stupidity. Distraction equaled trouble. Mistakes got made that way. So aye, his lack of focus was a problem—dangerous in more ways than one considering the killer he kept caged rattled his mental bars, begging for freedom . . .

Dying to get out.

The mere hint of battle—the pleasure of drawing his blades—always had the same effect. It invigorated him. Cranked the tension tight. Shoved the past back into the box where it belonged, allowing him to stay in the here and now. Except . . .

The usual wasn't working today.

No matter how hard he tried, he couldn't put the last few days behind him. His mind remained fixed on Cosmina. On the way he'd left her. On the note and what it contained. On the hurt he imagined flaring in her eyes when she read it. Goddamn it. Not good. He was a bastard for doing that to her. For not making a clean break. For leaving her with the knowledge that she meant more to him than a fast fling over a few days.

For telling her that he loved her.

He never should've done that. Never should have opened his heart, never mind admit how he felt about her. But it was too late. He couldn't go back and unwrite the note. And honestly, Henrik wasn't sure he wished to anyway. Which made him worse than a bastard. It qualified him as a first-rate fool. Acknowledging the truth, however, didn't stop the ache. It simply made it worse. Now he throbbed with it, the pain so persistent errant urges rose to taunt him. He wanted to go back. Right now. Say to hell with it, mount up, ride off, and return to her. If only to hold her one more time.

Henrik huffed. God, he was an idiot . . . for so many reasons. Not the least of which included—

"Henrik." Boots crunching through crusty snow, Andrei stopped alongside him. His friend threw him a measured look. "Pull your head out of your arse. We need you focused."

True enough. "I'm good."

Disbelief in his expression, Andrei's gaze bore into his.

"No need to worry," he said, meeting the death stare head-on while he lied to his friend. Andrei's eyes narrowed. Henrik ignored the perusal and, rolling his shoulders, glanced behind him. Kazim stood at the ready, dark eyes sharp, body loose. Shay, on the other hand, took a different approach. Wet stone in hand, he sharpened one of his blades. The familiar rasp of stone against steel settled Henrik down, calming him in ways naught else could. Dragging his gaze from his comrades, he met Andrei's. "We all set?"

"The horses are ready."

Henrik nodded and went over the plan one more time. Pictured the terrain in his mind's eye. Thought about each move. Visualized how Halál would react and marshal his assassins when he realized the horses galloped into the bottleneck on the narrow trail. By then, it would be too late. Henrik would already be in position, at the enemies flank, weapons drawn, lethal at the ready while Xavian moved in from the opposite direction. Tareek and the other dragons would seal the deal, cutting off any chance of Druinguari retreat.

A good plan. One that would get him what he most wanted . . .

Halál dead. And the Druinguari six feet under alongside him.

"Just so you know . . ." Henrik paused to check his blades one more time. Staring at spruce needles half-buried in snow, he palmed individual knife hilts, sliding each from its sheath, then back in again. Steel whispered against leather. He threw Andrei a sidelong look. "When this is done, I plan to go back for her."

"And you wish me to know this . . ." As he trailed off, Andrei raised a brow. "Why?"

Henrik shrugged. He didn't know. Feelings weren't his forte. Neither was admitting to having any, never mind sharing them. Years spent in isolation had taught him well. He knew the rules. Had accepted the curse of his kind long ago. Never show fear. Never surrender. Never allow anyone close enough to hurt him. All excellent entries in a belief system that kept him detached . . . out of harm's way in the emotional realm. With Cosmina, though, he didn't want to keep his distance. Instinct urged him to get closer instead. To claim her while opening himself up for her to do the same.

Odd in many ways. True in even more.

Which meant he couldn't walk away. Not yet. Not until he knew for certain. He wanted to give what he felt for her a chance. The why of it didn't matter. Happiness. Need. Desire. All took a turn, digging in, twisting him tight as hope collected inside his heart, making all the what-ifs stream into his head. What if she loved him back? What if she missed him as much as he did her? What if she forgave what he'd done and accepted him back into her arms . . . into her life?

Excellent questions. Every one of them in need of answering.

"'Tisn't a good idea, H."

Of course it wasn't. Henrik glared at his friend anyway.

"I do not say this to hurt you, brother," his friend murmured, his accent floating like a fragrance on the north wind. "There is no harm in wanting her. A dalliance is one thing, but claiming her?" Andrei paused for effect, the silence driving the point home before he shook his head. "You are chasing heartache, Henrik. She is a member of the Blessed, meant to serve at White Temple. You are one of us. Your home is Drachaven. 'Twill end badly . . . for both of you."

Polar opposites. Black and white. Her light colliding with his dark.

Henrik didn't care. Despite their differences, he wanted her anyway. Staring at the snow swirling between his boots, he sighed. Andrei was no doubt right. 'Twas madness to yearn for a woman he would only hurt in the end.

Thumping Andrei on the shoulder with his fist, Henrik pivoted toward the others. He met his comrades' gazes, each one in turn. "Make it count. Show no mercy."

"We never do," Kazim said, his voice little more than a growl.

Shay flexed his fists. "Let's move."

With a nod, Henrik walked toward his mount. Ice crunched beneath his boot treads as he left the protective cove of the large spruces. The wind picked up, wiping snow across frozen turf, making branches creak and his violent nature rise. The calm he wore in battle settled around him like a winter cloak, clothing him in silent aggression. Henrik rolled his shoulders, accepting its weight, relishing the emotional chill and the absence of conscience.

His warhorse pawed the ground, snorting in greeting.

Henrik murmured back and, gripping her mane, swung into the saddle. Leather groaned. His mount shifted, muscles bunching in preparation. His need to find a fight as great as his steed's, he set heels to his horse's flanks. She leapt forward, strides lengthening, hooves cracking through the underbrush toward the trail beyond the forest's edge. His comrades behind him, Henrik wheeled around a huge oak, then caught air, jumping over a fallen log. His warhorse landed in the middle of the pathway.

Sharp sound rippled, cracking through the quiet. With a quick flick of the reins, he turned his mount west. It wouldn't be long now. Gorgon Pass, and the low bluffs rising on either side of the trail, lay just ahead. One more bend in the narrow roadway. A single straightaway, and he'd be in the monster's throat. No turning back. Little chance of retreat. Weapons drawn for one purpose . . .

Killing the man—minion, beast, bastard turned Druinguari, whatever—responsible for a lifetime of pain. Which meant the more noise he made on approach, the better.

Stealth wasn't part of the plan. He wanted Halál to hear him coming. Needed his former sensei to make assumptions. Leap to the wrong conclusion. Believe he had Henrik beat so the Druinguari committed to the ambush and entered the canyon. The instant the enemy put boots on the ground, Henrik would make each and every one of them pay. Game over. No mercy. Just death as he brought an end to Halál and those who served him.

Urging his mount to greater speed, Henrik rounded the bend and reached out with his mind. *"Tareek, where are you?"*

"Cloaked and in position to the east of Gorgon Pass."

"Garren and Cruz?"

"Same . . . one north, the other south." Scales rattled, coming through mind-speak. *"Xavian and the others await your signal on the west side."*

"Get ready."

Tareek snorted. *"Born ready, fratele."*

In the straightaway now, Henrik leaned in, got low, and unleashed his magic. Cold air snapped. Snow flurries flew, whirling in his wake as he conjured the spell. The cloak of invisibility flared, moving up and over to swallow him whole. As he disappeared into thin air, he tightened his grip on the magical shield, expanding it to include those riding behind him. Senses keen, he heard his comrades murmur in appreciation. Henrik ignored the accolades and, eyes moving over the entrance into the canyon, scanned the forest on either side of the trail. Nothing yet. No Druinguari hidden in the bracken. No intensification of the buzz between his temples. Just a narrow roadway funneling past rocky outcroppings into Gorgon Pass. Worn by weather and time, twin columns rose on either side of the opening, jagged stone teeth rounding the corners into the gorge beyond.

"Almost there. Moments out."

Tareek growled. *"Give me a count."*

Gaze riveted to his target, Henrik kicked from his stirrups. His hand tightened on the reins. His feet touched down, one in the center of the saddle, the other atop his warhorse's rump. *"Three. Two . . ."*

Stone columns sped past.

Shaped like an oval, Gorgon Pass opened up, widening in the center only to narrow again at the opposite end. Inhuman snarls erupted, echoing off serrated walls and across the gorge. Movement flashed in his periphery. Sunlight glinted off sword edges as the Druinguari took the bait and gave away their positions along the bluff's edge.

"One!"

Teeth bared, muscles taut, Henrik made the leap. Wind whistled in his ears. The wide ledge along one side of the gorge rose to greet him. He landed with a bone-jarring thump. The cloak of invisibility warped, contracting around him. Bearing down, Henrik held the spell in place and—sweet Christ. It was working. He was doing it. His magic was holding, rendering him invisible, protecting his comrades, confusing the Druinguari as riderless horses thundered into the center of the canyon . . .

Drawing the enemy's fire.

Black-shafted arrows flew overhead. Druinguari leapt from their hidey-holes as the first flurry hammered the ground and the stone wall above his head. Ducking the barrage, Henrik skidded across the outcropping and behind a row of rocks. One knee down, the other foot flat on the ground, he palmed his bow and drew an arrow. The shaft rasped free of his quiver. Eyes narrowed on the nearest Druinguari, he steadied his grip and let loose. The bowstring twanged. The arrow flew straight and true, speeding across the canyon and—crack! It stuck hard, puncturing the right side of the Druinguari's chest. The enemy roared in agony a second before—

Pop-pop . . . snap!

The bastard disintegrated, dissolving into a pile of sludge on the canyon floor. Enemy eyes turned in his direction. Twin swords drawn, leading the others, Xavian charged through the opening at the opposite side of the gorge. Dark-blue scales glinting in sunlight, Garren set up shop behind the group, cutting off all hope of escape from that direction. Cruz appeared at the other end, huge talons ripping up dirt as Tareek flew in and circled overhead.

Perfect timing. Counterattack launched. Plan 100 percent successful. The enemy had nowhere to go and nothing to do . . . but die.

With a battle cry, Henrik let the shield of invisibility go. As it snapped, making him visible to the enemy, chaos ensued. Horses screamed, then bolted. Druinguari shouted and scrambled, looking for a way out. Too little, too late. Henrik loosed another arrow. As accurate as the first, it slammed home. Another enemy assassin fell as the arrowhead pierced muscle and bone, rupturing the empty space behind his breastbone. Black magic spilled out, clouding the air as the capsule exploded, severing the bastard's connection to the demon realm. Like fuel, the contents of the capsule kept the Druinguari alive, feeding each from the source, binding them to their master: Armand, the Prince of Shadows. Once cut, however, the tie lost its power and the bastards ceased to exist.

In any way, shape, or form.

Excellent information to possess. The sole reason he'd put Cosmina in Thrall.

With a snarl, Henrik launched a third arrow. And then another. Fast and furious. One after the other, each flying with more fury than the last—protecting Xavian, hemming the enemy in, pushing the bastards into the center of the canyon—as he tried to blot out the memory. Goddamned bastards. He wanted to obliterate every last one. Forget his vow along with his allegiance to the Goddess of All Things. Set aside his past and Halál's crimes. Here . . . right now . . . vengeance had naught to do with it, and duty even less. His rage stemmed from another source. One that struck far too close to home. He'd betrayed Cosmina's trust, unleashing his magic, using it against her with singular purpose . . .

To find the Druinguari's weakness.

Now he possessed the knowledge. Had the bastards in his sights and on the run. All thanks to Cosmina, so . . .

No mercy. He'd meant every word.

Stowing his bow, Henrik palmed the hilts rising over his shoulders. With a hard draw, he pulled the blades free. Steel zinged from the twin scabbards strapped to his back. Swords in hand, he leapt over the rock barricade. Free-falling to the canyon floor, he roared at the enemy. Fast strides took him across Gorgon Pass and into the thick of the fray. His sword tasted steel. Three Druinguari turned to repel his attack. Whirling beneath an enemy blade, Henrik spun, feet churning in the dirt, cloak whipping around him. His blade found flesh. Jamming it home, he cut through bone, bringing death as black blood flew. The enemy disintegrated beneath his sword. He shifted left. A quick jab. A lethal thrust. Another Druinguari down, one more to engage, and—

Christ. Halál.

The enemy leader lay within reach, just ten feet of hard fighting away. The distance, though, didn't matter. Neither did the assassins standing in his path. He needed to reach his former sensei. Yearned to feel the tip of his blade thrust into the bastard's chest. Before Xavian reached him first. Before his friend's blade struck home, and Xavian took what Henrik wanted most.

Halál's non-beating heart on a platter.

Moving with precision, Henrik kept ahead of his comrades. Two more Druinguari fell. Hemmed in on all sides, Halál pivoted and, swords raised, turned toward Henrik. Flame-orange eyes met Henrik's over the heads of the soldiers surrounding him. Henrik bared his teeth. The bastard's mouth curved a second before he sheathed one sword and fisted his hand. Time stretched. Perception warped. Frigid air heated as Halál cranked his arm back and, opening his palm, threw a burst of black mist out in front him. Thick as smoke, fog frothed into the canyon, obliterating his line of sight. Henrik paused mid-swing. Thunder boomed overhead and—

Halál disappeared into thin air, taking the mist and soldiers along with him.

Blade poised mid-strike, Xavian cursed. "Son of a bitch."

"What the hell?" Andrei muttered from behind him.

"Goddamn it." Turning full circle, Henrik scanned the canyon. Empty. No Druinguari in sight. Just black blood splattered on the ground. "The bastard retreated."

"Using an excellent trick."

"Not so excellent, Razvan. Black magic. Bad enough, but . . ." Trailing off, Cristobal sheathed his swords and stepped into the circle, flanked by two huge beasts. Paws the size of dinner platters, the pair growled, the guttural sound eerie in the silent aftermath of battle. Wariness slithered down Henrik's spine. Raising sword tips stained with Druinguari blood, he threw his friend a look full of *what the hell*. With a shrug, Cristobal stroked his hands over the beast's head and met his gaze. "I'll explain later. We've got a bigger problem."

"Right," Shay grumbled, pocketing his throwing stars. "Because disappearing Druinguari just isn't enough."

"What kind of problem, Cristobal?" Henrik asked, ignoring his apprentice's sarcasm.

"There weren't enough Druinguari here."

"*Rahat.*" Pale eyes nearly colorless in the daylight, Xavian joined the party. "How many individual boot prints did you track from the cemetery?"

"Twenty-one," Cristobal said, expression grim.

"Only fifteen sets here."

"Aye, Andrei, not nearly enough. We're six short," Cristobal said, a growl in his voice. The beasts snarled in reaction, bladed tails swishing, fangs bared, claws clicking as the pair paced a circle around him. "I lost the enemy's trail in the rocks before we reached the Mureş River, but . . . *rahat*. I mistook the signs. I thought they were simply covering their tracks, but—"

"Christ." Hands flexing around his sword hilts, Henrik frowned. Mind churning over the facts, he put two and two together. The news signaled disaster. If Cristobal was right, a group of Druinguari had backtracked, avoiding detection—and his friend's supreme tracking skills—with singular purpose. "The Blessed have been recalled to White Temple. What if six broke from the pack and circled back, intending to—"

Kazim cursed. "Set up shop inside the holy city."

"Lay in wait," Xavian said, sheathing his blades. "And kill them all."

"A move worthy of Halál." With a growl, Razvan shook his head. "One that will ensure the Prince of Shadows' victory."

No question. Excellent conclusion. And exactly what Henrik thought too. Halál sought to end the war—and eliminate the threat to his master—before it began. All hope rested with the Blessed and his sister, High Priestess of Orm. As servants to the Goddess of All Things, the rituals each Blessed performed would ensure the deity gained strength in the earthly realm. More worship meant greater power. The prayers fed the goddess, and the stronger she grew, the harder it would be for Armand to gain a foothold. Which was where he and his comrades came in. His mission was simple, his goal straightforward: Decimate the enemy before they assembled in great numbers. Ruin all chance for evil to take root and grow. Provide what the goddess needed to secure her hold and protect mankind through her magic.

As the goddess' conduit, Afina played the go-between, providing the bridge between worlds, spreading the healing energy that touched all living things, ensuring the planet thrived. His sister's role was an important one. Now so was his. But as Henrik stood in the rising silence, wind whistling through the canyon, the Druinguari's true intent struck hard. He'd missed a vital fact while pursuing his thirst for vengeance . . . and Halál's death. Had failed to see the enemy's real plan. Should've realized sooner all of the Blessed—not just Cosmina—had become targets. His heart picked up a beat. And then another, slamming into his breastbone as realization bloomed and all the nasty possibilities rose. Each played like a bloody piece of theater set on a real-life stage.

Sweet Christ. Cosmina was once again in serious danger.

Her intentions were no secret. He knew she planned to return to the holy city. She'd told him as much while they'd lain in bed talking. The ancient rite she'd performed days ago held sway. The magical tether tugged, urging her home—the draw so strong it couldn't be denied. Which meant . . . God help him. Cosmina might already be on her way back to White Temple.

"Tareek!" Spinning on his heel, Henrik searched the bluff behind him.

Magic snapped in the chilly air as Tareek uncloaked. Red scales and horned head glimmering in the sun, his friend tipped his chin. "What?"

"How long a flight is it to White Temple?"

"Balls out, no holds barred?"

Sliding his swords into the scabbards on his back, Henrik nodded.

"Three hours . . . minimum."

"Let's move." Violence in his tone, his command rippled through the canyon.

His comrades obeyed without hesitation.

Multiple footfalls rang out, obliterating the quiet as his friends sprinted for Garren and Cruz, and he made for the bluff. But as Henrik climbed the rock face, reaching the top and Tareek in record time, worry rose and fear for Cosmina hit hard. *Please God, let her be all right. Keep her inside the Limwoods with Thea and out of harm's way.* A plea filled with desperation? A losing roll in a game of chance? Naught more than a shot in the dark? Without a doubt. No question in his mind. He understood her well. Could practically hear her thinking from a hundred miles away.

Abandoned by him. Alone in her cottage. Angry and hurt.

'Twas a nasty combination.

One that made instinct rise and remorse circle. Three full days since he'd left her. She wouldn't have waited. Not an extra hour, never mind an entire day. Cosmina was a fighter, prone to action, not wallowing. So aye, supposition be damned. 'Twas no longer a guessing game. Henrik knew she was already on the move, headed back to the holy city and into danger. And as he mounted up and Tareek took flight, Henrik sent a prayer heavenward, asking for help, pleading for mercy . . .

Praying he arrived in time to shield and keep her safe.

CHAPTER TWENTY-THREE

Traveling through a cosmic corridor made of black magic and mist, Halál relished the roar of sensation. The whiplash of spine-bending speed clawed at his skin. He hummed, welcoming the rush even though it wasn't as satisfying as fighting. But Lucifer love him, it came awfully close. A definite second in a powerful pull rife with ferocious velocity. The ability to transport himself—and those who served him—over great distances with the wave of his hand. An excellent trick. Quite the magical coup. A gift courtesy of Armand, Prince of Shadows, and an exceptional skill to possess. Except for one thing . . .

He couldn't control where the mist transported him.

Not yet anyway.

Every time he unleashed it, the magic-filled fog always sent him straight home. To Grey Keep, the Al Pacii stronghold he shared with the other Druinguari. Disappointing in so many ways. Particularly since he didn't want to go home. He'd wanted to stay and fight—to transport himself out of Gorgon Pass to a prime shooting position atop the ridge instead of deep into the Carpathian Mountain Range . . . and far from the enemy. Not that he was complaining. Not really. He'd been in a vulnerable position inside the canyon, moments from seeing his soldiers slaughtered, and his own death. The thought left a sour taste in his mouth. Damn Henrik along with the rest. His defeat at the hands of The Seven surpassed failure. It represented disaster, a debacle of epic proportions.

The realization tweaked his temper.

Fury spiraled deep, making him long to draw his swords and return to Gorgon Pass. He wanted another chance. Needed to strike a telling blow and assuage his pride. But not now. It wouldn't happen today. Not while the vortex sped him through space, refusing to heed his request and change course. Halál swallowed a growl. Protesting was a waste of good breath. The facts remained. Until he learned to master the skill, the mist would do as it always did—determine the trajectory, control the velocity, set him down where it pleased instead of where he wanted. Which left him suspended in flight with nothing but time on his hands. Time to strategize. Time to imagine. Time to plot his revenge against the warriors who served the Goddess of All Things.

A beautiful death. One that included torture and eventual decapitation.

With a snarl, Halál twisted into a flip mid-flight, testing the confines of the vortex. The walls expanded around him, making room, adjusting its tempo, speeding him toward Grey Keep. Orange light flared along its curved sides, flashing into angry bursts, reminding him of falling stars. All without causing him any discomfort. 'Twas a marvel in many ways. A sight to behold. Just like the bastards at Gorgon Pass.

The thought sped through his head even as he tried to shut it down. He didn't want to think about it anymore, but . . . devil take him. He couldn't let it go. Or live with the humiliation. His lip curled off his upper teeth. What a catastrophe.

The Seven posed a serious threat. They were far too cunning for anyone's good.

Not surprising. To be expected even. Each warrior had been raised by the Order of Assassins. Fostered inside Grey Keep. Trained by him to be formidable assassins without conscience or mercy. He'd succeeded . . . marvelously. Add that to the magic he'd seen the bastards wield and . . . Halál frowned. 'Twas more than a problem. Set aside the combined viciousness of the group for a moment. Forget about Henrik's vendetta and the warrior's drive to make him pay for past pain. Combined, The Seven were impressive. But possessed of unlimited power derived from the Goddess of All Things? Well now, that signaled trouble. Throw a trio of dragons into the mix and . . .

Halál's eyes narrowed.

Aye. Without a doubt. He needed to find a solution to the scaly beasts. The Seven's alliance with The Three qualified as a huge advantage and a serious hurdle. One he must eliminate posthaste if he wanted to survive. And the Druinguari to thrive. Armand might accept an occasional setback, but not continued failure. Neither did Halál, under ordinary circumstances. These, though, were anything but *ordinary*. His former pupils knew his tactics well.

Proof positive lay in the aftermath of battle.

The betrayers had outmaneuvered him inside the gorge, turning his trap into their own. The ambush reeked of Henrik. The son of a bitch knew how to plan and execute, ensuring maximum damage in the process. A worthy adversary. On par with Xavian and just as lethal. He'd always liked that about Henrik. Until now. He'd lost three more Druinguari to the folly and the fight. Which meant he needed to rethink everything. All of his strategies along with how he implemented each one. Otherwise the assassins who now opposed him would gain more ground.

Unacceptable. Nowhere near optimal. Circumstances in need of change.

Mind churning, Halál flipped up and over, getting into position as his flight slowed. The vortex contracted around him. A pinprick of light expanded in the gloom, widening into a circle. Gaze locked on the opening, he spotted familiar terrain beyond the mist. A thinning forest, icy branches reaching for sunny skies. Jagged rock jutting from sheer cliff faces. Sloping valleys rising to meet snowcapped mountain peaks. Thick castle walls came into view. Muscles tense and body ready, he braced, preparing for impact. Any moment now. Just a few more seconds and—

The vortex funneled into a curve over the inner bailey and set down.

His feet thumped against slick cobblestone.

Hitting one knee, Halál bowed his head and waited for the fog to retreat. He heard his soldiers land behind him. Black tendrils released him one finger at a time, leaving him kneeling in the center of Grey Keep's courtyard. High winds buffeted his back. As it blew across the nape of his neck, he pushed to his feet and scanned the battlements rising beyond the Keep. No one stood on the high wall, awaiting him. Which meant Valmont had yet to return home. Halál nodded in satisfaction. His first in command's absence was an excellent sign. Adept at carrying out orders—even better at covert missions—Valmont must still be at White Temple . . .

Executing members of the Blessed.

The knowledge reassured him. The sudden urge to return to the holy city almost overwhelmed him. He cursed the vortex again. If only the magic would listen. If only he could find the key to controlling it. If only he could transport himself to White Temple and assist Valmont in the killings. But wishing and wanting never made a thing so. Practice coupled with the mind-ease of meditation, however, just might, so . . .

Time to put the day's disappointment behind him. And start making plans for the future.

Rolling his shoulders to work out the tension, Halál glanced over his shoulder. Flame-orange eyes met his. He nodded, acknowledging his second in command.

Beauvic tipped his chin. "Your orders?"

"Gather the eleven-year-olds," Halál said, the need for violence rising. He yearned for it more than an opium addict wanted a fix. Brutality always evened him out, and after today, he required peace . . . if not quiet. Watching the boys battle in the fighting pit would smooth out the rough edges left by a bad day. Well that, and something else too. Aye, he might owe his allegiance to Armand now, but Grey Keep and its traditions lived on. Boys would continue to be captured, kept, and trained as assassins, but for a new aim: filling Druinguari ranks instead of Al Pacii, ensuring his army grew. "Put them through their paces."

"Hand-to-hand?"

A kernel of excitement bloomed. Halál's mouth curved. "Round shields and short knives."

Silent per usual, Beauvic didn't say a word.

"Time to cull the wheat from the chaff, Beauvic," Halál said, holding his second in command's gaze. "Let us see who deserves to remain among us."

With a nod, Beauvic turned toward the barracks and the boys. Halál strode in the opposite direction, toward the Keep and his bedchamber. He longed to see Beauty. Needed to stroke her fine scales and feel her weight as he watched the fight from the rooftop overlooking the pit. Combat would begin within the hour. He wanted to assess each fledgling. Determine their strengths. Assess the weaknesses. Watch every move and knife slash. Witness all the damage done and each blood droplet fall, but . . .

First things first.

He must send out the call, request an audience with Armand. Probably not the wisest thing to do, but Halál refused to hide the day's setback. Or avoid his new master. Naught but disaster lay in that direction. The truth must be told. Questions needed to be asked and answered. Insight, after all, led to information. Knowledge equaled understanding, which precipitated power. The kind that toppled kingdoms and brought great men to their knees.

Nothing different there.

He'd lived long enough to understand every man possessed a fatal flaw. A weak spot, whether rooted in the collective interests or individual defects. He must discover each one to ensure he inflected maximum damage. Armand would supply what he required—insight and guidance, power and increased skill . . . all the spells Halál requested. An advantage to be sure, except for one thing . . .

Armand would punish him for his failure.

A great deal of agony would ensue. Halál shrugged off the certainty along with the threat. Pain wasn't the problem. He could handle anything the dark one threw at him. But as he mounted the steps, he left nothing to chance, practicing what he would say to his new master. Bad news first. Good news second. Aye, 'twas no doubt the best strategy. Particularly since relaying the news that Valmont sat at the heart of the enemy—inside White Temple, doing exactly what Armand expected, decimating the Blessed to ensure the goddess lost ground—would improve Armand's mood. Which without a doubt would see Halál's punishment reduced a hundredfold.

CHAPTER TWENTY-FOUR

Sliding to a stop on icy cobblestones, Cosmina took cover behind a small cottage. Back flat against its stone wall, she paused to catch her breath . . . and prayed she'd gone undetected. 'Twas hard to tell. She couldn't hear much of anything. Her heart refused to cooperate, pounding inside her chest, making blood rush in her ears and listening almost impossible. Nowhere near optimal. Even more dangerous. Cold nipping at her, she pressed her hand against the wall of her chest, willing her heartbeat to slow.

Gods, she needed to pull herself together. Right now. This instant. Before she gave herself away. If that happened, she wouldn't last long inside White Temple.

Not now that the Druinguari stood inside the gates.

Fear tightened its grip, squeezing around her rib cage. She fought the lockdown and forced her lungs open, refusing to let terror win. No matter how afraid, she needed to go on. Her mission left no room for hesitation. One way or another, she must find the others—intercept the Blessed, secret each one to safety, and ensure all arrived home in one piece. 'Twas a lofty task and a terrible undertaking, but she could do it. The goddess had chosen her for a reason, trusted her to be strong, well able to navigate peril and city streets crawling with enemy soldiers. Gritting her teeth, Cosmina stifled a huff. All right. So *crawling* might be overstating it a bit. She hadn't, after all, encountered one yet, but . . .

She knew the blackguards were out there. Somewhere. Surveying the whole city. Lying in wait. Preparing to kill her along with her sisters in the Order of Orm.

Panic threatened again. Cosmina shoved it aside.

A clear mind, not one clouded by dread, was an absolute must. The Druinguari weren't stupid. Master assassins with more skill in their little fingers than she possessed in her entire throwing arm, the group epitomized smart. The infernal beasts had spread out. One stood on the battlements along the east wall. Another atop the west and . . . well, she didn't know about the south. Hadn't seen one when she'd slipped through the postern gate to the north earlier. But that didn't mean an enemy assassin wasn't out there now. Concealed in shadow. Ready to sound the alarm the moment she came into view. Which meant she needed to find better cover before her luck ran out.

The realization made her stomach ache.

Ignoring the discomfort, balanced on the balls of her feet, Cosmina adjusted her shoulder strap instead. Her satchel obeyed with a persistent tug, settling against her hip as she contemplated her next move. A map of the city morphed in her mind's eye. She searched for the best way through the maze of streets, back alleys, and main thoroughfares. Her target? The rose garden abutting the south parapet. 'Twas a bold maneuver, a strategy that would put her under the enemy's nose . . . and the Druinguari keeping watch at that end of White Temple. But few other options existed. The wall at the rear of the garden—beyond the old oak—was the best alternative. She knew the terrain well and . . .

The door concealed within the wall even better.

A few clicks of her key, and she would be through, stepping out of danger and into the secret passageway. Deep inside the complex warren of underground tunnels beneath the holy city. Able to access every part of it without detection. An undeniable advantage. Particularly since it would allow her to intercept her sisters. Pull each one inside the underground labyrinth before the Druinguari registered their presence. An excellent strategy, but for one thing. She must save herself first and reach a secret door hidden in plain sight. Which meant . . .

She needed to move.

Remaining in one spot for too long wasn't smart.

Inhaling through her nose, Cosmina exhaled through her mouth. Frigid air picked up the current, turning each breath into a white puff. In. Out. Catch and release. The breathing method worked. Her heart slowed beat by beat, allowing her to hear again. Tilting her head, she listened hard. No scrape of footfalls. No murmur of deep voices. Naught but the whistle of wind through narrow alleys and empty thoroughfares.

Preparing to shift positions, she pressed her hand flat against the wall. Dirty snow pushed between her fingers as Cosmina peeked around the cornerstone. Main Street sliced between buildings, racing past stone facades with shuttered windows. She released a pent-up breath. No movement on the thoroughfare. Or in the large market square beyond it. Just trim houses set in row upon neat row. All shared the same look—whitewashed on the outside, thatched roofs overhead—every one of them abandoned, awaiting the day the residents returned and White Temple thrived once more.

Too much to hope for? A last-ditch effort in a losing game of chance? Probably. And yet, despite everything, Cosmina wanted to believe . . . so many things. That she could find a true home with others of her kind. That the new High Priestess would be nothing like the last. That the Goddess of All Things knew what she was doing—had a plan, one that included Cosmina living long enough to see it succeed.

"You listening?" she asked as she glanced skyward. Gods, she hoped the goddess heard her. Life with the Blessed, after all, was a whole lot better than death by Druinguari. Reaching for courage, Cosmina dragged her gaze from the heavens, and her mind from the Goddess of All Things. "All right now . . . enough stalling. Move it."

Blowing out a breath, Cosmina inched forward. Her fingers flexed around the dagger. The solid feel of it dragged unwanted memories to the surface as she scanned the street again. Henrik. His knife in her hand. His face in her head. Words written in a wretched note. *I love you.* Blast and damn him. Her gaze strayed to the wicked six-inch blade—sharp edge, beautiful lines, perfectly balanced, and . . . made for Henrik's hand. Carried in a sheath over his heart. Given to her with love . . . in a moment he would no doubt call weakness. It didn't matter. Whatever he chose to label it, Cosmina clung to the connection anyway . . . desperate to be more like him—strong, brave, and unafraid—while she remembered everything about him.

So many things. *Too many things.*

His kindness. The gentleness of his touch when he made love to her. The way he listened when she talked, as though she were the only woman in his world. The sound of his voice. 'Twas absurd, really. She was well past the point of redemption. Swallowing the lump in her throat, Cosmina shook her head. She must stop thinking about him. Henrik had chosen to leave her. Sad, but true. So enough with the heartbreak. She needed to face facts. She was on her own. Once again alone in the world. Free to make her own decisions. Unencumbered by another's opinions and . . .

Drat it all. She didn't need him.

Didn't want him either.

Her motto now. Words to live by. Now if only she could make herself believe it.

Her brow furrowed, Cosmina rechecked her position. Now or never. Do or die. A new mantra, and one much more pressing than the last. Pushing from her crouch, she stayed low and sprinted across Main Street. Boots scuffing against the stone pavers underfoot, she skidded in tight against the next building and listened. All quiet. No flash of movement along the battlements overlooking the city streets. Both things to be thankful for, particularly since the Druinguari assassin atop the east parapet held a distinct advantage. Dressed to blend in, his back flat against the tower wall, he crouched atop the high wall. The perfect vantage point for him. Not so great for her. One wrong turn. Too much noise. The slightest mistake, and his gaze would snap in her direction. Which would lead to all sorts of nasty things . . .

One of the beasts raising the alarm. Druinguari mobilization. Her capture by the enemy.

The thought prompted her to get up and go. Knifepoint leading the way, the midday sun upon her shoulders, Cosmina ran, slinking between stone facades and into back alleyways. Mind working triple time, she scanned each street, every deserted storefront, and all the rooftops while moving with stealth between abandoned wagons and overturned barrels. Almost there. A few more turns. Five, mayhap six, more street corners to negotiate. One last door to find her way through, and she'd be home free. Deep inside the underground passageway and headed for—

A scream shredded the silence.

Fear sliced through her, making her stomach clench. Cosmina dodged right, taking cover behind a pile of timber beams. A shout went up. Unearthly growls accompanied the rapid hammer of footfalls. As sound funneled through the empty streets, Cosmina slid into a crouch, held her breath, and waited. Another earsplitting scream ripped through White Temple. Cosmina squeezed her eyes shut. Oh gods. Oh nay. She knew what that awful cry meant. She wasn't the only woman inside the city. Not anymore. A member of the Blessed, one of her sisters, had heeded the call, returned to the temple . . .

And walked straight into the Druinguari's trap.

"Great goddess of the shadow and light," she whispered, falling into habit, reciting the prayer by heart as she turned back in the direction she'd come. No other choice. She refused to leave a member of the Blessed to die. Couldn't stand the screams, never mind the thought of abandoning one of her own. Following the gut-wrenching cries for help, Cosmina sprinted down one alley after another, heart pounding, fear rising, murmuring more of the prayer as she ran toward danger instead of away. "Grant me courage. Give me strength and allay my fears. Fill my heart with purpose and my mind with knowledge, shine your light upon me so that I might not only serve you well but succeed in the doing."

Old words taken from an ancient text.

Ones she hadn't recited in years. Yet in the moment, the prayer felt right, granting her what she needed most—know-how and enough nerve to move forward without fear.

Slowing her pace, Cosmina tracked the voices. She frowned and, creeping around the next building corner, stopped to pinpoint their location. Eyes narrowed, she followed the sound of a scuffle. A horrible crack echoed, the sound of bone striking bone. The bastards were hitting her sister and—

Another scream echoed through the city.

Her attention snapped to the left. Her feet followed, directing her toward the next intersection. Slipping in behind the milliner's shop, she took cover behind a half wall and, without making a sound, crept along its length. Her dagger tip glinted in the sunlight. The golden dome of High Temple rose above the rooftops. She peeked over the wall and . . . understanding struck. Goddess be with her. Double-damned beasts. The Druinguari were dragging her sister toward the courtyard outside the temple's main entrance. The location made sense . . . in a sick, twisted sort of way. A place of worship and ceremony, the quadrangle sat at the heart of the city, the perfect location to kill a member of the Blessed. Doing so amounted to the highest form of sacrilege—blood on the stones, shame upon the house of the Blessed and White Temple.

Revulsion rolled through her.

Cosmina shoved it aside and, using the wall for cover, slid to a stop at the edge of the piazza. Forever the same, the large rectangular courtyard projected power, anchoring High Temple, standing strong at the base of wide stairs that rose to meet an imposing row of doors. Sunlight fell over the frieze carved in marble above the entrance, depicting the history and the importance of the Order of Orm, cementing her purpose. And yet she waited . . .

A man strode into view, entering the courtyard from the street opposite her.

Cosmina's heart stalled mid-thump. Oh goddess. Not good. Armed to the teeth with twin swords strapped to his back, the lead Druinguari wore brutality like a scent. One hand clenched in the woman's hair, he dragged her behind him while she fought him every step of the way. Clenching her teeth, she suppressed the urge to yell "good for you . . . fight hard" at her sister and assessed the situation, searching for an opening.

None presented itself.

She was in big, *big* trouble. Smack-dab in the middle of an untenable situation with few options and no way out.

With a vicious yank, the Druinguari tossed his captive to the cobblestones. Long blond hair matted with blood—face bruised, clothes ripped, and hands bound—she hit the ground hard and rolled across stone. Coming to a stop in the center of the mosaic medallion, the woman pushed onto her knees. Raising her head, she leveled her chin, defying at the beast standing less than five feet away.

Cosmina drew a shuttered breath. Blast and damn. Nairobi.

She would know her face anywhere. Close in age, she and Nairobi had grown up together and been friends until Cosmina's imprisonment inside the north tower . . . and eventual expulsion from White Temple. Cosmina hadn't seen her since, but old friendships died hard and loyalty lasted forever.

"Make your peace, Blessed," the Druinguari said, voice almost melodic as he drew his sword. Steel scraped against leather, echoing through the stillness. A smile on his face, he rotated the weapon, twirling it in a circle. Light arched from the blade and sunlight winked, flashing across cobblestone. "You go to meet the devil."

The five assassins, arranged in a semicircle behind the leader, growled in agreement.

Still on her knees, Nairobi squared her shoulders. "What is your name?"

The Druinguari hesitated, blade stalling mid-twirl. "Why?"

"'Tis only right I know who sends me to my death."

"Valmont."

"Know this, Valmont." Tipping her head back, Nairobi looked him in the eye. "You will pay for spilling my blood. The goddess will avenge me."

He bared his teeth. "A plague upon your goddess."

"You have just sealed your fate," her friend said.

Indeed. Without a doubt.

If the bastard so much as twitched. Made another move. Just one more, Cosmina would let fly and bury Henrik's dagger hilt deep in his chest. 'Twould be easy enough to do. Despite being outnumbered, she held the advantage, the element of surprise along with a prime position.

An ugly expression on his face, Valmont double-fisted his sword hilt.

Shifting right along the wall, Cosmina improved her vantage point. With a quick flip, she rotated the knife in her palm. Blade poised between her fingertips, she tensed and got ready to throw hard and move fast. Stepping in close, the bastard took aim at Nairobi's throat. Muscles tightened along Cosmina's spine. Skill drew her arm back. Premonition flexed, then flared, telling her to aim for the right side of his chest. Confidence steadied her hand and—

Cosmina unleashed, launching the dagger.

Steel flashed. Its sharp tip spun over the weighted hilt. Time stretched, thinning perception, making her breath slow and her heart pause mid-beat. The Druinguari's gaze snapped toward her. But it was too late. She'd thrown hard and aimed well. Orange eyes widened in disbelief a moment before her dagger struck home. Steel pierced muscle and bone to reach the vulnerable flesh beneath. A sickening crack echoed. Black blood spilled down his chest a second before—

Valmont disintegrated with a sickening pop.

Sludge sloshed on the cobblestones next to Nairobi. Snarls of fury rolled across the courtyard. Already up and over the half wall, Cosmina unsheathed another dagger, drawing it from inside her boot mid-leap. Focusing on the five remaining Druinguari, she sprinted toward her friend. "Nairobi . . ."

Wide eyes met hers. Nairobi's mouth fell open. "Cosmina?"

"Run!"

Her command rang out. Her friend didn't hesitate.

Hands bound, Nairobi scrambled backward as the enemy came to life in front of her. Moving in unison, each pulled identical swords free from matching scabbards. Baring her teeth, Cosmina chose the Druinguari nearest her, took aim, and threw her knife. Just like the other, the dagger hurtled end over end to reach its target. With a flick of his sword, the beast deflected the weapon in flight. The blade hit the ground, clattering across ice and snow. As she watched it spin, terror hit full force. Gods, it was futile. She was doomed. Worse than dead the second the enemy got ahold of her.

Still, she refused to retreat. Or give up.

Running hard, she grabbed Nairobi mid-stride, lifting her to her feet. With a yank, Cosmina dragged her friend across the courtyard. She needed to get up the stairs and into High Temple. Once inside, she could take cover behind the columns and make for the back wall . . . and the Chamber of Whispers. Just like she had the last time. 'Twas their only chance. The only slice of hope in a situation filled with death. But as she sprinted up the steps, a bowstring twanged behind her.

A whistling sound followed as the arrow shot through the air.

Tears burned the corners of her eyes. Oh gods . . . please help her. She knew how much getting hit was going to hurt. Remembered the pain. Still felt the burn of impact and blood rolling down her arm. Anticipation tearing her apart, she waited for it to happen. Felt her muscles tense and suffered the fear as—

A Druinguari bellowed in rage behind her.

Losing her footing on slick stone, Cosmina stumbled, missing a step. Nairobi staggered into her, knocking her sideways. Her knee cracked against marble. Steel met steel behind her, the clash muffled by the blood rushing in her ears. Another Druinguari roared in pain. Shoving her friend up the stairs ahead of her, Cosmina glanced over her shoulder. The air swirled, warping into naught but a shimmer beneath sunlight. The enemy paused to take stock. The wind held its breath. A man materialized in the courtyard, stepping out from behind an invisibility shield.

Cosmina's mouth fell open.

"Good goddess," Nairobi said from behind her. "Who is that?"

"Henrik."

She whispered his name like a benediction. The tears she refused to shed, but couldn't stop, spilled over her bottom lashes. Gratefulness bubbled up, swallowing her whole as she watched Henrik engage the enemy. Rhythm sure, lethal skill on display, he whirled, ducking beneath Druinguari blades, wielding his own, bringing death with each parry and slice. Black blood arced, splashing beneath the sunlight. Druinguari heads flew a second before Henrik thrust his blade home, into the right side of their chests. As each pop reverberated through the courtyard, a group of warriors arrived to help him, coming from—Cosmina frowned—well, everywhere. Sliding down rooftops. Charging between the high hedgerows. Flying in on dragon-back before making the jump to land on the ground beside Henrik.

Not that he needed anyone's help.

Precision personified, he was already done. The last Druinguari lay at his feet . . . and Cosmina started to shake. She couldn't help it. Shock rode in on a wave and held her under, drowning her with unyielding emotion. It made so little sense. His arrival. Her rescue. The terrible yearning rising up from deep inside her. She thought she was past the desperation—the clawing need, the terrible want . . . all the heartfelt longing. One look at him forced her to admit the truth.

She needed him more than her own heartbeat.

Druinguari blood dripping from his blades, Henrik turned toward her. Expression set in fierce lines, his intense hazel-gold eyes met hers. And just like that the barriers between them fell away. Aye, she ought to be angry with him. Should no doubt make him pay for abandoning her the way he had, but as relief sparked in his eyes, the past ceased to matter. He was here now. She wanted him forever. So to hell with doubt. Say good-bye to her pride. She refused to deny her love, so instead of turning away, she held his gaze and sprang to her feet. Not wasting a second, she sprinted down the steps toward him.

No one moved. White Temple didn't even breathe.

Her footfalls rang across the courtyard.

Henrik murmured her name and, sheathing his swords, reached for her. Cosmina didn't hesitate. Not for a moment. She ran straight into his arms, feeling as though she'd finally come home as she settled in and Henrik hugged her tight.

CHAPTER TWENTY-FIVE

Silence settled like a net, blanketing the courtyard in front of High Temple. Déjà vu. Kismet. Call it whatever the situation warranted. The title didn't matter. Neither did the fact it always came down to this—him and White Temple, going head to head and heart to heart. But not this time. Henrik's mouth curved. Aye, *not this time*. Right now, he was exactly where he wanted to be—

In Cosmina's embrace. His heart pressed against hers.

Stifling a shiver, Henrik struggled to hold on—to distill the violent rush of bloodlust and slow the beat of his heart. It refused to listen, hammering the inside of his chest as he pulled Cosmina closer. A kind of sacrilege, actually. He shouldn't be holding her while the urge to kill still gripped him. He stank of death. Wore the scent like the predator he was and would always be. So aye, he should release her—long enough at least to get himself under control. But even as the thought surfaced, the needy bastard inside him rose, refusing to unlock his arms and let her go. He needed the contact. Craved her heat and the acceptance. Which left him flailing, unable to turn away until he knew for sure she was all right.

Asking her was no doubt the best tack to take.

Too bad he couldn't find his voice.

Christ, she'd scared the hell out of him. It had been so close. Too damned close. A moment later—a split second more—and Cosmina would be dead. Lying in a pool of her own blood. Sacrificed on the steps of High Temple. An arrow in her back, her heart no longer beating. The image made him draw a shaky breath. The reality of how lucky he'd been made him thank God. It could've gone the other way so easily. Could've ended in sorrow instead of . . .

Cupping the back of her head, Henrik pressed his face into her hair. "Cosmina."

"I'm all right, but, please, not yet . . ." she whispered against his throat. He shifted in her embrace, wanting to see her face. Her grip on the back of his tunic tightened. "I'm not ready to let go of you yet."

Fine by him. He wasn't anywhere near ready either. "Not to worry, *iubita*. We can stay here as long as you like."

"Are they g-gone? Are they all . . ." She shivered against him. "Gone?"

"Aye."

True. One hundred percent accurate. Henrik scanned the terrain over the top of her head anyway, looking for danger where he knew none existed. Proof ran in rivulets on the cobblestones, finding the cracks, marring the face of colorful mosaic tiles. Druinguari blood—black as pitch, evil as sin. He stared at it a moment, then turned the dial, fine-tuning his senses, wanting to make sure. Nay. Nothing to be worried about. The Druinguari who had invaded the holy city were dead. The absence of vibration between his temples told him so. The stillness creeping across the square confirmed it.

None remained inside White Temple. He'd killed them all to keep her safe.

"Henrik?"

"Aye, love?"

"Is Nairobi all right?" Another shiver racked her. Running his hands over her shoulders, he drew gentle circles down her back, absorbing her chill, sharing his body heat, providing the kind of comfort she gave him all the time. "I don't know how badly she is hurt. The beast hit her, Henrik. He *hit* her. Now she's—"

"Being well tended."

Cosmina frowned against the side of his throat. "By whom?"

"Cristobal."

Pressing a kiss to her temple, Henrik gave her a gentle squeeze. He didn't want her to worry. Nairobi was in good hands. And Cristobal? Well now, his friend was in fine form. Without lifting his chin from atop her head, Henrik glanced across the courtyard. His mouth curved. Halfway up the fluted staircase, his friend didn't notice his perusal. Crouched in front of Nairobi— hands busy, body tense, healing satchel open on the step beside him—Cristobal was too busy playing knight in shining armor to the damsel in distress.

Odd in more ways than one.

Particularly since Andrei usually handled injuries in the aftermath.

Blowing out a shaky breath, Cosmina uncurled her fingers from his tunic and lifted her head. Her hands slid over his arms, making pleasure hum and yearning rise. Christ, he wanted her. More now than ever, but instead of picking her up and carting her off, he clung to self-control. She needed time to calm down. So did he. But as she set her hands, palms flat, against the wall of his chest, he almost lost it. The heat of her touch. The beauty of her scent. All her lithe curves pressed to him sent him sideways, tearing apart patience, making his restraint falter.

He murmured her name.

Tipping her chin up, she met his gaze. The chaos in her eyes set him straight, shoving desire aside. Jesus. He didn't like that look. It contained so much doubt, as though she'd lost her footing along with her bearings. Henrik frowned, wondering for a moment if her uncertainty was somehow his fault. His leaving hadn't been kind. Aye, he'd left the note but . . . hell. It didn't mean much. Not here. Not now while he tried to get closer and . . .

She backpedaled into full-blown retreat.

All right, so she wasn't withdrawing physically. She still stood in the circle of his arms. Nor was she trying to break his hold. But Henrik recognized the shift into self-protection. Saw her guard go up an instant before she broke eye contact and looked away. Shifting in his embrace, Cosmina glanced over her shoulder. Her gaze landed on the pair halfway up the steps. Worry furrowed her brow. A moment later, she pushed against his chest and tried to step away. He held on tight, preventing her from leaving his arms and returning to her friend. She'd said it first: *not yet.* He wasn't ready to let her go yet.

"She's fine, Cosmina," he said, tone full of reassurance. "Cristobal can be trusted. He'll see to her wounds and keep her safe."

"Like you did me."

"Aye." Brushing the hair from her temple, he met her gaze, then turned his hand and cupped her cheek. Soft silk caressed his palm. Pleasure hummed, raising awareness as he traced her mouth with his thumb. She opened for him, parting her lips, inviting his kiss, but . . . goddamn it. As much as he yearned to taste her again, he couldn't. Too much remained unsaid between them. So like it or nay, he must hold the line. Make it clear. Bring them back to the point where trust took root, and she believed in him again. "Like I did you, *iubita*. Like I always will you."

Tears filled her eyes.

"Sweet love . . . please look at me."

She shook her head. "If I do, I'll be finished. Just done and . . . blast it all. 'Tisn't the least bit fair."

"What isn't?"

"I should be furious with you for the whole mind-invasion thing." She frowned, looking more confused than angry. "And the way you left too, but—goddess help me—I cannot begin to . . . I don't even know how to . . ."

Her voice broke. Henrik's heart along with it. He hadn't wanted to hurt her. Had known from the beginning making love to her—allowing her too close—would lead to huge complications and bad feelings. And yet, here he stood, acting selfish once again, holding on to her instead of leaning away.

"I want to be angry. I really do, but . . ." With a sigh, she thumped his shoulder with the side of a fist. A moment later, her forehead followed, touching down in the center of his chest. "I cannot seem to manage it. 'Tis the truth, I'm so happy to see you, I cannot think of one nasty thing to say. 'Tis pathetic."

"Nay, Cosmina . . . 'tisn't a bit pathetic," he said, stroking his hand over her hair. The tendrils slipped between his fingertips, encouraging him to delve deeper. He didn't hesitate. Murmuring his enjoyment, he played in the thick strands, loving the weight and feel, but mostly that she allowed him to touch her. "'Tis just the shock talking. As soon as it passes, you'll show no mercy."

She huffed. "Probably."

"I'm sure of it."

"I don't like feeling this way."

"I know," he said. "Would you like me to fix it?"

"Do you think you can?"

He knew he could. Three little words said out loud instead of written on parchment. That's all it would take. At least, he hoped so. Nothing in life ever came easy. Love least among them. Yet Henrik knew he needed to do it. To right the wrong he'd done to her, bare his soul and come clean. The truth must be told. Cosmina deserved every ounce of it. Knowing it, however, didn't make moving forward any easier. He hated that he'd hurt her. Despised all her uncertainty and pain. But as silence fell, he struggled to find his voice.

'Twas a helluva thing.

So brave in battle. Yet terrified by the power of his love for Cosmina.

So instead of baring all, he wrapped his arms around her, buying the time he needed to work up the courage to start the conversation. Cosmina didn't object. She snuggled close instead, wrapping him up, aligning her body with his, taking all the room beneath his chin. Gratefulness squeezed his heart tight. He loved the feel of her. Could hold her for days and never get bored. 'Twas inevitable, he guessed. Mayhap even normal. His need for her superseded self-preservation . . . along with the usual impulse to retreat. She made him feel things he hadn't thought possible— need, want, a yearning so deep it scared the hell out of him. Too bad he wasn't a coward. 'Twould be easier to deny the truth and walk away. But he couldn't go back.

Or even contemplate leaving her again.

Not while he held her close, and she clung to him. His desire to be near her was no longer a matter of choice or a simple case of want. He needed her now. Far too much to ever let her go. So instead of unlocking his arms, he tightened his grip and murmured her name. She whispered his back, making his heart hurt and his chest ache. Goddamn, she'd been unbelievable today. So smart. So strong. The best kind of accurate too, when she'd taken aim and let the dagger fly. An image of her skipped through his mind. Intense gaze pinned to her target. Perfect balance and form, even on the run. Courage and ability rolled into one. His mouth curved. He couldn't help it. His pride for her was an involuntary reflex, one he couldn't—

Someone cleared his throat.

Henrik cringed. Ah hell. He'd lost track of time . . . and his comrades.

With a sigh, he lifted his cheek from atop Cosmina's head and glanced over his shoulder. Jesus. 'Twas even worse than he thought. Standing in a semicircle behind him, boots planted and expressions set, his friends wore varying shades of *what the hell?* Henrik understood the surprise along with the charged pause. All the raised eyebrows too. He'd broken rank. Had gone half-mad in his quest to reach Cosmina in time. Add that to the fact he now stood holding her in the middle of the quad while his friends looked on and—aye, give the man a prize. His comrades' astonishment made sense. He wasn't, after all, the hugging kind. Open affection simply wasn't his forte. Or at least, it hadn't been . . .

Until he'd met Cosmina.

He met his friend's gaze. "Give me a moment, Xavian."

"Take all the time you need," he said, understanding and more in his tone. The *more* wasn't difficult to guess. His friend knew what it felt like to fall . . . to be deep in uncharted territory with a woman on his mind. "See to her. I'll see to the rest. With the dragons in the air, the city will be locked down in less than an hour."

True enough. White Temple might be large, but its design made defending the city easier than most. Throw in thick stone walls. Add on the square parapets rising like teeth across the battlements, then consider the double gatehouses complete with murder holes at each city entrance and—aye, a skeleton crew could not only man it, but hold it against an enemy for years. Not that three dragons qualified as a *skeleton crew*. The trio was a force unto themselves. One an incoming army wouldn't survive, never mind defeat. And as Henrik watched Tareek fly overhead, wings spread wide, bloodred scales gleaming in the sunlight, his heartbeat slowed, and he felt himself unwind.

Finally. 'Twas about time.

Taut muscles relaxing, Henrik exhaled in a rush, thankful as tension loosed its grip one talon at a time. Rolling his shoulders, he held Xavian's gaze and tipped his chin. The quick gesture carried a silent message. One wrapped in gratitude . . . sent by him, and received on cue by his friend. Xavian accepted his thanks with a nod. Seconds later, he was gone, leading the others across the courtyard, footfalls quiet, voice hushed as he doled out individual duties. As his comrades disappeared into the city, Henrik swung Cosmina into his arms.

She went rigid against him. "Hey."

Her sharp tone lightened his mood. Ah, good. There she was . . . the smart-mouthed hellion he knew and loved. "Humor me, *iubita*. We need to talk and there are too many ears and eyes here."

"Oh." Brows drawn tight, her attention strayed to Nairobi and Cristobal.

"They'll be fine."

She stared at the pair an instant longer, then looked back at him. Green eyes brimming with uncertainty met his. The impact hit him like a sucker punch, knocking the wind out of him. He went stone-still, wanting to say more, needing to explain. The compulsion to convince her nearly overwhelmed him. He forced himself to remain still instead, waiting for her to decide. Stay or go. Run away and hide . . . or hear him out. 'Twas her call. Not his. He couldn't force her to listen. He didn't deserve a second chance, not after the way he'd betrayed her in the Limwoods. But as the silence stretched, nerves got the better of him. His chest went tight. Henrik swallowed, combating the burn as pressure squeezed around his torso.

Jesus help him. Mayhap it was too late. Mayhap he couldn't fix it. Mayhap having her in his life was too much to—

"All right then," she said, voice so soft he barely heard her. And yet, it restored his faith, making him believe, infecting him with the possibility forgiveness existed a conversation away. Buoyed by the prospect, his gaze strayed to her mouth. Desire slammed through him. Unable to help himself, he leaned in. A quick kiss. Just one taste. 'Twas all he needed. But as he got close, Cosmina denied him, pressing her finger to his lips, shaking her head, warning him with a look. Looping her arm around his neck, she pointed to a building beyond the courtyard's half wall. "Talk first. The shoemaker's cottage is closest."

Cradling Cosmina against him, Henrik nodded, then put his feet to good use, and got moving. No time to waste. She'd agree to talk. He accepted the terms—no kissing until she allowed it. He could live with that. At least, for a little while. Pace even, he crossed the quad, skirted the wall, and stopped in front of the cottage door. Juggling her in his arms, he palmed the peg doubling as a handle. He lifted it free of its cradle. Wood scraped against wood. Neglected hinges squeaked as the door swung wide. Dipping his head beneath the lintel, he strode over the threshold and into a cobbler's paradise.

Tools lined the walls. Shoe molds sat in deep wooden bins, sharp tacks in shallower ones. Rolls of felt were stacked in one corner. Piles of tanned leather lay scattered in another, as though the shopkeeper had left in a hurry. No doubt close to the truth. The desertion of White Temple after Ylenia's death hadn't made for a tidy retreat. More of a mass exodus, by all accounts. So aye, the mess made perfect sense. So did the dust on the large table occupying the center of the room. Stepping over a pair of abandoned clogs, Henrik headed straight for it. Cosmina tensed as he set her down on the table edge. Taking the cue, trying to respect her space, he backed up a step.

"Nay," she whispered. "You don't get to back away, Henrik. Not yet."

Henrik blinked in surprise.

Hooking her calf behind his thigh, Cosmina brought him back, keeping him close, refusing to allow his retreat . . . messing with his head as she wrapped both of her legs around one of his. Her heat bled through his leather trews. Desire went on the rampage, elevating need until he throbbed with it. Taut muscles pulled at his hip bones. Unable to stop himself, he reached for her hips, pulling her closer as she raised her hand. Gentle and sure, her fingertips touched down, then drifted, tracing his cheekbone.

"You came back." Her voice shook a little. Swallowing hard, she cleared her throat. "I didn't think you would."

That made two of them. "I tried so hard to stay away, but . . ."

She raised a brow, asking without words.

Henrik gave it up without a fight. "I want you too much. I can't stay away."

"Good to know," she said, nearly breaking his heart. Jesus. For all her strength, she looked so vulnerable right now. "I seem to have a similar problem when it comes to you." She frowned. Her fingers stilled, then drew a gentle circle on his temple. "I could live without you, Henrik. I am strong enough to go on without you if need be, so be honest. Tell me true . . ."

She paused, her hesitation palpable.

"Ask," he said, heart thumping, hope rising. "Ask me anything."

"Did you mean it?" Looking worried, she released a shaky breath. "What you wrote in your note . . . did you mean it?"

"Every word. Every last one." Cupping her hand with his own, he turned his mouth into her palm. "I love you, Cosmina. I want to stay and build a life with you. I don't care where we live— here, Drachaven, the Limwoods. It doesn't matter. Please forgive me. Please take me back. Please be mine, *iubita*. I need you too much to ever let you go."

"'Tis forgiven . . . forgotten." Fingers playing with the hair at his nape, she tugged, bringing him even closer. Nestled against him, she whispered, "I love you too, Henrik."

"Then you'll have me as husband?" Bumping her cheek with his own, he turned his head and stole the kiss he craved. It wasn't much. The barest brush of his mouth against hers. Not even close to what he wanted, but 'twas enough for now. Raising his head, he met her gaze, trying to gauge her reaction and his chances of success. A pang tightened his chest as tears pooled in her eyes. So strong, yet undeniably soft too. She was a gift. One he didn't deserve, but he couldn't resist. "Will you wed me, Cosmina?"

"Anywhere. Anytime," she said, smiling through her tears. "Just tell me when."

Awe circled deep as gratitude hit hard. Inconceivable. Mind-boggling in so many ways, but he saw the truth in her eyes. She loved him. His throat went tight. He was lucky. So goddamned *lucky* to have found her. To be loved. To be accepted. To be wanted, valued, and needed. Naught compared to that, and as he set his mouth to hers—and she opened to accept him—Henrik thanked God for his good fortune and pressed deeper. Cosmina responded, tangling her tongue with his. Hot. Wet. Delicious. He accepted everything she gave, then demanded more. Kissed her hard. Skimmed over her curves. Craved without conscience as she caressed him back, pushing him past arousal into explosive need.

Breathing hard, he lifted his mouth from hers.

She grumbled, protesting his retreat.

"Goddamn, I want you." Sucking in a desperate breath, his love for her spilling into uncontrollable desire, Henrik looked around the cottage. Shit. Of all the rotten luck. No cot shoved into any of the corners. Nothing soft to lay her down on at all. "I cannot wait, Cosmina. We need a bed."

Eyes full of mischief, her mouth curved. "Well then, lucky for you . . ." Trailing off, she fingered the links of her necklace. With a tug, she pulled the delicate chain from beneath her tunic. Impishness blooming into a full-blown grin, she rocked her hand, making the chain—and what it carried—swing like a pendulum between them. "I have the key that unlocks every door inside White Temple."

"Keeper of the Key," he said, leaning in for another kiss.

Both hands buried in his hair, she nipped his bottom lip. "It does come with certain advantages."

"Beautiful."

And so was she. Beyond beautiful with her sassy mouth and quick wit. One hundred percent committed and all his. Every gorgeous inch of her. The fact she loved him added fuel to his fire, astounding him even as he thanked his lucky stars. Her forgiveness was nothing short of a miracle. He didn't deserve the second chance, never mind her. Henrik accepted both gifts anyway, feeling gratefulness rise as his love for her grew. His past no longer mattered. Neither did all the blood on his hands. His future began today. Every moment of it now belonged to her. And as he scooped Cosmina off the table and headed for the door, Henrik let his bitterness go.

His history with White Temple be damned.

The Goddess of All Things had finally gotten something right. And Henrik finally understood. The deity wove a crooked trail, pulling cosmic threads, adjusting outcomes, making amends in strange ways. All things happened for a reason. The goddess' mantra, not his. But as the heavy weight surrounding his heart lifted and Cosmina kissed him back, Henrik acknowledged the truth. His pain. All the strife. Every bit of uncertainty and fear couldn't touch him anymore. Not while he had Cosmina in his arms and the promise of her love to uphold.

A NOTE FROM THE AUTHOR

Thank you for reading *Knight Avenged*. If you enjoyed this book, I'd appreciate it if you'd help others find it so they can enjoy it too.

- Recommend it: Please help other readers find this book by recommending it to friends, readers' groups, and discussion boards.
- Review it: Let other readers know what you liked or didn't like about *Knight Avenged*.
- Lend it: This e-book is lending-enabled, so feel free to share it with your friends.

If you'd like to sign up for Coreene's newsletter to receive new release information, please visit: http://bit.ly/1fnnskF

You can follow Coreene Callahan on Facebook or on Twitter @coreenecallahan.

Book updates can be found at www.CoreeneCallahan.com

ACKNOWLEDGMENTS

This book took me on a journey. The characters challenged me. The world expanded to include things I hadn't anticipated. The love story touched my heart. I fell hard and fast for Henrik the moment I met him in the first Circle of Seven book, *Knight Awakened*, but I didn't expect Cosmina to make me do the same. Sometimes characters strike that way, becoming so entrenched in my heart and mind they feel real to me. Like old friends and comfortable playmates. I am so very thankful for that. Thank you as well to Montlake Romance and Amazon Publishing for helping me get this book into your hands. I hope you enjoyed reading Henrik and Cosmina's story as much as I did writing it.

Many thanks to my literary agent, Christine Witthohn. You are the best! You really are.

A huge thanks to Melody Guy. For your insight and honesty. For your dedication to getting the story right. You made this book better by making me work harder. And I am grateful.

Immeasurable thanks to my editor, Helen Cattaneo. Thank you for all your hard work and support. It means the world to me. And also to the entire Amazon Publishing team, but most especially to Jessica Poore, whose talents and enthusiasm never cease to amaze me. I so enjoy working with all of you!

To my friends and family. I love you all. Thank you for putting up with me and my distraction when I'm deep in Storyland.

Last but never least, to Kallie Lane, fellow writer, critique partner, and friend. You make me better. You always have. Thank you!

I raise a glass to all of you!

ABOUT THE AUTHOR

© Julie Daniluk, 2009

After growing up as the only girl on an all-male hockey team, Coreene Callahan knows a thing or two about tough guys, and loves to write characters inspired by them. After graduating with honors in psychology, and taking a detour to work in interior design, Coreene finally gave in and returned to her first love: writing. Her debut novel, *Fury of Fire,* was a finalist in the New Jersey Romance Writers Golden Leaf Contest in two categories: Best First Book and Best Paranormal. She combines her love of romance, adventure, and writing with her passion for history in her novels *Fury of Fire, Fury of Ice, Fury of Seduction, Fury of Desire, Knight Awakened,* and *Warrior's Revenge.* She lives in Canada with her family, a spirited golden retriever, and her wild imaginary world.

www.CoreeneCallahan.com